CO-ALJ-159

# WHITE *Heart*

# WHITE *Heart*

*a novel*

## Julie Caton

Tate Publishing *& Enterprises*

*White Heart*
Copyright © 2011 by Julie Caton. All rights reserved.

No part of this publication may be reproduced, stored in a retrieval system or transmitted in any way by any means, electronic, mechanical, photocopy, recording or otherwise without the prior permission of the author except as provided by USA copyright law.

This novel is a work of fiction. However, several names, descriptions, entities, and incidents included in the story are based on the lives of real people.

The opinions expressed by the author are not necessarily those of Tate Publishing, LLC.

Published by Tate Publishing & Enterprises, LLC
127 E. Trade Center Terrace | Mustang, Oklahoma 73064 USA
1.888.361.9473 | www.tatepublishing.com

Tate Publishing is committed to excellence in the publishing industry. The company reflects the philosophy established by the founders, based on Psalm 68:11,
*"The Lord gave the word and great was the company of those who published it."*

Book design copyright © 2011 by Tate Publishing, LLC. All rights reserved.
*Cover design by Kellie Southerland*
*Interior design by Christina Hicks*

Published in the United States of America

ISBN: 978-1-61777-053-1
1. Fiction / Historical
2. Fiction / Christian / Historical
11.01.31

# DEDICATION

To my heavenly Father, the Lord Jesus Christ, the Gift-giver,
whom I met personally on April 12, 1964.
And to my earthly father, Jonathan Allison Brown, Sr. (1914–1974),
who inspired my reading and writing from the beginning.

# ACKNOWLEDGMENTS

Many people encouraged and advised me as I worked on *White Heart*. A special thanks to Sharon Larsen and Eileen Charbonneau. Thank you to Ursuline Sister Suzanne Prince for her introducing me to the Reverend Mother Marie. Thank you to the early readers who plodded through 250,000 words without complaint and encouraged me to keep at it: Nancy Balbick, Julie Burgess, Joy Cooney, Elizabeth Crampton, Sheila Hess, Darlene Mieney, Iva McKenna, Michael and Char Mumau, Catherine Pettepiece, and Allison and Sarah VanderLinden. Thank you to John Steckley of Humber College for translating my English into Iroquois.

The following readers gave me continued support and suggestions: Loretta Carpenter, Sue Chiddy, Rhonda Cole, Leslie DeLooze, Loa Dunn, Ethel Ettinger, Peggy Friedman, Lynette Gilbert, Liz and Mark Houseman, Terri Marchese, Lauren Pahuta, Diana Radley, Vicky Ripple, Jim and Lynda Tait, Nancy Timbers, Brenda Weidrich, and Julie Wright. The suggestions of two booksellers, Bill Evans and Sue Brooke from Barnes and Noble, Naples, Florida, were invaluable. Chad Bierdeman used his artistic talents to create a map of Madeleine's New France.

The staff of Tate Publishing has been friendly, helpful, and faithful throughout the process. Special thanks to my conceptual editor, Emily Wilson.

My adult children, Elizabeth and Jay, supported and inspired me in ways that are beyond "the book." My prayer partners, Brenda Bierdeman, Char Mumau, Patty Shelhorse, Julie Watterson, and Nancy Wilson were always there for me. My clients' stories have touched my heart, and it is for them Madeleine is portrayed as victorious over her special issues. Finally, thank you to Rick Caton, for making our travels all they had been and setting up the platform of a home-based practice.

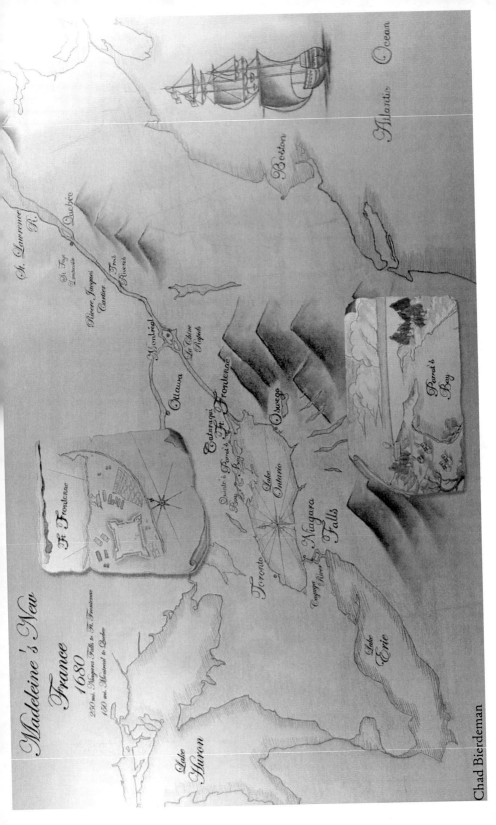

Madeleine's New France 1680

230 mi. Niagara Falls to Ft. Frontenac
160 mi. Montreal to Quebec

Atlantic Ocean

St. Lawrence R.
Quebec
St. Foy
Lorettville
Riviere Jacques Cartier
Trois Rivieres
Boston
Montreal
La Chine Rapids
Ottawa
Cataraqui
Ft. Frontenac
Oswego
Ft. Frontenac
Quinte's Parrot's Bay
Parrot's Bay
Toronto
Lake Ontario
Niagara Falls
Cayuga River
Lake Erie
Lake Huron
Parrot's Bay

Chad Bierderman

# Historical Note

On the King's Highway, ten miles west of Kingston, Ontario, a small park overlooks Parrot's Bay on Lake Ontario. Displayed in the center is a historical marker written by the Province of Ontario Heritage Foundation. It reads:

### Madeleine de Roybon D'Allone (1646–1718)

Of noble birth, De Roybon was the first European woman to own land in what is now Ontario. She came to Fort Frontenac (Kingston) probably in 1679 where she acquired property from Rene Robert Cavelier de LaSalle, governor and seigneur of the fort. In 1681, she loaned him money to finance his explorations, and about this time, he granted her a seigneury extending westward from Toneguignon (Collin's Bay). On this land she built a house, outbuilding, and a trading post; grew crops; and raised cattle. Marauding Iroquois, angry with the French for their campaign against the Senecas in 1686, destroyed de Roybon's establishment in August 1687 and took her prisoner. Released the following year, she lived in Montreal until her death.

# PROLOGUE

On that humid August morning in 1687, Francois, a handsome boy of Huron and French blood, led the stallion Tonnere as we hunted a mile from my trading post. Suddenly smoke rose on the horizon above Parrott's Bay. Seeing the plume of dirty sky, I wondered, *Is my hired man, Claude, burning brush? No. That can't be. It must be a thundercloud forming.*

But Francois knew better. And in my heart, so did I. Hadn't we both seen the moccasin print in the silt? It was one—not of our trading partners—but of France's foe, the Iroquois's Onondaga people from across Lake Ontario. As a woman of New France, I, Madeleine de Roybon D'Allone, would have no power to negotiate with them.

Francois leapt onto Tonnere's saddle despite his clubfoot. I sprinted after them, calling between gasps, "Don't let them see you!" A deformed child was worse than garbage to a native.

Stopping short of our property, I crept behind a tree. In my yard, Ellen stood frozen, clutching her four-year-old daughter, Midge. One warrior guarded them. Claude lay dead, an arrow through his chest, his scalp bloody. Smoke and soot filled the air as a dozen Iroquois circled our burning house, gathering bounty. Our trade goods were strewn on the ground.

From my hiding place, I smelled sweat and war paint. Midge peered around her mother's enfolded arms. Another Iroquois dragged a stunned Full Moon, Claude's Ojibwa wife, out of the barn. They fastened her wrists and hobbled her ankles with rawhide. For once, the garrulous woman stood quiet; soot-stained tears smeared her face.

Then a flaming arrow flew and ignited the shingles of the barn roof. Ellen raised her fists in the air and screamed. For that second, Midge was free from her mother's grasp. The warrior grabbed the child and tossed her to a comrade, who stuffed her mouth, trussed her, and laid her face down on the bottom of a canoe. Midge squirmed and grunted.

Ellen threw herself at the guard, scratching his face. His blood splattered her apron. The warrior slapped her and punched her gut. Her breath emptied out of her with a whoosh. Ellen's knees buckled, and she sank to the ground.

The warrior leapt on her like a starving wolf on a lamb. Pressing a large knife to her throat, he pinned her down. His free hand grabbed her thick skirts and undershirt, and he yanked them over her head. His face contorted with lustful exhilaration and hatred as he raped her.

She screamed again and again.

I tried to turn away but could not. Shame flooded me. Ellen had been my best friend for five years. We had seen the trading post prosper. Her gentle Huguenot spirit had succored me through difficulties. I had grown into a better woman because of her faith.

And I knew how her violation felt. Had I not fled France sixteen years ago because of my own humiliation? Had I not been devastated by my abuse while at Versailles?

What could I do? As the warrior ravaged Ellen, angry heat washed my body. I clenched my teeth, letting out a snarl. Then I felt for the hunting knife strapped to my leg.

# PART ONE:

## A Patch of New Ground

# I
# Fleeing Versailles

My timid mother, a queen's waiting maid, died in childbirth when I was small. After mentoring me in Court for several years, the Queen Mother, Anne of Austria, succumbed to cancer of the breast. My aloof father, the royal carver and king's own *chef de cuisine* introduced me to exotic royal dishes, the latest dances, and the king's peculiar interests. But my father also viewed me as his object, a prize to be shown off to arrogant courtiers. He did not keep me safe. By the age of fifteen, I lived like a mouse in a palace of cats. Court intrigues clawed at me, shamed me. And I yearned to escape.

Under the guidance of the Lady of the Royal Herb Garden, I gathered and dispensed herbs and medicines, and learned history and languages alongside the courtiers' children. When I read copies of the *Jesuit Relations* about Canada, I felt like a released falcon soaring over mountain peaks in the high country. These priests' tales were my haven amidst the artificial, play-acting coquetry of Versailles.

As I grew older, shame seared and confusion exhausted me, so I left Versailles for the Ursuline convent in Montagris. While protected there, my appetite for Canada was fed by vivid daydreams of the New World's wilderness and its native people. Catherine de Baillon, my friend from the convent, shared my desire to cross the Atlantic.

Then my father's death in 1670 forced me to return to Court. I had learned from Catherine about the king's plan of "adopting" young women as his "daughters." By my becoming one of these, a *fille du roi*, I could collect a modest dowry, receive transport to Quebec, and leave France. But I would have to marry a man in the colony and raise one child after another for the sake of the Sun King. Bold Catherine had signed on and left for the New World in 1667.

I was twenty-four years old and afraid.

But I grabbed hold of this lifeline too.

...

In 1671, I boarded the *Jeanne Baptist* and sailed for Canada. When our first storm struck one week out, I feared drowning and started gagging from the stink below deck, so I crawled up the ladder out of the hold. I begged an old sailor to tie me to the mast so I wouldn't get washed overboard.

White and black froth churned over the hull and drenched me, as I stood lashed to the mast. Towering gray cascades tossed our little ship into shrouded mist. Ominous clouds raced in the rain-sodden sky. Lightning swords slashed the steel horizon. During the terrifying night, I distracted my thoughts with rich, colorful images from Court. Gold embroidered gowns, gilded sofas covered with fine tapestry, mirrors everywhere reflecting back the powdered wigs of the courtiers. My proud father in his chef's uniform, carving the huge roast. A sumptuous spread of fresh pastries, crisp fruits, and cold wines. The herb garden smelling like lavender and strawberries. Delights had surrounded me as I grew up in the Sun King's Court. But, when I reached womanhood, my taste for Court life soured. As courtiers treated me like a possession, my soul wasted away.

A salty blast of the stormy Atlantic smacked me in my face, and I swallowed water. Why had I contracted to board this ship? Had I traded a nauseating security in France for a tantalizing vulnerability in the New World?

...

When the storm abated, the old sailor, smelling of kelp and looking like a dried up lime, hobbled across the slippery deck. "There ye go, milady." He grinned, showing rotted teeth as he cut my ropes. "Git yourself below 'for you ketch your death."

JULIE CATON

I stumbled down the ladder. My companions, twenty-nine *filles du roi*, were curled seasick in their hammocks. I stole a glimpse of myself in our one mirror nailed to the nearby beam. The storm's gale had blotched my cheeks, and stinging salt water had reddened my eyes. My bodice was plastered to my chest. My brunette hair, still moist and windswept, curled freely without a proper cap.

Unlike the women around me, I had chosen this role of *fille du roi*; it had not been forced upon me by lack of dowry or family connections. My father had left me a one thousand livres dowry. In France, my matchmaking aunt had found me a potential husband. The suitor, a barrel-shaped Frenchman, was a widower with three children. He had interest in nothing but his hounds and horses. In a life with him, I would likely shrivel and die. My heart and soul had yearned for a better life.

...

The ship's priest, Father Artemis, asked how I felt about marrying a man I would not know well. My throat clotted, and my stomach churned. I leaned back on the rail and locked my vision on the sky.

I sensed him watching me. Slowly, I planned my response.

"Father, why do you assume I will marry at all?"

"Are not all of you ladies obliged to choose a mate within a few weeks of arrival?"

"We signed no contract stating such."

"But," he sputtered, "it would be contrary to the royal behest and ... unseemly!"

"In our homeland, perhaps. But as I leave France, I long for freedom. I don't know what there is for me in the new land. But I won't settle for becoming a brood mare."

Father Artemis flinched at my outspokenness.

My neck reddened. I steadied myself with the ship's rail as I walked away, looking for a place to sit and read. The priest moved on to converse with some male passengers.

While reading *Jesuit Relations*, I wondered whether it was proper to call natives "*les sauvages*," meaning the brutal people, the wild, the untamed. These people in their natural state, caretakers of the land, had found a place in my heart. I envied their freedom from pretension.

I now overheard Father Artemis say the natives were not wild and would make excellent converts. But the ship's Captain Jamison disagreed. He believed the Jesuits were deluded; the natives were primitive, barbarous, and devoid of anything spiritual.

"We Jesuits believe the native is a creature of God," the priest maintained. "Conversion will help them in their survival and our economy. We Frenchmen will be able to trust them more if they are Catholic and partner with us in our trading."

Captain Jamison shook his head. "Ah, but often *les sauvages* lose their *joie de vivre* once they have taken up the practices of the Catholics. And our diseases kill them. Religious teachings cause bad splits, Father, when some stay native and others convert. The natives are losing their power as a people."

A plainly dressed man joined the discussion. "We need to learn the native languages and tribal symbols. Then we can translate the truths of the Bible into their culture. God can be a God for all people, as the Bible says. Jesus Christ died for everyone. All the native needs is to know Jesus."

I peeked up from my book to see a smiling Father Artemis slap the man on the shoulder. "Monsieur Bratten," he proclaimed, "even though you are a Huguenot, for once I agree with you!"

I thought long and hard on their conversation. Would this divergence of opinion be part of the conflicted climate in the new land? Did I believe in "a God for all people"? How would I come to understand *les sauvages?* Would their freedom, their cultural independence, their tribal simplicity give me what I had been missing all my life in Louis XIV's Court?

...

After four weeks on the Atlantic, we saw land. A few curious passengers and I were rowed to shore at fog-enshrouded Newfoundland. Ice floes drifted, pushed about by crested waves. The cold wind whipped through my cloak with just as much urgency as when we were on the ship. When I first walked on solid ground, I kept tilting from side to side.

The captain said the last part of our journey upriver to Quebec would be more dangerous than the ocean crossing. He needed to feel his ship's way through foggy mornings and overcast days and tack around numerous islands and icebergs without colliding.

One evening, fish as large as our ship swam along side us—whales, the sailors told us. They cavorted on the surface for a few minutes, then dove, flinging their majestic tails up into the air and splashing them down on the water before disappearing beneath the waves. Often water erupted from their blowholes. The captain told us *les sauvages* spear-hunted the whales from small boats and used the meat, whale oil, and other products.

A sailor pointed out a beach covered with pebbles shimmering in the light. As we drew nearer, the white pebbles erupted into life and soared upward. Thousands of birds rushed our vessel and divided into two streamers of glistening silver. They opened a path for our sails and then closed ranks as we passed their beach. En mass they swooped back down to their resting place. The sailor said these sandpipers were eating sand shrimp to fatten up for their migration south.

As we traveled southwest, I relaxed on deck chairs and ambulated with other passengers, but my mind questioned what I would encounter. My soul trembled in the face of the unknown. As swiftly as the landscape changed, my thoughts took flight. Cliffs along the St. Lawrence had been cut in dramatic designs of gray, maroon, brown, and white and were drenched relentlessly with seawater. As the swishing sound and fluid motion of the waves washed over my anxious thoughts, I discovered I no longer feared the water. I wanted to learn its secrets as intimately as those rocks and sand did. Some day I would be like a fish in these waters… when I learned to swim. What other skills would I need in order to survive?

# 2

# MAN HUNT

A multitude of eyes stared at us when we *filles du roi* were lifted out of the dories onto the Quebec shore on August 12, 1671. Some men tossed their caps and cheered. Others stood still, thoughtful, looking from one of us to the next.

I hiked up my skirt to avoid the mud and immodestly exposed my ankles and knees. Quebec smelled of codfish, wet garbage, and fresh-cut lumber. Rugged-looking men hovered in the expectant crowd. Some of the males wore fashionable wigs and felt cloaks. Bearded, pale-skinned Frenchmen tipped their hats. Priests sweated in black robes. A few women in homespun dresses with long sleeves and high necks spied at us from under their bonnets.

The copper-skinned people wore only leather aprons and neck-laces of glass beads. Some of the savages had ebony hair decorated with feathers, and others twisted colored twine through their long hair. Some had shaved their heads, and others had hair sticking up like a rooster's comb.

I pulled my collar up, my cap down, and brushed dirt off my skirts, feeling scrutinized with every step I took. My friend Jeanne and I clutched each other as we walked among the other *filles du roi*, our legs unsure of themselves after six weeks at sea. Jeanne, a pert redhead, had been raised as a dairy's maid on a large estate in northern France. She wanted a healthy, kind man who would provide for her. She had no interest in adventure or in learning about new people.

*How does one decide on the right man to marry?* I thought. *A man's heart is not evident from his clothes, nor his soul discerned by his posture. How were we ladies to make such an important decision?*

Jeanne and I stepped around rotted fruit, hardened mud ruts, and fly-infested horse droppings. We made our way up the hill to the Ursuline convent. Sounds at the brewery, the cawing of sea gulls, and the rattling of wagon wheels made it difficult to talk above the din. When we arrived out of breath, Madame de la Peltrie, the missionary laywoman, welcomed us to her two-story home on the convent grounds. She was plump and energetic, with graying hair and a ruddy complexion. A tall rock wall linked her cottage and the adjacent convent to the barnyard and grille for the nuns.

The second floor of Madame de la Peltrie's home was the *filles du roi* dormitory, with our sleeping cubicles lined up row upon row. Each girl had a bed and a small table, separated from each other by shoulder-high, black linen curtains, low enough to peek over but high enough to provide privacy while saying our prayers. Our sea chests sat at the foot of our beds, which were slender wooden structures containing a hemp rope sling covered by a horsehair mattress, rough linen, and a woolen blanket. Small iron-framed windows outlined the walls, not unlike the portholes on the ship.

Once we were settled, Madame de la Peltrie gathered us downstairs. "Ladies, our king has sent you here to marry and raise families for France. Word is circulating throughout Quebec to gather our eligible men here in two days, and you are invited to a community reception."

Jeanne nudged me nervously; others sucked in their breath. Tension mounted.

"I expect you to rest up, clean up, and look your best. And we could use some help in the kitchen baking." She scurried off. Her announcement heightened the anxiety we all felt.

...

Eligible men flowed through the gate, across the yard, and into the Peltrie parlor. I could see the Ursuline novices gripping the bars of their grille, peering through the iron slats. The domestics helped Madame de la Peltrie serve the tankards of mixed berry juice and plates of partridgeberry cakes. We women hovered along the walls, watching, wondering, and imagining.

Jeanne caught the eye of a middle-aged, red-haired farmer who was dressed in leggings, a well-cut waistcoat, and polished leather shoes. I studied his kindly face as he appraised Jeanne from across the room. When the bachelor offered her a tumbler of juice, she took it with trembling hand. Smiling from embarrassment, the two wandered off, their heads tipped toward each other, talking quietly. Several more of my companions also paired up. I made a pretense of straightening the napkins, brushing crumbs off the white tablecloths, and rearranging the cakes. Eavesdropping on two woodsmen behind me, I was shocked to learn what a strong influence the king and his government had in these New World marriages.

"The edict says we cain't get a permit to trade furs 'less we're married," the lanky lad said to his chum, scratching his chin and fingering his sparse, maple-blond beard.

His pal grinned. "Is dat why you're here? You want to go into the *pays d'en haut*, the high country, again? Why not just go? Why tie yourself down to a woman?" This older man was clean-shaven, weathered, and dressed in britches of cured hides, a rough cotton tunic, and knee-high moccasins.

"Gaylord just got let out from the jail for tradin' brandy to the Injuns. He said prison was worse than being on board a ship during a storm. No, I don't want to flirt with the government and end up in jail." The younger, bearded fellow stuffed two petite cakes into his mouth, looked around, and wiped his jittery fingers on his Sunday suit. "So I'm considering finding m'self a bride." He swallowed. "What brought you here?"

"The long, cold nights during the winter." The older man chuckled a deep throaty laugh. "Plus I heard dat His Majesty rewards the farmer and his wife for havin' children."

"Yeh, I heard that too. But, Paul, you have to have ten brats before the government gives you the fifty livres. Do you see any woman in this room lookin' strong enough to drop that many live ones?"

Sensing their eyes on my back, I blushed and then turned toward the door. Breathing was hard in the stifling room.

"Mademoiselle?" A well-dressed man, a head shorter than I, approached. He had trimmed his graying beard and tied his salt and pepper hair back off his balding brow with a leather thong. "May I have the pleasure of escorting you?"

"Very well, sir," I stammered.

I stepped into the courtyard with Serge LeDuc, the proprietor of Quebec's brewery. His first wife had died the previous winter, and he had two "eligible" sons working with him at his beer factory. Monsieur LeDuc had gained his position at the brewery through the authority of the Intendant Jean Talon, Quebec's representative of the king. LeDuc said, "Talon created a golden age here. He caused Quebec's population to grow from three thousand to six thousand in six years, and he also built up the shoe and shirt factories. This leader wants to keep centralizing and populating New France. The way people talk about Talon, one would think he was responsible for every birth in Quebec."

...

Only fifteen *filles du roi* remained at Madame de la Peltrie's several days after the reception. LeDuc came again Sunday evening and took me for a stroll. As we entered the lower city, he pointed out his brewery and the house adjacent to it. For a fleeting moment, I imagined myself being Madame LeDuc and smelling of hops and barley with stepsons nearly my age. Rarely would I leave Quebec City. While Monsieur LeDuc talked about his business, I could taste the sour staleness of his house.

My attention limped back when I heard him say, "To the natives, a drunken state is a mystical experience like a state of spirit possession. Alcoholic delirium is so coveted that if a group of savages has a small amount of liquor, they will not share it, but instead choose one person to consume it all. That way the selected person can enter into the state of 'religious experience.'"

Monsieur LeDuc enjoyed hearing himself talk. He continued, "But, Mademoiselle, a native who has had too much beer becomes wild—twirling, screaming, stomping, and flinging his hatchet. He and his people do not feel this to be bad behavior. No indeed."

I was fascinated, not by my suitor but by his tale. "Do the savages ever hurt anyone?" I asked. "At Versailles, drunkenness brought out the worst in the men. Often drink would lead to fatal duels for the silliest of reasons."

"*Mais oui!* Drunken natives have set fire to lodges, bitten off people's ears and noses, and stabbed others. Whatever crime he commits while drunk is blamed on the alien spirit occupying his head. The government wants to keep a good relationship going with the savages so it tolerates their drunken behavior. Recently laws were passed to hold the Frenchman who supplied the alcohol responsible if damage was done."

"That doesn't seem fair," I said, dumbfounded.

"Just this summer one of my brewery men stole a gourd of beer from me and sold it to a native. The native got drunk, attacked a sailor, and in a frenzy swung his hatchet, severing the sailor's left wrist."

I winced.

LeDuc went on. "It was not the drunken savage who was blamed for the crime. No. The fault lay with the person who gave the native the liquor. The lad from the brewery was jailed for a month, eating only stale bread and water."

Walking on, LeDuc continued. "When he was released, he disappeared. We think he has gone into the woods to become a *coureur de bois.*"

"A *coureur de bois?*"

"Ah, literally the phrase means 'runner in the woods,' of course. But a coureur de bois is a man who trades furs for wampum, kettles, and other items needed by the natives. He's a traveler, a loner. Carrying bales of pelts, he makes his way through the western rivers, the great lakes, and down the St. Lawrence to our grand city. There he turns in the beaver pelts, gets his yearly wage, and returns to his wife and children to settle in for the winter."

"Where does the money come from?"

"Companies of coureur de bois under contract with furriers in Quebec and Montreal pay their yearly wages."

"And these men have wives?" I asked in confusion. *Who would want to marry a man who would be there just three months a year?* I thought.

"They certainly do. And a passel of children too. In fact, to be legal and have a license to be a coureur de bois, one now has to be married in Quebec."

"Then the woman is left to tend the homestead by herself?"

"Some women like running their places without a man's direction. The inhabitants who live on land tracts along the river help each other. They share the plowing, harvesting, and expensive equipment. But not every farm is headed by a coureur de bois."

As my education continued, LeDuc led me up the granite steps on the cliffside of the city. As the hill got steeper, it was harder to walk and talk, so our conversation slowed. With shortened breath, he said, "Only one in five of the men in our community… take to that way of life. The other men supplement their farming… "—he turned to look back down the path and catch his breath—"with boatmaking, blacksmithing, rope manufacturing, and milling."

We did not talk again until we were on the peak of the cliffs. The city sprawled behind us, the Great St. Lawrence rolling far below. The sun slid down the western horizon, turning the sky violet and mauve.

LeDuc interrupted my reverie. "What do you think of life in Quebec?"

So many images competed for prominence in my mind: the drunken savage cutting off the sailor's hand; the brewery lad receiving blame for that crime; the cloistered nuns praying; the coureur de bois traveling down the river with his pelts; and the homesteader with her children toiling for a harvest.

"It's so new, Monsieur," I answered.

But the truth was, it all tantalized me.

...

After two weeks, Jeanne told the redheaded farmer, Sebastian Nolet, she would be his bride. The morning before her wedding, side-by-side on our knees, we washed the Peltrie cottage floor. Jeanne had chided me the day before, "It is foolish of you not to return LeDuc's interest. He's so well-to-do and an established part of Quebec," she said.

Jeanne had been silent since dawn. Preoccupied myself, I had barely noticed her as I scrubbed.

"Jeanne," I thought aloud midway through our chore, stretching the kinks out of my back, "I don't care to be married or keep a spotless house for some man. I want an adventure. I want my independence."

I realized Jeanne's eyes were red. "I understand," she said. "I have not slept all night, thinking about my responsibilities as a married woman. I am so frightened." Jeanne grimaced when she said "married."

I sat back on my heels and twisted dirty water out of the washrag. "What do you mean?"

"You know, Madeleine. Marital duties… with a man." She almost choked on the words as she brushed the floor vigorously.

I sucked in my breath. "Jeanne, you lived on a farm. You know the facts of life."

"Of course I know how babies are made. But I don't know what I'm supposed to do. You've been at Court. Do you know what the man expects?"

I reached for the suds bucket and slopped more water on the wooden floor, scrubbing hard. What does a man expect? An image of a courtier flashed in my mind and shattered like a black rock tossed into water. Suddenly a fog of the mind overtook me, and I collapsed, knocking over my bucket.

"Madeleine? Whatever is it? I didn't mean to upset you. Oh look, your skirt is soaked." She helped me rise and squeezed the soapy water out of my hem. "I'm sorry. I never talked to *ma mere* about, you know, lying with a man. I certainly can't talk to Sister Frances or Sister Anne. I thought you could help."

I shook my muddled head, trying to clear it. "I'm sure Sebastian will be gentle and patient. He will instruct you, Jeanne. You have nothing to fear."

Even as I said that, I knew I was afraid. But I couldn't bring the cause of my fear into focus.

# 3

# CLOISTERED

When I first met the Reverend Mother Marie, her unadorned cell smelled of eucalyptus and thyme. The esteemed seventy-one-year-old nun gently took my hand and raised me from my curtsey. And she smiled. Her nurturing face made me want to cry.

"Why, my dear, did you wait so long to introduce yourself?" she said.

I cleared my throat. "The other sisters said you were not to be bothered, that you were ill."

"The sisters have been instructed by my physician to let me rest. Time and work are finally catching up with me. Please sit down. Let us have some brewed chamomile. When you're refreshed, you may share what's on your mind."

She pulled a bell cord; a nun arrived and started to protest. Mother Marie's wave silenced her. "Dear Sister, this young lady has come from our Sister Ursulines in Montagris, France. I want to hear how those women are doing."

With that, the nun bowed and backed out of the doorway.

By the time a tray of chamomile and cakes arrived, I had described my life at the Court of Versailles and my experience at the Ursuline convent school.

The Reverend Mother was curious about every detail. "Why did you take this dangerous trip to Quebec, Mademoiselle Madeleine?"

"From reading the *Jesuit Relations* I felt drawn to *les sauvages*. Now, when I see your native girls in the refectory, they seem bright and eager, curious about everything. They want to learn my language and hear about my country. But ... " Here I sighed.

"What is this 'but,' Madeleine?" she asked.

"Well, I started teaching French to one little girl, Phillipee, but the Mother Superior told me not to talk with her. She said the child would sway me to her native ways," I blurted out. "The Mother Superior questioned me. 'Why have you not secured a husband yet, Mademoiselle?' she asked. 'Isn't that why the king himself paid for your passage to our land?'

"I told the Mother Superior I have come with the Sun King's blessing to start a new life. I hoped to work with the natives.

"She said, '*Les sauvages* can lure believers into their feral and sinful ways.'

"I asked Mother Superior how so lovely a child could turn me from my faith?" I paused to catch my breath.

"Daughter, why don't you refill our cups?" the Reverend Mother asked. My trembling hands made the cups clatter in their saucers.

After composing myself, I plunged in with my questions. "Reverend Mother, why is my contact with the native girls wrong? Doesn't the letter from the Montagris convent confirm my loyalty and say that the Lord has given me the gifts of language and teaching?"

"Ah, my dear, the Mother Superior means well. And yes, the Montagris sisters praised your faith and your gifts."

She sipped in silence.

Then, to my surprise, the Reverend Mother began speaking in Spanish. "So, daughter, you are adept at languages? Forgive me for this little test, but are you able to converse with me? Where did you develop your ability to speak Spanish, German, and English as the sisters report?"

In Spanish, I answered back, "I had the honor of serving the Queen Mother, Anne of Austria. She and her ladies said I had a quick ear and taught me these languages. I am best at Spanish, less good with German. My English is fair."

"Ah, yes?" Mother Marie said in English this time, "English is important in this part of the world. We are constantly in competition with the Englishmen on the other side of the Great Saint Lawrence for furs and native alliances."

Resting her porcelain cup on her lap, Mother Marie closed her eyes. Was she deep in thought, or had I tired her out?

The nun opened her eyes abruptly, looked at me, and spoke a musical and guttural language I had never heard.

"*Dexa yawenduten Wendat eatatiak. Yawendawatsi. Lyerhe aiwaton chienhwiha d'Wendat.*"

In French the nun said, "When you learn this Iroquoian language you could be a missionary to these natives."

She placed her cup down and continued, "Ah, child, for the last twenty years I have been compiling a dictionary of Iroquoian words to teach the natives the Catholic catechism in their own language. I believe the Lord has brought you here to help me."

...

During the winter of 1671, I worked mornings with Mother Marie in her tiny room, copying Huron words next to French words, repeating them aloud as I learned the Iroquoian language.

One Sunday morning in early November, our community was eating porridge at Madame de la Peltrie's expansive table when a domestic rushed in and whispered in her ear. Madame de la Peltrie's face blanched, and her reddened hands clutched the table edge as she rose. She rapped her knuckles to get our attention.

"My dears, I have some dreadful news! Last night one of the native girls died in her bed."

She lowered her head and sighed deeply. When she looked up, her eyes held tears. The silence in the hall was leaden. "Let us pray for her soul."

As I bowed my head, my thoughts raced. *A native girl has died! Here? Why?*

For several days, no one explained why the Huron child had died. Reports said there was no evidence of physical illness, no fatal injury. What explanation would the Reverend Mother offer if I dared ask?

JULIE CATON

...

Mother Marie greeted me from her bed one morning with her own question. "Tell me your intentions about marrying, my dear."

"Truly, the call of the new land, the needs of the natives, and a desire for adventure are more important to me than a husband," I explained. This conversation was not going in my desired direction. I wanted to know why that child had died.

Mother Marie's face lit up. "My daughter, have I told you I had similar yearnings for adventure? Sadly for me, my family insisted it was proper to marry." Tears appeared in her old eyes. "So I submitted myself to their will."

Putting her gray head back against pillows, the Reverend Mother told me her own story.

"I was born Marie Guyart to a merchant couple. My parents believed I should wed an individual similar to themselves. So by my nineteenth birthday I was married and helping my husband in the silk industry. During the first year of our marriage, Claude got in legal trouble due to his relationship with unethical creditors. This caused a deep rift in our union.

"Once aware of Claude's mistake, I needed to forgive him. I had been reading books of devotion. And now I turned to the sacraments to find strength to forgive him," she said. "Shortly after we reconciled, I found myself pregnant, and gave birth to our son, Claude Martin, on April 2, 1619." The nun smiled. "We enjoyed our life as a young family. But the Lord tested me that fall. My husband got sick and died suddenly. I was barely twenty years of age, a widow with a child just six months old!" Beads of perspiration clung to her crinkled brow.

"I despaired. My prayers seemed hollow. Then on the eve of the Feast of the Annunciation in 1620, as I was walking to the business office, I was struck motionless. The eyes of my soul were opened. All the imperfections of my life were revealed, and I saw myself plunged into a bath of the precious blood and cleansed."

The Reverend Mother reached up her bony hands. "Love surrounded me, so penetrating, so inexorable! I would have thrown myself into flames to merge with it."

Mother Marie's voice lost strength. Then she closed her eyes and rested. I took her cold hands in mine and massaged them. Her shadowed eyelids looked sunken in her face. When I heard her deep, rhythmic breathing, I assumed she had fallen asleep.

...

When I arrived in her cell the next day, the Reverend Mother resumed her story.

"When I was inducted into the Ursuline convent, my beloved son, Claude, then eleven years old, wept bitterly by my side as I walked down the chapel aisle. His sorrow tore my soul in two. I just had to leave Claude in God's hands. So I bade good-bye to him and smiled on the outside but wept inside. Claude became the foster son of my sister, who opposed my taking religious vows. To protect myself from negative thoughts, I kept repeating that God was dearer to me than all else, the only focus of my love."

I reached over to fluff her pillow and looked into her eyes. *How could a mother leave her son as Mother Marie had done?* Her expression conveyed peace and sorrow regarding that difficult decision.

"In 1633, I had a vision of a young widow woman and myself sailing together to this land and ministering to the natives. Six years later I met a stranger who expressed her desire to serve the Lord in New France. Immediately I realized this laywoman fulfilled my vision. So our beloved Madame de la Peltrie and I made plans for our new lives.

"As the time approached for our trip, my dear son tested me to the core. I thought he was with my sister and attending school. But at the Dieppe Harbor, I was shocked to find Claude running out to greet me. He shouted, 'Oh, Mother, is that really you, out of your cloister?' My sister had set him up to ambush my departure. I felt betrayed.

"My nineteen-year-old son clung to me and begged me not to go to North America. My heart felt the pain of my giving him over to the

Lord anew. I reconsidered my dilemma. I could stay in France, as so many people thought I should. Instead, I prayed in my spirit to ward off that temptation. After all, I was married to the Lord!"

"What did you do?" I asked.

"I drew him near me. 'Claude, eight years ago I left you for God. Have you ever been in need of anything?' He shook his head in agreement. 'Well, let the past be a guarantee for the future,' I urged. 'Those who fear God want for nothing.'

"Separating from him pained me. So great was the natural sorrow I felt as though my bones were being dislocated. My daughter, remember that in doing God's will, joy and pain are inextricably intertwined. But the peace that comes from obedience will always prevail."

...

A few days later, the Reverend Mother shared her memories of a Huron Christian named Teresa.

"Madeleine," Mother Marie enthused, "you have not seen greater zeal for the salvation of souls than in this young woman. When I think about her, I believe my work toward converting the Huron has not been in vain.

"Teresa was crossing the northern coast of Lake Ontario with her family in 1639 when they were attacked by the Iroquois. She hid in the woods while she witnessed her father and brothers being burned at the stake. After another year, Teresa and her mother arrived shaken and starving at our convent. She and I built a lasting friendship.

"In 1644, Teresa was to travel to the Huron village near Trois Pistoles and live as a daughter of the chief. She would teach the women to read and write and speak French. But the Iroquois pursued the Huron escort down the river and took twenty-eight prisoners. We heard later the Iroquois did not kill the female captives but married them to their own warriors.

"It has been twenty-seven years since I last saw this precious believer. I pray for Teresa every day. Somewhere in this vast country, Teresa is still living for Christ."

The Reverend Mother continued teaching me the language and the ways of the savages. "You see, my dear," Mother Marie said, "many of the French Catholic ways of living conflict with the principles of the natives. We expect the redskins to change to our morals. But they resist. For example, a Huron medicine man assured one of our priests that there were five fundamentals he would not give up: the love of women, the belief in his dreams, the eat-all feasts, the desire to kill the Iroquois, and the reliance on sorcerers. At the heart of the matter, the savages do not see physical self-gratification as a sin."

"Nor does Louis XIV's Court," I muttered, my stomach souring when I thought of Versailles.

My comment drove the Reverend Mother deep into thought. Finally, she said, "You're right, Madeleine. The unsaved savage and the unbelieving royalty are very much alike."

We sat quietly, hands still.

I gathered my courage and asked, "Reverend Mother, I am troubled. A while ago one of the Huron girls died in her bed. Will you explain to me what happened?" I ventured onto this forbidden topic.

"Sadly, Madeleine, every so often a dear one succumbs while under our care and for no apparent reason. No one really knows why. I have my suspicion that the prince of darkness does not want the children to see the light of Christ, so he snuffs out their souls."

I considered her mystical explanation. But I preferred my own theory: The girl's soul had dried up, starved for the freedoms and familiarities of her own culture. If I had been constrained to marry Quebec's brewery owner or the hound-lover from France, my soul would have died too.

# 4

# CLIMBING THE WALL

"Madeleine! We need you. Do wake up!"

In the predawn darkness, Sister Anne's black eyes peered over my privacy curtain, lamp held high. I pulled on my linen shirt and woolen skirt as the nun cried, "Phillipee is gone! The smart one you've been teaching. She's not in her bed."

My fingers, stiff from the cold November morning, hooked up my bootlaces. I seized my winter cape, headed downstairs, and grabbed a gourd of hot cider.

Soon I was rambling along in the convent's cart to the village of Sainte Foye because the nuns surmised Phillipee had escaped to her home. Madame de la Peltrie had recently died of influenza, and I was the only person left at the convent who could communicate with Phillipee's Huron family. The nuns were cloistered behind the grille, having vowed not to leave, and the domestics could not speak Iroquois. The burden of being the only person at the convent who could go to find Phillipee weighed heavily on me. But I had yet to see a native village so I entered Sainte Foye with anticipation. I walked through a maze-like path, a narrow, twisting entry built into the wooden palisade. Constructed of ten-foot-high saplings lined up side-by-side with four lookout towers at the corners, this palisade surrounded the village and protected it from both animal and human intruders.

The longhouses, about fifteen feet wide, were erected from saplings and overlapping bark. They stretched along a well-swept dirt floor for about thirty feet. The interior darkness blinded me at first, as small fires provided the only source of light. Despite fist-size smoke holes on the roof ridge, my eyes stung and my nose quivered from the cloying smell.

Warriors and wives with their babes all cooked, slept, and stored their food and belongings here. Tobacco leaves of different hues hung from the beams. Sacred masks—some comic, others grotesque—stared down from the cross poles. Bowls, tools, dried corn in woven baskets, and bouquets of drying herbs hung like ornaments on the walls. Children sat cross-legged on furs or squatted on hides along an upper deck.

Phillipee jumped down from the shelf above her family's hearth, skipped over to me, and gleefully described her escapade.

"I slept in my clothes and then snuck out to the courtyard. I knew where the footholds in the wall were, so I climbed up and over and loped home." Phillipee took my hand and kissed it cheerfully. "I'm so glad you came, and not the others. You understand that I can't go back. Your heart tells you I need to be with my people."

Chief Tree-on-the-Rock and his wife Sleeping Willow, Phillipee's parents, seated me at their fire. The chief packed tobacco into a long pipe decorated with shells and feathers, languidly lit its bowl, and inhaled. He passed it to me. To not smoke would be a breach of etiquette. So I laid the warm clay calumet on my lips and inhaled. A bittersweet drag, moist and pungent, caressed my mouth. Then a cough threatened to escape, and I choked. Sleeping Willow hid a smile with her hand.

"I picked yesterday because a full moon lit my snow-covered path so I could see easily," Phillipee chirped. She threw her arms around her slender mother. "I was home to *ma mere* and *mon pere* by the time you were doing matins."

I felt conflicted. The Mother Superior had asked me to convince Phillipee to return to our convent school. But why should Phillipee not feel free to live as she liked? I had felt ensnared at Versailles and did not wish to entrap this youngster as I had been.

When I told my young friend's family of the nun's desire, Phillipee spoke quietly in clear French. "My heart is hungry for my people. I did what *ma mere* and *mon pere* asked … to learn your language. Now I am home."

I turned to Sleeping Willow, whom I had been told was a devout Catholic. She looked to be of middle age, with soulful eyes and high cheekbones. Her skin was the color of coffee with cream and her thick, black braids were woven with blue-tinged shells. She wore leggings, a matching skirt, and a deerskin tunic. Her slight shoulders bore a rabbit skin cape. Speaking slowly in Iroquois, I expressed the nuns' opinion.

Responding in French, Sleeping Willow said, "My daughter Flower Eyes—you call her Phillipee—she can be a good Christian here, too."

I tried another tactic, turning my attention to the chief. Tree-on-the-Rock, a large man, wore a bear-tooth necklace and fur pelts over his tunic. His hair was styled in the way of the boar, spiked up in the middle with bald sides. The nuns had not known what Tree-on-the-Rock's beliefs were.

"Chief, your daughter is the flower of this village. Your longhouse is strong. Your village people are brave. What do you want Phillipee to do?

He smiled, displaying a missing incisor tooth.

I ventured further. "Chief, your daughter is growing up to be a fine young lady. Would you not want her to marry a Frenchman and live in a French house and wear French clothes?"

Silence.

I tried again from another angle. "Wouldn't her education in the French ways give you and your village better business connections with Quebec?"

The father's somber face scrutinized his daughter as he puffed on the calumet. Then he spoke in Iroquois. "For two years, during the good season, we let her learn with your people. She knows your language, your ways, your beliefs. Now our ways and our beliefs can revive her. If Flower Eyes wants to marry a Huron or a Frenchman, she can decide. It is her life."

"Do you not fear for her soul? That she will end up in hell?" I asked. Inwardly I felt like a hypocrite, parroting the nuns' words, not believing them for myself.

The man looked at his woman. Tension flashed across Sleeping Willow's face. Tree-on-the-Rock pulled Flower Eyes down onto his lap. He smoothed his daughter's black coil of hair and lifted it in his hand. He gazed at the fire and spoke.

"I, and now my children, have lived among the French. Your people have taught us their doctrine. But the more I try to fathom your mysteries, the less I see light," he said. "Your church gives us fear of this fire. Years ago my people were so numerous we were the terror of our enemies. Now diseases exterminate us. War kills our men. Famine pursues us. These misfortunes came from you French people."

Flower Eyes looked intently at her father. Sleeping Willow bowed her head. She knew what her husband said was true. But I reckoned she wanted to hold on to her faith in Christ and her hope of heaven.

"Honored Chief, I have been told that you, your wife, and your daughter have been baptized. Are you doubting the value of your conversion?" I asked.

"Ha! That sacred ceremony was done thirty years ago in Huronia. For me, it was a pledge of alliance to you Frenchmen. I escaped an Iroquois massacre five years later and fled to Sainte Foye. Here I found shelter and my wife." His face softened as he looked at his woman in the firelight.

Sleeping Willow's slender fingers gripped his shoulder. "We have seen our parents burn in the Iroquois fires and have heard their screams," she said. "If there is a hell, I do not want to go there.

"Husband," she continued, "the priests pray for rain in the drought, and it has rained. You see Christians plead to the Creator for moose, and we find moose to slaughter. You cannot deny this Christian God."

Without a sound, the father rose, took his daughter and some furs, and left. I excused myself to Sleeping Willow, who was gazing beyond the fire, and followed them out.

Some Huron women were restoring a small conical dwelling by replacing bark shingles ripped loose by wind. Others were scorching long saplings so they would break in half to use for repairs. A handful of Indian men were playing a competitive game while young boys watched them.

Tree-on-the-Rock and Flower Eyes sat on a stump by the village's center pole, which was decorated with an elk's head and skulls interwoven with feathers. The village also displayed a carved wooden statue of a life-size boy resembling Jesus. He sat cross-legged with his right hand reaching up toward heaven and his left resting palm up on his lap. A butterfly had been carved on his shoulder. The artist had portrayed the boy with a broad face, almond eyes, and strong, high cheekbones.

When she saw me coming, Flower Eyes slid off her father's lap.

"Mademoiselle, come join us," she said in French, tugging at my hand.

"Thank you, Phillipee—oh, er—Flower Eyes, but I don't want to disturb your time with your father," I replied in Iroquois.

"You don't disturb us," the father said in his native tongue.

The three of us sat in silence while the sun sank. When the sky turned dark lavender and the moon's crescent rose, a group of youths whooped and stomped into Sainte Foye. Villagers interrupted their activities to greet these four men carrying a large buck slung on a pole.

Quickly the buck was prepared and its quarters spitted over the central fire. Children vied for the job of rotating the large slabs over the logs, enjoying the smell of the roasting meat and the sizzle of grease dripping into the fire.

"We will eat well tonight," Tree-on-the-Rock said.

A brawny male approached Flower Eyes and her father and bowed. He smiled, displaying fine teeth in a wide, bronze face. "Father, it was a good hunt. And I see my sister has returned," he said, lifting her up into his arms. "Flower Eyes, you are not so little anymore." He pretended to stoop under the load. She giggled.

"Tonato, come meet my teacher, Mademoiselle Madeleine. Mademoiselle, this is my brother Tonato, which means 'born in a storm,'" Flower Eyes said gaily in French.

I pushed back a stray curl and smoothed my skirt as I rose. Tonato was startled at my height. Native women were not as tall as I. Tonato's deep voice resonated as he said in French, "You know our language as well as French? And it was you who taught Flower Eyes?"

"Oui. May I ask where you learned my language?"

"When I was my sister's age, my father sent me to the Jesuit school in Quebec. I learned the French language, mannerisms, and religion. When I was fifteen, I returned to my village. That was four winters ago. Now I hone my skills as a Huron warrior to protect my relatives from the Iroquois."

When the roast was cooked, chunks of venison and a large communal bowl of corn mush was passed around. The first time the bowl came by, I quickly passed it on. The next time I tentatively dipped and licked my index finger. How good the dish tasted! Each time it came around, I reached in deeper and chewed with increasing relish.

Once we had eaten our fill, Sleeping Willow led me to a small shelter, the village guesthouse.

I stretched out and looked through the smoke hole at the stars. My body should have been tired, yet I could not fall asleep. The day's experience had affected me deeply. The life of the Huron people contrasted with the glitter of Court with its showy manners and false compliments. When artificial Versailles had dampened my spirit, I had begun to doubt my values, my strengths, and myself. Would the simplicity here in the New World help me discover who I was and what I held to be important? Eventually I fell asleep listening to a chorus of natives, talking, laughing, and chanting.

...

The next morning I ate corn porridge peppered with elderberries and prepared to leave. Tonato and his father had fed our horse, harnessed him to the cart, and placed some furs as a most welcomed gift on the seat. Tonato, Sleeping Willow, and Tree-on-the-Rock stood in the shadow of the longhouse watching me depart.

I felt dispirited as I left. Twisting in my seat for one last look, I saw Flower Eyes waving good-bye from the eastern watchtower. Melancholy squeezed my heart as the Huron village and the little girl disappeared from sight.

# 5

## ANTOINE

Upon my return from Sainte Foye, an invitation to attend the governor's 1671 holiday ball awaited me. But I wanted nothing to do with a fancy party, a lifestyle I had left behind at Versailles. I considered my response as I went to help the Reverend Mother. The window's angular morning light illuminated the fatigue lines on Mother Marie's weathered face. During my short absence, her health had declined due to the intense pain from ear abscesses. Yet, she was as alert as ever.

"My dear, not going to Governor deCourcelle's ball? Why ever not?" the nun asked, reading my thoughts. "We Ursulines need you there," she insisted holding up a trumpet-shaped gourd that would help her hearing.

"Need me? Why, Reverend Mother?"

Her hands bustled around her tray table, organizing papers, filling the inkwell, and sharpening quills. She sighed. "Madeleine, you can act as the Ursulines' representative. We cannot attend because of our vows. But there will be important people there who control the financial and social decisions of New France. I need you to be my ears and eyes, to advocate for educating and acculturating the savages," she explained. "Only through our work can we solidify this country with one belief, one church, and one king."

Her fingers were warm to my flesh, as she tucked loose hair back under my cap. "You are God's gift to me in my old age, my dear. You have the energy and the linguistic ability to carry on where I am leaving off. Maybe that's why God has not planted the desire in your heart for an earthly mate. Maybe you are to wed the Lord."

JULIE CATON

The Reverend Mother dipped her quill and said, "Come now, write to the governor that you'll be there. Sister Frances will help you prepare your gown."

...

So Sister Frances took my one fashionable gown and dressed its outer skirt with an ivory lace apron, stitching up the mauve silk to display the green underskirt. She wove matching green ribbon through the lace collar. On the evening of the ball, the nun crowned me with a petite cap of green silk, pinned up my curls, and left lengths of lace and ribbon tumbling down my back. I stopped by Mother Marie's cell before the carriage came.

"God bless you, Madeleine," she said, squeezing my gloved hands. "You are beautiful."

About forty people had gathered at the spacious Chateau Saint-Louis, but I recognized only a few: Pierre LeDuc and his two sons; Monsieur Talon, the intendant of the colony; and the proprietor of the tannery. The other single women had each claimed a man and hung onto her escort's arm throughout the evening.

The Intendant Talon came quickly to my side and introduced me to Governor deCourcelle as "the linguist His Majesty sent us from Court."

The governor, resembling a ferret with bright eyes, a close-shaved beard, and pointy chin, bowed over my hand. "Ah, Mademoiselle, my pleasure. Monsieur Talon and I are hopeful we can squelch the Iroquois raids. We are calling up an extra one thousand troops to keep the savages at bay. May I call upon you if we need a translator?" the governor inquired.

Roast partridge, pumpkin squash, creamed corn, and fried apples completed the main course. My corselet, which I hadn't worn for months, dug into my ribs, making it difficult to eat and breathe. And to think I used to wear that fashion every day!

Talon escorted me the rest of the evening. I was put off by his arrogance, but I gave him full attention when he talked about two western explorers.

"LaSalle believes westerly rivers will lead to China and that Mexico has silver mines. He proposes to claim the Gulf of Mexico area for France. Joliet is convinced that the Mississippi River flows toward California. Who knows which man is right—Robert LaSalle or Louis Joliet? Both have courage." Talon tugged at his goatee. "Yet I have not heard from either of them for over a year. LaSalle has traveled to France to gain financial support, and Joliet has ventured into the high country. What, Mademoiselle, do their futures hold?" Talon mused.

After the meal, a fiddler, a mustached man on a harmonica, and a woman on the harpsichord played rondos and waltzes. Whenever Talon linked his arm around mine to lead me to the dance floor, I felt light-headed and unsettled. I tried to lose myself in his conversation, but my attention drifted in and out.

"Finally exporting our colonial beer to France … Six hundred and fifty babies born, all since my arrival in Quebec in 1665 … " M. Talon droned on.

I tried to fight off my anxiety. The tranquility and simplicity at both the convent and the Huron village suited me better. While I could manage the social graces, this frivolity disconcerted me.

During the musicians' supper break, a comely lad immersed us in paddling songs and Quebec ballads. Talon leaned toward me and whispered, "Monsieur Antoine LaBarge returned from Michilimachinac just before the snows. He is well known for his singing ability and his courage with the savages."

The guests drank punch, made idle talk, and danced and danced. I felt the evening drag on and on, boredom numbing my agitation.

Finally, when Talon led me toward a dimly lit hallway to retrieve my coat, bile rose in my throat. My mind began to enter a tunnel. I heard my heart pumping.

Julie Caton

A woman's voice brought me back to my senses. The servant girl was asking what my wrap looked like. Quickly I dressed for the cold night air, said "Good evening" to M. Talon and did not speak to the Intendant's driver as we headed back to the convent.

The next day I described to Mother Marie the strange panic that overcame me at the governor's ball, as well as similar incidents occurring on board the *Jeanne Baptiste* and at Madame de la Peltrie's. The nun's mystical explanation irritated me. She figured that demons or spirits of the air were disturbing my sense of reality. But I sensed my mind was unsettled by vague memories from Court, the men under Louis XIV's influence and their way of handling women.

...

A month later, Antoine LaBarge, the singing voyageur, sought me out at the convent. "Mademoiselle, I noticed your beauty amidst the guests at the holiday ball and have been interested in making your acquaintance."

His sandy hair and freckled face gave him a boyish look. As he limped toward me, I expressed sympathy. "Ah, an injury from a fall during that ice storm in January," he said. "Think nothing of it."

Hastily I tucked my curls back under the cap, balled up my soiled apron, and tossed it into a corner. I held out my hand in welcome.

As we sipped hot cider in front of the central fire, Antoine told me about himself.

"I am the only child, er son, we are all boys … remaining in Quebec. My two oldest brothers left for France as soon as they were old enough to be cabin boys, and the Iroquois captured my other two brothers. My father went after them, but we haven't seen them for ten years." He fought down his emotions. "This crushed my mother's spirit, but she is tough and is healing from the loss. You must meet her some time."

"I'd like that. And you, Antoine? Where did you learn those beautiful ballads? Intendant Talon said you have been in the high country?"

"I was blessed with a good voice and sense of rhythm. The boss of a fur-trading company hired me on when I was fourteen to be the *chanteur.*"

"*Chanteur?*"

"Aye, the man in the large canoe who sets the paddling rhythm and the tone of the vessel by the songs he sings." I must have had a puzzled look, for he continued, "Every fur-trading vessel has a chanteur. Without one the paddlers don't stay in rhythm and drift off into sulky moods when the trip gets boring."

Antoine made me feel comfortable, free of the haunting anxiety that plagued me when I was around most men. By the end of that afternoon, he and I had forged a friendship.

...

On my next visit to Mother Marie's cell, she was frailer. She reached out her hand but was slow to raise herself in the bed. Her bloated, stiff fingers felt cold to my touch. Seeing her condition, tears came to my eyes, so I turned and made a show of finding a cushion for my chair.

Holding her misshapen hand, I sat in silence. Her breathing was ragged. For the first time, I could smell the foulness on her breath and knew then her illness poisoned her whole body. I was reminded of the Queen Mother's suffering and her slow death, which I witnessed ten years before. This memory sparked a sense of foreboding.

"I have been praying God would show you his will," Mother Marie said. "Have you too been praying?"

I hoped the bedchamber's dim light and shadows obscured my blush. Not only had I not prayed, but also I now coveted the life of a coureur de bois, not an Ursuline. My conversations with Antoine had expanded my knowledge. New ideas piqued my curiosity and deepened my thirst for exploration.

"Reverend Mother," I spoke at last, "I cannot envision myself on a religious path."

"My dear, does your reluctance to make a commitment to God stem from your desire to marry? Has this Antoine turned your heart?"

My heart certainly missed him at this very moment. Did that mean I wished to marry him?

Sensing my hesitancy, Mother Marie forged ahead. "Madeleine, the wife of the voyageur lives a lonely existence. Imagine not knowing if your mate will return to you in one piece or at all. With children and the farmstead, you will carry all the work. Do not marry a coureur de bois."

...

Antoine took me to meet his mother on the following Sunday. Madame LaBarge's blue eyes twinkled as her son's did. I enjoyed a hot brew of mint leaves, and blueberry tarts in their little home.

Antoine did not seem as energetic and positive as usual. "My captain heard about my injury and insisted I see his physician," he explained. "The doctor does not feel I'll have enough strength to sustain the journey this year. Captain Beaulieu assures me he will hold my place in '73, but he is already looking for another chanteur." Antoine tried hard to keep the pain out of his voice.

The three of us sat sipping our drinks. We could see ice floes in the St. Lawrence moving languidly, melting under the late March sun. At his mother's suggestion, Antoine and I went out to walk along the river.

"What will you do this summer then, Antoine?"

"Probably work at the brewery," he sighed. "Madeleine, what are you going to do? Are you going to become a nun?"

I found myself pouring out my confusion about religion as we walked. "How could I? I'm not even sure if I believe in God."

I picked up a handful of pebbles. One by one I tossed them into the great river. Finally I confessed, "Antoine, I dream of being a coureur de bois."

I expected him to laugh. But he did not.

As we strolled along the riverbank, he took my hand.

"Tell me more," he said.

"At the king's Court, I was smothered with worldly elegance, rich food, human intrigue, and the politics of the courtiers, their wives, and mistresses. Seeing the vastness of this country, watching the natural world with its animals and abundant plants, I hunger for this primitive beauty. I want freedom to move when I want to move, to say what I want to say, to wear what I want to wear! That is what I want."

"And marriage, Madeleine? Don't you want a man who can care for and protect you? Don't you want to have a baby who will love you?"

"That idea sticks in my throat, Antoine," I admitted. "I feel a powerful discomfort when I think of marriage and babies. "But I'm twenty-five years old. What will be my lot in life without a mate or the church?"

"Ah, being single would be difficult, though not impossible. My mother has lived the last nine years as a widow, a single woman in this colony. Talk to her alone. See what she thinks."

As we headed back, Antoine added, "I'd hoped that you and I might have more than a friendship. But I won't keep you from pursuing what you desire." Antoine's suggestion comforted me.

Consequently, Patricia LaBarge and I talked for several hours while she embroidered and I hemstitched a tablecloth. She was well known in Quebec for her skills at needlework from which she earned a decent income.

"Are you a practicing Catholic?" Patricia asked.

"Yes," I answered, although I thought that question odd.

"The church teaches the sanctity of marriage and sexual union only in the marital bed. A good Catholic who is not married would have to forgo her sexual urges."

"I don't have any sexual urges," I admitted on impulse.

Her stitching hand poised in the air. "That is unusual coming from a healthy, attractive girl like you." She finished her stitch. We sat thinking.

When we continued, she told me that Quebec society assumed women were irresponsible by nature and should be dominated by men in order to curb their female passions. "But the wife is guaranteed protection this way," Patricia said.

"What does a woman do when the man is unfaithful, brutal, or habitually drunk?" I asked. "What if she needs protection from her own mate?"

"The Court gives a divorce only if the woman's life is in danger, if she has a venereal disease, or if she is mad. I can't say I agree, but it does represent the opinion of this new land."

Her comments made marriage seem like a trap. "Patricia, how did you feel when married compared to your freedom as a widowed seamstress?"

"Even when Raymond and I had differences of opinion, I liked our partnership," she said, her eyes tearful. "I still grieve for his loss. I liked sharing ideas with him, seeing beautiful sunsets together, hearing the geese come in to the fields while holding his hand. I have friends here, women and men, but no one who is beside me. I have found my contentment in recent years, accepting my losses as God's will, but nothing now is as satisfying as was the friendship and partnership of my husband."

From what I had seen in France, men assumed a dominant role and women were considered property—or at best an ornament for the man's pleasure.

Here in New France, the marital contract was different. To survive in this new land, one must partner in work and pleasure. But the unfortunate woman who was tied to a wife-beater would not find relief in Quebec courts. *Could marriage have a healthy balance of dominance and submission? What kind of man was Antoine underneath all? Would I be safe with him?*

# 6

# PASSING ON TO NEW GROUND

By mid-April, the nuns were spending much of their time in prayer for Mother Marie's recovery. Figuring that I was not skilled at prayer, I took up as many of their chores as possible. On my free day, I went down Quebec's hill to seek out Antoine.

One Saturday, we decided to walk through the town shops, although neither of us had an extra livre. The smells of nuts roasting, fresh-caught fish, dried grapes and apples assailed our senses. LeDuc's brewery was selling beer from a street stall. A young maid and one of the LeDuc sons passed out frothy, full mugs and called a jovial "hello."

Rounding another corner, Antoine and I walked into the town's green space, and twenty feet from us on a plank bench, a plump, blond doxy squirmed under the cumbersome body of a sailor. He'd crumpled her skirt up to her waist. I could see her pale thighs. I froze in my path and stared. My head swam as a gray mental mist descended.

The next thing I knew, Antoine was rubbing my wrists and calling my name. I shook the fog away and offered a weak smile.

"What happened, Madeleine?" He waited patiently for me to come to my senses.

I told him about my panicking, the unusual incidences, and how Mother Marie believed the events were demonic attacks blocking me from knowing God and his will. "She thinks the devil impedes one's efforts to do God's will by strange happenings such as these. What do you think, Antoine?" I asked.

"Madeleine, similar feelings overcome me," he said slowly. "Whenever I am in a hayfield with the light just so and the smell of summer coming from the mowed hay, I become dizzy and cold. I feel as if I'm no longer in my body. Sometimes I see my brothers being whipped and tied by the Iroquois and carted away. That bad summer of '62, I hid in the field with Iroquois just paces away from me when they took my brothers captive. Death's threat still sends chills up my spine when I'm reminded of that day."

I took some deep breaths and looked out at the river.

"Madeleine," Antoine said softly, "what terrible thing happened to you?"

I stood slowly. "I can't… I can't," I mumbled and trudged back up the hill to the convent, shivering.

...

"When you make vows of celibacy, the Lord himself becomes your All-in-All. You are never lonely. He gives you love and confidence in all circumstances."

"But, Reverend Mother, you can't be held physically by God."

"Indeed you can. It is a mystical experience beyond description. I have felt God's arms around me."

As we worked on the dictionaries, I thought about Marie Guyart as a young girl and then as a bride, nineteen years old.

I set my quill down. "Mother Marie, you have been married and borne a son. Did your experience of physical intimacy sate your appetite? Did being with a man make it easier for you to make that vow of celibacy?"

"On the contrary, Madeleine," the aged nun answered. "Once a woman has tasted the fruit of passion with a man, she is more likely to desire it again. Marital union may not be pleasant for the woman at the beginning. It takes practice. But as the woman experiences the sensations of carnal knowledge, she begins to crave that passion more." The nun's coloring heightened. "For me, only after I became a mother did I begin to find pleasure in the marital bed." She sighed and stared out the window. "After my husband's death, I yearned for the joy of our physical intimacy. But I felt guilty and ashamed of those feelings. Our Lord does not want us to dwell in areas of human passion.

"A virginal state makes commitment to the vow of celibacy easier for you. Simply put, you don't know what it is you are missing."

As Mother Marie spoke, a blush rose up my cheeks. Did I know what I was missing?

Lost in thought, I began doodling on a blank page, scribbling a narrow hall with no opening at the end. Then a small woman took shape under my quill, a circle of skirts and petticoats around her legs. She had her back against the wall. She had no face. In the foreground, my quill drew a large male, his enormous hands reaching down the hall. I designed a gray wig of curlicues on his head, darkened in his shoulders, and etched his belt black.

I studied the sketch. Then the picture made me sick, and I looked away. Out the window, the evening's clouds darkened the horizon, matching my spirit.

...

At the end of April, I carried a message to Sainte Foye about the Reverend Mother's health. The chief of the Hurons, as the leader of the native community, would need to decide how his people should respond to their revered missionary's passing. When I arrived, Sleeping Willow was roasting a haunch by the central fire. She rose and smiled at me warily. "Chief Tree-on-the-Rock will be home when the sun goes down."

Flower Eyes tugged at my arm. I spent the rest of the day with her and her friends chattering in their native language while I waited for the chief's return. Flower Eyes asked me to teach her friends about France, about the ocean, about the church. Six eager faces rewarded me with their enthusiasm as they listened to my descriptions of Louis XIV's coronation, when the fifteen-year-old king dressed all in white and gold rode his white stallion down the cathedral's aisle. Even though

I was eight at the time, I remember the spectacle and the arrogant look in the boy-king's eye.

The sun sank low in the sky. I told more stories about Versailles. Some of the youngsters became my teacher, saying native words at my request, my ears tuning to their pronunciation and cadence.

We heard a clamor of activity from outside the village. The hunters had returned! The chief and his people would eat until stuffed and then fall asleep. I would have to wait to see Tree-on-the-Rock the next day.

That night I slept on fresh hemlock boughs in the visitor's hut. Through the smoke hole I looked up at the stars and weighed how much I had learned since my first visit here five months ago. I felt so confident among the natives. I knew I needed to participate in adventure and become knowledgeable about the land surrounding me. Perhaps a man would join me, perhaps Antoine.

...

At sunrise, Flower Eyes woke me with a steaming cup of something that smelled of flowers and moss, looked like mud, and tasted like licorice. Her father would receive me.

We met by the Jesus statue. As was the Huron custom, the chief and I exchanged compliments and pleasantries. Then Tree-on-the-Rock became silent, waiting for me to speak. "The Reverend Mother is gravely ill and is not expected to live through another month," I said.

Even though I knew that truth, I had not spoken it out loud. The reality of losing my mentor overwhelmed me, tears stung my eyes, and a lump formed in my throat. I walked toward the fire. By turning my back on the chief, I broke etiquette, but I needed the fire to camouflage my emotions.

Flower Eyes heard my news, saw my sad expression, and ran up to me. "Who will teach us then, Mademoiselle? Madame de la Peltrie is gone to heaven. Mother Marie will follow her soon." She took hold of my hand. "You will teach us, *n'est-çe pas?*"

Tree-on-the-Rock approached us. "My daughter is right. Mademoiselle, come back when your nun passes to another world. Teach here."

The chief's invitation made my heart sing. Yes, I would come here to teach the native children. In exchange, maybe the Huron would teach me what I needed to know for success in their wilderness.

When I returned from Saint Foye, Mother Marie called to see me. I described my visit, leaving out news of Chief Tree-on-the-Rock's invitation. Yet, as if she read my thoughts, the Reverend Mother mustered energy and said, "When I am gone, Madeleine, teach the savages. No one in Quebec has your skills. And, my dear, I will be with the Lord shortly." A blissful smile settled on her face.

"I do feel it is God's calling for me ... to teach them," I said, holding her hand. The words came haltingly as I left out the part of Tree-on-the-Rock's request for me to go to Sainte Foye. I blushed at the omission.

"Good. Take your vows. Teach from within the convent as I have done."

My mind battled. Should I tell her my intention was to live with the natives, not the nuns?

But the Reverend Mother murmured, "I have given my all for the savages. There is nothing left." With those words, she sank back into her pillows.

All was silent.

Then I heard the nun's soft praying. "My God, my God, my great God. My life, my all, my love, my glory."

Rhythmically, while touching the smooth, wooden cross to her cracked lips, she repeated words of adoration.

Marie of the Incarnation died two days later, April 30, 1672.

# Part Two:

## The Bud and the Butterfly

# 7

# COUPLINGS

After Mother Marie died, without the church's blessing I moved to the Huron village in June. Dressed in a deerskin tunic, leggings, skirt, and beaded moccasins, I offered French lessons every morning around the central fire. The native women had collected large, flat stones and pieces of flint for the children to use for writing.

The native children loved to act out the stories I told them about France. The wooden statue of the boy Jesus looked on as I taught, becoming my silent friend. Their mothers feigned disinterest as they stitched moccasins, scraped hides, or decorated tunics with dyed porcupine quills. The men, less interested, were constructing another longhouse as Huron converts and natives from other nations kept arriving as refugees from Iroquois terrorism. Working together, the men felled pines, hacked branches off, and hoisted them against the seventy-foot center beam. They lashed slabs of bark onto the roof, being careful to leave five smoke holes spaced along the ridgepole.

Antoine's and my friendship deepened. He came often and stole me away on Saturdays so we could visit a lake and he could teach me to swim. The first time Antoine released his support, I sank. He pulled me up as I sputtered, and then taught me to fill up my lungs with air, hold my breath, put my arms out, and float on my back. Finally, I felt free enough to try swimming by myself. Antoine and I grew more comfortable together as I relaxed under the feel of his hands on my body and his gaze on my wet chemise.

The summer evenings were warm, but I had to light a fire in my tiny hut to keep away the bugs. Flower Eyes told me to rub bear grease on my skin for protection from the incessant biting of the mosquitoes, but I couldn't get used to its feel.

The Hurons' way of life fascinated me, particularly their ability to live daily in harmony with three or four families in one longhouse. Versailles courtiers and their relatives would have bickered. Maybe harmony among the natives happened because they had no sense of individual ownership. Each family cleared the land and cultivated the crops depending on what they could manage and what they needed. If they had surplus, they shared. If they didn't have enough, another family provided for them.

The longer I lived with the tribe, the more I learned of their culture. The Hurons were farmers by tradition, and their staple foods were corn, beans, and squash cooked in a variety of forms, and fondly called the "three sisters." Their young men supplied the meat. I tasted elk, venison, and bear from successful hunts. The people held dog-flesh in high esteem, but I could not develop a liking for it.

Their peculiar means of exchange, *wampum*, were elongated white and purple beads made from shells. They strung *wampum* into jewelry and used wampum to decorate the girls at the festivals. Wampum served a greater purpose than decoration. Neither contract nor speech was delivered without a belt of wampum, which sealed the transaction and also served as an aid for remembering the event.

The unmarried Huron female had a life of license, while the older married woman had a life of drudgery. I feared the same would be true for me if I married. The Huron tradition of experimental marriage confused me. A young woman could seal a compact, receive a gift of wampum from her suitor, and have him move in with her. Such a union could last a day, a week, or months. If the Huron maiden did not like her suitor after a period of time, she could end the connection and not return the gift of wampum. Flower Eyes pointed out three new brides who had collected many strands of wampum by going through several trial marriages before selecting their permanent mate.

Once the couple moved in with the girl's relatives and bedded down, there was no privacy for them, nor did they seem to care. If a couple wanted to be alone, they took to the bushes. One night Flower Eyes had me sleep by her in their longhouse so we could tell stories. I was unnerved by the sounds, smells, and smoky night images I saw. The natives' sexual freedom was one reason my little hut was an absolute refuge for me.

Once a young woman became pregnant and settled into a monogamous bond, her life became that of a slave. She was expected to gather the firewood, sew, and harvest, smoke fish, dress skins, and prepare clothing. The men were free to hunt for food, prepare for war parties, and govern their families. Many of the older women became shriveled and toothless, and their personalities suffered from their hard work. They became fierce in their language, and cruel with their gossip.

Religious tension crackled in Sainte Foye. A schism arose between the converted Christian Hurons and those who maintained the traditional beliefs. Only a few, such as Tree-on-the-Rock, held a middle ground and tolerated both factions. Because Sainte Foye was a mission town, a Jesuit visited often. The priest would exchange trade goods, such as a copper kettle, to a nonbeliever for some evidence of Christian behavior, like having his child baptized.

The traditionalists believed the Christians had turned their back on the people and sold themselves to the Frenchmen and the church. The Christians assumed the traditionalists were loyal to the "dark side," to demons and idols, magic and myth, and would end up burning in hell for eternity. Because of this belief, it was heartbreaking for a convert to see a loved one die who had not been baptized a Catholic.

...

Toward the end of July, Sleeping Willow took Flower Eyes and me to pick blueberries. Flower Eyes smeared bear grease on me to prevent black fly bites and sunburn. We picked late into the afternoon and stained our hands and mouths blue from our self-indulgence.

I needed to relieve myself, so I walked over the rocky ledge and around the blueberry bushes to find privacy. Mosquitoes buzzed around my head as I squatted. I looked up to shoo them away and saw a couple approaching the hillock. Dances-through-Leaves, a classmate of Flower Eyes, and a young warrior approached, their arms entwined, smiling. Dances-through-Leaves shed her vest and let her wampum necklace swing over her breasts. The girl looked beautiful and ripe with happiness.

The couple stopped by a large moss-covered rock. The male, with only an apron around his waist, stroked her hair, her neck, and her shoulders. The girl ran her hands over his back. Their mouths drank in each other.

I watched them from behind mountain laurel. The couple glowed golden against the afternoon sun. He pushed Dances-through-Leaves gently against the boulder and shifted his loin cloth out of the way. She closed her eyes and began to moan. Deep cries came from within her throat, and he swallowed her sounds, smothering her mouth with his. Their tension held; then they both started laughing and kissing again.

He bent down and picked a Queen Anne's lace for her, and Dances-through-Leaves put it in her hair. Arm-in-arm they walked back toward the village. The sun was behind them, and they faded into a haze of light.

I was breathless, and my heart began to pound. My moist body throbbed. Seconds later bile rose. I closed my eyes, and the golden image dirtied. A gray mist replaced sunlight. Instead of the wholesome smell of laurel and blueberry bushes, the sickening aromas of banquet meats assailed my senses. In the corridors of Versailles, I heard the noises of courtiers preening. I was against a wall—panting, blushing, terrified.

I could not breathe. A flood of emotion choked me into blackness.

Then Flower Eyes and Sleeping Willow were calling my name, moving me to the shade, offering me a drink. The water washed away some of my shame. After I recovered, we walked home, three of us laden with wooden baskets filled with early blueberries. Only I was burdened with sour memories.

Julie Caton

I tried to understand my emotional upheaval. Sleeping Willow maintained a companionable silence. But after three days she came, and we squatted together in the entrance of my hut, watching the pastel morning light fill the serene sky. Sleeping Willow was too respectful to ask a direct question. She began, "Madeleine, pain came to you when we went to pick blueberries. I am sorry."

*What should I tell her?* I wondered. The natives' attitudes toward one's body and the natural acts of copulation were so different from the French Catholics that I wasn't sure if she would understand. I didn't even know what my pain was all about.

Blushing and stammering, I told Sleeping Willow about the happening at the blueberry patch, and my other experiences. She said little. Her reassuring presence, understanding eyes, and occasional question helped me. As I talked, I remembered more: myself as a vulnerable girl at Versailles; a courtier touching me in a shameful but arousing way. I began to question myself. *Was that memory the key to my getting chills whenever I witnessed physical intimacy? Though I responded to the sweet lovemaking I'd observed, had my natural urges been tarnished?*

"What shall I do?" I asked my friend.

"Pray to Jesus," said Sleeping Willow, a woman of faith.

It was too simple an answer.

· · ·

After two months at Sainte Foye and one year from my arrival in this new land, I traveled to *Rivere Jacques Cartier* with a Huron escort for a reunion with Catherine Milville, my kindred spirit during our convent schooling six years earlier. Many afternoons she and I had swung in the convent garden and imagined living in Canada. Now we were living here, fulfilling our childhood dreams. I'd written her upon my arrival in Quebec via an itinerant Jesuit priest. Catherine, now heavy into her third pregnancy, invited me to come and help care for her two young children.

She wrote: "If you were to find it in yourself to become part of our family, you would be a godsend. Jacques is in the fields or doing farm work from sunrise to sunset. My time won't come for another few months, but my heart yearns for your cheerful presence and helpful hands."

A Huron runner took my message telling the Milvilles I would come in mid-August, and now here I was. Antoine had offered to escort me, but I encouraged him to keep his employment at the brewery. "I'll miss you," I said, but we were both too unsure to kiss good-bye. Chief Tree-on-the Rock had said nothing upon my departure, despite the tears in his wife's and daughter's eyes. My feelings were as changeable as the water swirling on the river—nervousness, sadness, and anticipation all running together.

The Milvilles had formed a small village, Rivere Jacques Cartier, with the LaCornes and six other families. Their farmlands, distributed like pieces of a pie, fanned out from a center point where their river flowed into the great St. Lawrence. Their houses were within a hundred yards of each other at the confluence of the rivers. A large community palisade protected the eight cabins from the woods. Outside the palisade, each family owned a tillable one hundred acres. Some of the families had been there for over a decade, and their fields yielded large harvests—enough to support themselves and help their newer neighbors.

Catherine plodded like a tortoise carrying a huge shell. Even though her face was puffy from her pregnancy and the August heat, her gray-green eyes still danced. If I gazed at them, she looked like the young girl with whom I used to play and share dreams.

And how glad I was to help! Nearly three-year-old Marie-Catherine, a cherubic blond with her father's eyes and her mother's smile, had mastered running and practiced another new skill: talking incessantly unless she was sleeping or eating. Charles, just over one year, tried toddling everywhere, yet his balance was unsteady, and often he landed on his fat bottom. But he laughed and grinned with each fall, clambered back up, and was off again.

Jacques had traveled the fur-trading routes with his partner, Samuel LaCorne, leaving Catherine home alone—the first year pregnant, the second year with her first infant, and the third year with

Marie-Catherine and Charles as mere babes. Other homesteaders, led by Suzanne LaCorne, supported her while their men were out trading. The village shared individual talents, breeding stock, and expensive equipment, as the Hurons did. Perhaps this community spirit, so different from Court, was a natural response to the need to survive and a way to deal with the terror of Iroquois attacks. Two years ago, fifty marauding Iroquois tried to break through the palisade at Rivere Jacques Cartier to steal the cattle and children. The attack had been thwarted, however, because the palisade held strong and the families had used their muskets freely. But this experience had raised Rivere Jacques Cartier's caution level. Now each person partnered up when working in the fields, one tilling and the other watching for intruders.

That spring Jacques had built Catherine a two-room house with a loft and two windows. He had trimmed flat edges on slender trees, aged and dried them so he could assemble a *piece-sur-piece* log building. Catherine's family in France would ship some glass panes nestled in a barrel of molasses to prevent breakage. Such a dwelling was a step up for Catherine, as she had lived in a rectangular shelter made of vertical posts, gaps between the woods stuffed with sod and a roof made out of branches. Now their livestock lived in their original shelter, and Catherine thought she resided in a palace.

...

"Run, Madeleine, and fetch Suzette. No, Charles, you can't sit on your Mama's lap." Realizing his wife's labor had started, Jacques shouted disorganized commands and rambled through their cabin.

Once Suzette arrived, she chased Jacques out, telling him to take the children. "No use the little ones hearing Catherine holler," she said. "We'll fetch you when her work's done."

I had been responsible for dispensing calming herbs or pain-numbing medicinals at several birthings while I lived at Versailles. My role there had been peripheral, but at least it had given me some experience attending a birth. Here Suzette, serving as the village midwife, used a native style of childbirth different from the more intrusive style used by Court physicians. She had Catherine squat over fresh straw, and she told me to support Catherine under her armpits. Suzette massaged Catherine's belly with hot compresses and urged the baby into the world. Catherine delivered her second son, Jean de Roybon Milville, around midnight on September 5, 1672.

When robust baby Jean wiggled his ten toes and bobbled a fluffy head of hair, I felt a tingle of pleasure, like I was somewhat responsible for this new life. Jacques peered into the infant's receiving blanket and grinned. Little Marie-Catherine didn't know what to make of her brother. She kissed her mother's sweaty brow and ran off to her trundle bed, crawling under her blanket next to sleeping Charles.

After Suzette left, I curled up in front of the fire, soothed by the sounds of baby Jean sucking at Catherine's breast and the mother cooing quietly to her newborn. I wondered, *would I feel elated if this were my child? Or would I hold myself apart from the babe, afraid of losing it within the year? Would I have to marry, or would these people of the new world accept a baby born who was a bastard?*

...

I took over Catherine's chores and tried to entertain the children. Marie-Catherine liked a family of cornstalk dolls I created with rawhide and linen scraps. Charles piled pinecones on top of one another and delighted himself by knocking them over. When there was time, Catherine and I chatted about our days in France and how different our lives were in Quebec.

"How do you find living in the wilderness?" I asked.

"I am content, Madeleine. Jacques's enthusiasm for this way of life sustains me. I don't mind being busy. But this life sometimes overwhelms." She paused in her mending and then continued softly, "I love Jacques deeply. But the second season, he left me alone with Marie-Catherine just toddling and unborn Charles weighing me down. I thought I would not endure the entire season." She stretched her shoulders and rubbed her distended belly.

"And my body had a mind of its own," Catherine reminisced. "Often I would have to put my feet up because my ankles were so swollen. When I should have been working in the garden, instead I would nap with Marie-Catherine tucked under my arm. If it weren't for the support of Suzette and the other women in Rivere Jacques Cartier, I might have gone mad."

The question plaguing me for the past year came to mind, so I asked it of Catherine: "How did you know Jacques was the man for you to marry?"

Catherine rethreaded her needle. "That's hard to say, Madeleine." She winced as she pushed herself up in the bed. "I knew I needed to respect the potential husband's vocation and goals. But most had respectable plans. So then I added that a husband would have to share my values and faith. Jacques is an upright Catholic. When I crossed over in '67, I found many men here had turned their backs on the church. Some had taken up drinking and running with loose women."

The newborn started whimpering and made sucking movements with his rosebud mouth. Catherine set down her needlework and lifted Jean to her breast. As she gazed at her infant, she was quiet, pondering.

Then she added, "But the decision went beyond these traits of character. I knew also I wanted to feel passion, attraction. Even though Jacques and I hadn't touched each other yet, I yearned to be in his arms, to wake up every morning next to him for the next forty years. I fell in love with him then."

"Have you ever doubted your decision?" I asked. My thread had knotted, and impatiently I yanked it. It snapped, forcing me to reknot and start again.

"Yes. Sometimes, when little things have gone wrong, I have doubted out of sheer exasperation. Like a fool I would think, 'Well, if I weren't married to him, then I wouldn't be in this mess.'"

"What were some of these little things?"

Catherine thought for a moment. "The first spring we were married I discovered that Jacques expected me to work in the fields. I took issue at first. But then Jacques explained as partners we had to work as an equally yoked team to get the most important work done first. As time went by, our division of labor would change.

"That winter, the chimney had clogged, and our shelter was filling with smoke. After he pitched the burning logs out the door, Jacques told me to climb up on the roof and drop ropes down the chimney to clear the blockage.

"'Why me?' I yelled at him. I hadn't told Jacques I was afraid of heights, even if it were only ten feet off the ground.

"'Well, my sweet, you are a hundred pounds lighter than I, for one reason. The thatched roof may hold you. I am not certain it will hold me. For another, I can boost you up there, but I doubt you can boost me up.'

"So I had no choice and went clambering up my tall husband's shoulders and halted, leery, before stepping on the thatch to clear the chimney. Later that day I confessed my fear of heights to him.

"Jacques told me living in this country has a way of chasing the fear out of you. That certainly is true. I am a much stronger and more confident woman now."

I pressed the subject. "Were there times when you wanted to leave the marriage?"

"Only two incidents caused me to doubt the wisdom of what I had done. As you can well imagine, the first time Jacques told me he was leaving for the pays d'en haut to trade for furs, I was shocked. While I knew that fur trading was a common occupation, Jacques had never mentioned his interest to me before we were married. I thought he was a farmer. I questioned his choice. He wanted to earn money quickly to build up our farm. I disagreed with him.

"'Deserting me is not part of the marriage contract,' I had argued with Jacques. 'I am too new at life in the wilderness to manage without you.' But he disputed me. 'I am not deserting you,' he told me. 'I am building up our homestead. Besides, the people of Rivere Jacques Cartier will help you.'

"I lost my temper," Catherine said. "Pointing my finger at him, I shouted, 'you're going only because you want other women! I've heard the voyageurs are loose with the red skin women. You're just like the rest. You're lusting after those natives!'

"Jacques became livid. He stormed out of the shelter and didn't speak to me for one whole day."

Thinking she must be thirsty, I poured Catherine some cider and seated myself on the foot of the bed. After she sipped, Catherine continued, "Jacques came to me apologizing. At first, I thought he had changed his mind about being a coureur de bois. But his apology was not for that choice, but for his insensitive way of telling me about his decision. As he explained himself again, in a more tender way, I fell back in love with him."

To examine my patching, I held up Jacques's shirt.

"Not half bad," Catherine said.

"And the other time you questioned yourself?" I asked.

"Jacques and Samuel had returned by mid-September of that same year, laden with beaver pelts. They wanted to see their families and rest up before taking the furs into Quebec to sell. I was deeply in love with Jacques during those few days, delighted to have him back and pleased he would be present for the birth of his first child. I took pleasure in washing him and shaving him, fixing him vegetable stews, and roasting a chicken for him. Our love-making was at first passionate and then leisurely and comforting."

Catherine shifted her baby to her shoulder and patted the wee fellow's back. His loud burp made us both smile. The new mother handed her infant to me, and I stood swaying with him next to the bed, feeling Jean's velvety cheek against my own.

My friend sipped some cider and resumed. "We shared stories about the adventures we each had while apart. I had become quite confident in my work as a farmer's wife. He was pleased he and Samuel had escaped some difficult encounters with the Algonquins and had kept their goods safe despite running through white water."

I settled into the rocker and held the newborn.

"Jacques and Samuel took off two days later to do their trading and selling," Catherine's voice tensed. "The third evening, Jacques came stumbling into our home smelling of ale. He could hardly stand and was singing bawdy sea ballads. He grabbed me up in his arms. I wiggled to get loose, repulsed by the smell of liquor. He laughed and held me tighter. I thrashed harder and screamed. Suddenly a black cloud came over his face. He threw me down and, kneeling over me, cussed and slapped me. 'Woman, don't ever scream like that at me again!' he shouted.

"I had never seen Jacques like that. I had heard of men being 'mean drunk' and supposed that was it. I wasn't sure what to do." She paused and took a deep breath. "I went limp, turned my face away from him, and closed my eyes. It must have scared Jacques. He started to cry, 'Oh, what have I done?' He fell beside me on the floor. Weeping, he stroked my face. As his fingers ran over the fresh welt, I held back a flinch and kept my eyes closed. Within minutes, he was snoring beside me on the cold earth. As I lay there, I doubted our marriage. Who was this man to whom I had committed my life?

"When I was sure he wouldn't awaken, I crept away and crawled into our bed. I prayed. I didn't know what else to do.

"The next morning Jacques was up stoking the fire, fixing tea, and looking sober—a very different man than the night before. When he saw the welt on my face, tears came to his eyes. 'I thought maybe it was all a bad dream, Catherine. But I did hit you, didn't I?' He got down on his knee by the side of the bed and took my hand in his. 'My father was a mean drunk,' Jacques said. 'I swore when I left France in '64 I would never be like him. Yet, I'm afraid that is what I was last night. Would you please forgive me?'

"I was still timid about how to approach him. So I waited, watching his eyes. He looked deep into my soul and showed remorse." She looked up at me while I rocked her infant.

"I hesitated to say 'yes' because I wasn't sure I knew what forgiveness entailed. Finally I said, 'Yes, Jacques, I will forgive you.' Then I added, 'But do not ever do that again—neither the drinking nor the hitting.' And Madeleine, even though I forgave him, I did not forget and still harbored fear and anger. But Jacques has never gone drunk on me since then."

I nestled lower into the rocker and luxuriated in the warmth of Jean's small body. "Catherine, how can you forgive him but still be angry with him? I thought one must give up her anger when she forgives? Isn't that what the church teaches?"

"It doesn't work that way for me," Catherine answered. "'Forgiving' is like the act of removing the splinter from your hand. Anger remains. That would be like the pus and infection still in the wound. It will take some time for the sore to heal. I had to will myself to fall back in love with Jacques after that experience."

...

When Samuel LaCorne and his Huron partner arrived in late September from the pays d'en haut, the village women fixed a welcoming feast and invited Antoine, who had paddled up from Quebec to visit me at *Rivere Jacques Cartier*. He was still working at the brewery. While we didn't discuss it, I sensed that he had missed me far more than I had missed him.

Antoine entertained us with stories about the new Governor Frontenac. "When he arrived here, the governor strutted down the gangplank with his freshly powdered wig on, his uniform buttons catching flashes of the afternoon sun. He is so short and thick that he couldn't keep his balance! As he hit solid ground, he grabbed the arm of Intendant Talon to steady himself. Nine seamen each dragged two bales of his personal belongings. A drummer followed with drum rolls."

I poked Catherine. "Eighteen bales of clothes! We *filles du roi* were allowed just one trunk apiece."

Antoine continued, "Frontenac talked only to Talon and the outgoing governor while his parade went through the lower town and then up to the Chateau Saint-Louis. I overheard Frontenac comment on how ugly and disorganized the lower town was with all the houses built any way the owners desired, much different from Versailles."

Soon the smells of people, bubbling stews, and the smoke from the bread oven fires at the LaCornes' stifled me, so I sought fresh air. Sitting on a pile of hay under the eves, I shucked ears of corn, listening to Antoine, Jacques Milville, and Samuel LaCorne share news of the high country. Antoine and Jacques were scraping kernels off the ears, and Samuel kept up a steady rhythm of grinding the kernels to cornmeal using a large pestle and crock.

I became lost in their words: A vast woodland where one might not see people for days. A chain of lakes, glassy and clear one day and windswept the next, perhaps with a cluster of deer grazing by an embankment. A cumbersome brown bear gracefully catching salmon with her thick paws. I could hear the roar of the white water, churning over rocks and rushing down sharp drops along the riverbeds.

As Samuel and Jacques reminisced with Antoine about the exotic birds and waterfowl they had seen, I could feel the whir of geese flying close overhead, looking for wetlands in which to build their nests. I remembered the magical swarm of sandpipers parting ways for our ship in Newfoundland. I looked at Antoine with new respect. He knew this high country. If I married him, would he take me with him into the wilderness?

As shadows lengthened, I left to walk around the palisade. *Why did the little ones—Marie-Catherine, Charles, and baby Jean, as precious as they were—not capture my heart the way the magnetic power of the wilderness did? How could I become a woman of les pays d'en haut? Would it be possible to explore nature and grow close to the Creator while supporting myself?* I gazed at the Great Saint Lawrence and yearned to get on the river and keep heading west.

...

Jacques and Catherine were embracing—no, they were coupling—when I walked into their cabin on All Saint's Day. I had left Marie-Catherine and Charles sleeping on blankets under the oak tree. Running into the house to get another quilt to put over them, I stumbled onto their parents' lovemaking.

Jacques's flannel shirt cluttered the wooden floor, and Catherine's linen chemise and dress formed a puddle by the bed. Catherine's hair, uncovered, flowed down her neck. Her face looked radiant, eyes closed, head thrown back, perspiration dripping down her throat as Jacques's hands caressed her.

I stopped, afraid of what I saw, apprehensive of what would happen if they discovered me. My insides heated. Out of embarrassment, I closed my eyes. But then I heard their passion even more acutely. Jacques's throat rumbled with satisfaction. Catherine moaned.

Dizzy, I began to sway. A mist encompassed me, and I saw myself running down a hall trying to get out, pounding at a door that wouldn't open to me. Arousal commingled with shame as I tried to flee.

The next thing I knew, Jacques was bent over me, his flannel shirt thrown on but not buttoned. He rubbed my wrists as Catherine, draped in a quilt, asked where the children were.

...

For four days, I felt embarrassed, ridiculous, and sullen.

Then Catherine and I were alone, a rarity. I didn't want to talk about the incident, but I knew I must. Because Jacques was visiting Samuel to discuss the building of a chapel—an idea that had grown since the priest's visit—and Marie-Catherine and Charles were asleep in their trundle bed, I cleared my throat. But it was Catherine who began.

"You have been so distant in the last few days, my dear Madeleine," she said. "Walking in on us is embarrassing, yet certainly not enough to cause you to clam up as you have. What is bothering you?"

I told Catherine how their lovemaking had aroused me and also flooded me with shame and panic. I described the strange mental narrowing of the corridor: myself filthy, running away. By the time I told of the closed door and not being able to get out, I was shaking and crying.

Catherine placed Jean in his cradle and came to put her arms around me. She rocked me and cooed as my tears turned to groans, coming deep from my belly. The image of the corridor and my banging on the door became so vivid I thought I would retch. Sobbing, gasping, hiccupping, I clung to Catherine, my fingers digging into her shoulders.

The fire died down. By then I had settled into her arms feeling drained and exhausted. Catherine shifted me to the cushion, rose, and went to build up the fire and make tea.

Over some chamomile tea, she said, "When we were together at Montagris' convent, I sensed something or someone had injured your soul. Now tell me what happened to you."

I took a deep breath. "It was at Versailles. I remember the tapestries and doors running along the dimly lit hall. I could hear the noises of the Court just a few paces away. But I was alone... except for him, a courtier, short and thick. His wig had the aroma of lavender, and his sweat reeked of garlic. His hands were large, clammy, covered with powder, and fleshy like a sow's cheek. Deep in the shadows, he pressed me against the wall. He held my chin straight in front of his face. When I didn't respond in a manner that pleased him, he pinched my neck and told me to 'behave like a lady.' Then he shoved my skirts up and touched me in a shameful way. As much as I tried not to, I could feel my body respond. 'Hey, my beauty. You love this, don't you?' he whispered. I swallowed down the gorge that threatened to spew over this creature. I felt so degraded."

As I shared with Catherine, an unburdening washed over me. Although shame and guilt still twisted my gut, my cloud of anxiety thinned. Jacques entered the room, but Catherine gave him a withering look, and he scurried back out. She refilled my cup. "You were a child, Madeleine, and singled out by an adult for his pleasure. That was wrong of him." She shook her head in dismay. "Did you tell anyone?"

Quickly I said "no." But as I stared into the fire, another image came. My body became flushed and trembled.

Catherine prodded gently. "Madeleine, what are you remembering now?"

"I… I told my father," I whispered. Fragments of the memory came together: My father at the carving table, glowering, turning his back to me, serving the next courtier a blackened slab of venison. My father wiping his hands on his apron and taking me aside.

"'A lady of the Court does that,' he said. When I told him that I would not, he slapped me. 'Do you want to ruin my place at Court?' he whispered two inches from my face. 'Do as he expects.'"

That memory of my father's betrayal was worse than my violation. He and I had never been close. Now I understood why; he was not a man to be trusted.

I don't know how long I cried with Catherine holding my head in her lap, but the fire had burned down to ashes.

...

Over the following week, Catherine and I talked more about Versailles. I told her how I found an imaginary place to go to while the man with the lavender wig ravished me. "It was a pine grove where I would perch myself on one of the branches and look down at the earth below. The afternoon sun would cut through the needles, making golden-laced patterns flicker. When I could no longer smell lavender, I would climb down out of the pine and find myself in the corridor, alone."

Despite Catherine's kindness and her help healing my spirit, I felt uncomfortable staying there. The Milvilles' primary chores for the winter months had been completed. Pumpkins, squash, corn, and parsnips had been stacked on wooden palettes in the shed. Burlap bags of dried peas and cornmeal were lined up under the chicken coop. A barrel of apples had been gathered. In the next few weeks, any food items subject to being frozen would be cooked or dried or stored in the warm rafters of the house.

I felt underfoot.

So I decided to accompany Samuel LaCorne and his son who were taking fur pelts to Quebec to trade for winter goods.

Catherine wept at our parting, and little Marie-Catherine walked around with a confused look on her face. Jacques helped me tie my goods into a bale for travel. While the trip was only a day on the river, a snow squall could prove hazardous. The western sky was already growing thick with gray clouds.

# 8

# THE GOVERNOR'S MAN

With no other place to consider home in Quebec City that November 1672, I knocked at the LaBarges' door. Patricia swallowed me in a big hug and drew me into the warmth of their rooms. Disappointment dampened my spirit when Patricia explained Antoine was at the Chateau Saint-Louis working for the new governor.

"My son was offered the position to assist the governor after Frontenac heard him sing at one of the receptions. Frontenac wasn't put off by Antoine's limp, as the governor himself has a gimp hand," Patricia explained. "But tell me what you're doing here?"

"I'm confused, Patricia. The Hurons said nothing about my returning as their teacher. I don't want to go back to the convent now that Mother Marie is gone. Maybe I should apply for work at the governor's mansion and get an inside view of the chateau like Antoine is doing."

We talked late into the evening sorting out my options, and I fell asleep on furs in front of her hearth.

On Sunday, Antoine came down the hill. His strong shoulders, his mop of sandy-red hair, and his smile filled me with familiar comfort. I had missed him, but my heart did not dance while around him, and nothing tingled with passion.

His mother and I had fixed a meal of roast goose stuffed with apples and breadcrumbs, along with honey-coated corn and blueberry cobbler with whipped cream.

Antoine talked about his responsibility pulling all of life's details together for Comte de Frontenac while the other governor's servants did the menial work. Along with the Intendant Talon, Frontenac and his lieutenants heard the colonists' complaints, investigated colonial concerns, and rendered a variety of judgments.

As Antoine served himself seconds on the cobbler, he said, "Most of us in Quebec hope Governor Frontenac will encourage economic and geographic expansion. After all, he has a reputation of being a brave solider and independent thinker. Perhaps the return of his explorer, LaSalle, will help the people realize the value of decentralizing. LaSalle is due back in a few days."

...

Antoine was not able to find me a position on the governor's staff, but I did get invited to the reception for LaSalle. When the new governor met me at his reception in late November, he commented on my helping him as an interpreter. "Your young man, Antoine, has told me all about your work with the natives. So you knew Marie of the Incarnation? My dear, you might be of use to me." I spent the first part of the evening at the Chateau Saint-Louis listening to Frontenac talk about his military experience in the war against the Turks and his successful defense of Venice. His philosophy was to continue to rule all the savages under his authority as his predecessor de Courcelle had done.

Because his hand was in his vest pocket during our conversation, I had not noticed Frontenac's right arm until we stood up to meet a guest. Frontenac rose, letting his arm droop, paralyzed. A courtly, blue-eyed man approached. Instead of shaking right hands, the new governor offered up his left to the newcomer.

"Monsieur LaSalle, your reputation precedes you. I am honored," Frontenac boomed, his voice carrying throughout the hall. Many of the guests turned to look. "How was your exploration? Was it successful? Have you found the China Sea?"

"Not as yet, Monsieur Governor."

LaSalle stood a head taller than Frontenac. He appeared reserved and reticent in the face of the novice governor's thrumming.

After an awkward silence, Frontenac shifted toward me. "Oh, pardon. Mademoiselle D'Allone, may I present Monsieur LaSalle?" I looked intently at the face of Robert Cavelier de LaSalle and sucked in my breath. His cheeks were clean-shaven and tan. He sported a chin-length brown mustache, waxed and curled at the tips. A small goatee emphasized his firm jaw. He wore an un-powdered, light brown wig. His regal nose broadened at the base. Dark brows and mahogany lashes accented his cerulean eyes. And his deep black pupils gazed back at me.

My stomach clutched as I returned his scrutiny. His look was wary and curious. When I gave him my hand to kiss, his lips brushed the back of it, which then tingled and stayed moist for several heartbeats. "Mademoiselle." The explorer's voice was low and confident.

LaSalle turned slowly to Frontenac and said, "Your reputation as a military leader precedes you, Governor. Your guests have been urging me to make your acquaintance. They believe you and I share much in common."

"Is that so?" Frontenac queried.

"*Mais oui.* Oh, yes. They say we are both passionately interested in expanding this country, in building its reputation for our good King Louis XIV, and in taming the savages."

"*C'est vrai.* That's true. If you are that kind of a man, I want to talk with you more. But tonight is not the time. These guests have traveled through the cold and mud in order to meet me. I must take my leave of you two and do my duty."

Frontenac made a military turn on his heel and reentered the reception. Within minutes, Antoine was escorting Frontenac throughout the hall, introducing him to more guests.

LaSalle cleared his throat and toyed with his mustache. His long fingers were roughened by exposure to the elements. Next to him I felt shy, ungainly, and yet pure female. He was in no hurry to either take his leave or talk. We both surveyed the room, shifted our feet, and watched Frontenac make his rounds.

I walked to the bow window with a view overlooking the St. Lawrence. When LaSalle followed me, I willed myself to be calm.

The light of a gibbous moon danced along a wave-tossed path on the great river. On its southern bank, we could see the natives' campfires. In Quebec's harbor, lanterns twinkled from the ships' masts.

"*Akewandawa?*" LaSalle said.

"*Oui.* Majestic," I responded, knowing the Iroquoian word.

He leaned his elbows on the windowsill, taking in the full view of the river. "*Kwindadaka,*" he added.

"Embracing," I echoed.

"You do understand! That gentleman,"—LaSalle gestured to Antoine—"told me you knew the natives' language."

"Somewhat," I stammered and blushed. "I learned from the Reverend Mother Marie of the Incarnation."

"So you were associated with the Ursulines? Are you a religious lady?"

"Well, my lord, I am a baptized Catholic. I know the liturgy of the mass. Is that what you mean by 'religious'?"

"What other meaning could there be, Mademoiselle D'Allone?" He looked at me quizzically. "I, too, am a Catholic and consider myself a religious man."

"With all due respect, Monsieur, my Huron friends would make a distinction between 'religious' and 'spiritual.' They do not believe that to be 'religious' is to be 'spiritual.' I am in a stage of exploration of these matters myself." I held my breath. Perhaps I had gone too far with my directness. LaSalle touched my elbow and turned me toward the nearest embroidered settee to sit.

I lowered myself next to him. "An interesting distinction, Mademoiselle. I have always been 'religious'—educated with the Jesuits, learning Greek and Latin, studying cartography and the history of the far East, and taking my vows of poverty when I was seventeen years old. I wished to be a missionary." LaSalle spoke with restrained pride. "But the Jesuit fathers found me too, too ... " LaSalle couldn't find the word. "Well, my free-thinking upset them."

LaSalle did not look at me but explored the room. Was he worrying about my opinion the way I fretted about his?

"Perhaps I was too rebellious toward authority for these Jesuits. I requested the Order assign me to China to see that country, but they refused my request. I asked for Portugal, and again they refused me. When my ongoing conflict with their authority became too much, I resigned from the Jesuit order." His openness surprised me.

He straightened his back. "Unfortunately, right after that, my father died, and his estate was distributed to my siblings. None of the inheritance came to me because earlier I had taken a vow of poverty. So my siblings started giving me four hundred livres a year. Not nearly enough."

"What did you do?"

"I came to New France and settled in the Montreal area. The Sulpician order there had thousands of acres of wilderness, and my brother Jean, a Sulpician priest, arranged for me to purchase a seigneury by the rapids west of Montreal. This land grant pleased me because voyageurs heading west on the St. Lawrence embarked at that very spot, and boatmen had to portage around those rapids. The place has been named 'Lachine' for "China" by my comrades because of my yet unfulfilled dream to find the China Sea."

I asked, "Where have you been exploring? Frontenac calls you one of our greatest explorers."

"Well, I want to see what the vast lands west of here are like. Where do these great waterways lead? Truthfully I can think of little else. Some say I am obsessed by my maps." LaSalle rose to look out of the window again. His eyes held a yearning in them, and his chin was stubbornly set.

"Tell me about your adventures." I jumped up to join him. "I've learned you just arrived from the upper lakes. Does the countryside resemble anything with which I would be familiar? What are the people like?" I sounded like a schoolgirl.

LaSalle spoke of the boundlessness of the land, the denseness of the forests, the power of the cascades, and the fickleness of the lakes.

With an artist's eye, he described numerous animals: the beaver, moose, elk, bear, otters, and raccoons. He recounted stories of his spotting them and their peculiar antics.

We talked of the diverse native peoples, some nomadic, some settled in villages with their crops surrounding them. LaSalle believed all savages respected their Creator and the creation, were loyal toward their own clan, and harbored a dangerous bloodthirstiness for those whom they perceived as enemies.

We conversed until guests started leaving. The LaSalle of the latter part of the evening was a different man from the quiet, reserved gentleman whom I had met two hours earlier. He now transmitted an aura of passion, ambition, and curiosity.

"Mademoiselle D'Allone, may I make an observation?" He went on without waiting for my acknowledgement. "The royal court has not spoiled you. It is refreshing to make the acquaintance of someone with your background who has stayed untarnished by the wealth and shallowness of His Majesty's circle. On my recent trips, I have been put off by that artificial atmosphere."

"Ah, Monsieur, if you only knew how that environment has influenced my life."

LaSalle looked around the room. "It appears we must depart. Perhaps we can see each other again and continue this conversation?"

"Indeed, yes. Your description of the western lands has stirred a fire in me."

He drew my hand to his lips and brushed my skin with his mustache. How affirming it was to have a man convey respect for my knowledge and curiosity. I did not tell him that he himself was sparking excitement in my heart.

When Antoine offered to escort me to his mother's, I was disappointed. Why hadn't LaSalle asked if he could do the honors or call on me? Perhaps he wasn't staying in Quebec and I wouldn't see him again. Would I hurt Antoine if he sensed my interest in LaSalle?

The back of my hand still tingled from Robert's kiss.

...

One morning in mid-December, Antoine arrived with a message from Governor Frontenac requesting my interpreting skills at a meeting of the Quebec leaders and the nearby Huron elders.

When I stepped into the Chateau Saint Louis's foyer, Tree-on-the-Rock was there and I forced myself to maintain diplomatic neutrality. Then I saw Sleeping Willow, and in my excitement I ignored protocol and moved into her embrace. When Antoine led us into the conference room, I was overcome with surprise and grabbed the edge of the large mahogany table. Robert LaSalle, engaged in a conversation with Frontenac, looked up just as I was sitting down. Our eyes met and held. But within seconds we both resumed our professional roles. I wiped my sweaty palms on my skirt.

LaSalle, several other Quebec landlords, and three unfamiliar native leaders sat around a polished table. The Hurons spoke only in their own language. I doubted Frontenac was aware Tree-on-the-Rock could speak French. Each of the natives gave his flowery, lengthy speech, praised Frontenac, and showered the king from "over the expanse of waters" with praise. When I interpreted, I stood beside each Huron as he spoke. Sleeping Willow had been permitted to remain in the room and sat cross-legged in front of the hearth.

Frontenac's impatience grew with the natives' verbosity. He twiddled his left hand's fingers, rubbed his right shoulder, and shifted in his chair. At one point, he made a gesture to rise, but LaSalle put his hand on the governor's knee and signaled with his eyes that Frontenac had better stay seated.

Toward the noon hour, a serving girl brought in tankards of ale, pots of tea, and loaves of mixed grain bread to eat with cheese and partridgeberries mixed with honey. Frontenac used his left hand freely to serve himself and to pat the behind of the buxom lass. I watched LaSalle. Frontenac's immodest gestures put a scowl on the explorer's face, increasing my respect for him.

When Frontenac adjourned the meeting, he and LaSalle left the room. Disappointment gripped me, and I let out the breath I was holding. Then I moved to Sleeping Willow's side, anxious for news from Sainte Foye. Chief Tree-on-the-Rock approached me. In his own language, he said, "We have noticed your absence. Our children should learn how to read and write the white man's way. Come back as our teacher. You are welcome in our clan's longhouse during the cold months ahead."

I accepted and felt at peace.

Upon hearing my plan, Antoine became sullen during our walk to the lower town. His good-bye was abrupt, his limp more pronounced as he walked back up the hill.

Over tea, I told Patricia about the meeting, the invitation from Chief Tree-on-the-Rock, and her son's reaction. I did not mention LaSalle.

"Oh, my dear," she said. "Antoine has been considering whether to ask you for your hand in marriage."

"Oh, no! How I must be hurting his feelings!" I jerked out of my chair. Pacing to the window, I thought hard. "Patricia, why didn't he say something sooner?"

"Perhaps my son senses your answer and didn't want to experience the disappointment of hearing you say 'no.'" She smoothed her mending out and started stitching again. "Madeleine, I don't think a union between you and my Antoine is wise. Do you?" She rose and joined me.

I looked out the window and answered, "No, probably not."

"Go and teach the natives. Learn of their ways, and become an ambassador between these people and us. Our fellow Frenchmen are trying to dominate the natives. The savages need you—honest, courageous, and knowledgeable in their language—to guide them. Come, now. Let me help you pack."

My sadness for Antoine quickly gave way to excitement. "Thank you, Patricia. Yes, let's pack."

Patricia and I shook out my few gowns and reorganized the linens in my trunk. I knew I might not see her or Antoine for a while.

Realizing that this might be my last conversation with her, I commented, "Patricia, my feelings about marriage have changed since we last talked."

"How so, Madeleine?"

I told her how I had regained some memories of Versailles. "After talking to Catherine, I'm not as afraid of intimacy and haven't had any anxiety, not even at the reception. I don't think marriage is so bad, especially if it is with someone you truly love."

"Madeleine! Were you touched by a man while at the Chateau Saint Louis?"

Recalling the feel of LaSalle's lips on my hand triggered a thrill throughout my body, a feeling of desire.

When I told the widow, she said, "Aye. You are healing, my young girl." She smiled. "Madeleine, I will deal with Antoine. One day he will understand."

# 9
# BLOOD ON WHITE SNOW

Time moved toward the winter solstice. At Sainte Foye, light snow fell for several nights. At first I slept beside Flower Eyes and Sleeping Willow in their longhouse, but the lack of privacy unsettled me. So I moved back to my conical "guest" hut. The small central fire made my home cozy. Sleeping Willow had even designed a reading lamp by pouring rendered beaver fat into a curved, bowl-shaped stone and running a string of linen through the oil and up the stone edge.

On the shortest day of the year, one-third of the village went to hunt deer for their winter festival. Joining Sleeping Willow's family, I marched to a place where the natives had built a V-shaped barrier of shrubs and sticks. This structure was a "trap" set downwind from the woodland acres where the deer lived. By the time we finished the trek, my boots were soaked and my toes ached from the cold. If my friend, Jeanne, had been with me, I would have complained. But with the Hurons I was stoic.

After the Hurons set up camp, the Christian natives erected a temporary place for worship. A shed, walled with brush and carpeted with spruce branches, displayed a carved crucifix in the center. The worshippers wore their best robes of beaver, elk, and black squirrel, each garment embellished with porcupine quills, dyed in scarlet. The women wore bracelets of shells, while the men donned collars of porcelain. By comparison, I was dressed plain; my woolen cape, homespun skirt, and tunic with leather boots were undecorated but functional.

I joined the two dozen believers, including Sleeping Willow and Flower Eyes, gathered around the crucifix. Tree-on-the-Rock and Tonato were not there. We knelt on the prickly boughs and chanted the Catholic liturgy in Latin. As there was no priest among us to sanctify the Eucharist, the natives omitted the sacrament of the body and blood of Christ. These Catholics then began to pray in Iroquois for the hunt the next day, calling on their Creator to provide an abundance of game.

...

The following morning, Chief Tree-on-the-Rock organized the hunt and requested the twenty womenfolk and their children to circle the woodland, corralling the deer. Thirty hunters were to take up positions, hiding behind the barrier or on a hillock above the makeshift pen. We were to chase the deer into the V, where the hunters would kill them.

The women and children spread out through the woods. Then Tree-on-the-Rock signaled the group with a wolf howl. Sounds of joy and high spirits rang out as the Huron women and children spooked the deer out of the woods into the trap by shouting and shaking rattles. At first I was excited watching the happy faces, red-cheeked with the cold, laughing as they ran.

Deer came, leaping with grace into the air; their white tails flashed against the gray-brown trees. Does and yearlings fled the commotion, their heads held high, sniffing the air in front of them for danger, not suspecting any.

The hunters were quick with their spears and arrows. Deer after deer fell to the blows. Men, wearing wooden armor on their chests, hauled the dead animals away from the melee as fast as they could.

Snow soaked up the blood. Deer kept running into the trap. By then, I was sickened by the sight and leaned against a tree for support, taking in deep breaths. Such beauty being destroyed!

Flower Eyes took hold of my hand, concerned. "Mademoiselle Madeleine," the youngster said softly, "we are blessed today. Do not be sad. These animals have sacrificed their lives for us. We will honor their spirits. Because of them, we will not go hungry this winter. Nor will we freeze to death. It is the Creator's will. It is good."

Each of the twenty families gathered a carcass or two, placed them on makeshift sleds of boughs and poles, and trudged back to the village.

As the sun set, women hung their kill, slit open the bodies, and cleaned the animals out. Most of the entrails would be used for household items: the bladder to become a water bag, the intestines to store roasted corn and smoked jerky, and the sinews for sewing and braiding. The hooves would be boiled and scraped out to make bowls and pipes. The heart, liver, and stomach would be stored overnight and cooked the next day for the winter solstice. Other sections of meat would be smoked to preserve them through the winter. Skins would be scraped and beaten and scraped again to use for leggings, moccasins, tunics, and vests.

I knew these people needed this harvest for their sustenance. I knew I should be thankful with them. But all I could see was the deer leaping and the blood-soaked snow.

...

For three days and nights, villagers feasted and danced. The little children watched wide-eyed from their sleeping platforms. Once the longhouse doors closed and the dancing started, it was considered impolite to leave until the celebration was over for that night.

The men with painted chests and made-up faces, dressed only in loincloths, performed a stomping dance while the women accompanied them with rattles, gourds, and bells. Young boys kept the fires going. The older children chanted in rhythm and yelped in excitement.

Hands passed around plates of venison and baskets of dried berries. When there was food to be had, Hurons ate past their being full.

On the first and second night of the celebration, I stayed through the ceremonial dancing. My woolen clothing itched and stuck to my sweaty skin from the heat. Smells of smoldering herbs and tobacco mixed with body odors thickened the air. But the primitive rhythm and joyous sounds of the festival captivated me.

Sleeping Willow handed me a music gourd, and I picked up the beat and rattled it in rhythm. Tonato's gyrations mesmerized me as he stomped and twisted to the drums, shaking his ankle bracelets of shells. His body glistened in the firelight. I felt like a moth drawn to that flame.

On Christmas Eve, I stayed alone in my hut feeling the drums and stomping through the ground and hearing the calls and chants from across the compound. Even the converted Hurons were participating in this ritual, for to do otherwise caused too much friction within the village. Sleeping Willow assured me nothing forbidden by the priests occurred in these Indian festivities, although the church discouraged face painting as it was considered playing with demons.

After the villagers went to sleep, I walked out into the cold toward the boy Jesus statue. This was my simple way of celebrating Christmas, away from the elaborate liturgy and special decorations of either Court or convent. Snow was falling. A few outdoor fires flickered, and I could see the statue: Jesus looking up into heaven, his hands open, the butterfly glistening with snow as it rested on his shoulder. Gratitude for Madame de la Peltrie filled me, for it was she who had commissioned this statue for Sainte Foye as a token of the union between the natives and the French.

As I looked up at the stars, I thought of the Reverend Mother and her love for the Savior born on Christmas. Was she looking down at me? Would she be talking to the Lord on my behalf? I felt closer to Jesus here than I ever had at Court or at the convent. But still, my spirit was restless. I could have joined Tonato and Flower Eyes in their celebration, but I had been remembering Robert LaSalle and our conversation, the light kiss on my hand, his meaningful look at the counsel meeting. What was he doing this Christmas?

...

On the first day of 1673, Chief Tree-on-the-Rock declared Onoharoia, a unique celebration intended to raise our spirits, to ease the burden of winter, and to help heal the sick. Flower Eyes explained that people, in the manner of childlike pranksters, went into the longhouses, upsetting items and rummaging through food stores. The tribe expected the sick and disheartened to roam and declare their needs by reciting their dreams or riddles to their friends. In turn, neighbors gave gifts, matching the symbols in their friends' dreams, to fulfill each persons' desires. The natives believed that when they were given what they were looking for, all their troubles were over.

On the festival's first day, Sleeping Willow remarked how glum I looked. So I told her about my dream the night before:

> I was in a darkened corridor at Versailles, when suddenly a hand covered my mouth. Panic soared. A second giant hand wrapped itself around me and squeezed. I grew smaller and smaller until I was so tiny I slid as blood out of that grasping hand, dripped onto the floor, and formed a puddle. I emerged with two legs and ran down the hall. My fear evaporated. I leapt through an open door and emerged into a new country with forests and flowers, rocks and water. My shift and shoes were white, and I felt unafraid and free. When I looked backward, I saw nothing, just a cloudless, pale sky with a warm sun shining.

Sleeping Willow encouraged me to seek support from the Huron to cheer my spirits. Word spread about the white teacher's dream. My young students brought me objects of red and white color, such as a feather from a redwing black bird and a smooth white rock. Others brought rabbit feet and bird talons, representing the hand. One woman brought me a carved-out hoof filled with deer blood, a drink she considered a delicacy. Sleeping Willow shyly handed me deerskin moccasins decorated with red and white glass beads.

But the most touching gift was a carved hand, the wood showing scars, perhaps depicting the hand of Jesus. The hand made me wonder if my dream was about transformation from oppression to freedom? Did Jesus' hands bleed for me, giving me a means of escape from the darkness of Versailles?

...

Thirty Huron children resumed school when the festival ended.

I saw Tonato etching words in the earthen floor of the longhouse during my lessons. When he thought people were watching him, he would pick up the flint arrowheads he was sharpening and continue his work. Priests had educated him, so why was he hiding his interest in learning from me? Was he ashamed of advancing his reading and writing under the guidance of a woman? Did he wonder about me as I wondered about him? His kind, deep-set eyes and copper-colored physique attracted me.

After school one day, Tonato pulled me aside and asked if I would review his vocabulary. I urged him to attend my school openly. But he shook his head and said, "No. Alone with you, I am better."

...

Father Pieter, a priest assigned by the church to minister to the converted natives, handed me a letter. When I saw LaSalle's seal on the packet, my stomach sang with excitement.

> Quebec
> January 17, 1673
> Dear Mademoiselle D'Allone,
>
> I was pleased to have met you at the governor's reception. I trust your teaching is fulfilling and this letter finds you in good health and spirits.
> I regret our discussion about my adventures was limited to that single evening. Few people in my acquaintance have shown as genuine an interest in our boundless land as you have. Therefore, I will summarize my travels of the last few years to satisfy your curiosity.
> My party of twenty-three Frenchmen and nine canoes started out from LaChine four and a half years ago, relying on three Seneca (Pro-French) Indians as guides. We traveled up the St. Lawrence toward Lake Ontario. When the great river became a boiling, foaming gorge of rapids, we portaged.

After two weeks of hard travel, we arrived at the eastern end of Lake Ontario where there is a confluence of the Rideau River and the St. Lawrence. A few Algonquin have established a small settlement there calling it Cataraqui. This location is the midpoint between Quebec, and the pays d'en haut and is an ideal place for a French fort.

We covered about thirty-five miles a day, along the southern shore of the lake, and arrived at the extreme western end called the Bay of Hamilton. There I met with natives whose language I could not speak but whose help I needed. With ten of my men, we ventured into their camp to refill our supplies and to gather information.

I had heard of the effects of liquor on the savages, but I had not witnessed it before. Suffice it to say, the dignity, reserve, and harmony of the savages disappear when they begin consuming rum. Images of hell come to my mind. The intoxicated people want to lose complete control of themselves. I pray you will never be a witness to this side of the natives.

By late August 1669, we resumed our party heading south toward the Alleghany River. As it had grown late in the season, we chose to bypass the great Niagara Gorge despite its allure. Two of the Jesuit priests left our party and headed north with the explorer Joliet. I cannot say I was disappointed by the abandonment of the priests because when I travel with Jesuits, friction develops.

Heading westward, we went down the Ohio River. At one of the villages, a Shawnee captive, Nika, attached himself to me. Because of his usefulness and loyalty, I traded beads and blankets for him, and he continued with me. He turns out to be a gift from God, as he speaks several dialects and is a sharp observer, good hunter, and man of integrity. It is strange to say this, but I find I am gruff and irritable with the Frenchmen traveling with me, yet even-tempered and affable with Nika. Why, Mademoiselle, would such a man, a native and not a believer, draw the good side from me, while the French Catholics release my tensions and my temper? Does my ill temper toward these companions stem from a sense they are not genuinely loyal to my vision?

The Ohio River was often clogged with rocks, tree trunks, and debris. To make progress, we had to walk our canoes in the water, with the murky, cold Ohio lapping at our armpits and our feet never sure of their foothold on the uneven river bottom. My men grumbled. I drove them onward and turned a deaf ear to their complaints. In late autumn, we arrived at the place where the Ohio drops from a great height into a marshland. Stopped in our tracks by the geography, we made camp on the high rocks. I needed to contemplate what to do.

The next morning, my guides and porters were gone! You must understand: desertion in the wilderness is tantamount to murder! No one stayed with me except for Nika.

The two of us had a musket for our defense, my compass, our canoe, and our strong, willing hands. What were we to do? We retraced our steps in the bitter cold. Snows set in before we reached the Great Lakes area. Nika wore eyeshades made of pieces of bark with slits cut in them to shield him from the blinding white snow. I thought I could cover my eyes with my hat brim and a kerchief. Within a few days, I was blinded and suffered an extreme headache.

A friendly tribe took us in and nursed me back to health. They applied pine needles, first soaked in hot water and then cooled, to my eyelids.

As I lay still for several days lost in thought, I realized the rivers on this continent flow south not west. It is unlikely I will find a way to China.

But there remains the Gulf of Mexico to explore.

As soon as I was able, I started off again toward Montreal to continue my life's work. This time I wore sunshades. Why had I been so stubborn about them before? We slogged through hip-deep snow even while we wore our snowshoes. We portaged our canoe when the rivers were impassable, skimmed over with thin ice. We made it to Montreal by mid-January 1670.

Exhausted as I was, I was impatient, so I trekked on to Quebec and approached Governor deCourcelle. I needed funds. But this was a waste of my time! He is committed to the king's vision, a French colony made up of a cluster of homesteads around the central government. He wants to keep our people close, living within miles of the governmental hub, not expanding throughout this continent. DeCourcelle had no more imagination than an ant. All he would offer me was his political support.

A half-year went by as I played political games with potential investors. By midsummer in 1670, I received sufficient financing. So six boatmen and four canoes were able to take off for the Great Lakes. We arrived at the Niagara River by the time the maples turned crimson.

As one enters the Niagara River, all you detect is a fast-moving current propelling one's boat back out to Lake Ontario. We portaged up an escarpment a tree's height above the waterway. But as we progressed up the river, the cliffs started to tower several hundred feet above the rushing water. The thunderous sound of the falls was heard before they were seen.

Below us a massive whirlpool swirled the river in a huge circle, catching trees, debris, and even a few animal carcasses in its vortex. The roar of the Great Waters became deafening. As we progressed south, suddenly mist covered the horizon like fog on a cool summer morning. Carrying our packs and our canoes, we climbed higher along the escarpment. We could not hear ourselves talk as we approached the cascade. Sheet upon sheet of white foam rushed over boulders the size of houses. There ahead of us and circling around us was the great Niagara Falls, almost two hundred feet high and one half a mile wide!

God spawned a magnificent wonder, something utterly breathtaking when he created that waterway. The falls emanated power beyond my imagination.

We built a winter camp and spent our time acquainting ourselves with the abundant wildlife and eating plentifully of their meat. We discovered more about the richness of the fur trading and trapping businesses. I improved my skills in their native languages.

Returning in June 1671, I immediately left for France for the purpose of raising more financial support from the Court. I am an adventurer at heart, not a courtier, and the time spent at Versailles was arduous.

I have built a relationship with our new governor, the Comte de Frontenac, this winter and am pleased to find he is a man of vision and ambition. He understands the value of exploration for the sake of France and this colony. He has already sent Louis Joliet and the Jesuit Father Marquette out to explore the Mississippi River further. Frontenac and I have enjoyed a dozen evenings together poring over maps of North America and eating pumpkin pies supplied by your friends, the Ursuline nuns.

I was encouraged to find you at the tribal counsel meeting in December. Your linguistic skills are impressive. Here's trusting that your Christmas holiday was blessed. Frontenac has me in his hand for the time being, and I await his bidding. I hope you have enjoyed my tale. If you would like to stay in contact, please send a response with the Jesuit priest.

Cordially, your humble servant,
Robert Rene Cavelier de LaSalle.

Intrigued by his descriptions and flattered by his attention, I read and reread Robert's letter.

# 10

# DISSENSIONS

When Father Pieter visited Saint Foye to propose the village build a chapel with government money, dissension permeated Saint Foye. Villagers needed to decide what they wanted. About one hundred Catholic natives supported this plan, and the traditionalists, only fifty in number, wanted nothing to do with it. The remaining one hundred and fifty Hurons debated this issue for three nights.

The priest reminded me of a pixie with his small size, tufts of blond hair, and sharp, blue eyes. His black robe contrasted with his fair skin and round, freckled nose. A nonjudgmental man, Father Pieter accepted my ability and role as a teacher, and the natives' way of life. He wanted the believing natives to have a place to worship according to their own cultural needs.

At the tribal fire, when the issue was debated, Tree-on-the-Rock's oration was the most persuasive. He took his place in the speaking circle, wearing porcelain necklaces and a fox cape over his shoulders. Red ochre covered his face. He wore rattles of bones around his moccasins. His speech resounded.

"We have seen the French come across the waters since my grandfather's days. These white men are here to stay in our land. They bring some good: kettles, iron stoves, metal for our hoes and hatchets. They bring brandy and beer, needles, and muskets as well.

"Because of the French our life is changed for the worse too. Our people have caught diseases never seen before. We have witnessed the slow bleeding death that comes when part of the body is blown off by buckshot."

Tree-on-the-Rock paused. He looked up at the sky and waited for the people's murmuring to settle. Then he continued.

"The French Black Robes have told us the big God in the sky has shown himself in the man Jesus, and belief in Jesus can take us to a heaven away from hell fires. I, for one, cannot declare what is true. But I have seen power in this Jesus, the way I have seen power in the leaders of our village."

Tree-on-the-Rock's voice rose and fell like waves on the river.

"The question is whether to say 'yes' so a priest can reside among us, so our children will learn the ways of the French."

The chief scanned the community, and resumed. "I say to you, what is the harm? I have talked to the governor about gaining French protection from the warring Iroquois. To be educated means we outsmart the Iroquois and their allies. We will understand the wig-wearing Frenchmen's conversations when they talk about us but think we don't know what they are saying. No longer will we be made fools."

As Tree-on-the-Rock talked, he accented his points by stomping his feet, rattling the anklebones, shouting "yipp" or "ayayay." By the time he finished, the people shouted "eyee," "yipp, yipp" along with him.

Finally Tree-on-the-Rock stomped once more and roared, "I counsel that you say 'yes' for our people's future." He then strode out of the firelight and left the crowd.

A silence fell. The traditionalists knew the matter had been settled. A priest would soon come to dwell among them. And a chapel would be built.

...

I rushed to write LaSalle a response, so Father Pieter would hand deliver it to him. *What should I say to the explorer? I admire your dreams, your perseverance? I want to see you again? I can remember your lips brushing the back of my hand?*

Monsieur LaSalle was a man of propriety and single-mindedness. My intuition told me he had little interest in romance but a strong desire to be understood and supported in his vision. Hence, I decided to write a brief, proper note of acknowledgment. As I sealed the letter, my heart uttered this truth: The future I desired depended on this intriguing explorer.

...

Sleeping Willow scratched on my hut's flap and waited to be invited in. I splashed frigid water on my sleepy eyes, ran my fingers through my disheveled hair, and said, "Come." Like a puff of white smoke, her breath was visible in the dawn's light. When I saw her red eyes and tear-stained cheeks, my stomach lurched. She had been more withdrawn and less joyful in the last few months, but I had thought her condition due to the strain of winter.

Sleeping Willow and I had bonded like sisters since I had moved to Sainte Foye. Over the year I had left behind the familiar. And this native woman had helped me. My use of comfortable chairs had been replaced with squatting. Instead of eating delicately at a table, I now reached my hand into the communal pot. While I used to tidy my sticky fingers on linen, I now wiped the grease on the fur of the nearest dog.

My friend hunched close to the small fire while I put on the kettle. Soon the burble of boiling water broke into our silence. I offered her a cup of herbal infusion and waited for her to speak.

Her hand trembled as she took the mug from me. She sipped the hot brew through her teeth, sighed, and said, "Oh, Madeleine, I dishonor God. I cannot talk to the priest. It is a woman's sin."

I drew her free hand into mine. Slowly through sobs and sips, Sleeping Willow owned that she was carrying a baby. "I am afraid. I had a difficult time with Flower Eyes. Perhaps childbirth will kill me."

"That was twelve years ago, Willow." I hesitated. "What have you and Trees done about this for all that time?"

"When I weaned my daughter, Trees and I discussed this. The church teaches that lying with your husband is not for pleasure but for baby making. But Trees began to do things, like withdraw when we would lie with each other. If he had spilled himself inside me, he went to the midwife and got me a bitter potion to stop life growing. I knew the church would think this act was wrong. But Trees insisted on his way."

Sleeping Willow absently picked up a stick and began stirring the fire. Red embers glowed and broke into flames. I added two logs and waited.

"I've missed three moon flows. I am terrified of telling Tree-on-the-Rock. He will blame me for what grows in my womb. He will think I chose to obey the priest over him, my husband. But I didn't!" She snapped her stick and flung the two pieces into the flames.

Looking up at me with agonized eyes, Sleeping Willow continued. "If the priest learns I have tried to prevent life by using herbs as my husband wished, he will judge me as having sinned. Perhaps God wants me to have another baby. But deep inside, I am afraid I might die."

I reached over and rubbed her shoulders. "Madeleine," Sleeping Willow whispered, "a woman must be prepared to face her time knowing that birthing might take her life. But Tree-on-the-Rock needs me. I must pray to see he is admitted to heaven. Flower Eyes is young yet, not quite a woman. She still requires her mother." Sleeping Willow put her head down. No tears escaped, but I could hear her trying to control her breathing. Natives thought it a sign of weakness to shed tears.

This sensitive woman was a mature believer compared to me. I understood her conflict. If he learned of the pregnancy, Tree-on-the-Rock might even direct her to end the pregnancy. The church taught that act was murder. But Sleeping Willow wanted to please her husband. Such a step would compound her guilt further. Her dilemma was even more complicated. A part of her wanted another child. Yet she was not ready to die or leave behind loved ones who depended on her. She was caught in a thorny tangle: the wishes of her husband and family, the demands of her church, and her own fears.

My mentor, the Reverend Mother Marie, would have said, "One should give all to her God and rely completely on him." My twenty-six-year-old mind believed Sleeping Willow should tend to her own body as the mistress of her fate.

I admitted my confusion and told my friend both ideas.

"I need time, Madeleine, alone. May I sit by your fire while you attend to the school children?"

And so I left Sleeping Willow deep in thought and prayer and went to Tree-on-the-Rock's longhouse for morning classes.

When I returned, Sleeping Willow had left a slate with a picture on it, the message conveying she had gone to fast and pray for a few days. I was to tell her family where she had gone but not the reason.

Tree-on-the-Rock took this behavior in stride, as it was the prerogative of any Huron to walk into the woods to seek wisdom. But Flower Eyes, never having seen her mother behave like this, was dismayed.

...

Toward the end of February, Father Pieter preached a midday homily about the night when Jesus had willingly given himself up to the Roman guards for arrest. When one of Jesus' followers sliced off a soldier's ear, he told his disciples to put away their swords. The Lord said, "Those who live by the sword will die by the sword." Father Pieter preached on Christ's pacifism.

Jesus' opposition to warfare stirred the ire of some of the young warriors, who were too old for school and games like fox-on-the-tail but too young to have seen the devastation of war. After the homily, Tonato and half a dozen young men remained in the longhouse talking. I listened, thinking of my friend Antoine, whose farm had been burned out when he was a boy, and the Milvilles and neighbors at Rivere Jacques Cartier who had the daily stress of watching the forest and river for marauding Indians.

Thickly built Turtle Back said, "I've seen fifteen winters. Yet, I have not had the chance to prove my manhood." Of late, he had taken to face painting and wearing porcelain bracelets. He had attended my schoolroom briefly but left the class for a midwinter hunt and returned dissatisfied. Turtle Back contended, "What good was that moose hunt? Even boys just off their mothers' tits can track and shoot at a moose. My success on the hunt does not declare me a man. I must go on a raiding party and bring back a prisoner for the village or some British scalps."

Tonato spoke up. "Turtle Back, killing or imprisoning someone does not make a man of you."

Some of the young men murmured disagreement and directed derisive comments at Tonato.

Tonato looked around the circle. "Brothers, gaining manhood means knowing your own spirit and marking out the path of life you're to walk. It's about finding a spirit partner, making a home around a fire and providing for your community. To create an incident to have a war party, so you can kill or be killed, is not proving your manhood."

The grumbling grew louder. Some slapped Tonato on the back while others shuffled their feet and mumbled curses. Finally Turtle Back sneered and said, "Tonato must be a Black Robe, a woman in black skirts hiding behind a gold cross, a coward afraid of going to war."

Turtle Back's derision did not ruffle Sleeping Willow's son. Wrapped in self-confidence, Tonato remained quiet.

...

Sleeping Willow slipped into her longhouse three days later while I was teaching. She resumed her seat and took up moccasin beadwork. She looked gaunt and tired but had a peacefulness emanating from her face. Later that morning, she told me she would bear the baby as God willed. She planned on telling Tree-on-the-Rock later in her term when she could no longer conceal her condition. I felt like a hypocrite when I smiled outwardly. Inwardly I fretted about her health and submissive attitude.

...

I strolled along Sainte Foye's palisades and breathed in the chilled air. Evening sunlight threw dramatic shadows against the wooden structures, and I enjoyed watching the black and gold designs. Then I rounded a corner and startled. Turtle Back was leaning against someone. I pulled back, unseen. A young girl had her head down, her arms crossed in front of her. Turtle Back pinned her to the wall. He forced her chin up. The girl was Flower Eyes! She kept her eyes shut, her chest protected.

My breath came in gasps. For a second, I thought I was going into that awful tunnel and would lose consciousness, but anger thrust me into action. I bounded forward, grabbed his wrist, jerked it back, and twisted his arm behind him. While he was much stronger than I, surprise caught him unawares, and he released Flower Eyes. She sprinted away. He yanked away. I told him sharply in Iroquois never to force himself on another girl. Without waiting for his response, I turned and ran after Flower Eyes.

When I couldn't find her, I sought refuge in my quarters, unable to control my shaking. I wondered, *Would Turtle Back retaliate? Would Flower Eye's father take revenge?* I built up the fire and tried to focus on the flame, willing it to calm my breathing and warm my insides. Images of another place came to mind. But now my thinking was focused. My fury belonged, not only to this arrogant Huron warrior, but also to the courtier who had violated me. For the first time, I believed that I had had no control over the situation as a young girl. With that thought, my guilt and shame flowed away.

...

Quebec
March 30, 1673
Dear Madeleine de Roybon D'Allone,

Knowing that Governor Frontenac has dispatched a new priest, Father Bart, to your community, I am entrusting this letter to him. I know the commitment of the governor to finance a chapel and a school will please you immensely. My influence with Frontenac figured considerably in this.

During our planning meetings, our primary concern was two-fold: to develop strategies that secured the loyalty of the native tribes and to organize a profitable fur-trade throughout the region. The latter requires forts to be built in a strategic band from east to west. I am hopeful I can participate in that expansion.

The governor is calling a massive meeting of all the northeastern tribes for July 1673, an idea I planted in his head. At this summit meeting, we will develop a peace treaty and fur-trading agreement with all of the natives and reinforce the loyalty to King Louis XIV. Frontenac will have his jamboree at Cataraqui, (This location was also my suggestion.) The tribal gathering will be held on the western side of the river, overlooking the lake.

Nika and I leave immediately to carry this news. As the meeting will be held the week of the full moon in July, I have three moon cycles to convince half dozen tribes located one thousand miles apart of the importance of their presence at such a gathering. Frontenac has supplied me with baubles and kettles to use as gifts when I seek out their villages.

Interpreters will be needed for that weeklong event, so I requested the governor to call upon your services. When the request comes, see if the chief of the Saint Foye Hurons will escort you. Travel to Cataraqui will be difficult for a woman even though you are strong.

Please petition God for my safety, as I will be entering the enemy camps of the Iroquois. If we Frenchmen can gain their loyalty and turn them from their alliance with the English, this will be a powerful move. I am trusting that my skill with their languages, my height, and clean-shaven appearance will win their influence. Did I tell you natives find hairy faces grotesque? So I have removed my mustache and goatee.

My experience with Father Bart suggests that your Catholic community will be in firm and disciplined hands. This Jesuit does not permit any superstitious nonsense among the believers. Father Bart is to supervise Father Pieter, a man considered to be a fledgling Osprey—alone and unpredictable.

If it pleases God, we will meet again. That is my prayer.

Courteously, Robert Cavelier de LaSalle.


...


In mid-May, Tree-on-the-Rock, Tonato, Turtle Back, and several other men from Sainte Foye journeyed with me to Quebec in preparation for the Cataraqui Summit. Father Pieter accompanied us. I was relieved to leave the village, for I did not care for Father Bart, the new priest. Bald, pock-mocked, and fleshy, he looked like an inky mushroom dressed in his black robe and wide-brim hat. The Huron Christians were hesitant around him.

Several weeks before, I had a run-in with this new priest. Father Bart reprimanded me when I had invited Tonato to share with the school children some native legends about the heavenly places. He believed I should not have allowed the youngsters to hear the thinking of a traditionalist.

I stood up to the Jesuit.

"Father Bart, your concern for the well-being of these children is admirable." I took in a deep breath and steadied myself. "But I believe God would want these maturing youngsters to make their own informed decisions. To do that, they need to hear all sides of a belief."

His face tensed, and the blood vessels around his chipmunk-like cheeks throbbed. He couldn't keep his eyes on mine. He walked away. All I could see was his dark cassock over his rounded shoulders and its muddy hem. But, in leaving, he said, "Mademoiselle, you are impertinent. When I have my chapel built, you will have no place in the school here."

Then he turned his face to me. "If you have learned these unruly thoughts from that saintly woman, the Reverend Mother Marie, then either you badly misunderstood her, or she was not the holy woman the church believes her to be."

Those last words hurt me more than anything. As he strode away, his black robe skimmed the ground and swayed side to side. I pictured myself booting him in the rump.

While I trekked to Quebec, I tried to understand the incident. Father Bart's arrogant attitude reminded me of the courtier who had shamed me. That feeling of my being squashed by a powerful male pulsated through me. Now, a decade later, I had stood up to a male authority, someone who was trying to hurt and control me. Was I finally courageous enough to face my foe?

...

When our group arrived dusty and tired at the governor's mansion, Antoine distanced himself from me while maintaining a professional friendliness. Each leader expressed his opinion to the governor about trade with the Dutch and the English. Some of the natives, such as Tree-on-the-Rock and Tonato, spoke with confidence about establishing a peace treaty. Others, such as Turtle Back, declared that the wealth and honor of the Huron would best be demonstrated by going on the warpath.

Governor Frontenac had learned the diplomatic necessity of letting each participant talk at length, but he often became impatient during their orations and interrupted.

By the afternoon, Tonato, fed up with the governor's bombast, whispered under his breath in Huron, "This is why we call the Frenchmen 'ducks.' They 'quack, quack, quack' all day long." Two of the chiefs who were within earshot began coughing to hide their amusement. Turtle Back laughed outright, a breach of Indian etiquette.

At the conclusion of the meeting, the governor educated the group about the strategy for the forthcoming Cataraqui jamboree, and I was commissioned to be one of Frontenac's interpreters.

On the evening march back to Sainte Foye, Tonato fell into step with me. We chatted in French, commenting on Father Pieter's absence in our group. He had stayed in Quebec because of his conflict with Father Bart.

"I also quarreled with Father Bart," I told Tonato and filled in the details.

Tonato was silent for a moment. Then he offered, "Do not trouble yourself about Father Bart's threat regarding 'his school.' If the Master of Life wants you to stay, you will. But perhaps God has got other things for you."

We walked on. Tonato then asked in Iroquois, "Madeleine, what do you wish?"

The caring look in his eyes warmed me. I stopped abruptly on the path to consider my answer. "Honestly, my friend, I don't know. I have much to learn about myself, the world around me, and my God."

Tonato took my hand. "Perhaps I can help you learn, Madeleine."

We continued side-by-side. I felt the energy in his body. His callused palm tantalized my skin. Even though Tonato was seven years younger than I, he displayed the wisdom of his father and the gentleness of his mother.

...

A few weeks later at dawn, I heard scratching on my entrance, and Sleeping Willow, holding her abdomen, entered without waiting. She had been laboring since the middle of the night.

"Madeleine, this is not the right time. My baby comes too soon. I am afraid." She didn't want to call on the Huron midwife or medicine man because the ritual surrounding a traditional birth conflicted with her Catholic beliefs. She would have to wear a false-face as a talisman and follow other superstitions. Sleeping Willow had come to me for help with a birthing based on our French Catholic ways.

I helped her onto my mat of furs and removed her tunic. She had tied a wooden crucifix around her neck. She was feverish. All morning I cooled my friend's forehead and breathed rhythmically with her throughout the labor. I wondered aloud about summoning the midwife, but Sleeping Willow refused, even though she knew I had never served directly in that role. If I had lived in her village longer, if I had held more authority with the Huron, I would have gone against her will. But I was unsure of myself.

We paced in a tight circle, hoping the movement would bring forth the baby. Intermittently I had Sleeping Willow squat and lean her back against my chest. In this position, she found some relief. Still, the labor didn't progress. Toward evening, she began vomiting from the pain.

"We need help," I whispered.

Sticky with sweat, she nodded for me to get her husband and a midwife.

Tree-on-the-Rock had been patching a canoe in preparation for our Cataraqui trip. All I had to say was "come," and he followed. On the way, after my brief explanation, he called out for Michipicta, a midwife, who fell in behind us.

The four of us squeezed into my tiny hut. Tree-on-the-Rock knelt by his wife, wiped her brow with his large hand, and whispered something that made her chapped lips smile. I glimpsed the pain he would feel if Sleeping Willow died during this birthing.

Michipicta respectfully waited and asked me in a low voice about Sleeping Willow's labor. The midwife then shooed the chief out of the tight space, washed her hands, and examined Sleeping Willow.

"I will need to turn your baby. He is trying to make it into the world sideways," Michipicta reported. During the next moment when Sleeping Willow's contractions relaxed, Michipicta's small hands entered the birth canal. She had asked me to rub my friend's belly in gentle, wide circles and breathe with her. I remembered some Latin chants sung by the nuns and began a quiet, slow song. Sleeping Willow let out a deep groan and clamped her teeth on her own hand.

"Ah, I've turned him," Michipicta sighed with relief. "Now push, Willow. Push your little one out into the world."

While Michipicta and I supported her in a squat, she pushed again and then again and out slipped a tiny boy. He was not much bigger than my foot and weighed less than my boot. Tree-on-the-Rock was invited back to hold his son. The infant mewed like a kitten. Michipicta pressed on his chest and breathed quietly into his mouth, encouraging the baby to breathe. But he was too weak.

Exhausted, Sleeping Willow, aware of how weak her son was, said, "Husband, I want my baby baptized." She looked up at Tree-on-the-Rock, who was holding the newborn. I gave her a sip of water. She ran her tongue over her cracked lips and whispered, "We will call him Matthew." The father bent over her and placed the son in her arms.

I rose. "I'll fetch the priest. You stay with Willow." Upon my return, Matthew was lying on his mother's breast. He was too weak to suckle, so Michipicta had placed some water-honey solution on a rag and was dripping liquid down the baby's throat.

Father Bart saw the finality of the situation and baptized Matthew without another word.

We three left after that brief ceremony so the father and mother could be together with their newborn, knowing their time was short. Soon we heard Sleeping Willow keening with grief and Tree-on-the-Rock comforting his wife. Matthew had died.

Baby Matthew was buried a few hours later by moonlight under the path leading into Sleeping Willow's longhouse. Each morning Sleeping Willow would kneel by the grave and spill her milk on the spot. Her milk would nurture the baby symbolically as he made his way into heaven.

Tree-on-the-Rock, Tonato, and I readied ourselves for the upriver trip to Cataraqui. Turtle Back believed the summit might make peace between the Indian tribes, so he didn't go. I wondered if he would foment trouble while we were gone.

Natives travel with few possessions. But I took one waterproof bale containing a tunic and moccasins, my woolen skirts, two linen chemises, French leather boots, and my winter cape. I did not know what I would need or how I should dress. I carried my medicine bag around my waist and with it my journal and quills. All else was left in Sleeping Willow's care. I had been holding in my fear of the unknown, and the strain now brought tears to my eyes as we paddled away. Would I see my Huron friends again? Tonato was traveling with me, and Robert would be at the Cataraqui summit. What would my future hold?

# II

# CATARAQUI

When Louis XIV was on the move through the countryside, hundreds of people would adjust their schedules, lands, and produce to meet the overwhelming needs of king and Court. And so it was with us colonists and natives in the summer of 1673 as our train of followers made its way from Montreal to the Cataraqui Peninsula. The native spectators on this spit of land saw one hundred and twenty canoes approach in formation. Governor Frontenac, in a blue and gold dress uniform, sat enthroned on a flatboat flanked by his military retinue. Their gold braids, brass helmets, and silver buckles sparkled in the sun.

The governor's honor guard, on a second flatboat, tried to stand erect in formation despite the rolling waters. Fifty natives in canoes escorted the governor on the left, and other vessels holding notables traveled on his right. Frontenac and LaSalle arranged for four hundred soldiers in their fighting uniforms to follow behind on flat boats. A half-mile downstream, vessels carrying carpenters and workmen completed the procession.

The drums rolled continuously. I heard the clinking of weapons, the shuffling of boots, and the cawing of nervous gulls. Hundreds of colorful tents, festive animal skins on tepees, and the smoke plumes of campfires made a variegated landscape. The moment the governor stepped foot on Cataraqui, the gold fleur-de-lis flag was hoisted in the name of King Louis XIV.

To provide me feminine privacy in the midst of this masculine melee, Tonato showed me how to erect a makeshift tepee on the lakeshore. He cut down two long, green saplings, bowed one over the other, and secured them at the center top. Leaning medium length poles up against this arched frame, he tied the sticks together with strands of sinew. Then he unrolled one large moose hide, draped it over the top, and tied it off. After we ate stew and cornbread, I withdrew into my tepee.

I could see out across the lake. Evening breezes whispered on the water, and the sunset's patterns of pink, lavender, and yellow shimmered on the surface. My spirit perked with a sense of anticipation as my thoughts turned to the men in my life. Antoine would have married me but our friendship held no physical attraction. Tonato pulled me like a magnet. But what would the French Catholic community think of my liaison with him? A Frenchman occasionally married a native woman, but I knew of no Frenchwoman who had married a Huron man. And what of the aloof, adventuresome Robert LaSalle? The mysterious explorer charmed me. Our common backgrounds and his apparent morality made me feel safe. His life choices of exploration and diplomacy intrigued me. But he probably would not want me as his wife because I would interfere with his goals.

...

"Children, Onondagas, Mohawks, Oneidas, Cayugas, and Senecas. What joy I feel to see you, your wives, and little ones here."

With these words, Governor Frontenac addressed the several hundred natives seated around the large council fire. He'd placed his weakened right arm at a military angle on his scabbard. His freshly powdered wig shone and flashes of light blinked off his brass buttons. Despite his lack of height, he made an impressive figure. He addressed everyone deferentially and with an underlying tone of menace.

Charles LeMoyne, a *donne* or a lay religious man, had replaced me as Frontenac's interpreter. No one offered me an explanation. But what should I have expected? I was a woman. And in this frontier community, even as it was at the French Court, the male had supremacy. I tried not to sulk.

Frontenac exhorted his audience to become Christians, to submit to the instructions of the Black Robes and the king of France. He asked the chiefs to chastise anyone who violated the goal of peace. He urged them to trade with the French and not the English. Then he presented the chiefs fifteen guns complete with powder and flints.

When the last chief took his gift and ended his long speech of gratitude, Frontenac resumed. "I will maintain a true and solid peace with you by settling Cataraqui, where I have already spread the mat and invited you to come and smoke. From here, our people can trade with one another."

Frontenac's staff then distributed twenty-five large overcoats and refreshments of biscuits, wine, and brandy to the men and dates and prunes to the women. The children were lured with trinkets of marbles and ribbons.

"Children! Onondagas, Mohawks, Oneidas, Cayugas, and Senecas. As I am the common father of all nations, how can I avoid reproaching you about the treachery and cruelty you have exhibited toward your brethren, the Huron? You even prevent them from visiting their relatives. How can I refrain from telling you that it is not good when you treat them as slaves and threaten to split their skulls?"

Frontenac went on, pausing to let LeMoyne interpret. "I invite you to give me four of your girls of eight years old and two of your boys, whom I shall instruct. I know it is not a trivial request that I make, but I shall take as much care of them as if they were mine own. I shall keep the boys by me and place the girls with the Ursuline nuns. The Huron will vouch that the children are well-reared living with the French."

I noticed Robert in the shadows. He was bouncing on the balls of his feet and clicking his fingers. What was causing his agitation? It had been due to his diplomacy that these multiple tribes had come together in a peaceful summit. Did he believe what Frontenac was saying, or did he see duplicity? I had a sinking feeling Frontenac would not be good to his word.

"I promise to restore your children when you require them back, should you not wish to have them marry with some of the French." The governor finished his speech with a flourish, praising the bravery and honesty of the Iroquois. He reminded them of his desire to make them prosperous.

The native men conversed among themselves at this proposal while the mothers pulled their children closer to their sides. Tribes exchanging children was a common practice when building alliances.

That same day, the site engineer and crew cleared the virgin land, harvested the timber for building supplies, and dug ditches to drain the swamp. The stockade was erected. The fort's construction would be completed within a week. The carpenters built a giant flatboat for transporting large quantities of men and supplies on the lake. The natives were impressed. Continuing his role as a diplomat, the governor invited different men to dine with LaSalle and his staff.

Tree-on-the-Rock, Tonato, and I watched all this from a distance. Frontenac had exceeded his ambitions.

I felt shunned.

...

"Mademoiselle D'Allone, good day." Robert approached my tepee, tipped his tricorn, and clicked his shiny boots together. During the conference, I had connected with him a few times and only in a professional role. My heart quickened as I anticipated a private moment.

Dressed in a fresh shirt, leather pants, and a buckskin tunic, he stopped a formal distance away from me. Because of the heat, he was wig-less, his light-brown curls secured with a buckskin tie. His mustache, grown back over the summer, was trimmed and waxed. I looked into his blue eyes and tried to hold them. But his gaze flitted over my face and moved on to the activity behind me. My excitement was swallowed up by disappointment.

"Governor Frontenac would like you to help the children he will be taking with him as we proceed down river. Once in Quebec, your role would be to see to the girls' placement in the convent and act as a liaison between them and the governor's staff," LaSalle said.

The homesickness of Flower Eyes came to mind. I did not wish to be privy to native children pining away in a strange environment. My own childhood had been sad enough even when the familiar surrounded me.

"Monsieur LaSalle, please thank him, but I must decline the governor's request. I am not convinced that to Frenchify the savages is the best for them or for us."

He scowled and turned to walk back toward the governor's circle of tents.

"Wait, sir," I said, catching up to him. "Tell me. What are your plans?"

"I leave for Quebec to raise finances for this new Fort Frontenac. The governor has asked me to supervise the fort's development."

As the hot sun baked down on us, he scrutinized my native tunic. Then, Robert removed a kerchief, wiped the sweat and some bugs from his brow, and said a brusque "Good day."

Robert left without asking my plans. Like a heavy rock sinking in water, my heart plummeted. I stood on the marshy bank overlooking the lake and studied the plumes of campfire smoke swirling up into the sky. Perhaps Robert had two sides to him—a proud, professional man, and a shy, reclusive male. Was he uncomfortable having a public relationship with me? Was I wishing for the unattainable with Robert?

I made my way down the boggy, weed-infested bank. At the edge, muddy pebbles pressed on my bare feet, forcing me to walk into the water gingerly. The contrast of heat with cold lake water sent a shudder down my back. I tossed my cap back to shore, hiked my tunic up to my thighs, and waded deeper. Unexpectedly the murky bottom dropped off. Swamp grasses entwined my toes. A fish nibbled me, and I laughed with surprise. I flipped on my back and floated the way Antoine had taught me the previous summer. Large bubbles of air played havoc with my tunic. Cool water soothed away my tension.

...

Montreal's fur-trading fair piqued my curiosity. Its noises and smells reached us even before we saw the crowds. Tonato, Tree-on-the-Rock, and I unloaded bales filled with basswood baskets, deerskin moccasins, and porcupine quill belts made by the women of Sainte Foye.

Montreal, a bustling town built up onto a steep hill from the St. Lawrence, differed from Quebec's French orderliness. In Montreal, the houses were primarily wooden, single-story dwellings with a sod roof. The diversity and clutter were evidence of its people's belief that appearances didn't matter.

French merchants, sailors, and natives of different tribes scuffed up dust clouds as they walked. Men in black robes circulated, expecting to be shown deference for their priestly vocation. Fur traders laid out pelts of beaver, wildcat, martin, and mink for customers. Deer, bear, moose, and wolf skins were displayed artfully on colorful woven blankets. Merchants hawked textiles, kettles, knives, guns and powder. Redskin women squatted by baskets filled with feathers of different birds and sold porcupine quills dyed a variety of shades.

People bargained in different languages, some of which I could understand. They communicated with hand signals and facial expressions and even drew ideas in the dirt. The French merchants, with their trimmed beards and colorful clothes, spoke a dialect that strained even my ear's ability to understand. Their women wore neat jackets buttoned up at the neck despite the heat and knee-length, dark-blue skirts. Many of the French wore moccasins. Each tribe had a different hairstyle. Tattoos of wild animals or other designs appeared on bodies, and feathers adorned their hair, ears, and clothing.

I smelled fires, sweat, and the cooking of sumptuous food. Customers bought roasted haunches of venison and legs of turkey on greenwood spindles. They counted out their change for aromatic corn-on-the-cob and toasted wheat cakes. When I saw a display of pretty flags paces ahead of me, I pressed through the crowd to examine them. Once there, I gasped. The flags were scalps—human scalps of brown, black, russet, and silver-gray.

Tree-on-the-Rock unloaded his bales next to someone's wagon, which was crammed with a large assortment of goods, including tonics, smoked fish, ink and paper, and French-made jewelry. A lumpy figure sat on the wagon bench and smoked a pipe of sweet tobacco. A full-brimmed, brown hat decorated with gray feathers covered white hair, but wisps escaped around papery ears. I could see sharp, blue eyes staring at me.

From beneath the brim, those eyes followed me as I shucked my shoulder basket off and helped Tonato unload his bales. Below the eyes was a leathery and lined face with broad cheeks, a pug nose, and cracked lips. The trader puffed on a pipe as if the tobacco gave life-breath. The left hand, gnarled and sun-blotched, tilted the hat back as the right removed the pipe. A smile greeted us, revealing a missing upper canine, leaving a hole just big enough for the pipe's stem. Short, stocky arms waved in welcome, and the trader jumped down from the wagon and sauntered over to us.

The voice spoke French with a jabbering in Iroquois. It belonged to a woman! Two breasts, the shape of gourds, filled out a tent-like top, and a big rump ballooned the baggy cotton pants. I couldn't help but smile at the short woman's easy manner when she wiped her hand on her hip and held it out to me.

I had met Annie Noleen.

# 12

# ANNIE NOLEEN

Annie invited me to be a guest in her shelter. She had mounted a wooden frame on the wagon and covered it with hides. Two feather tickings cased in deerskin functioned as beds by night but were stored underneath her merchandise by day. Trunks served as seats. We combined our resources, and along with the roasted meats the men purchased, we had a feast.

Annie Noleen would enter her seventieth winter when the snows returned. Born of a fur-trading Frenchman and his Ojibway wife, she appreciated all ways of life. She had taken over her deceased husband's general store five years before.

Annie peppered me with questions. "Where is your family, Madeleine? Why are you not married? Why have you taken to traveling with two redskins? How will you see yourself through the winter? Are you healthy? Do you mind not having children?"

My lack of material resources bothered her. "If you have no man, you must have money." That was her motto.

While Annie did not look or act it, the Noleens had laid up a good amount of cash. Annie's money could buy about anything she needed: medicine, housing, and even male companionship. Content with her life, she believed she would live a good number of years yet.

A Black Robe stopped by our booth to ask about Father Pieter and Father Bart. While the priest and I spoke, Annie became uncharacteristically reticent, climbed up on her wagon seat and puffed her pipe.

When the Jesuit left, she asked, "Are you a church woman?"

"What do you mean, Annie?"

"Are you Cath-thoo-lick and go to church?"

My answer didn't come easily. "I was baptized Catholic. But no, I don't go to church. Yet, generally, I do respect the work of the priests."

"You respect them Black Robes?" Annie asked.

"Why do you ask? Are you not a Catholic too?"

Annie said she had been baptized as a girl because the priest had pressured her parents. A few years later, the priest had left the mission village with no Jesuit to replace him. Her independent-minded parents taught her to straddle the white and the red cultures.

Annie's parents took their canoe and went trapping and hunting six months of the year. Annie learned how to swim before she could walk. She could patch a canoe with pitch and carve a paddle before she could cook. By the time she was ten winters, she could clean and skin out most of the small game and prepare their pelts for the market.

"The one thing a person needs, my folks taught me, is to believe in yourself, not a church or king," she said. "They revered animals and plants in the creation because each gives us life. Belief in God was not important to us."

Annie continued. "A year after I reached my full height—what little you see—and came into my womanhood, my ma came down with a wrenching cough. I nursed her best I could through a winter, but when the spring came, Ma got a high fever. She passed after a week of being out of her head."

Annie jumped down from her seat and straightened her wares. "My pa, he went up into the North Country right after burying Ma. I went with him to check the traps and help with the pelts. What else was there for me to do?

"My body muscled with the portaging and climbing. I got good with a musket and a bow and arrow. A knife became like another hand, and I could skin an elk and bear in an hour flat. I taught myself to be patient so I could stand still in the river shallows, waiting to spear the trout that chanced to swim under my spear. My hair grew long, and I braided it down my back, decorating it with basswood strings. I enjoyed feasts with my father when we caught game. When there was nothing to eat, I managed my hunger by sucking on rawhide, chewing roots, or scavenging for nuts and berries."

Annie puffed on her pipe and sat hunched in silence for some time. "Later we met a French voyageur at the Montreal Fur Fair. This Alfred Noleen was an honest and comely fellow. Pa offered him a part of our business. So Alfred, the old man, and I traveled for five more seasons and developed a place in the fur-trading world. Alfred, he taught me to read and write and cipher—a grand way to pass the time in front of camp fires. We talked about our business and how we'd seen too many natives barter their income of furs for a single jug of brandy. Then they'd turn drunkenly mad in one night and lose everything. So our trade was based on fairness and the avoidance of brandy and rum. We made quite a name for ourselves.

"Me and Alfred, we were married á la façon du pays, 'in the way of the country.' We chose the summer of 1625 and did it up on the lake escarpment, near Ma's grave."

"What does that mean, á la façon du pays?"

"Oh, it's a wedding ritual. It mixes the ways of the church and the rites of the natives. Alfred had to smoke a calumet with the Ojibway after paying a bride price to my Pa. And I had to go through a cleansing ritual with the women in the village. They scoured me, took off all my grease and paint, and handed me Frenchified garments. I got a blue linen gown coming down to my knees, a white cotton courtier's blouse, a muslin petticoat, and an embroidered vest of many colors. They washed my hair and plaited it—all tied up in red, blue, and yellow grosgrain ribbons, all the way from France!

"When I was all shining like an ocean-washed stone, the women presented me to Alfred. We went straight away to our quarters—that would be a tent draped over our canoe—so we could mate. From that point forth, man and wife!"

Annie chuckled, remembering.

"Did you love him?" I asked.

Annie cast her hawk gaze on me. "What, my young friend, is love?" she challenged.

I couldn't answer, but I pondered that question later in Annie's shelter, my journal open on my lap.

At Court, the ladies would chatter about love, read poetry about love, and sing about love. The courtiers portrayed love as an exhilarating feeling, worth pursuing at all costs. When one was "in love," the stomach churned and the heart fluttered. The troubadours would say love was a time when seeing your beau brings a flush to the cheeks and heat to the breasts. People in love were said to be out of their minds, thinking of nothing else.

At the convent, nuns described love as a commitment, a realization that the person was someone you would sacrifice your comfort for. If you loved, you would support your loved one in the worst circumstances. Love had nothing to do with feelings. Love demanded a code of behavior as seen in the life of Jesus and the saints. Love was a verb.

My friends Jeanne, Patricia, and Catherine's answers would not be the same, but their common ingredient was this: When a woman loved a man, she knew this man was her best friend, that he was someone who would provide for and protect her. These women would say their husbands were men who could complete them, and who would make them feel cherished.

I looked up from my journal and read Annie what I had just written. She laughed. "Provide, protect, befriend. Maybe so, Madeleine. But, my girl, don't walk through your life limping, waiting for that miracle of completion in a man. You're complete in yourself, *ma petite*. Now go to sleep." Soon she was snoring.

...

Tonato and I were wandering through the fair a few days later when suddenly five Iroquois pushed their way past, reeling with drink. One, a woman, squat and thick in the behind, found everything laughable. She could not walk a straight line and lunged into the male closest to her. He patted her rump. She laughed and swayed to the other side of the path.

When two of the savages veered by us, they were arguing about a bet, each man thinking he was the winner of a gambling game.

The woman focused on the tall one who wore an eagle feather in his hair lock. She wove over to him and spoke in a drunken mumble. He shoved her to the ground.

That caused the shorter, stockier man to let out a war hoop. He lunged toward the man with the eagle feather. But in so doing, he tripped over the woman who was sprawled on the path. After righting himself, he drew a hunting knife on his friend and threatened him.

Eagle Feather laughed and kept on walking. Hunting Knife became enraged and sliced through the back of Eagle Feather's vest, drawing blood. The other two men joined the fracas, and soon all were shouting, cursing, and attacking. Eagle Feather took a tomahawk from his belt and brought it down on Hunting Knife's head. Intoxication impaired his stroke, so instead of splitting the skull open, he sliced off Hunting Knife's right ear, who then dropped to the ground from the shock.

This violence drew the anger of the other two onto Eagle Feather. Within minutes, he was on the ground, bleeding from multiple wounds.

The woman struggled up and dashed to her man's side. Leaning over Eagle Feather's chest, she uttered an eerie, mournful sound. The three drunkards laughed and walked on.

Angry that the woman had been so abused, I moved forward to help. But Tonato put out a restraining hand. He said in French, "They are drunk. Very dangerous. Stay."

The bloody experience sickened me. Now I understood why Annie had tried to avoid trading with the natives in liquor.

...

On the last day of the fair, Tonato, Tree-on-the-Rock, and I packed for our return to Sainte Foye. I felt acute disappointment at leaving, as Montreal held so many possibilities. Teaching under the oppression of Father Bart rankled me, and I couldn't imagine what I would do in a relationship with Tonato in the native community. I felt conflicted about LaSalle. Before Cataraqui, Robert had been warm and approachable. Since the summit, he had been aloof and priggish. But Robert would be here in Montreal in a few months, and I was not about to give up on that relationship.

When I approached Annie with my thoughts, she grinned. "I'm getting old, Madeleine. Mornings are not easy to get out of bed. Why don't you stay? I'll teach you the trade. You're a bright young thing. And with your ability with languages, you can talk to most customers."

So I helped my Huron friends portage to the St. Lawrence River. Tonato took my elbow and led me to a rocky outcropping upstream. We could see the LaChine rapids to the west.

Looking into my eyes, Tonato said, "I must help see my family through the winter, to comfort my mother in her freshly cut grief. If not for this, I would stay close to you, Madeleine."

I swallowed back my tears. What could I say to Tonato? We were just friends, weren't we? So I hastened away, down into the town of Montreal and what its future would hold for me.

...

River smells riding on moist air wafted up from the harbor to Noleen's, a saltbox building covered with wooden clapboards and beautified by a wide front porch. The large front room centered around a stone fireplace with three smaller back rooms, two for storage and one for Annie's quarters.

We turned one room into my bedroom. I sneezed my way through years of cobwebs and rotten mouse turds. My back ached from moving crates and scrubbing wood. Annie bartered for a feather mattress. I found a straight-back chair in her storage and placed it in front of my window looking down the hill at the river. Sitting on a chair and sleeping on a bed felt strange at first, and several nights I pulled my mattress onto the floor, as I was more comfortable resting on that hard surface.

My doing the bulk of the physical labor around the store relieved Annie. She was free to put her effort into the cooking and baking.

People came and went at all hours. Annie taught me to cook over the open fire using kettles and hanging pots. We served hungry people stew or porridge for a franc and for another franc added a slice of fresh baked bread and some sweet cider. The customers usually asked for liquor, but so far Annie had avoided serving it.

Unlike most of Montreal's inhabitants, the Noleens had built an outhouse in their yard, in which we dumped our chamber pots. Using "the necessary" was quite the novelty, and our patrons loved it.

Barrels of apples, wheat, corn meal, and oats lined the walls, giving the store a rich, homey scent. The grain often spilled onto the wooden floor. My job, amongst others, was to sweep and sweep again—to sweep up mud from the street and feathers from the collection of down we had bagged, the spilled flour, and gray ashes. But I loved the smells assailing me as I swept—unless an unwashed voyageur or savage came in.

...

Annie challenged me one day, "You have no skills with a gun or your fists. You couldn't protect yourself or my store if you needed to."

She'd been leaving me to run the store on market days when she would load her cart and take baked goods and sundries to the wharf where the merchants gathered.

"Are you saying your store is vulnerable to robbers and brigands?" I laughed at the thought.

"Certainly it is!" Her face tightened in seriousness. "And drunken sailors and savages too. Do you know how to handle a musket?"

I did not and reddened a bit.

So the next day we locked the door just after sunup and hiked to the meadows. She taught me how to carry and load a musket and set up wooden targets. At the first report of the musket, I was thrown backward onto my behind. She laughed. Slowly the skill of using the gun came, and Annie took me hunting.

The first day I killed a living creature, a young buck, I felt powerful. Silently I did what the natives do, gave thanks to the creature for giving us his life.

And then I cried.

...

Noleen's was often the place for political debate and local gossip. I listened and watched while going about my chores.

"It is best to consolidate our colony and permit the governor to control the economy. How foolish of those settlers who built homesteads away from the river and more than a mile from their neighbors. When the Iroquois go on the warpath again, they'll be sorry." Monsieur Hamlin, a stout apothecary expressed his support for the king's policies.

"Ah, but Monsieur Hamlin, a man is more industrious when he works for himself without restrictions, *n'est-çe pas?* Beholden to the governor, his incentive to work harder gets thrown out with the slop." Roger Marceux, a tall, strongly built coureur de bois, countered.

Monsieur Hamlin's face reddened. "That man is not loyal to his king and country. He is only working for himself. How can this colony succeed with that attitude? You have been too long in the woods, Roger. You can't tell your nose from your back side."

Marceux balled his fist but kept his restraint. "What does Louis XIV know about this colony? Why, with his gilded chairs, golden robes, and silk-clad women, he has no idea about us. How does he dare to tell us where we may trade and when to marry? And who will enforce his laws here?" With that, Roger worked up some spittle from his gnawed tobacco wad and spat five feet over Monsieur Hamlin's boots, hitting the pewter spittoon.

"You're a traitor!" Monsieur Hamlin shouted as he turned toward the door. "You and that governor's lackey, Robert LaSalle."

The door banged behind him, letting in a waft of cool, October air.

*What did he mean about LaSalle being the governor's lackey?* I wondered. From that time forward, I made it my business to find out.

# 13
# MONTREAL

Several men lounged by the trading post's fire, waiting for the bread to come out of the oven. The smells of cinnamon and cloves from their hot drinks had relaxed me, so when I heard their voices rise and the cussing start, I was caught off guard.

"*Sacre Coeur*, I tell you, the redskin told me himself. Montreal's Governor Perrot bribed three natives to stop the furs coming in from Michilimachinac. Those pelts won't get as far as the fur-trading fair and will get a much higher price."

"Perrot wouldn't have the balls to do that. He's the king's boy and wipes the king's derriere," countered an older woodsman missing several teeth.

A sailor piped up, "I seen Perrot down at the dock last week overseeing a cargo of bales. Them was being loaded on the *Sainte Colombia*."

I imagined LaSalle's anger when he heard about the hijacked furs.

...

In the middle of November, Monsieur Hamlin came in for some fish chowder. Whenever the apothecary visited, I focused on learning what he thought about LaSalle. After serving him, I took a bowl of chowder over and asked if I might join him.

Monsieur Hamlin rose and dusted off the seat. The creamy broth mixed with scallions and salted cod warmed me, and I savored several spoonfuls before speaking.

"Monsieur, you mention a Robert LaSalle in not-so-pleasant terms. Who is this man?" I feigned ignorance.

"Mademoiselle, I thought everyone knew him. He has a way of making his presence felt."

As he talked I sat with an expectant look on my face, giving away nothing.

"He came to this country with the intent of expanding it to the western sea. He is never satisfied and wants to explore and conquer. He is a radical in his thinking. The one good thing I can say is the man has a way with the Iroquois. Perhaps under his influence, the redskins will stay in their villages and leave us alone. But, ah, Mademoiselle, he encourages the breaking of rules. This behavior will come back to bite him."

"'Breaking of the rules'?" I asked.

"That a man who wants to trap and hunt must have a license, and to have that license, he must be married. Robert LaSalle ignores these rules. He does as he pleases."

The apothecary lifted his chowder bowl to his fleshy lips and slurped the last of the soup. He looked around the store and then cleared his throat. "The governor also expects young women to marry. Have there not been men asking for your hand in marriage so that they could go into the pays d'en haut? Ah, I dare say, you will not be single for too long."

I frowned. Was I to be used to legitimize a man's freedom to hunt and explore? The turn in the conversation made me wonder what LaSalle's attitude was toward marriage. He had ignored the king's dictum!

When the store quieted that evening, Annie mended moccasins, and I shelled peas. The conversation of the afternoon still rankled. "Tell me your thoughts on that man, Robert LaSalle, Annie. Monsieur Hamlin does not think much of him."

"He used to come into the trading post a few years ago when he lived at LaChine, before he sold that land back to the Sulpicians in order to finance his travels. He was Frontenac's right-hand man at the Cataraqui conference. But you should know that, *oui?*"

"Ah, of course," I said, my face flushing as guilt surfaced. "But what do you think about Monsieur Hamlin's view that LaSalle is a traitor for wishing to expand our colony?"

Annie examined irregularities in the deerskin. "When I knew LaSalle, he was reserved but confident, a man who always had a purpose. LaSalle never let anyone know what he was thinking. His silence was difficult for some. They judged him to be prideful and cold."

"What do you think about the king's view of a consolidated settlement, where we inhabitants stay close and keep ourselves safe? Or do you feel as the coureurs de bois do, that this whole country is ours to explore, cultivate, and settle?" I asked.

"Ah, our land has a greatness." Annie paused to thread her awl. "And if we Frenchies stay close together, we will never discover its potential or its riches. I am all for expansion and growth. Life is always full of risks. It is foolish to govern one's choices from fear."

"What should we do about the governor's laws? What about the rule that coureur de bois who go into the pays d'en haut must be married?"

"Madeleine, I was born in this country. Who gave our government the right to butt into our daily lives? Truly I don't feel loyal to this king I hear about. I am committed to this country and her people, not some king six weeks away by boat. Do you feel loyalty to King Louis and his Court? You were raised there."

Loyal to the Sun King and Versailles with its elegance, stiff manners, and hypocritical spirits? A heavy weight pressed on my chest, and my heart thumped too loudly within me. Breathing deeply, I found myself telling Annie about Versailles and the history of my own fear.

...

The door clattered open and snow flakes mixed with dust on the floor. The white crystals left droplets of muddy water. I groaned, knowing I would have to get the mop. While I was looking down, I saw a pair of shiny, leather boots approach and stop just short of me. With the broom still in my hand, I raised my head.

Robert LaSalle smiled at me.

"Mademoiselle Madeleine. Tree-on–the-Rock told me you were befriended by Madame Noleen at the trade fair and had stayed on in Montreal."

He took my hand. My tongue babbled an incoherent greeting as I felt him lift my fingers to his lips, his shoulder-length hair titillating my skin.

"I just arrived at my cousin LeBer's." Robert looked around the store, giving me a moment to gather my thoughts.

Annie had gone to the apothecary; I was alone. Remembering my position at the store, I asked him how I could serve him.

He chuckled, a deep-throated sound, and said he was not here to purchase anything, that his needs were well met at LeBer's. "What I want is the enjoyment of conversation with you. *Kwindoewka*, let us talk. It helps to practice one's language skills, don't you think?"

Seated on a bench by the fire, mugs of cool cider in hand, we talked in the natives' language. He had arrived back at Fort Frontenac in early October with more soldiers and completed the fort's construction. Livestock supplied the men with eggs and milk, cheese and butter. Fresh produce had been stored, so his men would have plenty to eat during winter.

"I believe the fort can be turned over temporarily to my cousin, LeBer, and our friend, Monsieur Bazire. These colleagues are leaving tomorrow for Cataraqui before the river freezes. I'm staying in Montreal to raise funds for further travels. And it won't hurt to keep an eye on Frontenac's interests in the fur trade at this western end of the colony."

The apple wood gave off a sweet scent as Robert talked. I felt two emotions: exhilaration that he was sharing aspects of his life and a dismay that he was not asking me about myself.

When some customers came in to the store, LaSalle abruptly took his leave, saying he would return.

Did he mean tomorrow or in several months? What should I make of his change in attitude toward me—personable today, standoffish the next? Ah, I thought about what I had observed: When he believes he might be watched, he backs away from me. Was he afraid of intimacy?

...

Since Christmas was three days away, sailors and woodsmen were in the store gathering supplies and niceties for the holiday. They talked in low tones about Frontenac's men siphoning trade profits from Montreal for Quebec. "That new fort, down on the lake at Cataraqui, will block our profits. Why can't Perrot do anything to help us?" one coureur de bois said to the men.

"Ah, Perrot thinks he can manage Frontenac and overlook the Quebec policies, but he can't. Frontenac is a fox and a snake all in one. And his dandy explorer, LaSalle, has his hands out to keep profits for himself," a weathered woodsman complained.

Just then the door opened, and Robert entered. The door, sucked shut by the winter wind, slammed. The men dropped their voices. Coughs and chuckles covered the silence.

Robert walked over to the fire, turned to warm his backside, and surveyed the room. He caught my eye and smiled, then quickly nodded greetings to one of the voyageurs and took a seat on an overturned barrel.

"Pierre, how'd it fare this year?" Robert asked.

Pierre volunteered, "Da beaver's been plentiful. A small forest fire did burn out one of da bigger beaver' dams, but rains came and put it out before much damage got done."

The men talked further about some of the native settlements around Lake Nippising and the general calm of the intertribal disputes.

Then LaSalle asked, "Ah, Pierre? Is there any truth to the rumors about Perrot's hijacking a shipment of furs, keeping them for himself before they made their way to the Montreal trade fair?"

Pierre grunted a confirmation. "Dat Perrot is a two-sided scoundrel—blockin' free trade in the name of the Crown, den reaching his long arms into profits that ain't rightly his."

LaSalle's face reddened. He drew himself straight up off the barrel, thanked Pierre for the information, tipped his hat to me, and stalked out into the cold.

On Christmas Eve, I expected to see Robert in church as the service was filled to overflowing, but he didn't attend. Disappointment clouded my holiday joy, but I had no stake in Robert's life. Would I some day?

...

After the service I walked the darkened road alone to Noleen's and thought about God for the first time in a long time. The previous Christmas, only the boy Jesus statue at Sainte Foye had reminded me of the holiday's spiritual meaning. This year I had recited communal prayers in church. I felt a pang of sorrow that Reverend Mother Marie had died. Her relationship with Christ had inspired me.

*What will Sleeping Willow be doing tonight? Will she and Flower Eyes be worshipping in a pine-strewn hut, or has the new chapel been built?*

Annie had dressed a Canada goose for our dinner, and we enjoyed the afternoon together sharing memories from Christmases past. I was finding it easier to talk about Versailles—about seeing the autopsy of an elephant at the royal zoo, making fun of the courtier's lop-sided wigs and strained jokes, and tending the herb garden. Annie's presence steadied me as I described Court life. Her practical, down-home nature gave me a sense of safety and self-sufficiency.

...

During the first winter storm of the new year, a golden Labrador bitch, heavy into her pregnancy, sought shelter on our front porch. After I persuaded her to allow the dog inside, Annie gathered some old pelts and created a makeshift whelping box. Then we settled back and watched the miracle of birth. The mother pushed five pups into the world. Annie cut off the wet, gauzy birth sacks around two of them. Such a simple act of nature was awe-inspiring. We named the mother after her eye color, Amber. Four of the fur balls looked golden like their mother, and the fifth was a velvety black. We called him Midnight.

I watched Amber's puppies nuzzling her teats. Each would fight for purchase, and once it found the nipple, suck frantically, kneading its mother's belly with its tiny paws to bring down the milk. The pups would scramble over each other to get a better hold on their food source. Then they would fall asleep, bundled on top of one another. Life seemed simple and beautiful when I looked at it from the pups' perspective.

By springtime, we had found homes for three of the puppies and promised a golden one to a sailor. I wanted to keep Midnight, and Annie consented.

Robert had started visiting again. He and I often spent mornings poring over maps we had compiled of the western lands. He made a habit of stacking his charts like paper logs behind the counter, storing them here because his life was so itinerant. One day Midnight found one and was gnawing on it as if it were a bone. I snatched it away and reprimanded him with a smack on his nose. While the important details of the map were still intact, the parchment itself was wet and torn with tooth marks.

When LaSalle saw the defaced map, he lunged after Midnight, cuffing him across the head so hard that Midnight toppled over. Amber, her four feet spread and the hair on her back erect, growled at the man. I comforted Midnight.

LaSalle turned and lashed out, reminding me how important those maps were. Red in the face and seething, he grabbed his hat and cape and stormed out. I was shocked, having never seen that side of Robert before. What had really caused his rage? Surely not this innocent puppy and some singular map. Would I have the courage to speak to him about that behavior?

...

Later that morning, I was working alone on Noleen's accounts when Madame Bazire came in with her servant girl. Several gold bracelets dangled from the wealthy woman's gloved hand, complementing her ensemble of a magenta silk skirt and embroidered jacket. She ordered her girl to collect bolts of material, and then Madame Bazire charged thirty livres of new fabric.

"Madame Bazire, I am pleased to charge those goods," I told her. "But I trust you will be making a payment on your bill today as well. You are in debt to Noleen's for over two hundred livres."

While this was a small amount for the likes of Monsieur Bazire, one of LaSalle's primary supporters, it was over a half-year's earnings for a laborer. The servant girl coughed nervously and placed the yard goods back on the counter. Madame Bazire asked for Madame Noleen.

"She is at the market today," I replied.

Madame Bazire beckoned for the servant girl to put the bolts back in the basket and prepared to leave. "Tell Madame Noleen I will speak to her about this as soon as I find her." The matron swooped out of the store. Her blushing servant girl walked behind her, struggling with a heavy load of wool and damask.

When Annie returned, having heard of my "impertinence," she scolded me. "Madeleine, we allow these rich people to pay when they choose to."

"But you wouldn't think twice about asking some of the coureur de bois or the sailors to keep short accounts with you. And those men can afford your goods less than the Bazires. Why do you let the wealthy get away with unpaid bills?"

"Their scorn travels throughout the town like a poison in a water supply. It is not worth the trouble to get on their bad side."

Standing at the counter with hands on my hips, I challenged her. "But you told me that it is foolish to govern one's choices from the position of fear. You are doing that with Madame Bazire."

"That is not what I meant. We don't need the wealthy of Montreal affecting our sales with their negative attitude."

"So you're afraid they will withhold their business and turn others away from Noleen's?"

Annie tied off a twenty-pound bag of wheat and tossed it onto a pile. She said nothing more, brushed her hands on her trousers, and closed the door to her room with a bang.

Amber jumped up and looked at me. I shrugged, picked up the broom, and swept the floor. Annie didn't come out for the bowl of corn and bean sagamite stew I fixed at noon. I felt lonely, betrayed by Annie's attitude.

When the bedroom door opened later, my heart leaped, and I was caught between gladness my friend had returned and sadness we had had a difference of opinion. Her dark eyes, reddened by tears, looked right at me. "Madeleine. Give me that list of debtors, and we'll come up with a fair plan. To blazes with the snotty, poisonous tongues of the Bazires and folks like them."

...

Whenever Robert entered the store, Midnight hid and Amber's eyes stayed alert for trouble. Robert commented on neither his outburst nor on the dog's behavior. The first time I saw him after his outburst, I served him some hot cider and pulled out the map we had been working on. Now was the time to talk to him about his anger. Instead, Robert raised concern about Noleen's. "Since Annie has given you forty percent of the business, let's plan more ways to profit," he said.

"Why do I need more money?" I asked, forgetting my own agenda to discuss his treatment of Midnight.

"Because you're not satisfied with your present life. When we talk about the West, this kindles a fire within you. Without money, you will not be able to satisfy that burning." As he spoke, he ran his index finger over my cheekbone. His touch took my breath away.

Robert was not usually one to demonstrate public affection. Were the several customers milling around in the store noticing us? I blushed. His hand returned to the map, his fingers splayed across the Great Lakes. He talked about reconnoitering those western regions to establish more forts. He mentioned how profitable the trade in liquor was, insensitive to the fact this was a forbidden topic with Annie.

...

By Easter Sunday 1674, the St. Lawrence River had melted into a ten-foot-wide channel, a black, shimmering ribbon bracketed by thick, gray ice. Annie and I walked the dogs down to the harbor and along the well-trodden river path. In some places, slabs of ice as big as our hearth had been pushed up onto the rocky shore by the winds.

When we returned, Robert was waiting and requested our presence at Easter Mass. Annie declined but chatted with him in the fresh spring air while I freshened up. I put on a clean blouse and lace collar and wrapped a swath of light blue linen over my shoulders. My hair curled out from behind my lace cap. The feel of the loose tendrils added to my sense of delight of being with Robert.

Upon our entrance to the cathedral, I noticed Madame Bazire holding her gloved hand to her mouth, whispering to the woman next to her. That woman turned toward us. To my surprise, she blew a fingertip kiss to Robert. Having already removed his plumed hat, he swooped it downward and bowed slightly. Under his breath, he whispered, "That is Madame LeBer, my cousin's wife. And with her is Madame Bazire. Their husbands are overseeing Fort Frontenac on my behalf. Offer them a pleasant smile, will you?"

How did my effort at a smile appear to those women? Taking a hold of my elbow, Robert led me to the other side of the church. Were the looks on those women's faces disdain, hostility, or jealousy?

The service droned on. The homily began.

I was daydreaming when I felt Robert stiffen next to me. He began spinning his hat with his fingers. Father Fenelon raised his voice and rebuked Governor Frontenac for having arrested Montreal's Governor Perrot for skimming the best of the fur pelts before they reached the trade fair. The priest criticized Frontenac's lackey, LaSalle, for helping in the arrest. Fenelon said, "These men are cowards. They use the expanse of the Atlantic Ocean to protect themselves from the Sun King's orders."

Abruptly, Robert took my elbow in a firm pinch, raised me up from the pew, and ushered me out. We were a hundred paces down the road before I had a chance to catch my breath.

Robert muttered, "Why, that blown-up, self-righteous, arrogant pig. Who does he think he is, deriding Frontenac's management of the colony? Frontenac wants what is best for Quebec and Montreal: more lands, more money, more control over our enemies, and more independence from France. Only this way can our colony grow and prosper."

Later I reflected on Robert's recent reactions—his anger at his map being damaged and his strong opinion about this colony's expansion. He was a passionate man, but he kept his inner fire well hidden behind a rock façade. Why was he afraid of revealing his emotions?

...

For a week after LaSalle walked out on Father Fenelon's sermon, Annie and I kept our ears open for political gossip. Some of our customers agreed with Robert and believed Perrot and his faction were driven by economics, willing to lie and cheat in order to make money for themselves. But other people believed LaSalle was Frontenac's puppet, an adventurer solely out for his own gain. They thought Robert was siphoning money from their economy to invest it in his dream of finding the water route to China. To them, this was laughable and Robert was an arrogant fool.

I said nothing. But in my heart I was loyal to Robert.

# PART THREE:

## Seedling on the Wind

# 14

# BECOMING MAT-TEE

"I could never do that!"

"You're so wrong, my young one," Annie said as she rocked back and forth, stroking Amber's silky ear. "You're a fine one to make that trip."

We sat on Noleen's porch during a warm spring evening in 1674. "Is propriety standing in your way?" Annie probed. "Why, you're the one who told me to pay no mind to the Bazires of this world."

Having received Frontenac's orders to scout the western side of Lake Ontario for LaSalle, Tonato had arrived in Montreal looking for a travel partner. Annie had challenged me to volunteer for the position. Tonato's assignment was to find an area on the Niagara Frontier suitable for a fort. A vessel big enough to handle the Great Lakes would be built on the site.

"Annie, be sensible," I implored. "Neither Robert nor Tonato would think it a good idea. Tonato needs a strong and reliable helpmate. And Robert would never permit a lady to go."

Annie ran her hands through Amber's fur. "Then don't apply for the position as a lady, Madeleine. Cut off your hair or tuck it up under a cap. Strap your chest and don blousy sailor pants. You're a strong paddler. You know how to hunt and speak Iroquois. This way you can see the West."

To see the West! To spend time with Tonato! To join Robert in his explorations! My heart raced. "What about the store? Don't you need me?" I asked.

"I got along before you came. I'll be fine. But will I miss you? Yes, my dear. Convince Tonato. Robert wants the job done, and he trusts Tonato to do it. Robert won't stand in your way."

All night I pondered the idea. I could handle the water travel. My Iroquoian was strong, and I might even be of assistance to Tonato with tribal negotiations. If round, short Annie could pass herself off as a male, so could I with my tall lankiness. Tonato and I had built a deepening friendship over the last two years. Traveling with Tonato would transform me into a more knowledgeable companion to Robert. Who knew what an adventure into the unknown would bring for me?

•••

The next day, a broad smile lit up Tonato's face.

"You'll do *tres bien*, Madeleine," he enthused over my proposal. "You and I, we will teach each other." When he took my hand and drew it to his heart, my face flushed, and my belly tingled.

•••

Annie trimmed my chestnut hair to shoulder-length, pinned it up and pulled a linen cap with a visor over my forehead. Dusted with ashes, my upper lip gave an appearance of young facial hair. I bound my breasts tightly and wore a full-formed, white cotton shirt, a leather vest, baggy blue pants, linsey-woolsey stockings, and leather shoes.

When Robert bounded up the steps of Noleen's and pushed through the door, I was disguised, pretending to smoke a pipe on the front porch.

Tonato greeted Robert and said, "LaSalle, we leave tomorrow. Bring the bales of trade goods down to the harbor by sunset."

"You've found a partner, then?" the adventurer asked.

"An able-bodied sailor, young and green. Can paddle. Can speak Iroquois. Low wages too. Wants to travel west." Tonato came to the door and gestured for me to come in. "Mat-tee we call him."

LaSalle glanced at me. "Well, if you think he will do, it's your choice." Then suddenly Robert froze, turned toward me, held my gaze, and shook his head slowly from side-to-side.

"Madeleine, what do you think you're doing?"

I feared he would rage at me the way he had Midnight when the pup chewed the map. My hands started to sweat.

"A lady cannot make this trip," LaSalle growled. "Tonato, you need a strong paddler and a wise woodsman. Find yourself a worthy partner."

"Mat-tee is a fine paddler, a strong swimmer, and spirited partner."

"Mademoiselle… if I may still call you that?" Robert began sarcastically. "You do not have any idea of the perils awaiting you. Take off those ridiculous clothes."

He stood with his feet apart, glaring at me over the table. I felt like a child getting scolded by her father. Robert's opinion was important to me. Hesitating, my hand lifted toward my cap to regain my feminine self.

But then my desire to see the West surged and dissolved the fear. I inhaled and exhaled slowly, shucking off his intimidation. Let him get angry with me. I was doing nothing wrong. "Tonato has hired me. It is not your decision anymore." I stood more than erect. "But I would be grateful for your blessing." I then took off my cap, pulled the pins out, and shook my hair loose. Looking him in the eye, woman to man, I smiled. "Robert, I will be successful. And with this experience, I can appreciate even more what you do."

Robert appraised me for a long minute, took a deep breath, and moved toward the door. "Mademoiselle, it is true that I have delegated the trip to Tonato and his partner. If you be he, so be it." He turned to Tonato, cutting me out of his line of sight. "The harbor at sunset for loading," he said.

As he walked off the porch, we heard, "Bon chance, mes amis. Good luck, my friends." Robert's understated endorsement assuaged my anxiety about this crazy plan.

...

Tonato and I embarked from the Montreal pier at dawn May 1, 1674, our seventeen-foot canoe loaded with trading bales, our packs, and two extra paddles. Tonato had thrown a tarp over the load and secured it with leather ties.

When we arrived upriver an hour later at the LaChine rapids, I untied the tarp, preparing for the portage. A black, glossy coat and two golden eyes stared up at me. Midnight, the rascal, had stowed away! Released from his hiding place, the dog leaped out, jumped up on me, and licked my face.

Tonato laughed.

"Can that dog swim?" he asked. To see, Tonato grabbed the scruff of Midnight's neck and flung him in to the river. The dog flailed in the air, hit the surface with a splash, sank, and came up sputtering. He pivoted his body in the current, got his bearings, and swam a strong dog paddle back to shore.

Head held high, he trotted up the bank and shook himself off, spraying water all over Tonato and me. Tonato chuckled. "He can go." He itched behind the dog's ear. "Now let's make him useful."

Midnight had grown into a leggy, strong canine with big feet and broad shoulders. Tonato fashioned a travois of two saplings and several leather straps and attached it to Midnight's chest with an improvised shoulder harness. It took a few minutes for the dog to walk with this contraption dragging off his hindquarters. Tonato rewarded Midnight with a piece of pemmican each time he succeeded.

My dog was eager to please Tonato, and within a short time we had bundled two bales onto the travois for Midnight to tote. I was loaded with my pack plus some trade goods, and Tonato carried a bale on his shoulders and his pack on a tumpline. Thus, we made our way around the LaChine rapids. Before we reentered the river, the dismantled travois was lashed to the canoe's gunnels so that we could use it whenever there was a portage.

Evenings we camped on the river's shore. I set up our shelters while Tonato hunted for food. Midnight developed the skill of collecting firewood. Each evening we ate well, since Tonato caught fish, rabbit, or quail daily. He shared about his life as the chief's son and as a student with the Jesuits. I talked about my years at Court under the protection of the Queen Mother.

Julie Caton

One week into our journey we explored a minor river running out of the mountains into the St. Lawrence. Tonato emptied the canoe of our supplies, hoisted it onto his head, and trekked into the woods, following this unknown watercourse. We hiked upward for an hour and then found a path leading down to the tributary's tame shore. I was sweaty and tired but glad to embark again in the canoe to follow the stream back downriver.

Soon the current started to pick up speed, and the banks changed from level woodland into rocky cliffs. Tonato had been chanting Huron songs to keep our paddling in rhythm. His voice and the lapping current lulled me into relaxation. Midnight was riding in the middle, resting his head on the gunnels, and letting the occasional spray from my paddle drip on his nose.

Then we heard noise—a steady churning of water rumbled in the distance, getting louder as we approached. Rounding a bend, I saw scattered white caps in a rolling current. Downstream, granite cliffs loomed over us. As the banks rose higher, the river narrowed, forcing its water to run through a tight gorge.

Tonato, aware of my inexperience in white water, raised his voice above the surging sounds. "Keep a steady rhythm. Do not fear the water!" he shouted. Midnight flattened his body on the bottom of the boat.

Before I knew it, our canoe was pummeling into white froth, each wave growing bigger as we sped past the steep riverbanks. My heart pounded. A shriek escaped from my throat. A blast of cold mountain water hit me full in the chest. I gasped. And I kept paddling. Another drenched my face and hair. I lost my breath. I couldn't see.

Like giant hands, angry waters grabbed our canoe. They hurled us down the river. With every wave, we took on buckets of water.

I knelt forward, braced against the bow piece, my feet numb, my arms burning from exertion. Midnight, trying to keep his balance, rode with his four legs splayed out beneath him, water sloshing under his belly.

When I saw bigger rapids ahead of us, rising higher than the bow of our vessel, fear replaced my exhilaration. Tonato's paddling picked up speed. His chant was pitched higher and louder. I tried to keep a paddling rhythm. But with each swell I'd break my pace, first digging hard into churning white waves and next sweeping frantically through froth and spray.

Water broke over my head, throwing me backward onto Midnight. Gripping the paddle in my cramped, frozen hands, I fought to regain my kneeling position. As my eyes cleared, I saw the river spreading out, settling down, finally calming. Tonato steered for a bank covered with flat rocks and green shrubs.

As we neared the shore, Midnight jumped out, having had enough of the watery boat. Tonato followed. With his strong, lithe legs braced against the persistent current, he pulled the canoe onto the shore.

"*Atironkwa onnhetien*—strong woman," he said, smiling. As I stepped out, my numb legs took several moments to operate properly.

Tonato built a fire, and soon it spread its warmth. He stripped off his deerskin vest, muslin shirt, and leather britches. He hung those wet garments on the tree limbs near the fire, and I saw the back of his muscled, bronze form.

I moved closer to the heat, still shivering in my river-drenched shirt and pants.

"Take them off," he said and turned around to face me, "or you'll be cold."

Heat crept over my face. Tonato's carmine skin shined from the wet, the firelight, and the setting sun. His hairless chest looked like a sleek river eel. My breath caught. Buzzing filled my ears. I felt light-headed.

He stepped over the rocks to steady me. Then he tugged off my clinging shirt, shaking it once and tossing it onto a branch. *It is all right*, I told myself. *This is Tonato, my friend and my guide.*

His gentle hands unwound my soaked chest band. My breasts breathed free. At first, I felt embarrassed. But soon I became accustomed to the fresh air, the fire's warmth, and free movement, and I reveled in it all.

"Your britches too," he pressed and went for some more driftwood to stoke the fire.

I turned my back to him. He was right; we needed to get warm and dry, and natives handled nudity with no inhibitions. At the Huron camp, children often ran naked, and women displayed their breasts with no shame. Keeping my back to Tonato, I slipped out of the rest of my garments. Squatting, I squeezed the water from the cotton pants and spread them on the warm, dry rocks. Not knowing what to do next, I remained in that position.

Tonato returned, and all I saw was his sinewy legs and then his offered hand. I took it and lifted my head. I inhaled hard and sat back on a rock.

"What is wrong?" Tonato asked, raising an eyebrow.

"Nothing." My eyes sought the safety of the gray, flat rocks at my feet.

"You're afraid."

"No." I tried to laugh.

"What do you fear, Madeleine?"

I stared at his ankles, studied his toes, unable to look up.

"Tell me."

Instead I started to cry. He lifted me up and folded me in his arms. His warm body felt oddly safe. We stayed that way until my shivering stopped. When Tonato broke our bond, my nakedness then became awkward.

He placed more wood on the flames. "Let's sit. You talk." He gestured to the smooth, granite slab on the smokeless side of the fire.

My abuse at Versailles had not afflicted me for some time. But I had never seen a naked man before nor stood with my own body uncovered and vulnerable until today. I poured out my story and treated my fear like the river water. I rode through it. Tonato's presence reassured me. His face stayed calm and accepting when I told about the man touching me. He understood that I could feel excited and dirty at the same time.

Later, we feasted on a large rabbit, deftly skinned, gutted, and spitted on the fire. I prepared some peas and brought fresh water from the river. At first, self-consciousness plagued me while doing these chores *au natural*, but soon my nakedness became comfortable and freeing.

I bent over a shallow pool in the riverbed and saw my reflection: creamy white skin, wavy chestnut hair brushing my collarbone, and high, firm breasts. My body was different from Huron women, more angular than curvy. What did Tonato think of me?

Midnight, glad to have the rabbit carcass, went off to find more dinner. Tonato arranged the rocks to make a flattened sleeping area. He retrieved his vest and my shirt, spread them out, carried the canoe to the windward side, and suggested we sleep half tucked under it with our feet to the fire. Our other garments we used for cover.

We lay next to each other for the first time. Stretched out under the blue-black sky, the fire flickering near my feet, I found my relaxed state changing. I was becoming… What was the feeling? Nervous? No. Aroused? Perhaps.

I turned toward Tonato, and he interlocked his arms with mine. He smelled of smoke and sweat. After a moment, he took my hand, lowered it toward his chest, and guided it into a loving caress.

"Good," he whispered. Then he took my fingers in his and showed me how to do more to give him pleasure. I felt empowered when his manhood hardened under my hand. Ah, that a woman could make a man respond like this!

When he touched me in return, my body tensed. He felt that response and stopped all his movement. In that moment with that exact touch, shame and arousal converged and scared me. My mind cowered while my body surged.

I decided then to jettison my past. Let him do to me what he had me do to him. I breathed deeply. Excitement rose in my stomach and spread in my body. While Tonato made love to me for the first time, a strange, pleasant sensation swirled through me. For the rest of the night, I was transported. Tonato took me as his lover again, and his gentle care and sensitive caresses erased the lingering fears from my time at Versailles. He fell asleep on my shoulder, one leg flung over my thigh and his fingers splayed on my chest. I stared up at the black sky and experienced a sweet, internal glow coming from deep within me. Inky clouds, gliding past the moon, gave dramatic life to our silvery forms.

The next morning awkwardness overwhelmed me. I sensed I had lost a part of me in him and he in me. Tonato handed me my cap and ran his hands through my curls. "Well, Mat-tee, we need to enter these waters and get ourselves back on course."

As we rode the canoe onto the St. Lawrence, I knew I was a changed woman.

But I was also confused. Should I have waited for someone else? Robert perhaps? The church had taught me to save myself for my husband, preaching that God planned sex within the bonds of marriage for my protection. Yet lovemaking was pleasurable, natural. Tonato, a friend, had just become my lover. What would God find wrong with that?

No distinct answer came. I pushed my guilt away for the time being and moved on.

...

No one raised a suspicious eye as the twenty soldiers at Fort Frontenac welcomed Tonato and his traveling companion, the sailor-voyageur Mat-tee. The fort, with its wooden palisades, looked as it did a year ago, except that several cows with their calves roamed the central yard and the men had built a strong paddock for their bull. The soldiers were raising a herd of sheep that kept the grass clipped down. A proud rooster hovered lustily around the chicken coop.

A wooden dock jutted out into the bay to tie up several canoes. The native village, situated on the land northwest of the fort, teemed with activity. The noises of Cataraqui blended sounds of children playing, animals bellowing, and occasional musket firing. The fort had only five buildings: the kitchen with an adjoining common room centered on a large fireplace, a connecting bunk house for the garrison, captain's quarters on the other side of the wall, and a small separate building for the administrator. There was a barn of sorts.

The administrators, LeBer and Bazire, did not show up to welcome us, and I wasn't sure what to make of this. Was it a rebuff? We supped with the soldiers on beans and salt pork and were shown our places in the bunkhouse. Tonato and I slept in separate cots, an odd experience after the physical intimacy of the past week. Midnight curled up by my feet, providing comfort.

The captain of the fort, Wilhelm Jenet, was unavailable since his young Catholic-Huron wife was struggling that very evening in a long and protracted childbirth. Captain Jenet had turned his room into the birthing chamber, despite the protests of his Huron wife who wanted to deliver in a more traditional way.

No female voices came from the birthing room. Where were Mrs. Jenet's women? Whether native or French, traditionally a few experienced females gathered around a woman who faced the arduous task of delivering a child.

I overheard that Captain Jenet's pale skin, red beard, and attitude of protectiveness had predisposed his wife's people against him. Those Huron women were not about to come into the white men's fort to help one of their own in childbirth. If Mrs. Jenet had chosen to marry a white man, then she would have to embrace the ways of the white man without her native sisters' support. And there was no white woman at the fort. Or so they thought.

My heart went out to the young mother as I heard her moaning through the wooden walls of our bunkroom. The captain's voice was low and reassuring, but every few minutes we could all hear the woman's muffled screams. When the moon was high in the night sky, I could bear it no longer.

"Tonato," I whispered. Midnight, sensing my urgency, jumped up on his bunk, straddled the man, and licked his face. Tonato was up in an instant. We walked out into the cool night air. "I want to go to her," I said.

"Mat-tee, you cannot go into a woman in childbirth as a male." Tonato sighed but then realized I was digging in my heels. "All right. What do you suggest?" he asked finally.

"That we tell the men I was a medic on the ships and have attended women. But we can tell Captain Jenet the truth—after we learn if he wishes my help."

So I attended the birth of the baby boy, Francois Jenet.

Mrs. Jenet's broad cheeks, saucer-like eyes, and full figure reminded me of Flower Eyes. Captain Jenet and I worked until dawn to ease her labor. Francois came into the world head first, dragging a badly deformed right foot behind him. Mrs. Jenet recoiled at the sight. She refused to take the baby to her breast and told the captain to drown him.

Horrified, Captain Jenet slapped his wife.

I was dumbfounded and instantly protective of Francois.

Tonato frowned and then explained to the father that death for the deformed and weak newborns was the native way.

"Have you seen any deformed red-skinned children? Do you notice Huron who are slow or clumsy?" Tonato asked. "In her village, the midwives would have strangled your son before either mother or father met him. The corpse would have been buried quickly under the path leading to your wife's longhouse. This way his spirit would enter another baby's body and reappear on this earth as a healthy son."

Captain Jenet looked down on Francois, unswaddled and flailing on his mother's belly. The baby's face scrunched tight in a rage, and he wailed a high-pitched cry.

"But I am French, and I am Catholic," the anguished father said. "Our God does not permit killings. And I am sure God has a plan for this little one."

The new mother turned her sweat-streaked face to the wall; her hands clutched her thighs in anger.

His father picked up Francois and swaddled him in the receiving blanket. Handing him to his mother, Captain Jenet spoke in a commanding voice. "Marie-Anne, you will nurse him and raise him up as my son until he can be weaned. Then, if you wish it, you need to have no more contact with him. I will be both his mother and father."

As the dawn turned Lake Ontario peach and silver, little did I imagine the roles Wilhelm and Francois were to play in my life.

# 15
# GREAT FALLING WATERS

Having traveled for one month, Tonato and I were camping on the south shore of Lake Ontario when my dog awoke suddenly at dawn. He stood stock-still, the hackles up on his neck, staring into the woods. Unnerved, I touched Tonato and whispered to be on the alert. He put his hand on his musket, and we sat up in our bedrolls on guard.

A boy's face peeked from behind a tree about fifty paces away from us. Then another boy's face and another appeared. Their nationality was evident from the type of war paint and their shaved heads displaying long queues down their backs. We were under the watchful eyes of a band of school-age Iroquois Onondaga.

Tonato called out in Iroquois, "*Onywatenro*. We are friends. We come in peace."

Fortunately, Tonato was dressed in Métis garb, half native and half European. His clothes would not give away his Huron origin.

The boys made no sound. All we could hear was the sloshing of the waves on the beach and a few gulls cawing.

Tonato rose and stirred up the fire. He went about making cornmeal porridge and used some of our pemmican to flavor it. I looked into the cook pot. Why, he was making enough for a longhouse full of people! When the porridge was done, he called out in Iroquois, "Friends, your breakfast is ready." Then he beckoned Midnight to come and lie down next to us so the dog would not pose a threat to the youngsters.

Lured by the smell of the cornmeal cooking and seeing Midnight in a resting position, six budding warriors hesitatingly moved toward us from the woods.

I welcomed them in Iroquois. They relaxed when they heard both of us speak their language. Soon we eight were seated around the fire as the sun rose, eating porridge from the common pot with our fingers. We explained we were traveling the lake to see the famous cataract Niagara. Had they heard of the Great Falling Waters, or what we called Niagara Falls? What could they tell us of that area?

As the sun illuminated the rocks along the wood line, I saw a seventh youngster loitering on the periphery. He chose not to eat. He was larger than the others, tenser. He kept his hand on his weapons while the others had placed bows, arrows, and hatchets on the ground while eating. When the straggler turned to watch Midnight romp along the beach to fetch a stick, I saw an ugly disfigurement covering the left side of his face.

The boys stayed that morning with us. Tonato laid out his coastline map and asked them about inlets and harbors. Several of the boys were eager and friendly. They had been permitted by their parents to go off on a "war party" for practice. They had been told not to kill anybody but to report back to their camp should an enemy appear in their territory. Their camp was about a day's hike southward.

Because these youngsters were from the pro-British Onondaga tribe, I kept my few words to the best Iroquois I could remember and used the basic English I had learned at Court, further convincing them of our assumed British loyalties.

Toward the end of the morning, the boy with the scarred face became increasingly curious. I had gotten out our ironware and beads and was trying to decide what to leave with the urchins as gifts. "Scarface" came near and watched over my shoulder while I unwrapped a pack of bright-red, glass beads. Suddenly he grabbed up a handful and poured them into the medicine bag hanging from his waist.

The schoolteacher in me was annoyed by this selfish gesture of a spoiled child. But Mat-tee, the paddler who could speak Iroquois and a bit of English, wanted to guarantee a friendship. I erased any look of annoyance off my face and smiled. In Iroquois and then in English, I said, "They are yours. Thank you for sharing the shore with us."

This friendly gesture disarmed the lad. He sat down next to me. I passed him the pot of cornmeal, and he grabbed a handful of warm gruel and stuffed it in his mouth. After several lusty mouthfuls, he wiped his hand on his leather loincloth. Midnight took the opportunity to nuzzle him, so Scarface finished by running his hand over the dog's coat.

"Why you going to the Great Falling Waters?" he asked.

I indicated Tonato, saying, "My friend heard about it when he was your age. We wished to see its power and beauty."

As the boy became less skittish, I asked him about his tribe and his family. They were of the Turtle clan and lived in a village of five long-houses along the Salmon River. As he licked his fingers clean again, I dared to ask about his face.

"One night Hurons came on the warpath. They burned out my village, killed most of the men. They took the women and children captive. I was small and hid in a basket. Then I smelled smoke. Our longhouse, it was on fire." Scarface stared at the ground.

He took a breath and continued. "A burning cinder from the roof hit my head. My hair went on fire. I rolled in the dirt and screamed and screamed. No one heard me." Tears filled his eyes, and he quickly blinked them away.

"My parents found me wandering, long after the attack. They did not know me. My face was black and blistered. That was eight winters past. Now, I am almost a man." He drew his hand across his face. "I seek the Huron. When I find him, I kill him. Maybe not this year but soon."

I shuddered from the bitterness in his voice.

After I dispersed the gifts, Tonato filled an extra animal bladder with some leftover cornmeal for the boys. We loaded the canoe and pushed off. So tense were we from that encounter, Tonato and I didn't talk for many minutes. Tonato made a decision we would not camp at night but paddle continuously for several days, taking turns in order to stay away from the Pro-English Iroquois. Perhaps the boys would report our presence to their chief, and we would be hunted. We ate dried corn porridge and chewed on pemmican. I was grateful we were carrying Annie's chamber pot.

...

While Tonato and I paddled southwest on the great Lake Ontario, I thought of tiny Francois Jenet and what kind of life he would have with his clubfoot. I pictured Robert in command of the fort and wondered what life would be like with him.

But most of the time on the lake, I thought of Tonato. If the headwind were chilly, I pictured myself tucked into his arm, lying warm against his welcoming torso. If I needed to shut my eyes against the sun's glare, I would see Tonato's dark smoothness shielding me. I wondered what it would be like to bring Tonato's child into the world. What would the people of Montreal think were I to wed a Christian Huron? I knew of no precedent for that union, so I shivered within. Did I love him enough to be his wife? Would I want to wake up next to him when I was Annie's age?

On the third evening, we beached the canoe. As I hopped out, I felt a telltale trickle, signaling my monthly flow. Procuring moss and soft vines to tie around me took longer than I thought, and Tonato had the fire going and a freshly caught pike spitted on a stick when I seated myself. He gave me a come-hither look.

"Tonato, I ... have begun my monthly flow," I stammered.

He nodded his understanding and turned his attention to the fish, showing me how to debone it between two flat rocks. As the moon rose, Tonato moved his bedroll over to mine and said, "Mat-tee, shall I teach you something new?" He drew me down beside him and took my hand in his. He showed me new ways to give him pleasure by touch.

Suddenly a dark memory closed over my vision, stilling my hand. I was back at Versailles. My hand was being forced to stroke Monsieur, Monsieur—oh, my God, I could almost say his name and see his face.

My breathing accelerated, and my heart tightened. A surge of will-power focused my attention back on us, there at the lakeshore.

My lover's closed eyes, perspiring face, beautiful body, all tense with pleasure, was so different from Monsieur Galouis. There! The name had come to me!

"Mat-tee, what is it?"

I sat up and pulled my knees up to my chest. He took me in his arms. "You are remembering your hurt."

"Yes," I whimpered. "I'm sorry."

He held me closer.

"This is a good thing, Mat-tee. Good, like your bleeding is good for us."

I cuddled against him, questioning in silence what he meant.

...

Several days later we canoed up the Genesee River to a pro-French Seneca village. It had been erected in the belly of a green valley graced by meandering streams and multicolored woodlands. Acres of freshly planted corn, squash, and beans bracketed the village grounds.

I marveled at the way these plants, the "three sisters," intertwined with each other; the bean stalks just beginning to climb up the short corn stalk, which within a month would be up to my knees. The wide leaves of the squash plant were immature at this point in their cycle, but by the heat of the summer, they would spread out over the ground, protecting the beans and corn from an infestation of unwanted weeds.

The next day we joined in the Pro-French Senecas' seasonal celebration of the strawberry festival. The strawberry was the first fruit to ripen in the spring and had special importance, as it represented a good season ahead. To the beat of the drums, faithkeepers led the people in a ritual of thanksgiving and passed strawberry juice around. After this, the clans separated into two groups and competed in a rousing game of lacrosse. The children and the women watched and cheered, often yelling to their favorite players.

An unusually muscular person, with a mane of white hair and a headdress of gull feathers, sat on a carved throne in the center. A young girl fanned him with ferns while another served him refreshment whenever he raised his finger. Tattooed lines up and down his thigh made curious designs. Another young woman, who was trying to win my attention assuming I, Mat-tee, was an eligible male, saw my interest and explained.

"That is our Aharihon, the eldest and most powerful tribal chief. He has seen fifty winters. You wonder at his tattoos? Those lines are marks for the men he has killed."

"He must have over one hundred lines on his legs!" I exclaimed.

"Ah-yup. This is his right. When our chief was young, a warrior of a Lake Erie Iroquois tribe killed his brother. Aharihon spends his life avenging his brother's death. Sometimes he has thought of adopting captives into the tribe. Several winters ago he found a lad almost worthy of taking his brother's place. I remember well the ordeal."

I encouraged the maiden to go on.

"Aharihon had captured some white men and with them a boy. The chief thought boy might have the courage and the spirit needed to be his adopted brother. So the chief gave the boy the run of the village and led him to believe he would be adopted. Aharihon even started a feast and fed the boy the choicest of dog meat."

The pretty girl looked shyly over at me. Eager for the rest of the story, I nodded.

"But, in the middle of the festivities, Aharihon declared the boy unfit to take his brother's place. No one knows why he changed his mind. Maybe he had planned this all along. Shocked, the boy bolted for the longhouse door, but two warriors stopped him. Aharihon wanted the captive burned, roasted slowly. The boy was tied to a stake, and a slow fire was lit. They placed sticks and logs on it carefully because they did not want the boy to die of breathing in smoke. Then they watched as his feet burned, then his thighs."

Coyly, the girl watched to see if she were horrifying me. I tried to keep my expression neutral.

She continued. "After midnight, they took him off the stake and allowed him to rally his strength. Aharihon ordered women to bathe his wounds and keep him comfortable. But the boy groaned and shed great tears. He begged for his life. This is not customary for a savage. We glory in being burned limb by limb, openly showing our courage. This boy had no courage. Maybe Aharihon knew this and that is what changed his mind.

"The weeping got to the hearts of my relatives. My father requested permission to plunge a knife into the boy's heart to stop his suffering. Aharihon would hear none of that. The next morning, the boy was tied back on the stake and burned to death."

The girl had become pensive in the telling of the story. Did she sympathize with the boy?

I considered this kind of ending to my own life. Would I have the courage to bear the pain? Would I be able to sing myself through a death by burning? Or would I be like the boy and cry out for mercy?

Despite the Senecas' welcome and the joviality of the strawberry festival, we stayed but one night in that village.

...

Tonato and I began fighting when we arrived at the Niagara River. That evening when we were about to make love, he pulled something out of his bag. Baffled, I took hold of what looked like a slippery animal skin.

He laughed. "Careful, Mat-tee, that is a precious thing."

"What is it?"

"A sheepskin. I traded at the Seneca village for this. It catches my seeds and keeps you safe from bearing a child."

I glowered at him with raw annoyance. "Maybe I would like to have your baby." My eyes filled with tears.

"Mat-tee, we should talk with each other, but your French ways cloud your speaking truth. You get embarrassed, so it is hard to discuss things with you."

I wiped my tears. "You don't wish me to carry your child? That is why you said my bleeding was good?"

"Think about your desire to find your place among these French people. This dream will not come to be if you bear a redskin baby." He smoothed my hair off my damp forehead. "Do I speak the truth?"

I swallowed the lump in my throat and nodded. His words made sense.

...

At dawn we left our belongings on the shore where the river and the lake join and began to explore the eastern bank. LaSalle wanted us to determine the best path for a portage from Lake Ontario to Lake Erie. We knew the Niagara River dropped three hundred feet over twenty miles, and its current was treacherous. Ahead of me Tonato started up the rocky embankment, referencing LaSalle's map.

The rising sun heated the summer air. As bushes and boulders shielded us, no lake breeze made its way to us. Occasionally Tonato followed an animal path where bracken, vines, and low-hanging trees had been broken back. When we couldn't find such a natural path, Tonato would secure the map and hack our way through the undergrowth. My hot skin itched from bug bites, and the scratches of underbrush aggravated me.

By noon, we had nothing to show for our efforts—no map entries, no special locaters or trail markings. I said as much to Tonato when we rested overlooking the gorge. He gnawed on the corncakes and pemmican and grunted when I handed him the water bladder.

"At this rate, we won't get back to Montreal until winter!" I complained.

"Mat-tee, did you expect that exploration is easy? This drudgery is how LaSalle discovers the rivers he marks on his maps."

After that rebuke, I said little. We trekked on. That night I tried to fall asleep next to Tonato on a bed of pine needles and poplar branches, but my worry kept sleep at bay. Sure that he had lost our way, I stayed alert for an opportunity to peek at his maps.

The next day as we were hiking, we heard a persistent droning of thunder in the distance. It grew louder with each step we took along the escarpment. As the sun reached its afternoon ledge, we could see a cloud of mist like a gray-blue umbrella localized on the horizon. We continued our approach without talking, not being able to hear over the roar of the falls.

Seeing the Great Falling Waters left me breathless. Never had I envisioned a sight so wondrous, so majestic. Boundless water raced over a sharp cliff, dropping the depth of a dozen canoes to the river below. White water bashed into black, kicking up larger-than-life sculptures of foam and mist with power, defying imagination.

At the edge of the escarpment, I watched silver liquid rush over the edge. I saw myself as a small stick in the foam, thrown fifty feet out from the brink. Down, down, down into the torrential swirls below I fell. I could see myself churning beneath the falls, miniscule and helpless.

The experience fired up my heart. I was seeing the hand of the Creator—he the all-powerful; I, his insignificant creation. Oh, I craved to know God personally.

Placing my belongings on the grassy knoll, I propped myself on a boulder by the falls' brink and sat enraptured. Tonato grew impatient with my stalling, so he took Midnight to find a suitable place to set up camp. Other than my journal, my blanket, some pemmican, and a water skin, I was alone.

Yet not alone. The force of this cascade captivated me. The water had a magical draw, so I rested one hand on a boulder, and the rock became my anchor. I closed my eyes to better feel the vibrations and to hear the deluge roar. Thrilled, my body sang with a consistent quiver. I inhaled the moist odor of the river. I breathed again. And again.

Then I was sobbing, deep, soul-wrenching sobs coming up from an unknown place in my belly, surprising me. I only knew I was sobbing not by hearing, but by the strange movements in my throat and the feel of warm tears on my checks.

Why was I weeping?

The sobs continued. I was so tired of trying to figure out my life. Here I was a French woman, miles from my country and my new friends, with no known future. No husband, no child, no personal belongings worth naming. Was I sobbing because I felt sorry for myself?

Lying flat on my belly, I crept forward and reached into the rushing river just above the brink. The powerful current pulled my right hand away from me, and I strained to scoop water up to splash my face and wash away my salty tears.

Struggling, I said to my Creator, "God, I'm here on the edge of your majestic display. I am puny, a nothing, a cipher."

I leaned on the boulder and watched the sun sink behind the western sky. As I surveyed the Great Falling Waters, I uttered a prayer. "God, I offer myself to you." Then, as a practical afterthought, I implored, "Give me a purpose for my life. Thank you."

As the moon rose and the stars came out, I rolled up in my blanket and felt a peace unlike any I ever had. I knew, for the first time, that in order to discover my life's purpose, I had to discover God. Here, at the falls, he was just beyond my grasp.

…

We headed home, paddling during the long hours of sunlight. Our maps were safely rolled in watertight skins tied to the gunnels. We had marked an inland river, the Cayuga, as the ideal place for LaSalle's base camp and shipbuilding area. It flowed into the Niagara on the east side and provided a natural harbor, sheltered by an island one-half mile above the falls. Tuscaroras, friendly and helpful, had sketched out the route from Cayuga to Lake Erie.

As we skimmed along, I told Tonato about my experience at the falls. He understood my sense of finiteness in the face of the Creator's wonders. But as to my need to find a purpose in life?

"Mat-tee," he said, "waking up next to a dear one, capturing your night's dreams, eating well if there is food and not grumbling if there is none, joining your body to another's, serving your family, fixing, planting, hunting, dancing—this is living. And living is all we need. That's my way."

"Not for me, Tonato. I need a purpose, a goal, a vision. I yearn for some desire bigger than myself to live for."

"My people don't think like that. Is that what your Frenchmen do? Think about a goal, the future?"

I considered Tonato's question. "Some do. LaSalle's goal is to explore as much territory as he can and to map the way to China, or at least to the Gulf of Mexico. To do that, he trades his furs and builds up capital to finance his explorations. Other Frenchmen only live for their own needs and pleasures."

"So LaSalle thinks about his future and so do you? Is this what attracts you both? What happens to people like Robert and you when you can't reach your goal?" he asked.

The wind shifted and began to blow us out to the middle of the lake. We had to apply ourselves to paddling and ceased talking. That was fine with me, as I did not have an answer.

*What will I do if I set a goal, but then don't achieve it? Is the natives' way of living in the moment the best approach? Admittedly my respect for Robert is built on our shared goals. What values do Tonato and I have in common?*

...

For three days we progressed in a northeasterly direction with the sky dry and the waters choppy. But Tonato was ever vigilant since now we again traveled in Pro-English Iroquois territory. After our encounter with the boys' mock war party at the Salmon River, we were cautious about where we camped at night. We lit no fires. We kept our muskets at ready. We slept under the canoe with our bags packed for a quick departure. We trusted Midnight to be our watchman.

Our luck did not hold out.

On the fourth day, Midnight woke us with a low growl. We flipped the boat over, lashed our packs and travois into the hull, and pushed off. The predawn sky created a silvery glow in the east but did not give us enough light to see our enemy.

We paddled swiftly into the hazy, gray-pink sunrise. Shortly an uncommon, southerly wind began blowing us out into the middle of the lake. Gray clouds, thick and dirty like sheep's wool, saturated the sky behind us, threatening a storm.

We could go to the southern shore, but it was enemy territory, and we did not want to encounter the Iroquois. We could allow ourselves to be blown further into the center of the lake where the waves would be the biggest and most dangerous if a storm hit. That choice was life-threatening. Finally, we could put our backs into our paddling for the eastern shore, which Tonato estimated was about ten miles away.

We paddled east because our lives depended on it.

The weather grew worse and the waves higher. Midnight whined and hunkered down amidst our bales. I secured a blanket around my shoulders, pulled the hat down over my brow, tucked chin to chest, and poured myself into paddling. A crack of thunder sounded in the distant southwest. Midnight whimpered. Raindrops started, lightly at first. The waves kicked up two to three feet high, but we were not taking on water—yet.

Lightening licked the sky behind us, its reflection shattering on the water ahead. The inky-blue lake was transformed with light for an instant. More thunder cracked, this time closer. Trembling, Midnight sat up on his haunches and howled. Tonato spoke to the dog in a calm voice, and Midnight flattened down on his belly and placed his paws over his head.

The waves boiled up three feet high from trough to crest, then four feet. They started hitting us on the starboard side, so Tonato had to turn into them to keep the canoe from being rolled over. Pouring rain blinded us. The canoe would be lifted by the oncoming wave and then pitch down into a watery valley.

My face and hair were drenched, hat gone. My soaked blanket became a dead weight. My stomach flipped and churned—whether from the rush of the ride or from the motion of the sea, I could not tell. I swallowed my vomit. Paddling became awkward. When the wave lifted us above the water, I would scoop air and lose my rhythm. Tonato yelled for me to bail. Grabbing the ceramic chamber pot, I pitched out water. But we took on more than I was able to bail out. I bent harder into the task, scooping and tossing.

The waves were now more than five feet, the rain unrelenting. The thunder cracked and roared as if we were right at its source.

Lightening flashes revealed land somewhere in the distance.

A large wave lifted us up. The white curl of the crest broke across the boat. It flung me into the lake. Imprisoned by my heavy boots and pants, I sank. The blanket swirled around me, tangling my arms. My lungs were bursting. Panic seized my heart. I was drowning!

Then the words of the Reverend Mother, Antoine, Annie, and Tonato reverberated in my mind. They had each said in their own way: "Relax. Breathe. Trust. You are loved." These thoughts became a hopeful cadence. As I focused on trusting, I experienced the presence of my loving Creator.

Then I heard a voice directing me.

"Madeleine, pull the blanket off your head. Throw off anything hindering your swimming. Push up to the surface. Draw a breath of air. Yes. Reach down and pull off your boots. Good. Breathe. Don't panic. Swim with the waves. Good. Keep your mouth closed. Don't gulp in water. Breathe. Good. Keep moving. Breathe. Good."

Something knocked me on my side. A fish? No. In the pale storm's light, I saw Midnight butting my shoulder, offering me his haunches to hang on to. He was a good swimmer and buoyant. I held his neck with one arm to keep my head above the surface, and with the other arm, I stroked the water, kicking. We made slow progress as I cooed sounds of encouragement to Midnight through my chattering teeth and aching lungs.

A bolt of lightening illuminated the sky, and I thought I saw Tonato kneeling in the canoe and bailing, letting the wind drive him north to the Cataraqui side of the lake. I prayed for his survival. I prayed for Midnight's strength to continue and for the storm to quiet. "God, please let me live."

When my own strength was spent, Midnight dragged me through the water by my hair. I twisted to see if the canoe or Tonato were within sight. My heart sank when I saw nothing. But there was land ahead. The steady tailwind blew us onward. I clamped Midnight's tail in my mouth so we wouldn't get separated. At some point the rain stopped and the sun came out giving me renewed hope.

Finally, the lake's tide and the movement of storm debris washed Midnight and me up onto a rocky beach on the northern shore of Lake Ontario.

...

Was Tonato alive? How far east were we? After Midnight shook his mane and tail, he curled up on the windward side of me, pressed against the small of my back. I tucked into myself for warmth. We slept.

The sound of gulls awakened me. Debris was strewn across the beach. Broken branches, fish carcasses, wooden boxes, bird feathers, and algae a hand high carpeted the rocks. Midnight had gone off looking for his breakfast. I scavenged for human food, but nothing looked edible. Following the lakeshore, I began circling back to the north and discovered I was on a peninsula or an island.

Off in the distance, I saw a vague, shadowy figure waver on the horizon. Was it a moose come for an early morning drink? The figure straightened. I had no place to hide. Was this an enemy? Would I be captured and tortured?

When he beckoned, my heart leaped with joy. Tonato loped toward me. In a moment, we were in each other's arms. I laughed and cried and laughed again. Tonato clung to me and whispered unintelligible words. Midnight pranced up, wagging his tail. Behind Tonato I saw our canoe, not any worse from wear.

After we had filled our senses with each other, Tonato let go and handed me a roll of pemmican. I sat down next to him and discovered my legs were shaking. We ate and shared our stories as the early morning sun graced the sky.

Tonato thought we were on a large landform ten miles west of Cataraqui. The storm's gale had washed everything onto the island's beach, including Tonato, Midnight, and the canoe. Directly across from our position was a bay, several stones' throw wide, receding into a lush, green cove. I studied the way the cedar trees came down to the water and unfurled their roots amongst the boulders. The maples and oaks spread their green shade while ferns and wildflowers carpeted both sides of the inlet.

Colors of the sunrise transformed the blue-gray bay into turquoise, green, gold, and yellow. The sheltered harbor was decorated with streaks of black and white too, reflections from the trees and their shadows. The colors of the inlet reminded me of a large, elegant bird I had seen at Versailles. Courtiers had called the creature a parrot, his broad body festooned by plumage of blue, green, and gold, his piercing eyes composed of striking white and black stripes. The harbor and its surrounding land drew my heart in a way I couldn't explain.

"Parrot's Bay," I heard myself whisper. "I will make this land mine."

JULIE CATON

# 16

# THE LEAVINGS

Annie was so surprised at seeing us she nearly dropped the bin of wheat. We embraced.

"Oh, my dear, my dear. How I missed you," she said, holding me at arm's length. Amber jumped up, placed her paws on my chest, and licked my face.

Life with Tonato for the last two weeks of our journey had been idyllic. As we scouted out Parrot's Bay, bypassed the fort, and meandered back to Montreal, our passion went unbridled. I felt like a queen, desired and attended to morning, noon, and night. My understanding of the power of sex grew.

At Versailles, the ladies and men of the Court vied for sexual power. Monsieur Galouis coveted it so much he thought it reasonable to violate me. Sex was the draw even for the king, who publicly pretended to be a moral Catholic but fornicated with Louise de la Valliere and others behind closed doors.

Was it the thrill of pure pleasure that held all this power? Were we captivated by the dance of intimacy itself? Or perhaps we yearned to be attached, to bond emotionally? Why would human beings so freely give up chastity and fidelity, principles they believed to be morally right, in order to satisfy their sexual urges?

In the last two months, I too had left behind my Christian morality and become a fornicator. Did I care? No. I loved Tonato and adored being close to him. I enjoyed the way he made me feel and valued the pleasure I could give him. When I made love to Tonato, I often ignored God. In truth, my interest in God had been waning since the Reverend Mother Marie died. But my experience at the Great Falling Waters had kindled a fresh awareness of the Creator. Now I yearned to know God's power intimately. I wanted to share with God the same closeness I had with Tonato. Was this desire what the Reverend Mother referred to when she talked about Jesus being her bridegroom? Yet wasn't God spirit and Tonato flesh? My mind swirled.

The horrific experience during the storm, my being stirred like a wooden flotsam amongst the waves, indebted me to God. He had calmed me and given me the clarity of thought to manage the danger. He had sent Midnight into the water to give me strength and encouragement. And was it not he who answered my prayers and threw me up on the same island where my beloved Tonato had also landed, alive?

So here I was, a new woman, born afresh out of the depths of the storm, like Jonah coming from the whale.

...

When word spread Tonato and I had arrived, people gathered at Noleen's to get news of the West. My description of the Niagara Cataract awed them. When we reported the natives were in a season of peace and not war, Montrealers expressed relief. Now they might get through the harvest season without bloodshed. Tonato mingled, answering questions, barely glancing at me.

After our weeks of near solitude, the press of all the people was too much, and I retreated. While soaking in Annie's large copper bathtub, the front door opened, and I heard Robert's voice. "Tonato, where is this lady partner of yours?"

I scooted down into the water, sending a wave of suds over the edge of the tub. Hastily I rinsed off my hair and body.

Robert was here! I had not thought about the nature of this encounter with him. Would Robert see I was a changed woman? Would he sense that Tonato and I were lovers? Since Robert would not countenance a maiden consorting with a native, he must never know about us.

Yet I felt so different. Could I hide my newness from him?

These thoughts rushed through my mind as I buttoned my white linen blouse, the garb for proper women of this colony. I fastened the waist of my blue, woolen Métis skirt and smiled, confident that my firm body was attractive. I towel-dried my locks and drew a comb through my hair, wanting to impress Robert, not just with my courage and strength (which he had doubted) but also with my newly discovered sensuality.

Contrary to propriety, I left my cap on the bed, letting my damp curls hang loose. Upon seeing me, Robert smiled broadly and kissed my hand. His powdered wig tickled my wrist. I did not blush this time. I held his gaze and enjoyed this silent moment. Then out of the corner of my eye, I saw Tonato leave Noleen's. He didn't even glance at me.

... 

As suddenly as the storm's waves had thrown me into the raging lake, Tonato left me. We had not discussed our future. He had not said a word about his plans. I was stunned. Homesickness was the only explanation I could consider. But that was a frail excuse considering all that we had experienced together. I felt punched in the gut.

After Tonato's surprising departure for Sainte Foye, Annie tried to console me. He had neither said good-bye nor shared any last-minute intimacies. "All his words, all his actions suggested he wanted to be with me," I moaned. "Did I misread him?"

Annie was knitting socks while she rocked on the porch. "Natives don't think about the future." The air was thick with humidity. "Tell me, had you two talked about your plans?" She peered up at my crestfallen face. "I didn't think so. He's probably not even aware he's hurt you."

"He left when he saw me with LaSalle. Could he have been jealous?" I asked.

"Come, my girl. We may never know. Maybe he thought he was doing you a favor. Go shed a tear. Then remember, I need you here. There is work to do." The clicking of her needles picked up speed.

...

For several weeks, I struggled to readjust to my role as shop clerk. I also needed to shift emotionally—away from my closeness to Tonato and toward Robert. Maybe Tonato was right. My future was with LaSalle.

Robert collaborated with me over the maps Tonato and I had completed, and we marked the site of Parrot's Bay. I planted the idea of establishing a trading post there. I even invested my share of our trading profits for Noleen merchandise. Sweeping, stocking, selling, ciphering—these activities kept me busy. Work buffered my pain. Routine and ritual disciplined my thinking. Letting go of Tonato and my dreams about him was a healthy action to take. But the walls of my heart felt raw as if burned with acid. At night, my body ached with loneliness. I couldn't fall asleep. I tried to pray but doubted God heard. Was he silent because of my unblessed lovemaking? Had our passion been wrong?

...

On September 1, 1674, Montrealers buzzed. Intendant Jean Talon had issued a new decree: No adult male could return to France unless he was married with children. And his family had to stay here while he completed his business across the Atlantic. It was treason to do otherwise.

The women believed the decree to be wise, with only the well-being of this newly settled land at its core. Such a law guaranteed men would seek marriage, make the women pregnant, and commit themselves to their children. If they had to leave for France, they would return to their families here.

Others, like Robert, felt they had been imprisoned on this continent with freedoms curtailed.

...

Robert could not contain his impatience when he learned the two explorers, Louis Joliet and Father Marquette, had traveled down the Mississippi from the pays d'en haut. If they had gone further south, they might have traveled into the Gulf of Mexico. Because of their discovery, LaSalle's theory that a river route existed to the Gulf of Mexico had turned into a certainty. Instead of his being glad, Robert, jealous of Joliet and Marquette, commented under his breath that their discoveries should have been his.

Relentlessly, he studied his maps and conversed with men who had been west. Reluctantly he socialized with people so he could build up his capital to finance another exploration. With the additional information supplied by Tonato and me, he had more ideas about establishing a trade route. Because his capital flowed in slowly, he reckoned he had to approach King Louis XIV again for financing. Yet the Crown's decree about marriage blocked his way to leave this continent.

"Would you ever consider marriage, Madeleine, to a man who would be traveling most of your married life?" he asked as we strolled along the river.

"Would such a man want me for his wife?" I looked impishly at him. "I'd nag to travel along with him, would I not?" I bent to scoop up a stone, flipped it into the water, and winked.

We laughed together. He was not serious. But I was.

Robert petitioned for and received Frontenac's dispensation to travel to France without being married. As we waited for his departure day, I was learning to be content with the various roles I played on this stage of life. At sunrise, I was a woodsman, going with Annie to hunt for quail, geese, deer, and moose for our customers. When the sun rose high, I was a storekeeper and merchandiser, selling, bartering, buying, and parlaying to keep our patrons happy. When the shop closed, I became a socialite, invited to suppers with the prominent families in Montreal.

I was also LaSalle's lady, a female courtier, trying to entertain, encourage, challenge, and soothe this difficult man. I tried to imitate the Court ladies' facial expressions, their subtle but witty analyses, their proper but suggestive touches.

Why did I revert to Court behavior after years of loathing what I had seen at Versailles? In truth, I knew no other way. I wanted Robert's support and respect. And I wanted Parrot's Bay for my home. Robert was the key.

On November 30, 1674, Robert sailed for France. I had known his date of departure. But I had not anticipated how wretched his leaving would make me feel.

. . .

Melting ice, rising waters, and growing grass heralded spring. Increased river traffic kept Annie and me busy dawn to dusk restocking our low supplies with new shipments. I watched each ship come into port. Robert did not return from France.

. . .

"Mat-tee." I heard my old name as I bent over a new barrel of glass trinkets. Heat rose up my torso. I straightened to see Tonato on the other side of the counter.

My first instinct was to leap the counter into his embrace. My second was to slap him for having left.

I did neither.

He held up his hand in greeting and said he and Tree-on-the-Rock were here to pick up some goods for their venture west. I looked around.

He laughed. "My father is up at LaChine, waiting for me."

Tonato was as handsome as ever.

We kept our distance as I collected the items on his list: iron kettles, needles, bricks of pewter for bullets, ladles and bullet forms to make ammunition. Tonato also peered into the barrel of glass trinkets and asked for a pouch full of them. "They will charm the ladies." He grinned.

My stomach churned. I saw no hint of sadness or guilt in his expression.

"Mat-tee, my father and mother send their greetings."

Between clenched teeth, I wished happiness and health for his parents and sister.

"You can congratulate me too. At the end of the summer, I'll be a father. Remember Minnow? She was in your school." Ah, I remembered; the lovely, young thing with the hair down to her waist and slender arms and legs. "We were married last Christmas by Father Bart. It is good." Then he walked onto the porch and down the steps.

I leaned against the door as it closed behind him, shaking with hot indignation.

...

No Tonato. No Robert. Annie tried all sorts of tender, loving ploys to lift me out of my blue mood. She even tried scolding me.

"Madeleine, your mood should not depend on another person. You must find your happiness within yourself. What do you think a man brings to you anyway? Is it security from his strength? Or do you need his touch because you're afraid of being alone? Is it passion you want?"

I blushed and shook my head no.

"Well then, what is their attraction?"

I had no answer.

...

Rocking on Noleen's front porch one afternoon in late June, I looked down the road to the river and saw a courier coming up from the docks. He brought me a sealed letter posted six weeks earlier. I flushed in anticipation.

> Versailles
> May 5, 1675
> Mademoiselle Madeleine,
>
> This letter carries with it great joy. His Majesty Louis XIV has given me an audience. And he has authorized my explorations into the West! But his Court is only able to finance a small percent of the expenses, so I need to stay longer. With the king's backing, members of my family should feel secure investing in France's new colony.
>
> When I return, I will linger in Quebec long enough to clear my plans with Governor Frontenac. This letter is going out tonight with a courier whose destination is Montreal, and you will be reading it shortly. Then, my

friend, I will be at your doorstep. We have important plans to discuss!

    Cordially, Monsieur Robert LaSalle

…

Two weeks later, when I was expecting Robert himself, another letter arrived. I excused myself to read it alone, sensing it was portentous.

> Quebec
> June 20, 1675
> Madeleine,
>     The governor suggests I travel immediately to Fort Frontenac to secure holdings and stake my claim. Therefore, I will be unable to rendezvous with you as planned. May the Almighty look after you. I will arrive in Montreal before the autumn.
>     Salutations.
>     Your servant, Monsieur Robert LaSalle.
>     P.S. I have sworn an oath of allegiance to Governor Frontenac. His vision for this new land coincides with mine, and he is the center of political power. To do otherwise would be a foolhardy. RLS

I flopped over on the bed and pushed Midnight off with my feet. *Unable to rendezvous? Maybe. Then again, maybe not.*

…

Days later, I was seated next to Father Georgio at Madame LeBer's dinner party. Twelve of us were eating grilled whitefish with asparagus stuffing. A negative mood, directed at Robert, brewed among the diners. I sat quietly nodding my head in feigned interest.

    Father Georgio complained that the governor now required Jesuit priests to carry passports wherever they went, a curtailment of the freedoms Black Robes had had. "Frontenac and his lackeys feel they have a right to legislate our travels, investigate our policies, and limit our trading. With their support of liquor as a commodity of trade, they undermine the Catholic morality we priests have worked so hard to instill in the savages. The crown is taking power away from the people."

A guest inquired, "Aren't you Jesuits in the good graces of the governor?"

"It does not appear so. Governor Frontenac's goals and the Jesuits' pursuits are often at odds. For example, Frontenac wants to subjugate the natives so he can build up a trade with France. We priests have worked at saving these people for the glory of the church and the king." Father Georgio pushed his dinner plate away and propped his elbows on the table. The sleeves of his black robe were frayed at the wrist. Curly hair covered his thick arms.

The host, Monsieur LeBer, offered his opinion. "Indeed, Father, our governor is greedy and aggressive. I am sure you have heard he has sent LaSalle directly to Fort Frontenac to guarantee the governor's control of the fort?"

I heard gasps around the table.

LeBer reminded us if it had not been for his own gracious endowment of LaSalle last year and his personal guidance at Fort Frontenac, the explorer would have a limited reputation, if any at all.

As I listened to the conversation, I realized these Montrealers were jealous of LaSalle. Robert had moved himself into a primary place to manage the natives, become rich on the fur trade, and established a name for himself through his explorations. These pompous guests wished they were he! Their hypocrisy made me cringe. In their envy, these Montrealers were conniving for the comeuppance of my friend.

Should I leave Montreal to warn him?

# 17
# A Deal Is Struck

My plans shocked Annie. I was going to meet Robert at the fort.

"I thought you were angry with him for running on ahead to Cataraqui and forgetting about you?"

"Annie, if LaSalle has gained the king's permission for land ownership, I want to be first in line to purchase Parrot's Bay. If LaSalle is becoming the enemy of these Montreal and Quebec leaders, I want to warn him. Romance is not my motive," I assured her. When she eyed me skeptically, I blushed.

I traded for a canoe light enough to portage alone. I affixed ropes to both the bow and the stern and lashed several bales of belongings to the center thwart. I set off at noon on July 19, 1675, up the St. Lawrence. My savings were tied in a watertight pouch around my waist. I would not chance it ending up at the bottom of the river unless I went with it.

Looking back on my decision, my true motive was to prove I was independent. I needed neither man nor woman, and I had learned well my lessons of survival. Perhaps such an experience of being alone would help me clear up my confusion and draw me closer to God.

But I was not completely alone. Midnight rode proudly up in the bow, scouting for me. He would warn me about a deadfall or a large rock ahead by dropping to the keel and putting his paws over his muzzle. I paddled from sunrise to early evening, taking a midday break. I dressed in my most practical garb: my native tunic and moccasins.

My decision to depart came so quickly I had little to say to Annie. I whispered to her that we would see each other again, but my heart, heavy with sadness, realized Annie had outlived the number of days given most women. She might not be strong enough to come to me. And I did not plan to return—if I could get Parrot's Bay.

To keep the boredom away as I paddled, I played a game. When I paddled on the starboard side, I considered the reasons Robert and I should be together. We were both young, French, and eager to make a new life in this country. We were healthy and would make fine children. We were both educated and Catholic and could share in common experiences from Court life in France. Our intellectual curiosity and business acumen were a good match for each other.

Then I would shift sides. While paddling on the port, I reviewed the reasons I should stay single. Robert would be traveling most of his life and would not provide consistent companionship to anyone who wasn't traveling with him. And he had already made it clear he would not want a female to "endure" the traveling. Robert tended to be self-absorbed and had shown little interest in intimate details in my life—unless they directly affected him. Robert was controlling and domineering, expecting me to bend to his whims.

I tried not to think of Tonato at all.

...

"Mademoiselle Mat-tee, Mat-tee." Captain Jenet sprinted toward me. Midnight jumped on to the fort's dock and wagged his tail. "You've returned. I somehow sensed you would. You're looking well." He gripped my hand. "May I ask the purpose of your visit?"

I tucked some hair up under the hat and brushed my tunic off. "My dear captain!" I returned his enthusiasm but ignored his question. "How are your wife and baby?" I asked, recalling the birth of Francois. "Your son must be one year plus now. Is he walking?" Too late I remembered the tragedy of the baby's twisted foot and blanched.

Without answering my questions, Captain Jenet beckoned his men to hoist my equipment. We passed inside the fort's palisade and he offered to house me in his cabin. He explained the soldiers' quarters were full and the "government" quarters had been commandeered by Monsieur LaSalle. My stomach spun at the sound of that name.

Over the year, the fort's wooden structures had been replaced by fieldstone. The palisade had been made higher; the turrets stood twelve feet tall on each corner. In the middle of the courtyard, a well provided water. I knew Robert must be proud of these accomplishments.

But where was he?

We entered the newly built captain's quarters. The cabin had no bright colors, no decorations, no field flowers or artful dishes. When I could not hear the sound of a child, my heart sank. Was Francois one more colonial infant who died before his first birthday?

Captain Jenet walked into a little back room, put my belongings on the planked floor next to a cot and a chair, and left. A small window overlooked the courtyard. Stepping up to it, I noticed two women; one was drawing water and the other beating a rug outside the barracks. I could hear Captain Jenet building up the fire in the front room and hanging the iron kettle over the flames.

"You would like some tea, Mademoiselle?" he called.

"That would be very kind," I said, entering the front room.

The captain picked up the fire tongs and pushed the burning logs around.

I heard the shrill, happy cry of a child outside, and a soldier loped in with a tot perched on his shoulders. "Da-Da," the boy said and laughed as the captain scooped him up.

"Oh, sir, sorry. Didn't know you had a guest," the tall youth rattled. He had big, oddly shaped ears and bangs cut bluntly across his forehead. He would not look me in the eye. "Francois wan... wan... wanted you," he stammered. "Monsieur LaSalle sent me. He's returning from the native village any time now." The gangly soldier patted Francois on the head and left. The man was Robert's fetch-'em boy, Claude Leonine.

Captain Jenet tenderly brushed his son's dark hair, hugged him, and set him down on a blanket. Kneeling down to Francois's height,

Jenet said, "This lady, Francie, was here when you were born. Say 'hello' to Mademoiselle Mat-tee."

I squatted down and smiled as the copper-skinned, blue-eyed baby grinned and said, "Ma-ma-mat-tee."

Tousling his hair, I said, "Hey, Francie."

He was robust, well formed, and clothed like a savage in the summer. That is to say, he had nothing on. His right foot still turned inward.

We heard loud, gruff sounds from the courtyard. "A woman? Here? By whose authority?"

There were grumblings and mutterings, and a tall shadow appeared in the doorway.

Captain Jenet jumped up, knocking over his mug. "Monsieur LaSalle, the fort has a guest. Mademoiselle Mat-tee."

Robert took three strides into the room and looked at me quizzically. Reaching for my hand, he pulled me up. He started to smile, but shifted into a more military mode. "I know you as Mademoiselle de Roybon D'Allone, do I not? To what do we owe this surprise?"

I winced at his steel voice. Was my coming a mistake? I breathed deeply and looked up. "Why, to yourself, sir. You had planned on meeting me in midsummer, do you not recall? So our rendezvous takes place here, not in Montreal. Do you have any objection?"

Robert shifted his feet, glanced at Captain Jenet who was trying to mop up the spilled tea with his foot unnoticed, and turned back to me. His neck flushed. "I have business with my captain now, but perhaps you will dine with me at sunset?" He failed to look me in the eye.

"With pleasure, sir." Then I addressed Captain Jenet. "Perhaps I could give my regards to your young wife?"

"I regret, Mademoiselle, Mrs. Jenet does not reside here. She is in the village with her mother's people. I am Francois' sole parent."

"Well then, sir, I delight in reacquainting myself with Francois."

Jenet bowed. "That would be a pleasure for both of us. Francie? Stand up and walk over to Mat-tee."

Francie, now fifteen-months-old, stood unsteadily, held onto his father's pant leg to get his balance, and walked over to me. His clubbed right foot dragged behind him.

I marveled at the boy's strength and courage. His father added, "He is not going to grow up thinking of himself as a tragedy. Are you, Francie?"

The toddler reached my chair, pivoted on his good leg, faced his father, and threw himself forward into his father's waiting arms.

Robert fidgeted with impatience, waiting for Francois and me to depart.

In the next few weeks, I would learn that dinners with Monsieur LaSalle and his men were formal, factual, and devoid of emotion. But playtimes with Francois Jenet and Midnight were exciting, entertaining, and full of laughter.

...

Fort Frontenac had turned into a village with Robert as its head. Several of the soldiers had built single-room cabins along the northern palisade. Robert ordered his men to build a chapel because he expected a Recollet priest, Father Hennepin, to arrive any day from Quebec. Hennepin would bring copies of the dictionaries compiled by the Reverend Mother Marie of the Incarnation.

We heard reports the Iroquois had been defeated badly by the Susquehanna tribes. While these skirmishes took place on the south side of the lake, we wondered when trouble would invade our lands. Robert wanted me to keep up with my language skills so I might step in as peacemaker if difficulties with the Iroquois increased.

The day after I arrived at the fort, Robert and I took a walk together in order to gain privacy. Only then did he take my hand as we strolled. I told him about the dissension brewing against him in Montreal.

"Let them think what they will, Madeleine," Robert said as he threw a stick into the lake for Midnight to retrieve. "I have our king on my side." Midnight dashed up the bank, dropped the stick by Robert's feet, and shook, spraying lake water all over. I laughed. Robert scowled and backed up a few feet from the dog. But he then reconsidered and, grinning, tossed the stick again.

When we were away from the prying eyes of the men and the pressures of his command, Robert's warmth and affection peeked out from behind the clouds of his formal personality. He smiled, his eyes laughed, and his hand was warm. We discussed his time at Court, his financial difficulties, and his continued vision for finding a water route to the Gulf of Mexico. And Robert listened while I talked about my dream of settling in this area, although I did not mention Parrot's Bay.

When we spent time together alone, my body melted like a warm candle. However, no matter how feminine I acted, Robert behaved like a proper gentleman. I would rather he have taken me in his arms.

...

On September 8, Father Hennepin arrived on a flat-bottom boat. Guided by a Huron lad, the priest traveled with two soldiers, some cattle and chickens, and one beautiful horse, a gift from the governor to LaSalle.

The horse, the first seen in this area, drew the natives down to the waterfront. When the men tried to unload her, the mare dug her four feet in, braced her legs, and stood stock-still. She faced the gap of rolling water between the boat and the dock. So the men blindfolded her. When they got her onto dry land and removed the blindfold, she pranced for them, danced for them, and kicked up her heels. She had a sleek, chestnut coat, black mane and tail, and stood well over fifteen hands tall.

The men were getting used to my appearance, dressed as Mattee in my seaman's blouse and britches. All hands harvested the corn, squash, and beans or worked on the chapel. Between the two of us, Captain Jenet and I kept Francois entertained and out of mischief. Francois, who stood head to head with Midnight, got around by holding onto the scruff of the dog's neck. The boy, oblivious to his twisted foot, would chase Midnight in circles. I laughed whenever Francie and the dog wrestled, watching until the toddler ended up on his behind, and Midnight smothered the boy with licks.

Four of the stronger men rammed earth and straw into the stone foundation of the chapel, a process called *renchaussage*. Select timbers were dragged in from the forest for the building itself, and logs were cut and sawed for the chapel's siding. One day all the soldiers were ordered to the site to hoist with pulleys the exterior frames of the chapel. While Robert barked the orders, he stood apart from his sweating workers.

At the end of October, Robert and I were in his quarters drawing new landmarks on various maps. Since different explorers each designed his own maps, significant geographical discrepancies showed up among them. Robert compared existing maps, combining all the common landmarks, and then created his own. I placed my mug down, smoothed out his map, and ran my hand along the northern shore of Lake Ontario. Then I touched Parrot's Bay with my index finger. I had never told Robert about the storm and what I had discovered.

Now was the moment, I decided. "Robert, this area holds a particular spot in my heart. I call it Parrot's Bay for the colors it reflected during a sunset last summer. Tonato and I encountered it on the last leg of our trip."

Robert shifted the oil lantern so he could see the map better. "It is about ten miles from the fort. An interesting place for an outpost, perhaps. What is the geography like around it?"

"It's sheltered on the west by forests; on the east, between the bay and Fort Frontenac, with meadows and woodlands. The lakeshore is rocky but accessible. The bay is about three hundred yards wide and is fed at its north shore by a fresh water spring, making it marshy and a home for waterfowl and wild life. Approaching that area from the north would be difficult."

Robert looked up from his maps and lifted my chin, studying me. His thumb caressed my cheek. He smiled.

"Madeleine, you know that lake frontage in extraordinary detail. You are interested in it?"

I could smell his muskiness, the clover grass on his breath. We said nothing for several heartbeats but held each other's gaze.

"What would you do with it?" my explorer asked. He sounded pleased.

"I would build a wood-frame house and start a trading post like Noleen's. If this were successful, I would expand my holdings. I'd clear the land, plant corn, squash, and beans, raise cattle and chickens, and become self-sufficient. The creek flowing down from the north is ideal for a mill.

"If your dream of westward expansion comes true," I continued, "then the success of such a business as mine would be guaranteed. I would serve not only the settlers from the fort but any homesteaders who build along the north shore of the lake. I know the languages of the Iroquois and Huron and could welcome trade with all the native tribes."

This was the first time in a year I had discussed these plans with anybody. I knew Annie would support me if I said I wanted to fly to the moon. But how would Robert receive this news? As I spoke my thoughts aloud, a long-tied knot in my stomach unraveled.

Robert looked down at the map again and took out a measuring stick. He drew lines on the parchment from Fort Frontenac to Parrot's Bay and checked it against another document, one with the king's seal on it.

"Madeleine, the land around Parrot's Bay is within the king's concession to me. I will sell you that land. The purchase price will help equip part of my next venture to the Niagara area and beyond."

A flush of excitement spread over me. Robert rolled up the piece of parchment. "Let's walk, Madeleine. And you can make me an offer."

...

The full moon, low on the horizon, glowed like a yellow squash. Since the sky was clear, our shadows cast long figures behind us. The chilled autumn air tingled my nostrils. We saw the flickering of the outdoor fires in the village and their black smoke spiraling into the dark, silver sky.

The cows lowed and munched on squash vines. Sheep blatted and drifted around the grass. The fort's horse, her smooth flank reflecting the moonlight, grazed with her back to us. Robert whistled, and she loped over to the fence. He fondled her nose. I stroked her mane and pulled some burdocks out of her forelock. She smelled my raised hand. Her nose was like brushed velvet, and her warm breath kissed my fingers.

Robert stroked the mare's withers. His hands were gentle. "I've been training her so she can be ridden. I call her Tempete. She's going to foal this winter. I want you to have her baby to rear as your own. You will need a horse to work with you at Parrot's Bay."

"Oh, Robert. Parrot's Bay! And a horse. I don't know what to say," I blathered. He accepted my offer of one-half my savings, two thousand livres. As we walked, it took self-discipline for me not to skip and shout. I wanted to embrace Robert in my excitement. But who might suddenly appear and see us? As a substitute, I signaled for Midnight, who came and put his paws on my chest. I wrestled with him, burying my smile in his fur, imagining I was nuzzling Robert's rich-brown locks.

# 18

# UNDER THE GLASS

"Mademoiselle, Monsieur LaSalle said to come git... git you," Claude Leonine said. "Father Jean Cavelier, that Sulpician monk, you know, Monsieur LaSalle's brother?" He took a quick breath and continued as I placed Francois on his blanket. "Father Jean came down from Montreal on the supply boat before noon. He and Captain LaSalle have been closeted for hours. Please come."

"Why do they wish *me* to come, Claude?" I asked.

"Monsieur LaSalle wants you to prepare a supper for him and his brother. 'A fine feast' were his words, M'me."

"Can't you or Sally prepare their dinner? Captain Jenet expects me to stay with Francois until late tonight."

"I'll mind Francie. You pre... prepare the meal. Captain LaSalle thinks your cooking is the best at the fort and told his brother your father was the royal carver for King Louis!" Claude began twisting his shirttail. "Oh, Mat-tee, the captain's got a bur... burdock in his britches. Do come. You being around calms him!"

Claude hoisted Francois to his shoulders, grabbed the boy's blanket and some wooden toys, and started out. I stoked the fire, wrote Jenet a note, and hastened to catch up with Claude. Francois bounced gleefully on the young man's shoulders while Midnight trotted ahead.

When we arrived, Sally and Maude had already built up the fire, and cut into a venison haunch. We worked together, sautéing the meat, boiling the potatoes, and polishing the tablesetting Robert had brought with him. I sent Maude to fetch some beets.

As we prepared the meal, I kept wondering if there was more to LaSalle's summons than his wanting food prepared like the royal table.

After dinner, LaSalle sent Claude to retrieve us. Maude didn't even try to tidy herself up. But Sally and I threw off our smeared aprons and straightened each other's caps before we went to meet the men.

The brothers could not have been more different. Where Robert was tall and angular, Jean Cavelier was round and soft. Where Robert's voice had a commanding tone to it, Jean's sounded liked he had a stuffed nose. Where Robert was sitting erect in his chair, tense and alert, Jean was slouched, the paunch of his belly filling out his priest's robe of dark-gray wool.

Robert stood and introduced us, but the priest did not rise and barely looked us in the eyes.

"Jean," Robert cleared his throat. "You wanted to meet the women at our fort. Ladies, my brother has come all the way from Montreal to clear up some unseemly business."

"Unseemly?" I queried.

"A rumor has surfaced in Montreal that the soldiers and I are residing at Fort Frontenac for no other purpose than to forni—… um … er, to entertain inappropriately the three women who are here. I asked my brother to speak to you ladies about his concerns." Robert was using all of his willpower to keep his temper in check.

Father Jean Cavelier hocked the phlegm from his throat, smoothed his cassock, and patted his belly. He asked each of us our names, where we had come from, and our purpose for being at the fort. Both Sally and Maude described themselves as married women. Their answers satisfied the Sulpician, and they were dismissed.

Until that hour, I had never given my housing arrangement with the Jenets any thought. "I'm here to establish a trading post," I told the priest. "This is a service Governor Frontenac has expressed interest in, as I am conversant in Iroquois. While I wait for that business to be established, I am 'nanny' to the captain's son. Little Francois was abandoned by his Huron mother because of his club foot."

Robert strengthened my statement by adding he and I had known each other for several years and that I was a woman "with many talents."

"This winter, before she begins her business venture, Mademoiselle will be involved teaching the natives," he continued as I raised my brow. It was the first I'd heard of this! "Once Mademoiselle D'Allone makes some profit in trade, I may request her to invest in my westward exploration."

"Yes, Robert. Now I am satisfied," the priest said. He took a letter from his voluminous robe with a look of distaste and handed it to me. "To you, Mademoiselle, from Madame Noleen. You seem to be following in the footsteps of the one who asked me to deliver this letter. Though why you do not engage in more womanly pursuits like marriage or the veil is beyond my comprehension!"

The men went on to discuss western trade routes and Robert's accounts. As I had not been dismissed, I remained standing like a servant girl, ignored.

Finally I turned on my heel and left.

Hours later, Robert sought my companionship at Jenet's.

"The maddening Mesdames up in Montreal have these stories going around about my 'flirtatious and lascivious behavior.' Imagine! They insist that you came here for no other purpose!"

Seated in front of Jenet's fire, with Francois sleeping peacefully in his trundle bed, I tilted my head in response, but thought, *Oh, Robert, how dense you are!*

"Have I told you how Madame Bazire threw herself at me last year?"

"No, Robert, you have not."

"It's true! Whenever I was around, she painted herself up handsomely and dressed to seduce. You know, I believe they wanted me to succumb to her flirtation. If I had given in, my whole reputation would have been lost."

"You're so right. Remember how jealous LeBer and Bazire were when you recalled them from the fort a year ago? They wanted to denounce you. But does your brother not know you well enough to have spoken up for you?"

"Jean is not a man who thinks for himself. I am sure LeBer and Bazire not only suggested this trip, but also donated extra funds to the Sulpician Order!"

Robert adjusted the logs on the fire. "Madeleine, your answers to my brother were perfect. You told the truth without revealing controversial information. He has loaned me money for my ventures, and I have not yet paid him off. If he had learned about the king's land grant, there might have been a serious problem. Thank you for being so circumspect."

"You're most welcome, my friend."

He hesitated before he spoke. "Tell me, are you just a nanny for Jenet's young son?" He emphasized "just."

The heat of the flames reddened my cheeks. A surge of excitement rose as well. Had his previous coolness stemmed from his thinking that I had romantic interest in Captain Jenet?

"I told your brother the complete truth in that regard. I am Captain Jenet's housekeeper and surrogate mother to his child. But my heart is committed to Parrot's Bay and establishing a trading post."

I stood and stepped toward him. More boldly, I added, "If there is any one person who has drawn me down to Fort Frontenac, it is you, not Wilhelm Jenet."

At my subtle declaration his eyes clouded with hesitation. I added quickly, "Your vision of this continent stirs my heart. Let me share that with you." Robert's blue eyes softened with relief. He could handle our common passion for the land, but not a potential passion of the heart. Was he afraid of being intimate?

...

As I dressed the next morning, Annie's forgotten letter rustled in my pocket.

> Montreal
> October 29, 1675
> Mat-tee,
>     Father Jean Cavelier said you were living at Fort Frontenac in a compromised state of morality. He asked

me to write a "parental epistle" to you so your reputation wouldn't be "lost."

Knowing you, my dear Madeleine, you may have compromised your morality in the eyes of the church if LaSalle would have you in that way (which I doubt), but I am sure you are being true to yourself.

So are your dreams coming true?

I was grief stricken when you left. Yet I know you will create a productive life. You have a great deal of inner strength. Never forget that.

This existence in Montreal would have dried up your soul. You won't be coming back. So I invited Alice, LeBer's service girl, to move into your room. She cleans and stocks for me and serves the customers.

Of course, you're welcome back, but I believe you've found your home there in Cataraqui.

Is Parrot's Bay yours yet?

Love, Annie

I wrote to Annie, blessing her plans with Alice and telling her I didn't know what Robert thought of me. His brother's arrival might have stirred an idea in Robert's head.

Several days later Robert made a comment that encouraged me. "Madeleine, I've been so focused on my pursuits, I hadn't thought of you as… as… er, well, a lovely lady." His fingers tightened around my forearm as we gazed at the colorful sunset.

At a candlelight repast that night, we indulged in a bottle of wine, a rare commodity at Fort Frontenac. Robert, comfortable in his own home and without curious soldier eyes present, began to expose his feelings—regarding westward expansion.

"I know Colbert and Talon echo Louis XIV's desire this country become centralized. They believe Frontenac and I push against their wishes. But they're wrong! We need to expand and spread the influence of France into strategic places. Don't you agree?"

"Yes, Robert."

He stooped down to stir up the hearth fire. He had an appealing, lean physique, with no spare fat. I liked how his tawny hair curled around the nape of his neck. His mustache was long and a shade redder than his hair. I so wanted the evening to be informal, personal, maybe intimate.

Robert acted as if closeness to me was dangerous. He continued to talk about his personal concerns. "Sometimes I wonder if I have the necessary ability to understand people and to command a brigade for an exploration. My men respect me well enough. But I feel detached from them." He paused. Was he wishing for my opinion?

"Perhaps that detachment is beneficial, a professional distance?" I tried.

"At night, though, when I'm reviewing my actions, I wonder if it is good. If I were more in tune with their rhythms, would I get more out of them?"

I knew how distant I felt from him sometimes. Yet I said nothing. Robert did not like to be criticized, only encouraged.

"And you, Madeleine, are you comfortable here? Is this life what you want?"

I took small sips of my wine and studied him.

"Thank you for asking, Robert. I'm content here." I swirled my glass and added, "For the time being."

He smiled. "I know your heart's desire—to establish the Parrot's Bay trading post. But are you not afraid of what you'll be facing?"

"I am skilled in survival. I have experienced profound loneliness and the dangers of Mother Nature. I don't believe I will have trouble with the savages. I speak their language and understand many of their ways. What would be my source of fear?"

"Hm," he reflected. "It's true that the Iroquois conflicts are settling down. Incessant raids have stopped. Last week we heard the Susquehanna and the Iroquois in the Genesee area were having peace talks."

We sat quietly lost in the fire's glow. I pictured him taking me in his arms and kissing my neck. He did place his hand over mine, but his excursion into intimacy stopped there.

# 19

# THE RED, WHITE, AND DIRTY

On a misty December dawn, Tempete grazed with her newborn colt at her side. The rising sun burned off the haze, dried the green grass, and warmed the newborn's black coat.

Then a few days later I stepped out into fresh snow and had to close my eyes to the brightness. Scattered snowflakes dusted my skin and frozen ground squeaked under my feet. Tempete nosed the snow and rummaged for remnants of grass. I placed the bucket down, and the mare lipped up the grain while her foal butted his mother in the side, trying to establish better footing to suckle. I crept closer and stroked his soft rump. He did not break off his feeding, just twitched his tail. His fur was a darker shade than his mother's, his mane black, and his hooves decorated with white markings.

I promised to feed them every day as long as the grain held out. The colt kicked up his heels and looked up at me with a bright challenge in his eyes. He dashed off.

I named him Tonnere, "thunder" in French, for his strength and quickness. By spring, I would have Tonnere trained to feed from my hand. In two years, he could be ridden. My experience with horses as a girl at Versailles was paying off.

...

In anticipation of the Christmas holiday, Sally, Maude, and I were asked to make breads, pies, and pickled vegetables for the soldiers. To manage Francie while we were in their kitchen, I created a "house" for the child under a table. For a while he played there, but shortly he was toddling around, fingering this and tasting that.

I was rolling out my piecrusts when I heard Maude say to Sally under her breath, "She so dotes on that crippled savage!"

Francois only grinned and asked Sally to play, tugging on her apron. She tried to shoo him away, but he persisted. Sally pushed him and said, "Go away, boy. Go back to your people."

I picked him up to stop his crying.

Sally turned to me. "Really, Madeleine, he'll have your scalp when he grows up." She and Maude snickered.

Only Robert, Captain Jenet, and Claude Leonine overlooked Francie's mixed blood. Sally's soldier husband, Thomas Bowers, often made racial slurs and mocked me for caring for him.

On Christmas Eve Captain Jenet invited Robert and Claude over for hot-spiced cider. We ate fresh pumpkin bread and enjoyed watching Francois and Midnight, curled against one another, sleeping by the fire. Robert, with an awl, sinew, and a large iron needle, took up repairing one of his boots. Claude whittled on a stick, trying to make a flute for Francie. Feeling guilty about my idle hands, I picked one of the child's shirts out of the mending pile and stitched a torn seam.

As we settled into our activities and the warmth of the home, I asked the men if they had heard the racial comments about our Francie.

Robert bristled. "I haven't noticed anything of the sort."

Claude blushed. "I hear it and see it. But do nothin.'"

Captain Jenet looked sad. "Madeleine, that arrogant attitude has been among the Frenchmen ever since I have been at the fort and chose Marie-Anne as my wife. The soldiers were cruel to her after Francois was born. They went so far as to say her people had cursed her, causing her 'half-breed' son's twisted foot. Bowers said, 'That was one of the few good ideas you savages have, kill off the weak and crippled,' he said.

"I wanted to beat the life out of him. But he is under my command, and we are a long way from any replacements.

"That next morning, my wife wasn't in our bed. When I went to her village, her father declared his grandchild dead to them. He beseeched me to give my wife up quietly so she could go back to live with the Huron.

"I don't go over to the village. I am raising Francois as both my son and his mother's son. He is the first of the mixed-blood children born here at the fort. As time passes, more of our men will seek the comfort of the native women, and others will join Francois. I want him to be proud of who he is and to take the best from both cultures."

I assured Captain Jenet that he was a wonderful father. Claude listened as he whittled industriously on the stick. And Robert? He seemed pensive, perhaps back to his own explorer's dreams.

In my heart, I did not agree with Jenet. The presence of more mixed-blood children would not do away with the prejudice. Tonato had been right. If we had lived as husband and wife and had a child, not one of the three of us would have felt "at home" anywhere. Each of us would have been an outsider—me as a French woman among the savages; Tonato as a Huron among the French; and our babe caught between two cultures, as Francois was.

...

Marie-Anne Jenet's father, a gray-haired Huron, had a chest covered with tattoos, blurred by scars and wrinkles. In Iroquois, I told the chief I was his daughter's friend who had helped at her birthing. He sullenly nodded and spoke with difficulty in French. "My daughter, she no speak French, no see French. Please go."

I answered in Iroquois, "You are a kind and protective father. She has often been on my mind and in my heart."

This compliment softened the Huron. As I turned to go, I added in Iroquois, "Please tell Marie-Anne I am no longer French but a woman of this new land."

When I passed back through the fort's palisade, Robert came striding over to me. He demanded, "Why did you go to the native's village?" Without waiting for my explanation, he went on. "I am the commander here, responsible for French and native relations. You should have cleared your decision with me." He took my arm roughly and escorted me to Jenet's.

"I was trying to win the friendship of Marie-Anne Jenet, one woman reaching out to another." My resentment toward Robert was building.

"You're aware her family's relations with Jenet and the soldiers are precarious?"

I jerked my arm away. I was cold and didn't want to squabble in the courtyard, so I quickened my stride. Robert caught up. "Madeleine, what is it?"

I kept walking.

When my hand was on the Jenet door latch, I said quietly, "Shall we speak privately of these matters?"

He noticed the soldiers' eyes on us and entered the cabin.

For an hour, we discussed our feelings about French and native relations. I said we needed to build a bridge between our cultures and learn each other's language. Robert, in contrast, felt his country's role was to control the tribes, in part by learning diverse languages. "We must show the natives how to manage the land, build an economy, and gain eternal life through the church," he added.

Since my arrival in Quebec five years ago, I had heard that philosophy many times, but I hadn't realized I disagreed with it until now. "Robert, I'm surprised at your opinion. You are usually so respectful of the natives. Are white and red men not on equal footing?"

"If I did not show them respect, we would not have been able to build an economic liaison with them. Being respectful to the natives is the basis of the safety they guarantee us. Do you think if I treated them as subordinate they would permit me these freedoms?"

So he had been placating the natives with respect, even though he didn't feel it? To gain the upper hand economically? Shocked speechless at Robert's hypocrisy, I moved forward and stirred the fire. Robert was not a man to be criticized. If he were in the right mood, he could only tolerate being challenged. Poking at the embers, I decided not to turn this into a confrontation. I stooped and hefted a log on to the coals.

"Robert, I would like to start teaching the soldiers some basic Iroquois, as you suggested to your brother. This will keep their minds busy during the winter. What do you think?"

Robert concurred.

I then said, "In addition, I would like to try again with Marie-Anne Jenet's family and see if they would like to learn French. It'll take several months to earn their trust, but such efforts can't hurt. Can they?"

With that, my role as teacher resumed.

...

Cataraqui buzzed with disastrous news: On February 27, 1676, forty miles west of Fort Albany, the Iroquois Indian Chief King Philip led five hundred followers against the Mohawk. The Mohawk retaliated, killing seventy-nine warriors and driving King Philip back to the Massachusetts Bay Colony. These tribal wars were far from us geographically, but their impact created a silent tension between the white people and *les sauvages*.

...

Going to the native village to teach French felt like swimming in a warm lake on a sunny day—relaxing and joy-filled. But teaching illiterate soldiers to speak Iroquois was like trying to swim in a river where you could not find solid footing—frustrating and precarious.

The twelve men spread out at the mess where a roaring fire provided light and warmth. Francois sat with Claude. Midnight, always my companion, curled up by my feet.

The men varied in intelligence and willingness. On one hand, Thomas Bowers, proud of the fact he could write French, had limited knowledge of reading it. Thomas often got Pierre LaGauche fooling around. I'd lose control of the class.

Claude Leonine learned with difficulty. When the class got unruly, he looked sheepish at first, as if he were responsible for his comrades' foolishness. His attention would turn to Francois, and he would speak simple Iroquois to the little boy.

Robert chuckled at my distress in the classroom. "Oh, Madeleine, the men aren't used to having an attractive woman to look at. Nor has anyone expected them to pay attention for more than twenty minutes. Don't worry about it. As they get used to seeing you, they will settle down."

After that, I dressed in an unfeminine woolen jerkin to be less of a distraction. The altered costume did little good. A few weeks later, I mentioned my continued problem with Bowers to Robert.

"I'll take care of him," was all LaSalle said.

The next day Thomas sat sullenly at the table and made no effort to learn. At least the class stayed in control.

...

On March 16, 1676, Midnight rescued me for the second time in my life.

When I dismissed class, Bowers snarled about my "savior" Robert, complaining about my being "holier than thou."

Standing so close I could smell his rancid breath, Bowers said, "Tell LaSalle how well mannered I've been."

I laughed.

Infuriated, he shoved me against the wall. He clutched my face and pushed my head back. His other hand grabbed my skirt and hoisted it. When his rough nail raked my skin, I cried out and tried to pull away. The nightmarish royal corridor, unvisited by my mind for two years, closed in around me. I froze, my knees buckled, and I slid down the wall.

In a fog, I saw Midnight spring at my attacker and grab his calf. Bowers, cursing and thrashing, tried to shake the dog free. Then Claude was there, extending a hand to raise me off the floor.

Mortified, I couldn't breathe. I fled for my cabin, shuddering, overcome by disgust. Bowers' groping had humiliated me. But my childhood shame's return was worse. I thought I had grown past that abhorrence.

Midnight loped after me. In the distance, Bowers swore, "I'll kill that damn dog."

Robert found me on my cot, trembling. Midnight, still protecting me, growled as Robert entered.

"Madeleine?" Robert leaned toward me. Captain Jenet brought a basin of water, and Robert wiped my forehead and my neck with a soft cloth. Then he helped me sit up.

"Breathe deeply." He took the woolen blanket offered him by Jenet and covered me. "Claude said he saw Midnight attacking Bowers with you slumped on the floor. What happened?"

I told Robert and Captain Jenet some of what had transpired. About the hand violating me, the weakness in my knees, and the sickness in my stomach—I kept that buried. I said nothing about my mind and its revisiting of the dark Versailles corridor.

Still shivering, I asked, "Will Midnight be all right? Bowers said he wanted to kill him. Don't allow it, please! Midnight saved me from ... from ... "

I curled up, turned to the wall, and over and over counted knotholes on the wall's lumber as I begged sleep to enshroud me.

Robert stayed with me all night, stretched out under a blanket on the floor. When the glow of dawn challenged me to face another day, I found him asleep. Morning light threw interesting patterns on his face. He looked much younger. Could he—would he—possibly understand my humiliation?

...

Francie wiggled up onto my cot and stroked my hair. He made sounds of endearment in French, Iroquois, and baby talk. His father came and shushed him.

I rose up on an elbow. "Francie can stay."

"Madeleine, you haven't spoken or eaten for three days. We're worried."

The door banged open. Midnight let out a watchful growl and trotted out of my room. Hearing Robert's voice, the captain left to greet his commander. Francie began to bounce in my arms, wanting me to get up and play.

Robert appeared and scowled. Francie giggled and walked out of the room, dragging his right foot with confidence. Midnight returned from taking stock of Robert, licked my hand, and settled on the floor.

"Madeleine, would you like a bowl of porridge?" he called, "Wilhelm, do you have hot water? We could make Madeleine some chamomile tea."

I pushed myself up and balled up the extra blanket for support behind my head. I looked at Robert. My brain felt like dirty cotton as though I were wakening from a nightmare. The tea Robert handed me burned as I sipped it, but the tingling pain felt good and brought me back to myself.

"Robert, thank you. For the tea. And for being here."

Silence.

Minutes passed. "Can I do anything for you?" Robert asked quietly.

I shook my head.

He continued, "Bowers has been reprimanded for speaking with disrespect. He laughed when I told him you don't remember the conversation."

The hot mug comforted my trembling hands. "Thank you for keeping Midnight safe." Sighing, I pulled a blanket over my shoulders.

Robert brought the Jenet rocker in and settled himself into it. He drank some tea. "Madeleine, what in the devil happened?"

I said nothing.

"You don't want to discuss it. All right then." He sipped the tea and rocked. His tense body relaxed as though he had resolved something. He said, "Until a few days ago, I didn't realize how much your companionship meant to me."

I closed my eyes and balanced my mug on my lap. Images of Tonato came to mind. Tonato sitting next to me before the fire. Tonato stroking my hair and my shoulders. Tonato looking at my nude body. Then I remembered Bowers hiking up my skirt, his dirty fingers seeking my flesh. Bowers blurred, and the courtier Joseph Galouis's face came into focus. He had me pinned in the corridor. Laughter, music, human voices were in the background. His lavender cologne assailed my senses. His gloved right hand stroked me and his left pulled my bodice down.

Shivering, I opened my eyes to see Robert grabbing the mug from my hand. He picked up my wrist and rubbed it. I pulled away, faced the wall, and pulled the blanket up to my nose. "Robert, go. Let me be."

Despite my misery, I was pleased that Robert was taking care of me.

...

Five nights later I had a strange dream.

> Voices echoed around me as I sat between the latrine's wooden walls. Whispers of "For Your Use" rebounded in my head. At that point, I metamorphosed from a girl to a woman and slid down into the stinking latrine's hole.

When Robert visited that afternoon, I responded with pleasantries even though I was thinking about the dream: *Is he another man who is going to "use" me?*

Over tea, Robert told me about chapel and Father's Hennepin's homily. He talked freely about himself. "Because I was the most intelligent and best looking of the children, my father doted on me," Robert said. "When I was ten years of age, he gave me the properties of LaSalle as a special gift. He wrote out the transfer of property on the day Louis XIV was coronated king. Imagine, only fifteen years old and he was king of France, and I was just ten and a property holder!

"You're too modest," I bantered.

Robert grinned at my tease. "True. But my brothers ridiculed me and harassed me with pranks—probably out of jealousy. As the youngest, under the laws of primogeniture, my birth order would block me from inheriting my father's wealthy mercantile business. So my parents bundled Jean off to the Sulpicians and threw me in with the Jesuits. I learned astronomy, navigational theory, and ancient and modern languages. The Jesuits taught me cartography and the use of the astrolabe. I grew fascinated by foreign lands and imagined myself gaining fame by making some grand discovery.

"So you're achieving your life's dream, eh?"

"I'm getting there, Madeleine. But I had to pay a price. The priests were harsh and cold and criticized me relentlessly. I learned early to not trust anyone. I would arise at five a.m. and study until lights out. They did teach us basic skills like hunting, sailing, and accounting, but their tone was one of duty, not one of pleasure. I guess, Mat-tee, that's why I must seem so driven and constrained some times." I blushed at his use of my nickname. "Did you know I am but three years older than you?"

I drew my knees up under the blanket. "Are you?"

"It's true!" He rocked and continued to unveil himself at a leisurely pace. "The Jesuits encouraged me to take my vows when I was seventeen. Ah, those years. I thought the world was a good place. That God was a good God. I made my vows of celibacy and poverty. In so doing, I had to release my father's properties back to my siblings. The Jesuits provided a morality and structure to my life that made my decisions easy. The Society of Jesus assigned me to teach grammar in various towns. I submitted to their authority but asked about opportunities to be a missionary.

"The priests wanted me to mature spiritually before assigning me somewhere. In 1666, I entreated them to send me to China, even telling them my father would pay my passage, but they withheld their consent. I pleaded to teach mathematics in Portugal, anything to see a different land and new people. Again they refused.

"I soon resented their use of religion to keep control over me, and I left the Jesuit life. Even today my anger is provoked when people try to control me."

As Robert talked, I caught glimpses of his emotions and understand more about the man he was, because of the things he'd experienced.

He went on. "My father died at the time I left the order and my brothers and sisters agreed to provide me four hundred livres annually. I felt cheated out of what should have been mine. So in the summer of 1667, I came here. It's been nine years."

Robert exhaled.

"Robert, tell me about your religion. Is God no longer a good God? Do you still believe in him?"

"I believe in God. Religion provides structure and meaning. But we Catholics cannot force our religion onto others. My interest in the mission field was not for the purpose of converting 'lost souls' but to expand my knowledge of the world. I yearn to improve our ways of doing things by learning from others. God can deal with each person's religion. That's one reason I don't ask you much about your personal beliefs. For me, it is good enough you are Catholic and will go to heaven. *N'est-ce pas?*" He took my hand and held it.

...

Time inched forward. Each day got longer and warmer as we drifted toward spring. LaSalle disbanded the language classes without consulting me, saying planting needed to be done. I was glad, not wanting to return to the guard's house where I had been dishonored.

Francois brought joy to my heart when he roused me out of bed mornings, eager to play or to speak "Quois" with me. He walked with confidence and speed; the clubfoot made no difference to him. Robert's men built a split rail fence so Tempete and Tonnere could be out of the stable all the time now. In the afternoon, Francie and I spent time in the horse paddock. Tonnere liked to suck sugar lumps from our fingers. The colt would stand while I rubbed my hands all over him, teaching him not to be shy of a human being. But the first time I placed a rope halter around his ears and muzzle, he kicked up his hind legs, almost tossing me into the fence. Francie, perched on the top rail, laughed at the sight. But soon, the colt settled, and I could lead him.

After we celebrated Easter, all occupants of the fort tilled the fields outside the palisades and planted, the few women working alongside the several dozen men. Our food supplies were scarce. This was the hardest time of the year to find food. It was too muddy to hunt effectively, and the stored roots and fruits were depleted. We existed on peas—ground, stewed, sweetened, or made into a gruel—and fish from the lake.

...

Robert approached me May first while I was leading Tonnere around the paddock with Francie astride the colt's withers. Midnight trotted a respectful distance behind. "Madeleine, are you strong enough to plan your departure for Parrot's Bay?" Robert asked.

Defensive about my set back I barked, "Of course I'm strong enough." Then, in a more apologetic tone, I said, "Thank you. Yes, let's plan." With that, I swung Francie down and slapped Tonnere on his backside. He ran off to his mother.

Robert, in his organized style, had thought through the practical matters of establishing a fur trading post. I had written Annie six weeks ago requesting supplies for planting and building, as well as a new musket and ammunition, some bolts of linen and cotton, my own iron kettle, and a tinderbox.

When Robert, Francie, and I arrived at Jenet's, we took advantage of the sun angled low in the sky to examine the layout drawings and fine-tune the details for establishing the Parrot's Bay Trading Post.

...

A letter from Noleen's Trading Post, Montreal, dated April 15, 1676, arrived May 7. With the letter Annie had sent me another dress, some candles and preserves, and tucked in bars of soap. She was thinking of turning the trading post over to Alice. In my return letter, I urged Annie to come and spend the last chapters of her life living at Parrot's Bay.

On my thirtieth birthday, May 9, 1676, I felt blessed. The next day I would leave for Parrot's Bay and with friends develop my life's dream: my own property, my own business, and my own independence. What more could a thirty-year-old woman want?

# PART FOUR:

## The Cultivating

# 20

# STRANGE VISITORS

With my feet spread wide and arms held high, I shouted with joy. My land, now—after five years! I surveyed the three-hundred-yard inlet and surrounding woodland and marsh. I turned and faced the single building, ready for the trade business. My heart swelled.

When I had arrived at Parrot's Bay along with Wilhelm Jenet, Claudine Leonine, and Robert LaSalle, we built one wooden dwelling centered on a stone hearth. Francie and Midnight romped with each other, making us laugh with their antics. The men helped till an acre of ground to the north of the trading post, which I would soon plant with "three sisters." To provide a makeshift dock, we secured a barge to nearby tree roots. I even built a "necessary," digging a hole and covering it with a small-planked enclosure.

The men and child stayed for one week and then left me to fend for myself. Midnight became my sole companion. My head and my heart were split. On one hand, saying good-bye to Francie and Robert was particularly sad. The child's tears quickened my desire to cry.

But then I thought, *Robert must be so proud of me. I am the person in charge. I belong here at Parrot's Bay. I now have a home. My very own home.*

...

Solitude refreshed my soul for the first half of June 1676. The lack of other people's demands, implied or stated, freed me. Fox, woodchucks, and squirrels entertained me. Waterfowl colored the bay, and their squawks and hoots lent music to the silence. Each day I thrived on taking up my hoe and planting my field. At noon, I'd walk back to the trading post; throw off my tunic, skirt, and moccasins; and pad down to the water's edge. Off would go my linen shift, and I would plunge into the lake.

The cool water shocked me at first and then relaxed me. I would swim out with Midnight scudding along by my side and float gazing at the clouds.

I thought of Francie and Wilhelm. Before Francie had returned to the fort, I had taught him to swim, just as Antoine had taught me when I first came to this country.

I wondered about Tonnere, grazing at the fort with Tempete until he was weaned.

I daydreamed about Antoine. Had he taken a wife?

Governor Frontenac flashed across my thoughts. Was he succeeding at quelling the native uprisings?

I missed Sleeping Willow and Flower Eyes and the simple Huron way of life.

Faces of old friends floated into my mind. Did Jeanne have a baby or two by now? Was Catherine's boy a walking, talking four-year-old?

When the sun's white rays slashed through the gray-blue clouds, I thought of heaven and my beloved Reverend Mother Marie. God was becoming an endearing reality to me ever since my encounter with him at the Great Falling Waters and my near drowning during the storm.

When the water slid along my stretched-out body, Tonato trespassed into my thoughts. How exhilarating it had been when the river rapids drenched us, and we stripped by the fire and made love. Did I know what I was doing then? I wondered if we had used each other. Maybe I needed his manhood, his sexual willingness, as much as he needed an outlet with me. I had not let any morality stand in my way. Had our actions shown disrespect for each other, knowing our "oneness" wasn't permanent?

After a week of the quiet, I started talking to Midnight. "Heh, buddy, what shall we fix for supper?" Or, "I know it's raining, but shouldn't we go swimming anyway?" Once, when I was building a shelf inside the trading post, I hit my thumb with the hammer, and my mouth popped out an obscenity. Immediately, I turned to Midnight. "Oops, don't tell Robert. He'll think that's very un-Catholic."

Talking to my dog made me laugh at first. But soon my laughter turned to frustration. "Admit it to yourself," I said, "you are lonely. You were not created to live by yourself."

Yet there I was, alone at Parrot's Bay. Should I summon Antoine and tell him we should marry? Or call upon Captain Jenet, who had expressed an interest in forming a "partnership" with the prerogatives of marriage. Though we were friends, neither of us loved the other one. Consider Claude then? No, he was too young and too simple.

And then there was Robert: the visionary with his gift of seeing the land as it would be in the future. He was influential in the colony, stirring up hopes that our country would stretch southwest to the Gulf of Mexico. Marriage was the farthest thing from his mind, an action that would hinder his dreams. If he were married, he would have split loyalties: his vision or his family. Such a conflict might be too much.

I had once thought the night cry of a single loon calling for her mate was beautiful. But, after a month by myself, the loon's mournful call brought a lump to my throat.

...

A canoe rounded the corner of the bay and came toward me as I swam *au naturale*. Scrambling up the rocky bank, I pulled my shift over my head, shook my hair, and smoothed it with my hands. Who was approaching my dock?

The canoeist was a single male in a plain birch bark vessel with no decorations, so I surmised the paddler must be French. Midnight began to yap. I ran into the trading post and dressed in my deerskin tunic and tied a band around my hair. My heart beat rapidly. *Mon Dieu!* A human being to talk with!

But alas, it was Claude who came bearing troubling news. Two days before, LaSalle had fallen critically ill and was asking for me.

In ten minutes, I secured the dwelling, gathered the necessary belongings, grabbed my paddle, and joined Claude in his canoe. Speed was paramount. From Claude's description, Robert was at death's door.

...

Robert's eyes were sunken and his voice raspy, his moustache matted, and his forehead, a chalky white. Despite the fact he couldn't sit up, he welcomed me with a smile.

At my request, Claude made a chamomile and ginger drink to try to break Robert's cycle of cramping and vomiting, and warm broth for his nutrition. I soaked rags in a basin of cool water and applied them to Robert's brow. We spent the rest of the day with my holding his head, either to soothe it or to support it as he continued to vomit.

After two days, Robert still kept nothing solid down without retching. He looked corpse-like. When he told me he thought his servant Jolycoeur, a lay Jesuit sent to Fort Frontenac, had poisoned him, I worried about his state of mind.

"I have seen hemlock poisoning before, Madeleine, when I was studying at the hospital in France. It causes stomach cramps, painful retching, and then death—if the amount is lethal."

"But why poison you, Robert?"

"Jolycoeur was sent me as a 'gift' from the businessmen in Montreal, including my brother. Perhaps they planned his crime. They all envy me. If I were killed, they would control Fort Frontenac and the western fur-trading business. Their profits would soar."

"How did Jolycoeur find the means?"

"I found it odd when he offered to serve me a meal in my quarters last week. He roasted a hare and made a fresh, mixed-green salad. I suspect the hemlock was tucked into the greens.

"Fortunately for me, as I was eating, one of the palisade walls caught fire. My soldiers called me away in the middle of my meal." Robert paused, somewhat breathless. He laid his head on his pillow. "I didn't feel well when I got back—so sick, so quickly. To think... if

I had finished the meal." He gripped his stomach where he had been cramping. I handed him the chamber pot.

When he'd recovered from the bout, I asked, "Robert, what are you going to do with this Jolycoeur?"

"Mat-tee, I don't know." He closed his eyes and didn't speak the rest of the evening.

...

After ten days, Robert confronted Jolycoeur. The sniveling man confessed, blaming LeBer and Bazire and Robert's brother, Jean Cavelier, for the attempt on LaSalle's life. "They all want you out of their way, Monsieur LaSalle. They think you're crazy." Jolycoeur pleaded for his life and swore allegiance to LaSalle.

Robert sent him under guard to Quebec for imprisonment with the orders to bypass Montreal and not to report back to those scheming businessmen. Robert's leniency toward Jolycoeur restored in me a sense of my friend's humanity. Or perhaps LaSalle was too weak to get angry.

His strength returned slowly. I cooked delicacies and easily digestible items. While he rested, I visited Francie and watched Tonnere frolic in the pasture. The colt let me wrap my arms around his neck and feel his soft nose on my cheek. He had grown! I had to stand on tiptoes to clean the gnats out of his ears and rub in protective bear grease.

While watching Robert nap, the idea of his recuperating at Parrot's Bay came to me. If we told no one but Captain Jenet and Claude of our plans, then Robert might be spared another murder attempt, as well as the demands of fort leadership.

So, in the middle of August, LaSalle and I moved to the trading post.

Residing together and working as partners shed light on our true personalities. I learned I could be self-protective and unyielding when it came to my property and my business. As he tried to find a niche for himself, Robert's competitiveness and perfectionism were unveiled. Tension sizzled between the two of us. During this first season at the trading post, only occasional natives and even more rarely a white coureur de bois stopped to barter their furs for necessities. One idea Robert and I both agreed on: It would take several years to establish a flow of traders and a wide-spread reputation for the Parrot's Bay Trading Post.

...

Millions of grasshoppers overran the wheat fields and other crops at Cataraqui, on August 30, 1676. Robert and I left Parrot's Bay to join the settlers in digging and tending fire trenches, hoping to stop the green-winged, leggy insects. The nearby natives helped with this crisis. Side by side, Frenchmen and savages swept the creatures into trench fires.

But as fast as we worked, more of the jumping insects appeared. The children found this a great game, as roasted grasshoppers were a delicacy to them. We all faced the hovering fear of a winter's famine.

When I returned to my trading post alone, my stomach knotted with worry that my crops, too, were destroyed. But, when I approached my dock, the festive caws of hundreds of gulls filled the bay. The gulls I had been feeding over the summer had taken it upon themselves to eat the grasshoppers instead. White and black feathers and gray gluey bird dung covered my property, and the "three sisters" remained standing. My crop had been saved.

As the shorter October days crept up on me, solitude weighed me down. So I made my trading post safe from potential intruders, the two-legged wanderers and the four-legged prowlers. When the seasonal chores were done, I packed up remaining food, my belongings, and returned to the Jenets' cabin to live through the winter.

...

By March 1677, food stores from Parrot's Bay and those that had been shipped from Quebec were running short at Fort Frontenac. Daily the villagers stood in line to get their meager ration of grain and stored corn, peas, and squash. People's tempers ran short. The winter was wearing on us all.

Wilhelm and Claude saw that Francie got enough to eat. He was growing out of his baby fat. His fine, black hair was cut in a bowl shape around his bronze face, and a smattering of chocolate freckles on his cheeks and nose set off his dark-blue eyes. Even though he limped, all his actions were quick and coordinated. I loved to watch the playful attachment between Wilhelm and Francie while I stayed in their home.

In the last year, Fort Frontenac's population had grown. About forty people attended the Catholic service on Sundays. We women selected our best dresses and wore clean caps. Our dressing up for church was a high point of color in a monotone week. Father Hennepin preached against the fashionable low décolletage, urging us females to dress modestly "for the morale of the entire fort."

...

Ice floes thunked against each other, and the smells of spring wafted in the air. I knew my return to Parrot's Bay was imminent and began making plans.

"I'm tired of orders, Madeleine. I'd like some freedom," Claude explained as we walked back from teaching. He wanted to ask Captain Jenet's permission to resign from his duties at Fort Frontenac and come to Parrot's Bay.

"Claude, we may not have the regimentation like the soldiers do, but the chores are demanding, particularly for just two people."

"I don't mind hard work." Claude puffed his chest out.

"And, Claude, I'm the proprietress, and there will be orders from me."

"Proprietress?"

"Yes, it's my property and my business. What I say goes. Like Monsieur LaSalle here at the fort."

We were silent. Geese flew overhead, their honking heralding the planting season. Claude was a strong youth, simple and hard working. Perhaps he would do.

We both talked to Robert, and he arranged for Claude to draw a commission for his service and be assigned to Parrot's Bay as a lookout point for Fort Frontenac.

After we arrived at my home, Claude went to bag fowl for our supper. I built a fire in our central room, made up my bed in the corner, and set up a cot for Claude against the wall. When Claude returned, I spitted the geese over the fire. I visited the "necessary" next, chased the winter spiders away with a broom, and placed cotton wicks of camphor around hoping this smell would discourage rodents.

An hour later Claude had laid out our supper: goose, peas, wild scallions, and roasted chestnuts. We sat down to enjoy our first meal at Parrot's Bay. But Claude lacked curiosity. Almost illiterate, he couldn't discuss books, and he was disengaged from politics, except for a fierce loyalty to Monsieur LaSalle. Simply put, Claude was boring.

I helped him clean up, and then I retired to my bed. A half hour later, while I was reading by my oil lamp, Claude stood at my bedside dressed in his long johns. Before I could say anything, he pulled the covers back and got in with me.

"Claude, what are you doing?"

"Sleeping with you, Madeleine? No? I guess not?" He shook his head as if to clear his confused thoughts.

"No, Claude. What gave you that idea?"

"That's just the way people do things. No?" A blush reddened his neck and ears. "But I'm wrong about this, eh?"

"Yes, Claude, you're wrong. Now go to that bed."

Claude stumbled into the cot on the other side of the hearth. I settled under my covers and sighed.

...

By June first, some Ojibway, Abenaki, Mohawk, Mohican, and others had stopped to trade, part of a steady stream going east on their way to the Montreal Fur Fair. My location, ten miles west of Cataraqui, allowed me to strike lucrative deals on the choicest furs.

When trading for brandy or rum, I passed liquor in a sealed gourd and required my native patrons to imbibe only after they were a half-day's travel away. I'd seen "firewater" cause too many problems.

On July 3, 1677, two visitors arrived unexpectedly: Annie in a canoe with Robert, and Tonnere, blindfolded and tethered, on a barge. We quickly put Tonnere into the pasture and hobbled him. Annie wasn't as I remembered her. Her robustness had given way to an unhealthy lumpiness. Her hair had thinned, and she wheezed as she moved. But she had the same old sparkle in her eye. Her hug warmed my heart.

Annie took quite a liking to Claude, appreciating his simplicity and industry. Claude, whose mother put him out to work when he was six, soaked up all Annie's nurturing. Despite the imbalance in their relationship, their contentment with each other was transparent.

# 21

# ANNIE'S STRUGGLE

That September LaSalle summoned me to act as hostess for the governor's 1677 inspection of Fort Frontenac. Claude and Annie would manage the trading post without me.

Governor Frontenac had aged but still presented a striking figure. A powdered wig framed his fleshy face. His voice resonated. His handshake, with his healthy left, was strong and welcoming. The governor's conversations focused on the fort's physical changes and its tribal relations. The palisade had been expanded and reinforced, with each corner displaying a turret standing two stories above the ground. From those vantage points, a soldier could see vessels or people approaching from a mile away.

A village bloomed outside the perimeter. Drainage ditches had been cleared in the marsh to make the land arable. Several wooden docks were built into the soggy bank, secured by strong hemp ropes and pine pilings. Two large flat-bottomed boats stood ready to transport troops or livestock. The path between the fort and the native village was well worn. With help I prepared as many rich and varied dinners as this wilderness permitted: stuffed partridge, roasted squash lacquered with honey and raisins, creamed peas, trout fried with scallions, pickled beets, berry pies, and corn bread. Governor Frontenac had brought several kegs of brandy.

On the governor's last night, the gentlemen invited me to join them at a formal dinner. LaSalle talked about his rival Louis Joliet. Joliet had capsized his canoe at the LaChine rapids and lost some important maps, which LaSalle had been hoping to study. Robert said, "Joliet found a shortcut from the pays d'en haut. When he was on the Mississippi River, natives guided him to the convergence of the Illinois River, and he canoed it north to the southern shore of Lake Michigan. The geography around there is flat and fertile and will do better for farmers than the land here, giving us numerous prospects for settlement."

Captain Jenet nodded. "Joliet married last year. I surmise he is anxious to establish a colony in that location and settle down."

Governor Frontenac interjected, "Joliet sailed to France to obtain royal permission and funds to explore the Illinois River. I wrote asking our king to endorse Joliet's venture."

Robert's face reddened. He sat forward in his chair.

"Oh, calm down, LaSalle," Frontenac growled. "You know I believe you're the best explorer, far surpassing Joliet and more willing to take risks. And you command better diplomatic relations with the natives. I merely wrote him a letter of support." Frontenac swirled his brandy glass with his good hand and sniffed the rich liquor. "More importantly, Robert, when a French man finally builds an outpost between Lake Erie and Lake Ontario, you will claim far more fame for France than Joliet."

"That's what Tonato and I reconnoitered for you, Robert, three years ago," I inserted myself into the conversation.

Robert said, "What was the name of the minor river and the sheltered island you discovered, Madeleine, just above the Falls?"

"Cayuga."

Robert began pacing the room. "Governor, why did you wait until now to tell me? At least, don't let Joliet step in and proceed to do what I believe is my destiny."

"I waited, my young friend," the governor said as he lit his pipe, "because I wanted to confirm the progress you have made here at Fort Frontenac. Indeed, your leadership skills and industry have proven excellent. Now, what we must plan are new tactics, a strategy the king will embrace."

The rest of the evening we discussed the underlying wishes of His Majesty and how we colonists should support them. The king wanted colonists to form military units on the model of the French army, including daily drilling on the village square. "But the reality is, we have no solid populated bases, except for Montreal and Quebec, and no village squares, except for small plots of grass on which our livestock feed," said Frontenac. "Warfare, when it must occur, has to adapt to the natives' style: hiding behind trees, tracking the enemy in the mud, and watching for telltale signs of human presence in the behavior of the wildlife. Surprise and retreat, slaughter or capture, these are the natives' methods. We must learn their ways, or we will be annihilated. Louis XIV and his minions do not understand this."

"But, Governor," LaSalle protested, "we cannot contradict the king. We must present the need for exploration in a different light."

After more discussion, the gentlemen agreed LaSalle should request permission to search for the mouth of the Mississippi with no mention of trading or colonization. He would obtain authorization to build forts wherever necessary. Their hidden purpose would be to spawn villages.

"That's concluded. Well done, men," the governor said, rising and stretching. "And our excellent cook-explorer, of course!" He nodded toward me. "Now, Robert, you must convince the king of this plan."

My heart sank. With this trip to the French Court, another winter would pass without him in my life.

...

When Robert and I parted on September 8, he handed me a note. I read it and reread it so the parchment wore thin.

> My dearest Madeleine,
>     Tomorrow we will go our separate ways yet again. I feel a wrenching in my heart as if part of me is being left behind. It appears God keeps drawing me to you. And then he challenges us to live separately.

You are rare—someone who understands my vision, tolerates my idiosyncrasies, and shares my faith. I am complete when I am with you.

As you know, I am a man of few words—when it comes to ladies and matters of the heart at least. (Instead, give me a Huron chief to converse with, a politician to sell an idea to, or an explorer to draw up a trade route!) But when you sat across from me, dressed in that crimson gown with your hair curling out from under your cap and your cheeks flushed—ah, you were radiant in my eyes.

I will hold that image in my heart as I cross the seas, trusting our Creator will see to my safe return. Until then, your friend, RLS

...

Annie and Claude were sleeping in the same bed! I discovered this upon my return to Parrot's Bay. "Why not?" the old gal said. "We give each other company, warmth, and comfort, *n'est-çe pas?*"

While I tried to sleep on my side of the room, Annie and Claude cuddled and cooed on the other side. Their companionship quickened a deep ache in my soul. I missed Robert. Would we ever be together? I could not find out until he returned from France.

I harvested, traded for furs, kept up the buildings, and cooked for Claude, Annie, and the voyageurs that joined us. White and red men alike brought news of skirmishes happening on the south side of Lake Ontario. Somewhere near Albany, Iroquois captured eighteen Abenaki Indians. The voyageurs debated the likelihood of these captives either being tortured and killed or being adopted into the conquering tribe.

One gnarled man, who had been traveling the trade routes for the last ten years, settled the argument. "It all comes down to this: if the mother of the conquering warrior is lonely or needs help, or if she likes the look of the captive, that person will live. She'll adopt him as her own to take the place of a lost family member. But if she is as surly as a bear that day, she'll order him put to death."

"Aye, and the deaths these Iroquois matrons choose! Being burned to death is the most pleasing. At least the poor person suffocates on the smoke before he experiences too much pain," a weathered fur-trader added.

Their grizzly tales were hard for me to believe. I dealt with the pro-French Iroquois, the Huron, the Mohawk, and the Abenaki every day. Most were gracious to me. Some were sullen and quiet, but I never felt threatened by any of them.

...

That winter Claude and I attached two eight-feet-long iron blades to the canoe's keel, and the three of us "ice skated" our way to the fort for Sunday services. The westerly wind would blow us to Cataraqui by filling a linen sail hoisted on a small mast. In the late afternoon, the breeze calmed; we used poles with iron teeth fastened to their tips to cross back to Parrot's Bay. Because winter brought us social isolation, Annie, Claude, and I were pleased to see Francie and Wilhelm Jenet, who would invite us for a hot meal and a game of quoits after church.

At Sunday dinner, Wilhelm Jenet began talking about the Widow Gelanis with irritation. I wondered if he had a special interest in her.

"She remarried just three weeks after her husband succumbed to an infection from an ax wound. Shouldn't she have waited the traditional year of mourning? But she up and moved her one-year-old child in with Monsieur Michelson just last week. And she is obviously pregnant."

Wilhelm had picked Francie up onto his lap and was holding him and stroking his hair. Filled with good food and warmed by the fire, Francie's eyes were closing. I challenged my friend. "Wilhelm, what do you expect a young woman to do for protection living in a place like Cataraqui?"

"Mat-tee, I know I still hold ideas from our old country. I can barely accept the changes in tradition such as 'mariage à la gamine.'"

"What is *mariage à la gamine?*" Claude asked.

"It's a form of marriage when the couple doesn't have the benefit of a Catholic wedding ceremony," I answered. "For example, if the bride's family opposed the union and refused to involve a priest, or if the couple didn't have the certificates needed and the priest declined to marry them, the couple might marry *à la gamine*."

"I don't git it."

"Claude, the couple believes they can be united in the sight of God when they make their declaration of marriage privately during mass. They wait until the priest raises the wafer and recites 'hoc est enim corpus meum,'" I said.

"What does that do?" Claude seemed confused.

"Those are Latin words for 'this is my body.' We believe the wafer is changed into the body of Jesus when the priest says that."

"Oh, that's a lot of hocus-pocus," Annie said and then belched. "Good stew, Captain Jenet."

"Annie," I said, "Protestants don't think the bread is actually transformed, but devout Catholics believe this. So in this manner of 'marriage,' God in his body is present at the union of the couple. Sometimes a couple will declare their intentions to each other at the time the priest is blessing the congregation. That way the couple believes the benediction falls on their alliance as well, so they can see themselves truly married in the eyes of God."

The conversation shifted when Wilhelm shared the news that native skirmishes were settling down in the area around Albany and Montreal. "But we hear raids continue and blood is shed farther south in the English colonies."

Annie rose, her short, squat body moving stiffly from old age. "When you white people see the savages as equals, as humans, as friends, peace will follow. Now, Captain Jenet, I would like to stretch out on your little bed for my nap before we make our way back."

...

The winter months took their toll on Annie. She lost more weight; her ankles and wrists became bony and her eyes, sunken. Yet she stayed lumpy around her middle, as though she were unnaturally pregnant. When I arose in the morning, she was up before me, stirring the glowing coals into flames. She rocked in her chair and stared into the fire, brooding.

In early April, we smelled the spring thaw as snow melted. I cleaned my musket and prepared to hunt. Annie grabbed her fur cape and struggled to pull on her moccasins. Soon we were out the door, leaving Claude behind the counter.

I handed Annie a pair of native sunglasses, birch bark masks with six tiny slits in them to filter the light. Only by wearing these would we be able to see the game against the white landscape.

Annie started out with enthusiasm.

The cattails and marsh grass waved golden-brown heads sticking above the snow. As we walked, quail and ducks flew up. Midnight, well trained to fetch and carry, retrieved six fowl I brought down.

As the sun slid below the trees, I saw a beautiful buck at the water's edge, and I put my arm out to stop Annie's forward movement. The wind blew our scent away, and the sun's angle prevented him from see-ing us. I raised my shotgun and took aim. I pulled the trigger back. Just as my finger moved, Annie shoved the gun off target. The ball bashed into a tree. The buck ran off.

"*Mais bon sang*! Annie. Why did you do that?" I cursed.

Annie put her face in her hands. She and I had hunted plenty of times together. Annie knew well our meat supplies were low and we had a strong market for smoked venison jerky. What had come over her?

The sun's last rays splashed the western sky with colors of peach and violet. Already the air was wintry again, the cold prickling my nose.

I sighed. "Come on, Annie. Let's go home. We've got enough."

She sat, frozen.

I rubbed her hunched shoulders. She lifted her head and stared toward the water's edge. Quietly she said, "Mat-tee, I did not want to see him die."

"*Ça va, Ça va*. Annie, he's alive," I cooed as to a child. "Let's go. It's getting cold and dark." I urged her up and led her down the path.

At supper, Annie nibbled her food while Claude and I devoured roasted partridge and creamed peas and enjoyed apples kept crisp in our fruit cellar. I helped Annie to her rocker and sat down on the floor. Claude retired to their bed, and within minutes he was snoring.

"Annie, talk to me," I urged.

"I've lived long, Mat-tee. But in all these years, I've thought little of death. Even when it took my Alfred. I've enjoyed the energy of being alive, its tastes and sounds, its smells and touches. But today, death became real. That buck—no longer free to run, to drink of that fresh water, to eat tender grasses, to mate with his doe—I could not bear it. So I pushed your arm."

Persimmon flames danced out of the blue embers of the hearth fire. Annie whispered, "I'm afraid, Mat-tee."

"Of what?" I hugged her knees. "You have me and Claude. We're all safe."

"I'm dying."

Where could I find words of comfort? She had rejected the Catholic faith years ago. She had never embraced the Ojibway belief that death was a passage into another realm to be reunited with loved ones.

I sat back and thought. "Annie, what does dying mean to you?"

As she stared at the floorboards, Annie answered in a frail voice. "Death means nothingness."

"You believe your soul ceases? How can that be?"

"How can that *not* be? Why should my soul continue? I have been practical for years and have given no respect to religions of any people. I can't start now." She snorted.

I rose to stoke the fire, went over to give her a good night hug, and said nothing more.

Going behind my screen, I stripped off my tunic, skirt, and leggings; pulled the flannel nightshirt over my head; and crawled into bed. Did Annie wish to have faith? I prayed, "Dear God, I don't want Annie to be afraid of dying. Tell me what to say. Show me what to do."

...

The next day I took Tonnere for a run. We both enjoyed the freedom of galloping along the meadow and on the deer paths in the marsh.

Midnight loved to race us, trying to stay on the heels of the stallion, but was often pulled off the path to scout out a new scent.

I thought of my conversation with Annie. Her voice in my head repeated the words, *Why should my soul continue?* Maybe that was her fear—not that she would die, but that she did not want her soul to live forever.

Just then Tonnere's hocks broke through the marsh bed, and he sank in mud up to his knees. I jolted forward in the saddle. The muck made a sucking sound. Tonnere, unable to turn around without making matters worse, had to slog forward until we got to solid ground.

The wet earth was jet black from years of decay. Its stench assaulted my nostrils. Tonnere put his head and shoulders into the task of getting out of the bog. The mud was filled with detritus all mixed to a thick soup, like the pit of hell. All one would need to experience hell was heat and flames, along with this foul miasma. I looked around, marking the landscape well so as to not come this way again.

At the thought of hell, Annie's dilemma became clear to me. Was she afraid of eternal life because she had no hope of heaven? Perhaps it was practical and comforting for her to believe there was no God, no everlasting life, no heaven or hell. Did she believe she deserved hell?

...

A letter arrived May 2, 1678.

> Versailles
> January 20, 1678
> Dear Madeleine,
>
> Oh, that you could be here to pass the time with me. Each morning I request an audience with the king and wait in his antechambers with other hopeful citizens. Colbert acts like a snake in the grass, smiling face-to-face, but as soon as a man's back is turned, he sabotages.
>
> I watch my words with extreme care. When I present my inquiry to the king, I want my vision and my enthusi-

asm to be fresh, not sullied by another courtier who thinks to gossip about me.

As I stroll through the gilded halls here and marvel at the Chinese ornaments and colorful flowers, I imagine you as walking these same corridors. Were these good times for you? Or when you crossed the Atlantic, were you turning your back on the artificiality and gildedness of Versailles?

In a few days I hope to win the king's audience and support for my petition. Keep my maps safe, my friend. Keep my creditors at bay, my business partner. Keep France's flag flying at the fort, my brave soldier.

Until we meet again, RLS

Was Robert being influenced by the wealth and the superficiality of King Louis XIV's Court? Should I worry that he wouldn't come home? Or when he did return, he'd bring a woman with him?

...

Annie's struggle with her mortality unsettled me. But how could I help her if I couldn't help myself? What was the nature of my faith? It often took on the shape and color of the person around me. With Robert, I was a good, social Catholic. With Sleeping Willow, I was a converted Huron. With the Reverend Mother Marie, I was a devout missionary. And with Annie?

This crisis of Annie's impending death firmed up my belief in a loving God, one who hears prayer and answers, who promises us heaven and preservation from hell. I wanted Annie to believe this, too.

When I dumped her chamber pot that morning, my stomach flipped and my heart froze. She had passed blood! Annie, age seventy plus, was bleeding. Where did she stand with God? What could I say to her?

...

A late spring blizzard hit us that May when our defenses were down. All traveling stopped. Two feet of snow blanketed our landscape, making a false covering over random ice floes on the lake and the crusted marsh. Where was the ground solid and firm? Where was it weak, half melted, and about to give way? Because no one knew, no one moved.

The storm provided time for Annie and me to talk. At first, she was annoyed I brought up her health.

"If I were still young and strong, I'd be emptying my own damn pot, and you'd never know. So let's not talk about it." Annie glowered at me as she rocked in jerky movements.

I was twisting soaked basswood bark into string, a popular commodity that brought us a good income. The pungent marinade stung my hands. "Annie, when I first met you, you cared for me. Let me return the help. *Bien?*"

Silence.

Annie's rocking slowed down and became more rhythmic. I took that as a qualified willingness to discuss the subject.

I continued, "I wish I knew of helpful herbs, but I don't." I sighed. "Perhaps you do? I could go collect them for you, *n'est-çe pas?* Or we could ask Claude to get them?"

"Don't tell Claude, Mat-tee. He is just a boy and wouldn't understand. He thinks I'll live forever. When I am with him, it is such a comfort. His faith in me and his love of life make me forget my frailty and mortality, even for a night."

"*Bien.* It is between you and me."

We heard the wind blowing snow off the trees. Every few minutes a mound of fresh powder thudded to the ground. The logs of the cabin creaked, and the firewood crackled.

"Annie, recently I learned of an event in the life of Jesus. A woman who had a hemorrhage for twelve years went to Jesus. She snuck up on him, afraid about going to him directly—he was so popular, and she was just a lowly female. When she was near him, she reached out and touched his cloak. Immediately her bleeding stopped.

"She was about to fade back into the crowd, but Jesus halted and said, 'Who touched me?' Jesus had felt power go out from him, you see.

The woman spoke up and told how the simple touch of his cloak had stopped her bleeding. Jesus said to her, 'Daughter, take courage, your faith has made you well.'"

I smelled the fragrance of apple wood burning and the mutton soup simmering. I smelled Annie, perfumed soap used carefully to mask the rotten stench of her illness.

My fingers moved quickly as I twisted the wet basswood bark strips together. I watched my red, chapped fingers dance.

Then I heard Annie's sob. She tried to muffle it, but another groan burst into the hushed room. Putting down the string, I wiped my hands and went over to her chair. She stiffened when I placed my palms on her shoulders. But I kept my fingers there and kneaded her neck muscles.

"It's all right," I offered.

"No, it's not." She wept.

"I love you, Annie."

"You shouldn't. If you truly knew me, you wouldn't love me." She slumped lower in her chair. I sat cross-legged on the floor, looking up at her. Her thin, white hair was flying loose from under her cap. Her eyes were bloodshot and her jaw set. Her cheeks, in the past quite fleshy, displayed predominate high bones, markers of her Ojibway parentage.

It took her a few minutes to thaw. But then she talked in a low, soft voice that shifted in and out of sobbing.

"Mat-tee, I gave faith up fifty-five years ago. I regret that now, but I don't know how to change. You talk to me about Jesus, who healed this lady because of her faith. Well, I don't have faith, so I can't get healed. But I would want to. I don't want to die."

"Are you afraid that you won't go to heaven?"

Her tear-filled eyes looked straight at mine. "How did you guess that?"

"Remember when you said, 'why should my soul continue?'"

"Oh, *sacre coeur*," Annie cursed and then wept.

I trusted her tears would be cleansing. Soon her heart-wrenching sounds calmed. She told me about her life after her mother died when she had just entered womanhood.

"Father and I headed north to continue our trading. He sought comfort from me at night. I thought nothing of his lying close to me for my warmth and companionship. But one night, something came over him. He twisted my tunic up, yanked his belt off, and pulled his britches open. Oh, my God. My own father."

Again, sobs emitted from her chest. She had to release this painful story. From my own experience, I knew that.

"A few weeks later, I realized I was carrying his child. What could I do? We wintered at the Ojibway Mission village. The Jesuit priests impressed me as educated men, and I respected their religion, their healing abilities, and their resourcefulness. So I confided in hardworking Father Anthony, hoping for practical advice. The priest was appalled I considered terminating the baby's life. His kindness disappeared in a flash. 'If you end your pregnancy, you will commit murder in God's eyes. Your soul will end in hell. You, a baptized, French woman, should know that.'

"He swooped up his black robe, smoothed his long beard, and paused to say, 'If you turn your back on God's ways now, you might never get another chance. He will turn his back on you.'

"A loving God would turn his back on me? I hadn't chosen to make the baby, to be involved with sin. After I recovered from my shock, I sought out the help of an Ojibway midwife. We did the job. The herbal drinks she gave me eased the pain. But I bled for several days. She must have pierced part of my womb with the bone needle. I have never been able to conceive a child since. I've wondered if God punished me."

Annie covered her eyes. Her shoulders shook. Her fists clenched. She struggled with her soul.

I did not believe God had forsaken her.

"Jesus can forgive you now even for something you did years ago, dear one."

Shifting to rest on my knees, I reached up and took her hands in mine. Part of me believed what I had said; my other part still wondered. But for Annie's sake, I would play the reverend mother, encouraging her repentance and her step of faith.

"Mat-tee, I didn't know you believed in Jesus like this. When we have been going to chapel at the fort, I thought you went to visit the people or to see Robert and Wilhelm. Do you go because you believe?"

"The Reverend Mother of the Incarnation taught me about Jesus, his love, his truth, and his forgiveness. But after she died, what I had learned withered. Since you and I have been discussing life and death, heaven and hell, I've been thinking through my beliefs. There is a personal God who loves me. Reading the Bible strengthens my faith. God became Jesus so I could connect with the Creator in human form. The reason our perfect God permitted his son to be crucified was to do away with our sin. And I believe there is a heaven we will all go to after we die if we trust Christ."

What I didn't say was how difficult it was for me to believe these ideas every day. Now, this moment, Annie needed to hear words of faith to kindle her soul.

"Mat-tee, you think after all these years of rebelling against God— and I certainly did a lot of that those first years after I took my child's life, before I met Mr. Noleen—you think that God will forgive me?"

I squeezed her hand. Annie continued to ponder and stayed deep in thought for a few minutes.

Then she added, "And when I wasn't being rebellious, I was indifferent to the Creator. I spent most of my adult life ignoring God, helping people but not thinking about God. You think he'd forgive me for that?"

"I do, Annie."

She leaned back in the rocker and closed her eyes. Tears slid down her cheeks. Then her sobbing gave way to deep breathing and mutterings. Perhaps she was praying. I offered up my own.

## 22

# THE RED CAPE

Earthy smells, vibrant greens, and other promises of new life gave us hope amidst our humdrum spring chores. We rock-lined three trenches to draw off excess moisture before we tilled our land. Tonnere, trained to pull a sledge, walked the field while I pitched off forkfuls of manure. Claude followed, breaking up the clots and shaking around the fertilizer. At last Annie helped us plant the seeds.

In early June, I received a letter from Robert.

> March 1, 1678, Paris
> Dear Madeleine,
>
> The slow pace and ineptitude of the Royal Court chafes my soul. "Tomorrow His Majesty will hear you," they say, but tomorrow and the next day come, and I have not been called into his presence. Colbert has heard my position so often, he considers me arrogant and obnoxious.
>
> If the king gives me his imprimatur to continue exploring, I will need more funds. So I have approached my older sisters for capital…
>
> I am grateful for you, my dear. You understand these dreams of mine. You respect the subtleties of our relations with the natives, the common laborer, and the government because you have had your ear on the diplomatic pulse since your arrival in 1671.
>
> I try not to feel lonely as such feelings serve no purpose. But in those rare moments when emptiness begins to steal over my soul like a gray cloud, my thoughts turn to you. When my mind is filled with your image, my heart grows strong.
>
> Until we meet again. By God's will, it cannot be long now. RLS

...

"Mat-tee, I am so tired of your fretting," Annie said. "Do something for Robert to encourage him when he returns."

So I designed a special cape for his travels and made it from crimson wool and gold braid. Robert would look regal, a French "chief" when he wore it in the natives' presence.

Keeping my hands busy on Robert's behalf helped my impatience. But my heart's rhythm was erratic. One minute it pounded with anticipation of seeing a successful Robert, and the next it slowed to a foreboding cadence worrying that the king would reject Robert's proposal.

Then June 29, a letter arrived.

> Versailles
> May 9, 1678
> Dear Madeleine,
>
> I have done it! His Majesty Louis XIV has granted me the right to operate as many forts as necessary to expand France's territory to the Gulf of Mexico. He has also given me a monopoly on the trade of buffalo hides, something I didn't request. And finally, my dear friend, he bestowed on me a title of nobility, the Sieur of the region around Frontenac.
>
> I am sending this letter by ship post-haste, but I need another week to get my business matters in order. I believe, with the king's backing, my cousins will advance me capital.
>
> Soon, my friend, I will be home and can commence on my exploring. RLS

After reading his letter, my head contained proud thoughts of Robert and, in some small way of myself, for helping with this grand vision of his. But my disappointed heart sank because he had not once mentioned plans for us. Was he afraid to include me in his future?

···

At the end of August, I convinced Wilhelm Jenet to accompany me to Quebec so I could see Robert. Our canoe, filled with mail and packages for loved ones, took off with Wilhelm paddling in the bow and a young native in the stern. In the middle, Francois and I sat facing each other, surrounded by packs, food supplies, and Robert's cape, secured in a waterproof pouch woven from resin-soaked reeds.

Four-year-old Francois entertained us with questions, stories, and outbursts of glee when he saw wildlife along the shores. My job was not only to keep Francois safe but also to set up camp, tend fire, and cook when we stopped in the evenings. We all had to wear that dreadful bear grease to protect us from the insects and the sun.

···

I was shocked when I found LaSalle abed at the governor's mansion. Robert could barely raise himself off the pillow. I stepped forward and grasped his hand.

"Robert." I smiled. "Has all the wining and dining at Court depleted your strength?"

"Madeleine." He chuckled with effort. "I feel much better than I did a week ago." He tried to grin, but his bloody gums made the effort painful. "On the ship voyage, we ran out of fresh produce within the first week. My steward had not anticipated the thirty Frenchmen who squeezed on the ship at the last minute to join me. I did not consume a fresh potato or piece of fruit for many weeks. But the governor's cook has found a variety of fresh vegetables for me."

Pulling up a chair, I smoothed hair off his forehead. He was feverish, and I made a mental note of the herbs that would make him more comfortable. "Go to sleep, Robert. Governor Frontenac has given me permission to tend you. I'll be here when you waken."

His eyes closed, and his breathing deepened. I was tempted to put my cheek down on the pillow next to him. I took his hand in mine instead. Dare I ask him why his letters were so one-sided?

LaSalle recuperated by consuming daily cups of brewed birch bark for his sore gums, bowls of chicken soup, and several apples a day. He took increasingly long walks with my help, first in the mansion's corridors and then outside along the river's edge.

As Robert's energy increased, he spoke passionately about his new plans. Occasionally he asked about Parrot's Bay and myself, but after I started to respond, he would interrupt me and put forth another one of his ideas. My heart rejoiced in his recovery, but my head kept asking, *why am I putting up with his one-sidedness?*

...

Governor Frontenac insisted LaSalle represent the interest of the traders west of Quebec at the Brandy Parliament to be held October 26, 1678. I was invited to participate. The issue of trading brandy and rum to the savages was a disconcerting topic. Some natives wanted the liquor, while others believed it was detrimental to their health. The governor had to balance the interests of the religious groups opposed to alcoholic beverages with the merchants' belief that trading in brandy stimulated the economy. The governor wanted the fastest way to make a solid profit—liquor for furs.

Since my concerns about Robert's health and loyalty were assuaged, I wanted to get home to Annie. An occasional falling leaf wafted its way onto the coverlet through the wide-open window, reminding us that winter would be here soon. In this climate, one never knew when the first snowstorms would hit or when the river would be frozen over, stopping all movement.

"After the parliament, Madeleine, we must be off to Cataraqui and Parrot's Bay. I want to see how the fort is doing before I leave with Tonty for the Great Falling Waters," Robert said as he sat on his bed looking over the gold and red landscapes of the St. Lawrence River.

At Robert's mention of Tonty, I felt a pang of jealousy. Young Henri de Tonty had attached himself to LaSalle while at Versailles. Robert was pleased that an intelligent soldier assisted him. When LaSalle first met him, Tonty had been recovering from a grenade wound that had blown off his hand. The royal physicians had replaced Tonty's hand with an iron device that had many practical uses. The two men had taken an immediate liking to each other.

"Robert, Tonty is clearly devoted to you," I ventured. "And this project you have him working on? What is that all about?" I asked, trying to suppress any sound of envy. I coveted the role of LaSalle's assistant.

Robert replied, "Tonty is collecting supplies to build a brigantine to carry our loads of fur on the great lakes. When we head west next week, we carry with us a 450-pound anchor, rigging, and hardware out of which we will construct our vessel. Would you like to see the plans?"

He drew out a parchment with sketches of various angles of the brigantine. As I watched him point out facets of the ship, I felt a surge of excitement. Even if I couldn't go with Robert in person, I could travel with him in spirit.

I said, "Your letters go into such detail. Through them I share in your adventures. But Robert, why did you not write asking me about my activities?"

"Oh, no, Mat-tee. I don't ask because our letters are not private matters. Their content can be read and gossiped about by anyone. My lack of reciprocity is for your protection, my dear. I wait expectantly for my time with you when I will hear all about you, every little detail." He smiled and clucked me on the chin.

"Well, fine. But while I've been here, you rarely ask about my experiences or thoughts. Am I boring to you?"

"Oh, no." Robert looked chagrined. "Of course, I am interested in you. You are my inspiration." He took my hand and kissed it. "I often think about our future together."

Once he affirmed his affection, I simply couldn't wait to give him my gift. I opened the drawer of a nearby bureau and drew out my homemade package.

"Mat-tee, what is this?" Robert asked, taking the bundle.

"Open and see." I felt like a schoolgirl on her birthday.

He untied the rawhide straps, reached into the bag, and lifted out the crimson cape. He sucked in his breath while he held the garment before him. I thought I detected tears in his eyes, but they were quickly masked.

"Try it on, Robert." I bounced on my toes.

"Help me." He held it out and turned so that I could place the cape on his muscled shoulders. I let my hands linger for a moment before fastening the gold clasp at his neck.

"Come," he urged, "I want to see what it looks like." We hurried down the stairs and opened the doors to the ballroom full of mirrors. Robert looked at his reflection and swished the cape left and right. He unclasped it and took it off, regally throwing it over his arm. Then he shook it out and artfully covered his shoulders. He turned so that his back was to the mirror, and he looked behind and grinned.

"Where did you ever find this?"

"I made it," I said with shyness. "When I was waiting for you to hear from the king. Its pouch is water-proofed so you can take it anywhere."

He drew me to him. I was hoping for an embrace. But he pivoted. With his arm over my shoulder, as though we were comrades going into war, he posed in front of the glass.

I saw a tall, handsome man with wavy brown hair and a neatly coifed goatee and mustache wearing this crimson robe with pride. An attractive brunette, tall and slender with a shapely bosom and full hips, stood next to him, wishing she might become the center of this man's world.

The window's settee beckoned me. My hand urged Robert forward, and he sat down, his back rigid against the embellished wooden arm. I placed his cape behind me. He realized my intent. His breathing sped up. Capturing his cheeks between my tremulous hands, I drew his mouth to meet mine. Robert grasped my sides and pulled me tight against him, his kisses now deep, moist, and uncontrolled. His response excited me. I abandoned myself to kissing him.

My ears were ringing when I came up for air. Robert blushed, lifted me off him, and cleared his throat. He picked up his gift, pecked my cheek with a dry kiss, and left me sitting there—stunned.

*Intimate and aroused one minute, and then gone! What is it with Robert? Is he afraid of our connection, our passion? Is his abrupt departure his way of maintaining control?*

...

In early November, Tonty, Nika, and seven explorers paddled our canoe up river toward Montreal. LaSalle gave commands, steered around obstacles, and chanted songs to keep a rhythm going. We left Wilhelm and Francois in Quebec.

A thud startled me when our boat hit a boulder unseen below the surface. I was stiff from cold and inactivity and nearly asleep. I shook my head to clear it. Seconds before I had been dreaming...

> I was meandering along a lakeshore and then into a meadow. I kept rambling, seeking someone. The terrain changed, and the surroundings transformed into mossy, gnarled trees, with patches of stagnant water. I felt increasingly desperate as I looked for a person.
>
> In my dream image, a tatter of red appeared in the distance. The patch of color grew larger and became the back of a man dressed in a crimson robe. I ran toward him. "Robert!" I cried.
>
> Slowly the man turned around. I gasped. Blood dripped from a hole in his head, slid down his brow, and stained his cloak. His face had a startled look. Then he faded into the swamp's fog.

The sound of the canoe hitting the rock was not unlike a gunshot. I struggled to make images of my here-and-now replace the dream. Craning my neck, I saw Robert paddling in the stern with a focused and contented expression, dressed in his buckskins and fur vest, conversing quietly with Tonty. When I caught his eye, he nodded in my direction. Nevertheless the horror of the dream lingered.

...

Upon return, Annie pressed me to her bosom as I stooped over. She had grown thinner and weaker over the last six weeks. But her familiar smile filled me with joy. She gestured to the floor in front of her rocker and invited me to sit and "tell all."

"Is Robert with you, Mat-tee?"

"He stayed at the fort to finish up his business. He is bound and determined to leave for the Great Falling Waters before Christmas," I said.

My old friend shook her head in dismay and clucked like a hen. "He'll have to battle ice floes and snow storms."

"Yes, he knows that, but he's pigheaded. It was quite the life, coming back. A blizzard assaulted us at *Trois Riveres*, and we lived, ten men and one woman, under our large canoe with rawhide walls for three days. It's getting treacherous on the water. As I paddled up here today from the fort, the lake is starting to freeze up. Twice I ran onto new ice, almost invisible. I had to crack the thin layer with my paddle, go backwards, and weave around the ice patches."

There was a companionable silence between us. Claude was out doing chores in the barn.

I asked, "How are Tonnere and Midnight? Life was dull without my friendly animals."

Claude had been riding Tonnere with some success, and Midnight had taken to being Annie's watchdog and companion. The stream of voyageurs had dried up to a trickle, and shipments of supplies had ceased.

I told Annie about Robert's illness. "I was hoping for time with Robert alone, but when he is around other men, he doesn't communicate thoughts or feelings. He is rarely encouraging or demonstrative, except in his letters." My inner core warmed at the memory of his kisses in the ballroom.

"Still, will you marry him someday?" Annie asked.

"I don't know. Sometimes I believe he loves me and wants me. Other times he pulls away. It's confusing."

"Do you want a life with him?

I sighed and leaned back against her knees. "Annie, when I am with him, listening to his plans, helping him with his maps or his language skills, I feel like we're hand in hand. Then he'll act distant and remote, especially around other people. The pain is so tender, I wish I'd never met the man."

"Is that pain worth bearing for the pleasure of loving him?"

Quickly I said, "Oh yes." In that moment, I realized I would have to endure his difficult ways in order to have the pleasure of his company.

I got up and poured water over fresh tea leaves.

"Do you still take lots of honey in your tea, Annie?"

"More than ever. Need my energy."

Annie was silent and sipped her tea.

"Each day I grow weaker, Mat-tee."

I sighed in sympathy.

She went on, "But I am not fighting against it any more, thanks to you. I have been afraid of God, of his judgment, and the reality of hell for sixty years. While you were gone, I took to reading that Bible. What you said about Jesus is true. I do believe he loves me. And after thinking about it for quite some time, I believe he forgives me for the murder I committed. I have experienced more peace in my heart in the last four months than at any other time in my life."

She took a deep breath, straightened herself in the rocker, and went on. "You know, the Bible says we will see him face-to-face. I'm looking forward to that."

Annie had found a peace and an intimacy with God that I envied. I still did not have that kind of personal faith. Even when I faced possible death in the blizzard east of LaChine, God was not in my thoughts.

...

When I spotted the loaded brigantine coming from the fort the day before Christmas, I galloped the stallion back to the barn, hung the saddle on its peg, and ran to the dock. Stomping my feet to ward off the cold, I waited for the vessel to land. Robert, Tonty, Nika, and several other men jumped out. I ran up to Robert but restrained myself at the last minute and just shook his hand and then Tonty's good hand as well. "Come. We'll heat up that cider for you."

Father Hennepin also came with news from the families at Fort Frontenac and was going west with LaSalle.

Robert had come to say good-bye. I lured him into the barn for privacy.

"Robert, please stay to celebrate Christmas with us. Let Father Hennepin say a mass. It would mean so much to Annie. One day won't make a difference."

"Ah, but it may, Mat-tee. I must catch up with LaMotte, whom I sent ahead to negotiate with the natives. I need to set up a fort at Cayuga, that in-land river you discovered. Plus I'm anxious to get another brigantine built to sail the Great Lakes."

"When will I see you again?"

I thought of my dream and trembled.

He reached up to pet Tonnere's nose and placed his cheek against the horse's muzzle. Then Robert drew me close and enveloped me in his arms.

I breathed in his scent. "I wish I could go with you."

"And I know you're more than capable of handling such hardships." He held me tightly and then sighed. "Sometimes I feel as though I were two men."

"Robert, perhaps you'll figure these two out while we're apart." Looking up into his eyes, I risked saying, "I have seen both. One is standing here with me, enjoying this closeness, this companionship. He is the visionary, both passionate and humane. The other Robert is the accomplisher, one who must work to feel right about himself. This one sat with me under a canoe for three days and barely exchanged a word."

Robert fingered my curls. "Madeleine, I can manage tribal negotiations, witness scalpings and drownings, and handle the perils of the sea with more courage than I can face my feelings for you."

He leaned over and kissed me. His lips were firm and dry, but as he turned me into his embrace, moist heat rose from our bodies. I responded with a deep kiss of my own. Time stopped as we drank in each other.

Too soon he pulled away and said, "I must go and rouse my men." Then he walked off toward the house.

# 23

# FAITH AND FEAR

As I did my chores that holiday, I brooded. Should I attach my heart to a man who thought mostly about himself and his objectives? Travel at this time of year was hazardous, and I worried about him. How would I feel if Robert did not come back? Heartbroken? Angry? Or just plain numb?

Claude and I prepared a festive meal while Annie read aloud from the Gospels about Christ's birth.

While we ate, Annie told of discoveries she had made about Jesus. I listened, never having heard Jesus spoken of in such personal terms, not even from the Huguenots I met on the *Jeanne Baptiste*.

"Imagine. His mother was newly into her womanhood when she gave birth to Jesus! And she had no one around except Joseph and the stable animals. Did you know she wrapped him in swaddling clothes? Why had she carried them with her? Swaddling bands are what people use when a person dies. Did Mary know her baby was born to die? Can you imagine having a child and knowing from the moment he was conceived that his purpose in life was to die?"

She picked up a lamb chop and licked the juices from it and then put it back on her plate. After a moment, Annie thanked me for giving her the Bible.

I said, "Annie, you're lucky. A Huguenot family gave it to me when we left the boat in 1671. I tucked it away as a memento but have rarely read it myself. The Reverend Mother Marie said priests were supposed to read the Scripture and not lay people because we might misinterpret it."

"Oh, hogwash," Annie said. "Priests are more worried we common folk will discover the truth for ourselves and not need them in their robes, with their rituals, telling us what the truth is."

Claude carved into his lamb and covered the piece with pickled beets. He said, "Annie, I believe what the church teaches me, that Jesus is the Savior. I've heard that all my life. But, so what? What difference does that make?"

"My dear boy. You pro'bly done nothing so bad you feared you're goin' to hell. Well, I have. And let me tell you, when that happens, your soul slinks down into a dark hole and lives in fear. Jesus is God, and yet he is man. He knows about these bad things we humans do, and he still forgives us—me that is, if I admit I'm wrong. Because of him, I'm not goin' to hell, Claude." Annie spoke with renewed energy.

"Ah, Annie, what have you done to hurt anyone?" Claude probed.

"M' boy, this old heart has silently spat on God, ignored God, and mocked God. And my heart did deserve hell. That is, until Jesus said, 'Annie, let me take your punishment on my back so you and God can be right with each other.' That is why I am so excited today. This is the first Christmas I've ever celebrated in which I believe God turned human and lives right here with us. This is the first winter I've felt peace and joy in my heart. And you know what, my dear friends, I welcome my death. I will pass into heaven and see this Jesus whom I love face-to-face."

...

When Annie fell into a coma January 17, 1679, Claude became distraught. Because she discharged blood and other bodily fluids, keeping her clean and dry used up our energy. Washing linens in winter was difficult, as we had to melt water over the fire and hang the bedding to dry in the main room. Our store looked like a sailing ship as we walked between wet sheets each day.

One of us sat with her all the time. Her closed eyes and softened mouth had a peaceful look. I read from the Bible when I was with her. She was awake when I read:

> Let not your heart be troubled, ye believe in God, believe also in me. In my Father's house are many mansions. If it were not so, I would have told you. I go to prepare a place for you. And if I go and prepare a place for you, I will come again, and receive you unto myself, that where I am there ye may be also.

When I finished, she squeezed my hand.

We sat in silence. Claude came in from the barn, pulled off his moccasins, and shook the snow off his cloak. He smiled when he saw Annie resting so peacefully. As if sensing his presence, Annie opened her eyes. She held Claude's look for a few seconds, shifted her eyes to my face, and then looked up to the ceiling. With effort, she raised herself from the bed, beaming. Then she extended her hands upward as if to greet someone. She whispered, "Jesus. Oh, Jesus." At that moment, air escaped her lungs, making a hollow, rattling noise. She relaxed into the pillow, still smiling and staring at the ceiling.

Her smile did not shift. I smoothed her gray hairs off her forehead and ran my fingers over her lips. She no longer breathed. Annie had departed for heaven.

...

The day after Annie died, Claude left. Dressed in his fur cloak, he resembled a loping, brown bear. He slung his musket over his shoulder and said he had to be alone for a while. I didn't question him.

My first week of solitude permitted a period of mourning. Annie filled my thoughts. When I was in the trading post, I rearranged items Annie had introduced to me: plaid woolens from Scotland and iron utensils from Britain. When some of the stock reminded me of her practical advice, I would cry, filled with sorrow for having lost her friendship, guidance, and support.

During the second week alone, anger rose. Claude had left me with all the chores. Robert had not only decamped but was indecisive in his interest toward me. And I was irate at Annie for her dying. I swept the floor with fury and manhandled the shelved items. While cleaning up Tonnere's manure, I stabbed it with the fork so vigorously one would think it were the object of my disdain. I flung hay into the colt's trough as though he were my enemy and his feed, bullets. I booted the hens out of the way when they got underfoot.

Toward the end of that week, I looked into the loft and saw the dusty shroud holding Annie's body. "Damn you, Annie, for leaving me. Damn you! Why?" My shouting became louder and louder. Tonnere started to whinny and turned skittish. Anger gushed forth as tears. I sat down in the straw, hugging Midnight, and cried and yelled and groaned until nothing else would come.

The third companionless week I was tired and dazed. In the morning, I would pull the quilt up over my head to block out the early light, hoping sleep would swallow me up again. Midnight would snuggle against my back. But the sleep and the dreams left me feeling drugged, apathetic, in a stupor. Then I would get up, walk stiff-legged to the fireplace, and kick up the embers with some tinder and logs. Several mornings the fire was almost out, and I had to find one hot coal and nurse it to life. All day long I would go from one routine chore to another with no interest, as though I were still dreaming.

By the fourth week, Claude seemed to have abandoned Parrot's Bay, leaving me profoundly alone. How I wished for conversation. As the weeks moved along, the sounds of nature substituted for voices. I improved my ability to distinguish one bird song from another's. The trumpeting of a moose, the nickering of a deer, the mewing of a fox, all entertained me. The bay lapped against the shore, sometimes gently caressing it, at others times abrasively hammering the rocks.

I took Tonnere for rides and enjoyed talking to him as we watched the snow decorating the lakeshore. Midnight trotted along, chasing a rabbit or squirrel every now and then.

To enforce some discipline in my life, I turned my mattress so the sunrise caught my pillow through the oilcloth window, shined on my eyes, teasing me out of bed. I ate three meals a day; wrote letters to Robert, Wilhelm, even Sleeping Willow; planned my future trading business; and studied the previous year's accounts. Midnight's companionship was a blessing.

Despite my best efforts, nothing filled the emptiness and loneliness within me. Desperate, I picked up the Bible and asked Jesus for help. As I read it, a strange, new freedom settled on me. This Jesus whom Annie saw during the last moments of her life became increasingly real to me. Every minute of getting to know Jesus was a delight and a source of fulfillment.

...

Claude returned with a wife, Full Moon, a demanding, full-bodied Ojibway girl of seventeen winters. He glowed with pleasure. She was a reluctant worker with a sour temper, but she was besotted with Claude. She giggled and blushed when it came to sharing his bed. The sounds coming from them not only kept me awake at night, but also stirred up images. Would it ever be like this with Robert?

...

Midnight's bark signaled the arrival of Robert and two men on snowshoes. I didn't even recognize them. The trek from Niagara Falls had iced up their bearded faces and caked their furs with frozen mud and debris. Even though they were traveling with light loads, they stooped under the weight of their packs. I sensed something ominous had happened.

Full Moon and I helped the stiff, cold travelers out of their frozen clothes. They were weak from not having eaten for several days.

While our mutton soup simmered, Full Moon flirted with the two men. We served hot cider and fresh baked bread.

Robert resembled a classic voyageur, his inquisitive, sharp eyes hiding in a forest of facial hair. I was used to seeing him in leather breeches and linen shirts, but stripped as he was, he looked gaunt in his gray, linsey-woolsey underwear.

"What day is today, Madeleine?" he asked.

"It is the fifteenth of March, 1679."

Robert groaned. Before speaking, he hung his head. "We left Niagara Falls two weeks ago, making our way along the ice-covered northern shore. We slept in snow caves and hunted small game and fowl. Several days ago our strength ran out. Despite the bag of wheat we carried, we didn't have the energy to even make a fire." He still shivered as he bit into the warm loaf, ripping the bread off in his teeth.

I yearned to reach across the table and cover his hand in mine. "What brought you back?" I asked, nervous with anticipation.

"We lost the brigantine. It's at the bottom of Lake Ontario at the foot of the Niagara River." Were those tears in his eyes?

"Oh, no! Robert, how did that happen?"

Claude and Full Moon hovered so they could hear the tale.

"That damn foolish captain. I warned him about sudden storms on the lake. But he didn't take me seriously. As a newcomer from France, he thought of Lake Ontario as just another lake, not the inland ocean we have come to know. So he slept on shore with his men. One night the winds kicked up. Powerful waves tossed the brigantine, unmanned and anchored off shore, like a twig on a raging river. The anchor line broke. The captain awoke to hear the hull being smashed against the rocks. Our cargo of rigging, sails, and lumber, not to mention the trade goods worth hundreds of livres, got washed away. Our anchor was the only item saved because we had gone to great lengths to remove it from the brigantine so as to lighten the ship's load."

Robert slouched in his chair, dejected and exhausted. Silence surrounded us as we took in this news.

"I came back because I have to start over," Robert growled.

I moved behind his chair. Despite the presence of the other people, I rubbed his shoulders. "Were any lives lost?" I asked.

"No. No, Mat-tee."

"That's a blessing."

"*Oui*," he concurred with reluctance.

As we ate our soup, I asked Robert how long they would stay.

When he proposed they leave at dawn, his men collectively groaned.

He glared. They stopped.

My heart despaired. "Robert, there is no need to hasten away. Recuperate. You're all weakened. Tarry a few days to gather your strength."

Robert thought. "We will stay until dawn on Sunday. Then we will head to the fort, attend services there, and push on to Montreal. I must discuss this situation with my creditors, rebuild some capital, purchase new supplies, and head back to Niagara Falls. That sailing vessel must be completed as soon as possible so we can head west within the year."

...

On Saturday, Robert and I went to the barn to be alone. My private time with Robert was so limited that I started our conversation where we left off on Christmas Eve Day, almost three months ago.

"Do you remember saying you often feel like two men? One person who wants to be close to me, and the other who wants to accomplish goals as an explorer? And you can't decide which one you are? Do you still think this is a problem?"

We were seated with our backs to Tonnere's stall. Robert carved on a piece of wood, keeping his hands busy. The sweet hay, horse sweat, and rich manure smelled comforting. Sounds of hens clucking, sheep braying lightly, and the colt nickering helped me feel safe as I challenged Robert.

"Mat-tee, the man with a vision who overcomes obstacle after obstacle is the LaSalle of the daytime. Only in the night's wee hours do I slow down and think about you. When I do, my heart is warmed by memories of our companionship. But I am also grieved." He sighed and stopped whittling. "Mat-tee, I am not ready for taking on the responsibility of a wife."

"Robert, don't think of me as a wife then. I am just as capable as any man to hunt, forage for food, cook, and tend fire. I am more capable than most in dealing with fevers and rashes, aches and pains. You know I connect with the natives, as I understand their language and customs."

Robert put his knife to the wood again. "Your presence would distract me from my duties or weaken my resolve to endure hardships. My men winter in bark shelters. They eat bear paws, squirrels, and porcupines. They go without bread, tea, and cider for the entire season. I must provide for you better than that."

"But I don't need those things. I only care about being with you. It breaks my heart when you come in and go out of my life so unexpectedly, so frequently. Today, I am thrilled you're here. Tomorrow, you'll be gone. Can I set a date when I can expect you back again? No. I would rather sleep on the ground in a bark shelter and eat bear paws but be with you."

I let out my breath and smiled. He grinned back and took my hand in his, not saying anything.

I reached up and stroked his beard. Then I pulled his head down so his lips met mine. The tip of my tongue caressed his soft inner lip. For a heartbeat, he moved against me. Then suddenly he pulled back, shaking his head. It was as though he had just wrapped his physical warmth in a tight box, afraid of letting it out. Perhaps he was afraid if he started loving me he wouldn't be able to stop. Certainly that might threaten his life's goals.

I would have to wait… yet again.

When Annie was alive, she urged me to discover how to live without needing a man. I was learning and relearning that lesson.

# 24

# LETTING GO

One white-hot day at the end of July, I was floating in the middle of Parrot's Bay, studying clouds, when I saw a tall male paddling a canoe toward me. I started swimming toward shore wearing only my chemise.

But the canoeist sped up in order to overtake me. "Ho, Mat-tee, slow down. It's me, LaSalle."

Blood rushed to my face. I treaded water and turned to greet my friend. "LaSalle, indeed. Address yourself by your Christian name, Robert, or I'll think you're here on some military errand." Scooping my arm across the lake's surface, I splashed water on him.

"Feels good in this heat." Robert wiped his wet face off and smiled. "Do you want a lift to shore, or shall we race?"

"Neither. Call Midnight to follow you so he won't try to wrestle with me on the way in."

As I stroked toward the dock, I composed myself. What was he doing here? How long would he stay? Had he succeeded in rebuilding his reputation while in Montreal?

Close to the shore where an occasional lake-bottom boulder was found, I stood up. How many nights had I lain awake wishing Robert would see me like this and desire me?

I would not let this opportunity go by.

Robert had tied off his canoe and was playing tag with Midnight when I stepped onto the dock. Without hesitation, I walked up the rocky embankment, squeezing water from my chemise and shaking drops from my hair.

Robert scanned the full length of my body. His mouth twitched at the corners. We held each other's gaze. The breeze whipped my hair and tugged at my shift. He appraised me again. I felt beautiful and light. As much as I wanted to take the initiative, this had to be his choice.

Then, abruptly Robert turned toward the house, calling, "Mat-tee, I'll see you on the porch after you get some clothes on."

Disappointment sank down into my feet like a weight.

When we met, I wore a demure cotton blouse and a knee-length Métis skirt. My dark hair was tied back in a red ribbon. I swallowed my pride, concealed my hurt, and smiled. "How wonderful it is to see you, Robert."

Reaching for his hands, I pulled him toward me. He softened and folded his arms around me, his fingers caressing my blouse.

"You're a welcome sight, dear friend," Robert said. "My enemies surrounded me while I was in Montreal."

"Were you successful in squaring up your accounts?"

"It took much time in the colonial Court, but two weeks ago the matters settled, and I got my furniture back from those men who had bid for it in auction. My belongings are being stored at Noleen's until my return." He sounded tired.

We drank cold, spring water. I rocked back and forth on the wooden swing we had mounted to the porch roof. As I pushed against the planks with my bare feet, Robert sat next to me and watched my toes closely.

"When are you heading west?" I asked, dreading the answer.

"I stopped by to pick up some of those multicolored glass beads you keep in stock."

I laughed and touched his moccasin with my toes. "You could have gotten plenty of those beads in Montreal or at the fort, for that matter."

His mouth twitched in a half-smile, and he took my hand. "Mat-tee, you're my mainstay. Seeing you means a great deal to me. My time in Montreal was an ordeal. Don't they realize there is a huge world out there to discover, to harvest, to convert?"

With his finger, he touched my palm, drew it to his mouth, and kissed it. He then laid his palm against mine and commingled our hands. His free hand massaged our interlaced fingers. I felt his warm skin moving against mine, arousing a tingle throughout my whole body.

I heard myself gasp. A blush heated my cheeks.

"Robert, take me with you," I blurted out.

He released my hand and looked back down at the planks and my bare feet. "The morale of the men would be injured if their captain had a woman while they themselves did not. Madeleine, I am afraid your coming with me would not work."

So Robert was back on the lake within a few hours, having forgotten the glass beads. I had filled him up on a meal of cold duck, beets, and fresh apples.

Once again my heart saddened as he paddled out of sight. Dangers faced him on his explorations. The memories of how Robert looked at me in my wet chemise, the ardor of our embrace, and his caress of my palm gave me hope for a future together.

...

Six months later, in December 1679, a letter arrived at Parrot's Bay.

> St. Joseph's, Lake Michigan October 27, 1679
> Dear Madeleine,
>
> I have hired a Jesuit courier, heading from St. Joseph up the Kanakee River to Quebec, to carry this letter.
>
> So much has happened! I can only write briefly. Soon with your hand in mine, I will share these adventures with you.
>
> When I arrived at Niagara Falls and Cayuga Island, Tonty and Nika had completed the building of the fifty-foot-long Griffon.
>
> Our first challenge was getting the Griffon up the Niagara River to Lake Erie. The Niagara River shoots over the boulders with the speed of an arrow and has an unfathomable power. But we defeated it by using the Griffon's sails. Wind blew the craft south to Lake Erie while my men

pulled the ship along the river's edge with cables. Within two weeks, twenty-five men and I were sailing west across Lake Erie to the strait connecting to Lake Huron.

Ah, Madeleine, our time on Lake Erie was heaven compared to the challenges of Lake Huron, which kicked up her waves within a day of our being on her. A storm tipped the Griffon violently. My men threw themselves on their knees praying to God. I felt powerless. I told God that if he would deliver us, I would erect a chapel to Saint Anthony as soon as I reached land.

And by God's grace we made it to Michilimackinac, an island commanding the passage between Lake Huron and Lake Michigan. This Jesuit Mission reminds me of a simplified Montreal.

A year ago I had sent out an advance party to Michilimackinac to trade on my behalf, but in my absence, some of these men decided to trade for their own profits. Then they absconded with four thousand livres of my profits in furs and fled north. Only four of the men were found and put in irons.

The trustworthy remainder of my advanced party showed up; they had accrued twelve thousand livres worth of furs as profit from their trading. My financial problems will soon be over! Thanks to the Griffon, I can load furs on to that new vessel and send it east to the Niagara River. There I can transfer the furs to a boat down river from the Great Falls, and that ship will sail on to Fort Frontenac and finally Quebec.

After leaving Tonty in Michilimackinac, Nika, Father Hennepin, and the rest of my men headed south with me on Lake Michigan in large canoes.

The natives have been suspicious of my business dealings in their territory. As a means of getting their attention and respect, your crimson and gold cape has been indispensable. The chief of the Pottawatamies, a friend of

Frontenac, had given me a special calumet. This two-and-a-half foot long pipe is made of handsome red stone, highly polished and decorated with feathers and human hair of all colors. Such a calumet is a passport of safe conduct to all the native allies. Each chief is convinced great evils will befall his people if he violates the calumet's protection.

With the robe on and this calumet raised in peace, I have made our way among the tribes, and there has been no aggression against us. We trade for corn, our staple food, and grapes, which my priest turns into communion wine.

We have made our way down the east coast of Lake Michigan and await Tonty's arrival with the Griffon at Fort St. Joseph's where my men are building a boathouse.

My heart wishes you could be with me, my lady. Sometimes I play with the idea of your coming along as my first mate. You'd be disguised as Mat-tee, the young sailor boy. Only at night you would unveil yourself for me. But this is impossible. My Christian conscience does not allow those thoughts to linger for long.

Soon, my dear, I will have explored this area of the world sufficiently and secured my fame and fortune. Then I will tackle that one last part of my dream: finding the route to the Gulf of Mexico. After we have accomplished this, my dearest Madeleine, I may want to settle in one place and enjoy the world right under my feet—with you by my side.

Keep up your strength and your faith. If you partner with me, you will need both. Respectfully, RLS

. . .

On the crystalline Sunday morning of January 20, 1680, Claude, Full Moon, and I "skated" our canoe to the fort. The deterioration of the place over seven months shocked us. Two of the cabins had collapsed, and icicles on the eaves of the chapel window had grown long and heavy, splintering the glass.

Four soldiers had commandeered the Jenet cabin, and it was filthy, messy, and crowded with makeshift furniture. Homesickness for Wilhelm and Francois unsettled me. How were their lives going?

Fewer people socialized outside the church, and the women were modestly attired, making the chapel service dull. As the priest gave the Latin mass and a homily on spiritual obedience, I squirmed. How does one surrender everything to God? Stubbornly I held on to the idea that Parrot's Bay was God's gift to me. What did God want for Robert and me? Why wouldn't the Lord change Robert's mind about marriage? Couldn't I design my own plan and do what I wanted? Suppose God and I didn't want the same thing?

I balked at yielding to God. Better that I keep some control over my life. Yet, when I thought like this, the flame burning brightly with faith in my heart would flicker and threaten to go out.

...

An Ojibway runner delivered a letter from Robert on March 15, 1680.

> Fort Crevecoeur, Illinois River
> January 20, 1680
> Dearest one,
>
> My heart is breaking. The Griffon has disappeared, presumed to have floundered and sunk in Lake Michigan. No one, neither white man nor native, has seen the "floating fort" as the savages called our ship. Twelve thousand livres worth of furs have been lost! God must still be holding me to my vows of poverty.
>
> January first we entered an Illinois tribal village with four hundred and sixty huts, much bigger than any village seen in your part of the world. To convince the chief of our value, I had our blacksmith demonstrate the portable forge. Indeed the chief could not resist the prospect of having his hatchets repaired, and soon the tribe softened and shared their corn and smoked meats.

I set my men to work building another fort that I have called Fort Crevecoeur. When we were half done, the Miami tribe arrived in the Illinois village and created dissension. While the Illinois chief sees our exploration as an advantage to his people, the Miami chief thinks we are usurpers. One of their chiefs painted horrifying pictures of the Native Territory. On rough boards, he had sketched bodies mounted on spikes, their hearts ripped out of their chest. On rock faces, he drew huge cooking pots with arms and legs protruding. These caused six of my men to desert.

We are short-handed and need a dozen able-bodied Christian men to continue this work. Madeleine, if you come upon any capable, morally upright men, please share our vision and recruit them. My heart sags with these setbacks, but I trust God wants this country explored, the savages influenced for Christ, and the path to the Gulf of Mexico mapped clearly.

Continue to intercede on my behalf.

In anticipation of the future, yours faithfully,

RLS

More losses. Men and equipment, and most precious of all: time. He had lost at least a year of his life. Robert would have to rebuild the Griffon. He had named his newest fort *Fort Crevecoeur* or Fort Heartbreak.

Spring planting started earlier than usual because of a premature thaw. With Tonnere harnessed to the drag and the extra hands of Full Moon, Claude and I cultivated and seeded our fields by mid-May. This work kept my mind off Robert and my future.

. . .

"I mustered my last supply of energy to cross this lake and come to you," Robert's hoarse voice confided a few days later in May. "I've pushed myself over the last six hundred miles, Madeleine." He sighed deeply and looked worn, thin, and tense. He had arrived on foot with three men. "I had to see you. I've lost Fort Niagara too!" Robert choked.

"Fort Niagara? What happened?"

"A dozen men mutinied and burned down the main building, so only a few loyal men were still there when we returned from Fort Crevecoeur." He cleared his throat and stared out toward the bay.

I rose from the swing and walked around Robert. Placing my hands on his shoulders, I kneaded them to the rhythm of his rocking. His muscles did not yield to my ministrations. But Robert himself gave in to my invitation to stay and recuperate while his men left for Fort Frontenac. Maybe our being together would restore him.

We discussed other challenges. To avoid facing hostile savages, he and his men masqueraded as a band of natives. They left carcasses of butchered animals behind, giving the sense they were careless and powerful and did not need to take the usual precautions. They posted charcoal drawings of human figures on tree trunks to symbolize their prisoners and drew scalps to indicate the number of their captives.

When he finished sharing his tale, I handed him a mug of cold cider. Then I knelt and took his hands in mine. "Robert, a messenger came Tuesday." A knot stuck in my throat.

His blue eyes held mine. He waited.

"The ship bringing your cargo from France foundered in the Gulf of Quebec. Your creditors say you are cursed, even mad, that it is folly to invest in your schemes."

He jumped up and walked the porch, clenching and unclenching his fists, the tension in his body that of a lithe cat about to pounce. He caught my hand and grabbed it to his face, kissing the back of it. He turned it over and kissed the palm, holding his dried and cracked lips to my skin. "Mad? Madeleine, I am not mad. Am I?" Tears reddened his eyes while he stood rigid in silence, awaiting my answer.

. . .

After recuperating, Robert left by himself for Montreal. He would have to face his creditors, justify his losses, and negotiate more loans to continue his exploits.

Was Robert mad? He had faced one defeat after another. What kept him going? He had a deep-rooted faith that God's hand was directing his explorations. Only his ideas of God's sovereignty and purpose could explain Robert's perseverance and unstinting focus on accomplishing his goal.

My own faith waxed and waned. If daily life were going smoothly and if I had slept well at night, I thought little about God. But when Tonnere stumbled in the ravine and his knee had swollen, I prayed for God to heal him. When Claude's simplicity and thick-headedness irked me or Full Moon's disdain rankled, I prayed for patience.

...

When I saw Robert paddling up the bay, grinning and waving, at the end of July 1680, joy washed over me. He had been successful in his business dealings. Most of his creditors had realized a shipwreck was no one person's fault. Robert, with his usual enthusiasm, had outlined his accomplishments, minimized his losses, and rebuilt his capital base. All he needed now was another twenty-two hundred livres to be off again.

The first night Robert camped on the front lawn while I stayed awake in my room. I laid out the account books over my bed. The success of this trading post now permitted me to invest in Robert's activities. Should I loan him the twenty-two hundred livres? Would he accept this and go into debt to me?

The next morning, while Robert and I worked side by side, I stocking items on the shelves and he bagging twenty-pound sacks of seeds into burlap, I made my offer.

"Mat-tee, I can't accept all your savings."

"I'll earn more. Parrot's Bay is successful, as you've seen for yourself. How many traders came through here yesterday? Seven? Ten? Every day during the good season it is like this. I want to help you." It was dusty work, and I was thirsty. "Come," I said. "Let's go wash up and have some spring water. We'll toast to our new partnership."

Kneeling on the dock, we sloshed the grime off our faces and rinsed our arms. I struggled to hold my silence. If he accepted my loan, I would be the first woman to invest in his westward explorations.

As we sat on the boulders by the shore, Robert surveyed the land around us. "This is all yours, isn't it, Madeleine?"

"Yes. You know that."

"There are widows who hold property bequeathed to them when their husbands died, such as Annie Noleen, but you are the first woman in this colony to own her own land. Yes?"

I smiled. What was he thinking?

"My dear, I will accept your loan. Who is to say one of my creditors cannot be a woman? Parrot's Bay will continue to succeed and turn a profit." Robert took hold of my hands. "Thank you, Mat-tee."

In an unguarded moment, he lifted me off the ground and spun me around, exhilarated, then placed me down and steadied me with a quick embrace. "Come. There is work to do. I'll leave day after tomorrow." With a boyish grin, he bounded up the bank.

The gray-blue sky was shifting to pink at the horizon when Robert paddled me out to watch the sun set. Orange and red rays shot through the clouds. Some billows seemed lined with gold, their rich blue exterior a sharp contrast to their dazzling underbelly.

"Move into the middle of the canoe," Robert suggested. "Come sit by me." I turned and inched forward from the bow to the stern, folded my skirt under me and rested on my knees, facing Robert.

Robert smoothed an errant curl away, ran his finger over my cheek, and lifted my hands. "Mat-tee." He cleared his throat and gestured to the west. "Madeleine, when all this is over, would you become my partner for life?"

My heart swelled so I thought it might burst.

"It will take several more years," he went on. "We are in good health. You can continue to build up Parrot's Bay, and it will become our home. We can have children here. Once I have found the route to the Gulf of

Mexico and secured this country for France, you will be my wife until death. What do you say?"

"Oh, yes, Robert. Yes."

He leaned over and kissed me. He pulled my cap off and seized my hair to thrust my mouth on to his. Our tongues danced together wet and hard, anticipating what was to come. Loons called to each other in the distance. We broke away to get air, and I turned and leaned against his strong legs, nestling into his arms. Evening breezes whispered across the water and lapped against the canoe. The sounds of dusk told us creatures were settling in for the night.

Later that night, I couldn't fall sleep. I tiptoed out on to the porch and found Robert also awake. Pulling my shawl over my shoulders, I stood by him. He drew me down onto his lap. His right thumb circled my palm and glided up each finger, thrilling me. Firmly, his hand lifted my lips to his, and he kissed me. He put his hand on the back of my hair and ran his fingers through my curls, kissing me again and again. I could feel his breath quicken. I shifted closer toward him. He gripped my shoulders, exhaled on my neck, then found the soft spot on my throat with his lips and left his mark. He was panting now, and I felt him underneath me. I shifted on his lap, hungry for more. My lips were hot and wet.

In the next breath, Robert stopped and groaned. "Oh, Mat-tee, this is not the right time for us."

I exhaled. "Robert, no. It's fine. We are betrothed." I stood up. "I want you."

"And I want you. But we should be married in the eyes of the church. God will bless us for waiting."

"Then let us be married tomorrow. Isn't there a priest at Fort Frontenac? I want you before you leave. I want to make a baby with you."

As soon as those words came out of my mouth, I knew I had made a mistake. Robert broke all contact and rose to leave. "And I want to be there for the birth of my son. We must wait."

Our bodies had urged us forward while our morality held us back. The loneliness I felt lying in bed that night cut deeply. My betrothed was respecting my body, and the decision was physically painful. Yet a sense of rightness and security wrapped itself around the ache and drew me deeper in love with Robert.

...

The next day Robert was set to leave for Niagara, when a fast canoe paddled by three men rounded the corner, the soldiers breathless and flush. I ran from the dock back to the trading post to get water for our guests. Upon returning, I saw the look on Robert's face. A soldier took the water gourd from my trembling hands.

"These men from Fort Frontenac say mutineers are heading this way to murder me," he said.

Stunned at the idea of someone murdering Robert, I cried out, "Why?"

"Mutineers have turned their fury against the Fort Crevecoeur and taken the portable forge, the plank saws, and other supplies and abandoned it. Some of the traitors are fleeing to Albany. But twelve are crossing the lake to do me in. They think I'm vulnerable, that the best way to avoid punishment is to kill me off first."

Robert, Claude, and the three men gathered up their arms; stocked their canoes with ammunition, food, and water; and pushed off into the lake. Two other canoes would join them within the hour, and they would move into Quinte's Bay, west of us by thirty miles. They would wait for the mutineers.

My old dream, where a man in the crimson cloak was shot in the head, came back to haunt me. Then God's word came to me: "Yield. I am in control."

But I couldn't submit. I was not about to loosen my grip.

# PART FIVE:

## The Burgeoning

# 25

# FOREBODING OMENS

Two weeks later, an invigorated and confident Robert leapt onto my dock and squeezed my shoulder like a comrade-at-arms. Five other canoes trolled in the bay waiting for him to make this brief stop.

"We have triumphed! Ten prisoners were taken. I killed two at the ambush. These coureur de bois will pay for their crimes. Messages have been sent to the governor in Quebec and also to the New York governor in Albany to insure these prisoners will be punished."

With these tidings, Robert lowered himself into his canoe, swung it around to meet his companions, and paddled off.

Relief swept over me. LaSalle would drop the prisoners at Fort Frontenac and then make his way west to start over again.

I would wait, bide my time through this year's harvest, and suspend my life through yet another winter.

...

On December 20, 1680, a comet blazoned the clear, ebony sky. The large, bright ball swam across the night's atmosphere trailing a long, filmy, white tail, like a rich lady's bridal veil.

The natives believed comets brought bad luck. Claude had to console Full Moon as she was convinced the comet was a foreboding omen. I remembered the Reverend Mother Marie thought comets were signs from God about his activity in this world, signaling either an unusual blessing or a powerful judgment. Robert, wherever he was, would probably be studying the comet with his telescope and astrolabe and making scientific notes about its location and appearance.

As for me, I marveled at the comet's beauty as I stood under the ennobled heavens. I felt at peace.

...

A letter came March 25, 1681.

> Fort Saint Joseph, Illinois River, January 2, 1681.
>
> Oh, my heart of hearts. Fort Crevecoeur is completely in ruins. All is destroyed!
>
> When we arrived there a month ago we found a mysterious inscription engraved on the planking:
>
> We Are All Savages, On This 15 A... , 1680.
>
> The evil of the Iroquois surrounds us. We often come upon villages with nothing left except a few ends of burnt poles. On these charred ends are the heads of dead men, their eyes and flesh eaten by crows. In the fields are half-devoured corpses, skeletons pulled from ransacked graves, ripped to fleshy shreds by wolves. In some villages, we come upon kettles, rusted and scummy, filled with the boney remains of human captives.
>
> Tonty has disappeared. I force myself to examine every scalp and every corpse, looking for his telltale blond hair or his iron hand.
>
> My men wanted me to continue south on the Illinois River, in search of the Mississippi. But my loyalty to Tonty consumes me. I have to travel north until I learn news of my captain.
>
> Please sustain me with your prayers. I watched the strikingly beautiful comet and wondered if you were marveling at it too. Some of my men feel it was a sign of doom and that we must vacate this territory. Others follow my lead and take a more rational approach.
>
> Persevere with me, my dear. While a thousand miles separates us, we still look up at the same sun and the same moon each day. The stars create a shared canopy in our

heavens. The next time you see the sunset, a melting of purple and orange on the western horizon, think of me. I will be watching it and dreaming of you. Ever yours. RLS

P.S. I have given this letter's courier some glass beads for his trouble, but would you please augment his gift with something more substantial, say, a frying pan or a pair of tweezers? RLS

...

During the last week of April, ice cracking joined the symphony of trumpeting Canada geese coming up from the south. We became hopeful spring would arrive.

A courier navigated his canoe around the ice floes toward our trading post. He handed me a letter from LaSalle. While we served the man a hot meal, he reported a tough winter in the pays d'en haut: snow falling every day, little sunshine, and below zero temperatures.

I let Full Moon serve the courier while I left to read Robert's letter.

Miami Tribal village, Western shore of Lake Michigan. March 7, 1681.
Dearest Madeleine,

My heart is warmed thinking of you, my partner, my muse. This has been a very cold winter, but I will not complain. I have chosen to walk down this road no matter the conditions.

Madeleine, I want you to discuss this idea with the right people at Fort Frontenac. We need to form a defensive league of the western tribes in the Illinois Valley. The tribes here, when they stand alone, are too small in number to be effective against the powerful Iroquois. My mission should be to strengthen France's alliance with the Miami, the Illinois, and the Ojibway. Together we can defend this country against the violence of the Iroquois.

A brief description of my diplomacy with the Miamis and the Illinois may give you an understanding of my work.

When it became known the Iroquois were gathering on the southern shore of Lake Erie to prepare for war, I knew the smaller tribes needed to stand in unison. I have developed a reputation for being a great orator because I speak the savages' words and understand their metaphors. Two days after giving them gifts, I donned the crimson cape, raised my calumet, and took my place in the chief's lodge. There I spoke of my loyalty to France and asked them all for justice and unity against our common enemy.

Madeleine, the natives' response exceeded my expectations. I was feted and revered and covered with wampum necklaces.

Now I need to get support for this defensive league from my creditors and from Governor Frontenac. *Au revoir.* RLS.

P.S. My lips are finally healing from exposure to the cold, and the cracks in my fingertips have stopped bleeding. I used some of that salve you gave me. Thank you for your foresight. R.

...

In July, I journeyed to Montreal at the time of the fur fair for several reasons. Claude and Full Moon needed private time, as Full Moon blamed Claude for the lack of fruit in her womb, while he remained silent in the face of her assaults. His stoicism angered her, and her sharp tongue irritated me.

I also wanted to hear the news of the country, especially opinions about the defensive league of the Great Lake tribes. All I knew was Robert's perspective. Plus, an iron object called "scissors," just two knives bolted together to cut rope or fabric, was a popular item, and I wanted an ample supply.

The Montreal of 1681 had changed from the time I had been a resident. The waterfront teemed with people and ships, houses had gone up everywhere, and a dozen dirt-packed roads ran from the river up the mountainside. I set up an area at the fair—a deer hide canopy under which I placed some of my best furs, along with the collection of beaded moccasins, vests, and capes we had received from the Cataraqui natives.

On my first afternoon, I saw a Sulpician priest approach, walking with intent toward me. At first, I watched with curiosity. But then my heart sank. He was Jean Cavelier, Robert's brother. The last time I had seen him was at Fort Frontenac when he had come to investigate his brother's "morality." How many years ago was that? Five?

"Mademoiselle D'Allone?" The overweight, gray-robed priest addressed me. "I didn't expect to see you here." He made a jerky, shallow bow at his thick waist. The Sulpician had put on weight over the years, and the flesh in his round face was sallow and flecked with blood veins. But his blue eyes made my heart leap as I thought of Robert.

"Ah, yes. Father Cavelier." I held out my hand as a courtesy. When he didn't take it, I shifted my posture quickly and began to adjust some of the items in my booth. The priest's wolfish gaze made me uncomfortable.

"What news do you hear from my brother, Mademoiselle? I have heard nothing since the winter closed in on us."

I was cautious, not sure what Father Cavelier wanted from me. "His last correspondence reached me in March, Father. He expressed good spirits."

I sensed he was scheming.

The priest pushed. "When do you expect him back? In '82 or '83?"

"Sometime this summer, Father, he may journey to the Fort Frontenac area."

"This year? So soon? I don't understand why he expends his energy coming the hundreds of miles back from the pays d'en haut every year. He should be building up his physical and financial reserves at his newest fort."

The priest's tone put me on edge. "I believe your brother thinks the effort of traveling back is warranted by his need to keep his communications open with you and his creditors. And of course, he needs to report to his leader, Governor Frontenac."

"If you see my brother before I do, tell him I appreciated his letter from last September," the priest said with sarcasm."It certainly clarified a concern I had." The priest shuffled around in his pocket and pulled out a well-worn parchment. Silently, he eyed me, baiting me. Like a wary fish that senses the hook in the bait, I held back.

But when my hunger overcame my sense of caution, I bit. "Is that a letter from the Sieur de LaSalle? I would be interested in seeing it."

"Why of course, Mademoiselle. You are welcome to read it." Cavelier handed it to me with a twisted grin.

Then I read in Robert's own hand:

> So you are uneasy about my pretended marriage. I had not thought about it at that time, but I shall not make any engagement of the sort till I have given you reason to be satisfied with me. I must say, dear brother, it is a little extraordinary that I need to render account to you on a matter which is free to most men in the world...

My heart constricted and blood rushed to my face. *"Pretended marriage... I shall not make any engagement..."* Forcing myself to breathe, I returned the letter to Robert's brother."How kind of you, Father. Now I must tend to these traders."

I pulled away to talk with a few customers and forced myself to keep my composure. Cavelier watched me. Finally, the priest lumped away, looking like a well-fed rodent.

I seethed with anger on my way back to Duprays,' formerly Noleen's. When I arrived at the trading post, Alice offered me supper. But I mumbled excuses and sought refuge in my room.

Confusion blinded me. Had I misunderstood Robert's proposal? Was this a trick on Cavelier's part? Or had Robert changed his mind about his commitment to me and chosen not to tell me? Was this all a matter of money? If Robert reneged on the marriage proposal, was he afraid I'd pull away my credit? In fact, had he asked me to marry him because he needed my money?

I wanted to scream. Covering my head with a pillow, I threw myself on the bed and cried until hiccups got the best of me. I must have slept, finally, because I awoke when the moon was high in the sky and the waterfront quiet. A dog barked in the distance. Tears crusted my eyes, and I could taste salt around my mouth.

Standing at the window I thought back over all my times with Robert. He usually talked about his dreams and visions, rarely inquiring about mine. His mind schemed as in a game of chess. Was I another part of his calculations? Was his interest in me solely to further his strategy of western expansion? Or were his words placating his brother, as Robert needed Cavelier's credit as well as mine?

No matter how I turned the problem, the fact remained: Robert had lied. He had either lied to me when he said he wanted to marry me, or he had lied to his brother when he said he would not become engaged unless his brother approved.

My heart turned cold. Had I made a colossal mistake when I said "yes"?

...

The next day, the Montreal fairgrounds bustled, and the crowd hummed with excitement. Two French soldiers were marching in the direction of my booth; a tall man with a full head of red hair reminded me of someone. Oh, my heart, it was Wilhelm Jenet accompanied by a shorter, swarthier comrade.

"Wilhelm, Wilhelm!" I waved. Dressed smartly in his uniform, he saluted in my direction. "Mademoiselle Madeleine, you are a far way from home!" He bowed and clicked his heels. I would have hugged him hard except for the reserve that had settled over him and the curious eyes of his mate-in-arms.

"My friend!" I offered my hand. His partner stood in a military pose as Captain Jenet and I exchanged courtesies.

"I'm boarding at Dupray's Trading Post. Perhaps when you are off duty we might visit? I'd love to hear all about Francois."

Wilhelm came by on June 20, 1681. He had aged, having more wrinkles and some graying in his red hair. He was stationed in Montreal at Governor Frontenac's request. "The honorable governor believes I should be on the frontier to keep the savages at bay. He's impressed with my knowledge of Iroquois—thanks to you, Madeleine."

So pleased was I to see him, my questions ran away with themselves. "But where is your son? And your wife? I heard you had remarried?"

"I had to leave them in Quebec. Ellen cares for her father and Francois. The lad's seven now. The government expects me to stay in military quarters while on the frontier. They assign us in six-month stints. I'll be returning before the snow falls." He gave me a moment to digest his news. "Now, tell me. How is your little corner of the world?"

"Satisfactory and out of harm's reach. We have a good business. Despite the rumors of trouble with the natives, Parrot's Bay welcomes them and the French men alike. If we see trouble, it is petty."

"I hope it stays that way. I have my concerns about our Governor Frontenac. He can be two-faced. He'll outline a policy one day and renege on it the next. I guess that is a common trait of a politician, but I don't like it."

My tongue felt dry. Those very words could describe LaSalle. "Wilhelm, would you like something cold to drink?"

Returning with two large mugs of sweet cider, I handed one to Wilhelm. "Tell me about Francie. Is he doing well? Have the people in Quebec accepted him?"

"Ah, he misses you." Wilhelm sipped. "And my boy wants people to call him Francois now. He feels he's too old for 'Francie'! His most happy memories are of you, Midnight, and Tonnere. How are they?"

"When last I saw them, they were healthy. And as loyal as ever." I settled myself into a porch rocker.

"Francois is getting used to Ellen and Captain Migault. Some Quebecois still have difficulty with my son's native blood, but he has learned to shrug off ridicules. More importantly, he is developing his strengths passed down from both his French and his Huron heritage. He's proud of his ability to speak the native language. Occasionally we've traveled to Loretteville, a half-day's walk, so he can mix with other native children. Ah, did you know Sainte Foye took its village and moved there so they could have more space?"

Wilhelm took the other rocker and stretched his long legs out. "Ellen is intrigued by native culture. In my absence, she opens her home to some of the girls to teach them French or to sew and cook in the French, all in exchange for learning their way of doing things."

The mention of Loretteville stirred my memories. For a moment, I wondered if he had met Chief Tree-on-the-Rock and his children, Flower Eyes and Tonato. While I was curious, enough pain lingered in my heart about Tonato's abandonment that I remained quiet.

I asked Wilhelm about Captain Migault. "Was he a seafaring captain, who brought his daughter over from France to wed you?"

"Yes. Sadly, during Captain's last visit in June 1680 to his French village of Mouton, royal dragoons beat him up for his religious beliefs. He hasn't been the same since, forgetful and moody. He tried to captain the last voyage of 1680 back to Quebec, but his first mate had to take over.

"When his ship arrived in port last December, the captain was released into Ellen's care and has been with us ever since. He's only in his late forties, but he acts much older. The Catholic bullies smashed his head with clubs, shattered his knee caps, and broke his arms."

"My God, what was the fight about?"

Wilhelm looked around for people within earshot. Seeing none, he explained. "Ellen Migault and her family are Huguenots. The captain was defending his right to worship as he chose, a principle guaranteed in the Edict of Nantes. The Catholic dragoons wanted to convince him to do otherwise."

I recalled the caution the Huguenots had exhibited when we crossed the ocean ten years earlier. Judith Bratten and I had spent hours walking the ship's deck and talking about Jesus. Where were the Brattens now? I looked warily into my friend's eyes and asked, "Wilhelm, are you now a Huguenot?"

"I am." Wilhelm held my gaze. The corner of his mouth twitched. Hesitating for a moment, he asked, "Does that disturb you, Madeleine?" Catholics were expected to shun the Protestants.

"No, my friend. Annie became a follower of Christ before she died. She would read the Bible to me and tell me we didn't need the church or a priest. She died content, anticipating heaven. I believe it was her personal relationship with Jesus that gave her such peace. But I have often wondered about the Huguenots' form of religion. I have many questions." I sipped my cider slowly. "Why did you convert?"

"After my first wife, Marie-Anne, rejected our son and me, I found no solace or understanding in the Catholic Church. The Catholics were the people most offended by Francois's mixed blood, as if God never intended the white man to mingle with the red man. I didn't want to bring my son up worshipping the white-robed, holier-than-thou Christ of that church.

"During the winter of '78, we took a room near the Quebec harbor and got to know Captain Migault. At that time, he was in his prime, a clear thinker, a lover of God. He knew his Bible. He stripped away the trappings of the church and focused on Jesus of Nazareth. The captain taught me how to repent without the intrusion of a priest and how to be cleansed spiritually without doing acts of contrition. I receive forgiveness as a gift from God now. Then Captain Migault revealed to me the power of the Holy Spirit that flows to us from the resurrected Christ.

"It took a while, but the more I read the Bible, the more I believed in Jesus. I yielded to the Lord's energy. That supernatural power has been indwelling me since 1679. I am a new man because of it." Examining Wilhelm's face, I could see that same peacefulness that had clothed Annie during her last days. What was it that gave them such deep joy and contentment? What was this "power of the Holy Spirit"?

...

While the fair was winding down, Wilhelm and I met often. On the closing day of the fur fair, we strolled along the riverbank, knowing this would be our last visit for some time.

"More persecution in France, Mat-tee—soldier against Huguenot, Catholic against Protestant. The king has published a declaration excluding Protestants from all public offices, so many can't earn a living."

Wilhelm's mouth was set, and his neck turned red as he continued. "My brother-in-law, a schoolmaster, had to move his wife and ten children to the village of Mouton. His wife, heavily into her eleventh pregnancy, wasn't doing well. The royal dragoons had spread out into the countryside to enforce obedience to the king's orders and curtail the rights of the Huguenots.

"The Migault family feared for their future. Fortunately the town of Mouton is tolerant. As of April this year, the Migaults have been managing fairly well. But I worry about him and my other brothers in the Lord. Madeleine, should I return to France to help them?"

"What would France offer you? What could you possibly do for them?" I asked. "Besides, how would you support yourself? At least here you have Governor Frontenac's endorsement and will always have a post in his military, *n'est-çe pas*? Certainly Francois would have a difficult time fitting into the old country. His mixed blood would be tolerated less there than in this country, don't you think?"

"I suppose you're right." Wilhelm remained pensive as we moved along the path, watching the river current send debris to the Atlantic.

After a while, he said, "Madeleine, you haven't mentioned Sieur de LaSalle."

I didn't respond. Turning upriver, I looked to the west and wondered how to answer. Wilhelm probed. "I thought you two had a future together."

A knot formed in my throat. Who better than Wilhelm to discuss my confusion, the letter, the "pretended engagement"?

So, seating myself on a boulder, I told him of Robert's proposal, the content of the letters I had received this winter, and then the recent, painful encounter with Jean Cavelier. I sighed. "So I believe Robert is a liar. He's either lying to Jean about me or to me about the engagement."

Wilhelm sat down, saying nothing. The slapping of the waves against the river's edge muted my crying and calmed me.

"You knew Robert well. What do you think is going on? What should I do?" I asked.

Wilhelm picked up pebbles and studied them as if they held the answer. "Ah, he was probably trying to keep his brother off his back." My friend began tossing stones into the St. Lawrence. I watched as each rippled on the surface. "You do realize, Madeleine, LaSalle is closed up tighter than a hatch in a storm when it comes to revealing himself. He may think a commitment to a woman is a weakness. Certainly, you know I don't believe such an idea. My Ellen has become my life. I would be a fool to pretend otherwise. But your Robert is independent and proud, as you know."

He brushed soil off his palm and sat looking out on to the water. The sun, below the horizon now, signaled we needed to be heading back, but he continued. "When can you talk with LaSalle about this? Soon? Will he come back this summer?"

I hesitated. "I never know when he'll come into my life. You think I should ask him about his lying, Wilhelm? I'm not sure he can be trusted."

Jenet pushed shore pebbles around with his toe. "Have you ever lied, Madeleine? I certainly have. I'm not proud of it, but there have been times where a lie has helped me get out of a tight spot. Perhaps LaSalle justified the lie in order for him to accomplish his goal. He does need both yours and his brother's support, right? Maybe Robert knew you would forgive him but thought Cavelier would not be as tolerant. So he had to tell his brother he is not planning on marrying, even though he is. And I suspect that LaSalle never once imagined Cavelier would show you his letter."

Wilhelm helped me up. I brushed off my skirt and wiped my tear-stained face. Jenet had a good way of putting my problems in perspective. Reaching into my apron pocket, I drew out the letter I had written to Francie. Half of the words were in French and half were in Iroquois.

"Wilhelm, will you see that Francie gets this? I want to be sure he knows I am thinking of him. I don't have a quill with me, but would you please change his name to 'Francois'?"

"He won't care if you call him Francie. But you'll be surprised how tall he is, how old he seems. Francois fits him better. And if you don't mind the delay, I'll carry it with my personal effects for the next few months and then deliver it in person. That way it is sure to arrive, and I'll have the pleasure of seeing my son's face when he reads it."

"Wilhelm, next summer, please bring Francois to Parrot's Bay, will you? Let him see what the wilderness is like again. He may be forgetting the beauty of the lake and the forest, what with all that citified life he's leading in Quebec."

# 26

# MANAGING MUCK

"Madeleine, stop this." Robert yanked my shoulder hard so I had to rise and face him. I pulled back and crouched down to attend to the garden.

"Stop what, Robert?" I said, gritting my teeth.

"Your attitude, your coldness. You have uttered barely a word to me since my return."

Two days before that hot July day in 1681, LaSalle and his captain Henri Tonty had arrived by canoe. Robert's welcome was constrained, so I kept busy with chores, the whole time my heart dying inside.

"And you?" I challenged him. "You've welcomed me with open arms? You've expressed gladness at seeing me?"

He blanched. "Well, no. But I am neither expressive nor ebullient. Ask Tonty. Even when I found him after a year and a half, I could do nothing more than shake his hand. Displays are not in my nature." He wiped his brow.

"Well, in your absence, I've thought carefully and decided that if you are going to be cool and standoffish, I'll meet you in kind."

"But that is not you!" Robert nearly shouted.

"I'm adapting to the role you place me in." I wrenched another large burdock out by its roots, shook the soil off, letting the breeze carry flecks of dirt onto LaSalle's britches.

"The 'role I place you in'?" With his left hand on my elbow, he drew me up to my full height. This time I did not resist. His other hand lifted my chin firmly, and he looked me in the eyes. "What is going on?"

Summoning my courage, I said, "You want me as a business partner? A business partner I will be. I believe in the work you are doing. But I am not sure I can trust you."

"Why can't you trust me?" Robert let go of me.

"Let's walk," I said. "Tonnere needs a visit." With that, I turned my back and strode to the pasture.

He kept pace.

As we walked, I unveiled my encounter with Jean Cavelier at the Montreal Fur Fair.

"*Sacre Coeur!* Oh, Mat-tee, I'm so sorry! Please let me explain." His face reddened. "My dear heart, in my not making you my wife legally, my creditors will not hunt you down if my mission fails. I need people like my brother to know that, or you become vulnerable."

"Then why did you ask me to marry you?"

"I want us to join together in legal marriage after I have succeeded."

"And what is your definition of 'success'?" I demanded. "One more fort established? Another ten thousand livres in the treasure chest under your bed?"

"You know my goal is to claim the Gulf of Mexico and that part of this continent for France."

"Well, you have already done that!"

"Mat-tee, I mean to locate the Gulf from both the northern route and then the southern route. I'll chart a clear passage from the Gulf to Quebec on a map and claim that western region for King Louis. I plan on leaving for Louisiana as soon as matters are resolved here."

"What matters?" I sounded whiney, a little child pouting.

"You, for one." He sighed and let out another breath before adding, "My dearest." And he held out his hand to me. When I didn't respond, he let his fall lifelessly to his side. Then he leaned against the rail fence and watched Tonnere languidly chomp on the summer grass. Finally he whispered, "Don't be angry with me. I returned to Parrot's Bay for you. To fill up my well. With you."

"And which well is that, Robert? Your pocket book? Your stomach? Your reputation?"

He took my face in his hands and kissed me on my lips, lingering. "You are my source of joy, of my well-being, Mat-tee. Your soul fills up my spiritual well." He pulled me into his arms and stroked my hair. "You complete me."

My heart thudded against his chest. I had yearned to hear those words for years.

But his endearments didn't negate the fact Robert had lied. What was I doing melting into him?

Robert spoke softly. "I need your love and respect. Your friendship is priceless. I believe we're soul mates."

With the fence supporting me, I looked into the distance. He inhaled, steadied himself, and continued. "Please forgive me. I did lie, a bit to you and a bit to my brother. When I wrote the letter, I had hoped the way I phrased my words was truthful. But I know now it was not."

People say forgiveness means you cease to resent the other person for the wrong he has committed against you, but you may not forget the wrong. I wanted to be able to do this with Robert, to forgive him for his self-protective lie. But it was not coming naturally.

"Robert, why would I commit to a man who does not tell the truth?"

"Madeleine, I've never lied to you before. As God is my witness, I believe lying is a sin." He stood taller and asked, "Is there a penance I could do?"

"Promise you will never lie to me again."

"That I can do. Mat-tee, I won't lie to you again."

"So tell me you don't want me to be your wife *now*. Did you not write to me about the advantages it was to you and your travelers that the natives took their squaws with them on the trips?"

"Those squaws functioned as servants and bedmates. You and I are above that."

Tonnere meandered over to the fence, and Robert rubbed his nose on the muzzle of the horse. Robert's long hair fell forward, tickling the beast's velvety snout. The horse pulled back his lips and blew out a sneeze. Tonnere, startled at his own sound, jumped back and eyed his former master with surprise. I laughed.

LaSalle remained serious. "Madeleine, if we join our fortunes now, it could be downright dangerous. If I fail, you might lose all you've worked for. I've already written a will making my cousin DuPlet the executor of my estate and passing my savings on to you. This plan will keep you safe from the creditors."

*And cut me out of your life*, I thought.

On impulse, angry and confounded, I scrambled up the split rail fence, grabbed hold of Tonnere's mane with my left hand, bunched my skirt up, and threw myself onto the horse's back. "Let me think, Robert!" I shouted. And with that, I kicked the stallion in the flanks and loped off.

The horse ran hard. I concentrated on staying seated as I rode bareback with no bridle to control my mount. I molded myself into Tonnere's body and clung forward to his neck. We ran. And ran. I loved feeling the wind on my face. But I knew I would have to sort out the conflicting feelings from that morning's conversation.

...

The next day I left Claude and Full Moon in charge and canoed onto the lake to avoid LaSalle. Rounding the end of Parrot's Bay, I tied up to a low-hanging tree. Robert did not have the courage to tell his brother that I was his soul mate and he desired to marry me. I felt so hurt, so unable to forgive. Was this another time in my life when men were using me?

If I did forgive Robert, then I should forgive Tonato. But Tonato used me for his release with no sense of commitment to me as a woman and little respect for my feelings. Was it homesickness that enticed him away? Or was he afraid of our relationship? That I would have driven a wedge between his people and himself? And if Robert and Tonato should be forgiven, then I should forgive Bowers and his wretched debauchment at the fort. And what about that knave who stole my innocence, Galouis? Never! I was nothing more than a girl when he used me for his own pleasure and left me feeling shamed and dirty. Forgive him? Impossible.

What did I know about forgiveness? Reverend Mother Marie had experienced both the need to forgive and to be forgiven. To hold true to her faith, Mother Marie had to find the way to forgive her sister and family. She also struggled with her own feelings of guilt when she chose to give up her twelve-year-old son when she entered holy orders. By the time I met her, she was well practiced in God's power of forgiveness. Mother Marie was confident that forgiveness was the essential reason God sent Jesus to mankind. Her words explained this. "We humans cannot ever make things right with God. There is no forgiveness without Jesus' death on the cross. There is no power to forgive without Jesus' resurrection from the tomb. To forgive, we must have the unleashing of his Holy Spirit."

Annie had lived over sixty years carrying a baggage of guilt. Yet she came to accept Jesus' forgiveness for her abortion and rebellion against God. In so doing, she had found peace with the Almighty. I envied these women.

Sprawled on the bottom of the canoe, I gazed at the sky. Cottony forms mesmerized me as they drifted across the clear heavens. Waves slapping on the hull of the canoe soothed me into sleep.

I dreamt I was alone in a small boat, comfortable and secure, Suddenly storm clouds burst forth in the western sky. Waves swelled. Within minutes, I shivered with cold, wet, and fear as water washed into the boat. I clung to the sides. Foam writhed and churned. My heart clutched and pounded. My breath quickened as the angry lake lifted my boat up and threw it down.

Then a boiling wave came right at me. In it I could see Joseph Galouis winking at me. That wave broke over my head, throwing me off balance. I grabbed again for the gunnels. Another wave, rising five feet above me, twisted its white effervescence and became the sneering face of Tom Bowers. As that wave slammed down, the canoe bucked. Another frothy image rose up. And it was Tonato—not just his face, but also his hardened body. That wave slapped me hard. I fought to clear my eyes and catch my breath.

When another huge wave rose in front of me, I cringed. In it was my father dressed in his finery, reaching his hand out to take me to the courtier. That wave broke over me, and my ears roared. Then all was quiet. As quickly as the storm arose, the wind died down, and the waves calmed. The sun, dazzled with silver and white, broke out from behind purple-blue clouds. The glare hurt. I had to close my eyes.

I awoke then. My heart raced, and sweat drenched my bodice. I sat up. My hair was dry, and the bottom of the canoe held no water. From the angle of the afternoon sun, an hour had gone by. My sense of unreality seeped away.

I saw a small black object moving toward me in the lake. As it came closer, it grew larger. Ah, Midnight! This loyal dog had swum all the way out of the bay to find me. His presence brought me out of the nightmare. I reached out for the scruff of his neck, hauling him up. Midnight flopped into the boat, splattering water.

As I hugged him, I pondered my dream. Perhaps the men who had used me were nothing more than storm waves in my life. They could threaten me, but they would not drown me. Maybe I could forgive them. God had been using them to make me a better, stronger person. He was redeeming the damage they had done in my life.

I decided to tell Robert I would forgive him with God's help. With that decision, a holy peace swaddled me. As Midnight and I watched the sun slide down the horizon, all was serene.

...

LaSalle wrote a formal acknowledgment on August 24, 1681, of the credit I extended him. This paperwork was a symbol of how we had resolved our differences. To the public eye, I was one of LaSalle's creditors, a respected merchant. Robert felt it necessary to put this relationship on record primarily to protect me.

And I accepted that publicly. But I knew in my heart what transpired privately between us. My forgiveness of his duplicity strengthened our bond, as if the metal in our relationship had been thrown into a refining fire and had come out cleaner and purer.

We worked side-by-side, preparing his maps, refreshing his language skills, and organizing his supplies. I collected medicinal herbs for his pack and pounded together ointments for everything from insect repellants to wound salves. We set up bales of smoked meat, corn meal, and dried peas, all wrapped in animal bladders. Claude found some fresh feathers for the ceremonial calumet and refurbished it. Finally I cleaned and mended the crimson cape.

Evenings Robert and I would sit on the porch discussing our future. He remained reluctant to show his affection for me. The occasions in which he reached for my hand were treasured moments.

Robert dared not talk about our old age, what our lives would be like a generation forward. His foreshortened sense became a knot in my stomach.

He left the next day.

...

A courier arrived in November, bringing my first correspondence of the season from Robert.

> Fort Niagara, the Great Falling Waters
> October 1, 1681
> Dearest Madeleine,
>
> Niagara Falls is cascading over its brink and as the mist spews up, I think of your pioneering work in this area. Now, at this halfway point in my five years' concession, I must hasten to complete my plans.
>
> The Iroquois are restless. Frenchmen are often taken prisoner and burned alive. If we are going to dominate this country, we need an alliance with the Iroquois, not their

warfare. The small northern tribes fear these Iroquois and sit quietly listening to my ideas of a defensive alliance.

Unfortunately, these same natives have become lazy because their countryside is so bountiful. They barely have to get out of bed to have their needs met. I use unremitting energy to persuade the tribes to stay organized.

We will be leaving the Niagara frontier and will make the difficult portage to Lake Huron and then paddle to Lake Michigan. Tribes there are ripe for recruitment to the defensive alliance.

Continue to look heavenward, my dear heart. Right now, I can only count on you and Governor Frontenac to be true advocates.

I place my hand in yours. RLS.

...

On March 30, 1682, I received a letter from Wilhelm Jenet via Montreal and Fort Frontenac.

Quebec
March 1, 1682
Dear Madeleine,

The political situation here in Quebec is growing increasingly difficult because of Governor Frontenac's unpopular policy of encouraging expansion and native alliances. The French people are feeling unprotected and vulnerable. They favor Colbert's concept of a close-knit colony, centralized around Quebec City. They believe the savages are unrepentant and vicious, and the government should push them westward. Rumor has it that Frontenac will be recalled any day.

My father-in-law has lost his mind and wanders off frequently, much to Ellen's dismay. Both Migault in his dementia and Francois with his native blood are often ridiculed here in the city. News from France is that the king's soldiers continue to persecute and torture the Huguenots. Protestantism is now stigmatized around Quebec. My people are turned away from employment opportunities, and the merchants won't serve us for fear that they themselves will be considered silent supporters of the Protestant faith and fall into disregard.

How we yearn for the natural quiet and social comfort of Parrot's Bay. When my military commission is done, may we come live with you?

Your friend, Wilhelm.

P.S. Francois has sent you a letter in his own hand. WJ

Dear Mat-Tee, I am learning to read and write French and to speak it better. But I miss learning Iroquois from you. Will I see you soon? When I am sad, my father reminds me of Parrot's Bay. I remember Midnight. How is that old dog? Still swimming with you? Then there is Tonnere. I rode him a few times with my father holding me on, didn't I? How big does a boy have to be to ride a horse by himself? I will be eight this May. And I am tall, my stepmother says.

My best friend here is my Grandfather Migault. He will play games and laugh with me. The town's people call him "Crazy Captain." Soldiers once beat him on the head and made him crazy just because he believed in Jesus differently from them.

Please write back. Your friend, Francois Jenet

How sheltered we were at Parrot's Bay compared to the Jenets in Quebec! I could not imagine being persecuted for my faith, such that it was. The idea of Francois and his parents coming to visit, perhaps even staying here, lightened my heart and gave me pleasant images to ponder while doing my chores.

...

A letter arrived on May 15, 1682, and I took a break from spring planting to read it.

> Gulf of Mexico
> April 10, 1682
> My dearest Madeleine, my soul mate in this endeavor,
>
> Wearing the scarlet cape, I have planted a wooden cross and proclaimed the Gulf of Mexico to be France's territory. Thus Louis XIV is the ruler of the entire Mississippi basin from Texas to the Atlantic, from the Great Lakes to the tropical shores of the Gulf of Mexico. One of my goals has been accomplished!
>
> Now I need to map the Gulf of Mexico so that the entire geographical area can be presented to the king for future colonization.
>
> But, between you and me, Madeleine, this southern area is wild and close to being uninhabitable, with extensive marshes and bayous. The Mississippi blends into the gulf with no clear land mass, only swamps and thick canes of greens forming an ever-changing curtain. The silty bottom of the river merges into the gulf so gradually that it is difficult to find landmarks to use for mapping.
>
> The men grumble because there is no real land, no hard earth surrounding us. We have been eating alligator and turtle for the last few weeks, sleeping in our canoes. The men find these creatures repugnant, even in the manner they must kill the alligators—by cracking their skulls open with an ax. They gripe there is no air to breathe as they stretch out in the boats, like sardines in the crowded hold of a ship. I, of course, must keep up the appearance of contentment and bravery so as to encourage my men by example.
>
> Look to the brightest stars in the southern sky, and remember me in your prayers. RLS

One of Robert's goals had been achieved! I gritted my teeth and crumbled the letter. Robert was planning another trip! I groaned. Would he ever be satisfied?

I could not take all this news in. The barn offered me solace even though Claude had turned Tonnere out and the stallion was not there to be curried and petted.

So I took to mucking out the horse stall. With a three-tine fork, I speared manure and straw and tossed it into a barrel. The rich, rank odor of horse urine assailed my nostrils. I speared again, vigorously. The stall had not been cleaned out for a good while. By sprinkling clean straw on the top of the damp refuse, the real mess had been covered up. The whole process made me think of government: how the rulers and authorities have a way of making circumstances appear clean on the surface, but underneath, toward the foundation, they leave smelly, steamy excrement.

# 27

# ELLEN

Francois stood by me watching Tonnere run around the corral. The Jenets had arrived at the end of June—Wilhelm, unchanged, with his lovely blond wife, Ellen, and eight-year-old Francois. The boy was tall with glossy black hair and intelligent, graphite-blue eyes accented by round, bronze, freckled cheekbones.

Before the family left Quebec, Ellen's father, Captain Migault, had wandered off while under Francois's less-than-watchful eye. The senile man disappeared for two days, and finally, his naked corpse floated to the banks of the St. Lawrence. Francois still struggled with remorse and grief over the loss of his step grandfather. So far his time at Parrott's Bay had not restored his *joie de vivre*.

Tonnere trotted to the rail and nudged the boy with his large, soft nose. Placing his hand on Tonnere's head, Francois leaned his brow on the horse's cheek. Tears started, and soon the boy wept openly. I rubbed Francie's back as he sobbed and told me, between sobs, why he felt so wretched.

"Francois, you made a mistake falling asleep instead of watching the captain. Do you think God forgives you?" I dared ask, still wondering what the child's faith was like.

"I guess Jesus forgives me."

"Do you forgive yourself?"

With that question, Francois fell silent. I waited.

"I don't know, Mat-tee."

So I shared the fact that even Jesus' disciples had fallen asleep on the job. Jesus had forgiven them. "If Jesus can forgive you, shouldn't you forgive yourself?" Annie had taught me this.

"Forgive myself because Jesus does?" He thought quietly and wiped his nose on his sleeve. "Maybe." He hugged me, his lanky arms reaching around my neck and his cheek nestling against my midriff.

...

Our trading post flourished that summer of 1682. Harmony and good will existed among the Indian tribes. All were interested in consolidating LaSalle's defensive alliance. The Iroquois did not trouble us. When they skirmished, they stayed on the southern shore of Lake Ontario and moved toward Virginia and New England.

The six of us at Parrot's Bay formed a family—part native, part French, part Catholic, part Protestant, part literate, part illiterate. But we all supported one another and respected our differences.

Ellen hadn't developed the skills of a farmer's wife or an Indian squaw yet, but she never complained and was eager to learn. Her size and strength enchanted me—a petite, fragile-looking woman, yet able to lift a forty-pound lamb with no trouble. She easily beat me swimming across the bay, a skill in which I thought I excelled. Wilhelm and I trained her to handle a musket, an ax, and a skinning knife.

I marveled at the dissimilarity in the two marital relationships. Wilhelm had a firm hand on Ellen's movements and brooked no disagreement from her. She submitted cheerfully. In contrast, Full Moon pushed Claude about like a puppet. He tried to please her in every way. His easygoing personality was a necessary complement for Full Moon's need to overbear.

When I thought about marriage to Robert, I saw us as equals, partners in decisions, with neither one of us being the dominant one. Or was that wishful thinking given Robert's personality?

Whenever a man approached Parrot's Bay, my mind considered the possibility that he was Robert. My heart would soar with anticipation and then sink with disappointment.

...

On October 20, I received a letter.

> Michilimackinac
> September 1, 1682
> My dearest one,
>
> Don't let the unsteadiness of my handwriting trouble you. My strength is returning. Since April, I have been fighting a mortal fever, and I must winter here.
>
> We have been upset upon hearing of Frontenac's recall and LaBarre's designation as the new governor. I will send LaBarre a copy of the patent given me by the king. The new governor cannot argue with that evidence. He must understand the rightness of my being here in the west.
>
> Madeleine, help me curry LaBarre's favor. Often I am criticized for harshness against my men, but those in government don't understand these men I must employ. One cannot simply "make merry" with these woodsmen as I have been asked to do. They need a firm hand. Please pass the word I treat my men with respect.
>
> Since I worry about confidentiality, I send only snippets of how we fare. Who knows when my seal will be broken while the letter journeys to you? When I return, dear heart, I will share all with you. The heavens declare his wonders. RLS.

"Oh, Ellen." I groaned. "He is wintering in Michilimackinac! How can I keep waiting? I feel sick."

"Waiting," Ellen said softly, reflectively. She paused in her craft to push her blonde hair off her forehead. "Ah, we are often asked to do that. I think God has something special in mind for his people when he asks us to wait." Ellen was weaving a basket from marsh reeds, a skill Full Moon had taught us. I was shucking cobs and crushing corn kernels with a pestle.

"Tell me what you mean," I said.

"'Time' from God's point of view, and 'time' from man's perspective are different, I think. We human beings want things right away. We are ruled by time, by immediacy. We have no sense that waiting is valuable.

"God, on the other hand, says one day is as a thousand years. He alone is housed in eternity, where time does not exist. Waiting is a spiritual attitude, a mindset given to us by God." She pulled another reed through the frame and tucked it into the rim. The basket would hold a bushel of apples when done.

"When we have to wait, the experience shifts the way we see things. Our reliance changes from depending on the things we think will make us happy to relying on the Creator whom we know can make us complete. Waiting refines us spiritually."

I paused in my work. "'Waiting refines me spiritually?' I don't understand." I pressed the pestle into the kernels.

Ellen looked at me. "I think God wants us to be content in all circumstances. Waiting is the instrument he uses to help us arrive at that acceptance."

"You're talking about giving God control of the events and their timing in my life?" Chuckling quietly, I said, "I have no choice, do I? But, Ellen, I have such a difficulty giving control over to God."

...

Ellen's face radiated serenity, and Wilhelm strutted like a peacock when they told us a baby would be born the next spring. Sadly, this announcement heightened the tension permeating the trading post. Ellen and I had planned on going to Fort Frontenac for the Christmas services. But at our noon meal on Christmas Eve Day, Wilhelm said, "Of course, Ellen, you won't be going across the lake."

Ellen was walking from the oven to the table with a pan of baked apples when she heard her husband. A sudden flash of anger followed by a resigned sadness settled over Ellen's face. She stopped midpath, gripped the pan hard, and stared at Wilhelm. "What do you mean, husband?" She held herself erect, proud, silently waiting for his answer. Claude and Full Moon were still helping themselves to the stew and bread, licking their fingers with relish.

The former military captain and now expectant father said, "Travel at this time of year can be dangerous, Ellen. You know that. I don't want to risk our baby's health." Wilhelm ripped off the heel from the warm loaf of bread.

Ellen slammed the baked apples on the table and remained standing. "I have not stopped doing all the other responsibilities around here. Plus Mat-tee and I have been looking forward to seeing the people, hearing new gossip, and eating festive food. Haven't we, Madeleine?"

My new friend turned to me with a beseeching look, calling me into this argument with her husband, who was my old friend. Francois looked uncomfortable, unaccustomed to his parents' disagreeing. The boy asked to be excused, cleared some of the pewter plates off the table, and disappeared. Full Moon picked up the baked apples, using the corner of her apron as the pan was still hot, and spooned one onto Claude's plate. She gestured to me, but I declined. I had lost my appetite.

I squelched the urge to state my opinion. Pregnancy was a normal condition, and the status quo shouldn't shift just because the female's womb was growing and nurturing an unborn child. That was God's plan for her body. Wilhelm's directive was selfish, biased, and narrowly masculine.

But for the sake of our larger family relations, I shouldn't say anything offensive. With as much diplomacy as possible, I said, "We ladies have been wishing for a change of scenery by going to the fort. Catching up on the news there and truly celebrating the holiday excited us. But, perhaps, Wilhelm, you've a better sense of the upcoming weather. You're skilled at forecasting storms and weather shifts."

Wilhelm put his hand over Ellen's and held on as she tried to draw her hand away. "I don't want to argue about this, Ellen. We will plan a celebration here. Mat-tee, would you and Full Moon prepare some special dishes and string berries and corn kernels for a garland? Claude, you and I will go out this afternoon and cut decorative pine boughs." He reached for the dessert. Ellen pushed her chair in hard as she left. The table shook. Tears were in her eyes.

We tried to enjoy our small Christmas dinner. Full Moon made delicious corn and cranberry pudding and baked a squash. I trapped several hares and stuffed and roasted them. Wilhelm read from the Bible while we ladies stitched and mended. Claude whittled pieces for a chess set. Francois sat close to the firelight, braiding Tonnere a new rawhide bridle.

Despite the hominess of our Christmas Day, friction crackled in the air. Ellen was drawn-in, saddened and confused by her husband's attitude. Wilhelm, sensing his wife's displeasure, didn't know how to make matters right. Francois was trying not to be sullen, but he was disappointed in this plain Christmas. Claude, ever quiet, had little to offer. Full Moon, who had ignored the state of Ellen's health up to this point, started to say mean-spirited things under her breath about Ellen's pregnancy. Full Moon was jealous, as she and Claude had still not conceived a child. In my heart of hearts, I too had wanted to get away for a day and was miffed with Wilhelm.

...

The day after Christmas, the sky was brilliantly blue, and the snow sparkled as if crystalline lights were sprinkled on the earth's surface. Ellen and I bundled into our furs and strolled along the bay. When I drew in my breath, my chest hurt; it was that cold.

"Mat-tee, I'm sorry you were disappointed about yesterday," Ellen said as she took my arm for support on the rocky, ice-mottled shore.

"I was sad. But we did have a nice day, didn't we?"

"I didn't," Ellen said. "What we did was harmless, but boring. And I wasn't right with God, because I was angry with Wilhelm. I think he didn't want to go to the fort for other reasons."

"Such as?"

"Wilhelm still struggles with his leaving the Catholic Church. He's comfortable in his relationship with God, but he is sorting out how to worship and what to think of priests and masses. Going to Fort Frontenac would have brought up that whole question because he'd be attending a Catholic service."

We had walked to the south end of the bay, and the lake stretched out in front of us. "Ellen, what about you? Doesn't attending a mass confuse you too?"

"Not as much. I was raised a Protestant, but I am not offended by the Catholic service. I know what my relationship with Jesus is all about. If I happen to worship in a Catholic chapel, I accept it for what it is: a different form of worship but conveying the same message. On the other hand, Wilhelm is still irked with the Catholic Church, unforgiving of its practices. If we wish the Catholics would be tolerant of us Protestants, why shouldn't we Huguenots be forbearing of the Catholics?"

The cold air made my nose drip. I fumbled into my furs' pocket, pulled out a kerchief, and blotted. "Can't you talk to Wilhelm about this if you think this was the underlying reason for his not letting us go to the fort?"

"I tried, but he shut down. He knows he's wrong to not forgive the Catholic Church and accept the priests as they are. But he can't do that yet."

"He shut down? Robert does that with me often. Is this something men tend to do? They shut down when the topic causes them too much emotional discomfort? Maybe God should let men become pregnant and give birth every now and then and experience real discomfort?"

Ellen placed her fur-mittened hand on her belly and chuckled. "I don't know about that discomfort yet, Mat-tee. This is my first baby."

I told Ellen I had participated in the birth process of various ladies of the court, Sleeping Willow and Wilhelm's first wife. Reassured by the news I was somewhat familiar with delivering a baby, Ellen peppered me with questions. Soon our noses and fingers tingled from the cold, and we headed back.

...

On March 27, 1683, Governor LaBarre seized Fort Frontenac in the name of the king! We worried that LaBarre, one of LaSalle's adversaries, might come the ten miles west to confiscate Parrot's Bay as well. Devastated by this report and scared for our future, we began discussing our course of action. Should we close down the trading post and head into New York to avoid hostilities with our governor? Or would our trading post's insignificance appear unthreatening to the governor? Would he ignore us?

After hours of discussion and prayer, a decision was made, based on the fact my paperwork proving rightful ownership was in order. To flee a flourishing business would be foolhardy. We decided to stay.

...

"My legs are long enough, Mat-tee. They can grip his sides. Please let me try." For his ninth birthday, Francois insisted he ride Tonnere bareback.

At the paddock, the stallion jogged to us. I held his halter while Francois clambered up the split rail fence, fastened the bit and bridle around the stallion's neck, and vaulted onto the horse. The boy's agility and quickness hid his handicap. Tonnere accepted the feel of Francois on his back. I swung the gate open and watched as the two walked tentatively into the field.

Francois nudged the stallion, leaned over his neck, grasped the mane in one hand, and controlled the horse by the bit with reins in the other. Tonnere shifted from his walk to a lope and then with grace broke into a run. The two became one, boy and horse relishing the freedom. Francois yipped with joy as they disappeared in the distance.

...

When Ellen's water broke, Wilhelm asked me to attend the delivery. I told Full Moon that Ellen's time had come. "Would you please heat up two tubs of water and bring the linens from the chest?"

Full Moon glared at me, made a snorting noise, and left the house. Claude followed her. We didn't see them for the next month.

By mid-afternoon Ellen hadn't made much progress, so I suggested she walk, a technique I had seen the native women use. She was pacing around the bedroom with my arm supporting her when Wilhelm came in.

"Ellen, what are you doing out of bed? Mat-tee, my wife is going to have a baby!" Sweat glistened on his forehead. He lowered his wife on to the mattress and sat down on the bed, barricading me from Ellen. Wilhelm's muttered endearments broke her concentration, making it difficult for her to breathe in rhythm.

Ellen grew more uncomfortable. Finally I had enough. "Wilhelm, this is a woman's job. Would you leave me with Ellen, please?" I looked the captain in the eye. "Go and look after Francois, who must be wondering what is going on."

Wilhelm hesitated and then left. I ordered Ellen up. "My friend, walk. It will make your delivery come faster."

"But, Mat-tee," Ellen started to protest, "Wilhelm told me to get in bed. What about obeying my husband?"

I kept walking her. "Ellen. God gave you a sound mind. Now use it."

Anne Migault Jenet, healthy, red and wrinkly, came into the world early the next morning, May 15, 1683. The infant cried with volume, wiggled ten ruddy toes, and grasped my thumb with her petite fingers miraculously crowned by miniscule nails. Captain Jenet was enamored with his daughter. Ellen fell asleep after naming her daughter "Midge," a nickname for Migault. Mother and daughter lay peacefully with no thought to the dangerous world into which Midge had been born.

# 28

# THE STING OF THE ROPE

A smug-looking Full Moon strolled into the trading post five weeks later. She chatted about visiting her tribe and announced with pride, "I'm growing a baby inside me. And Claude, he says, 'Moon, you don't need to work the fields. Ellen can now work. Francois, too. He do the work of a man now.'"

...

Robert looked like a ghost when he arrived from the Gulf of Mexico in mid-August 1683. His fever spiked every afternoon, and he broke out in sweats and collapsed in the hammock. Robert's latest illness made his eyes sunken and gray, and his beard matted.

Nursing him back to health became my full-time goal. I fed him corn pudding, oatmeal, apples, and blueberries. We swam in the midday heat. On the fourth day after his arrival, when our whole group gathered for the noon meal, Robert felt strong enough to answer questions about his trip.

"Louisiana is much different from Quebec—marshy and wet, filled with strange animals, snakes, and insects. The air is so thick it is hard to breathe. The forts that remain were rundown but gave us limited refuge. The natives slowly began to form an alliance with us French." He sipped his cider and continued.

"When I heard LaBarre had seized Fort Frontenac, I was overwhelmed with despair. Of course, I had to hide these emotions from my men. Besides Tonty and Nika, you're the only ones who know of my desperate feelings. I trust you not to sully my reputation."

For several days Robert was distracted or preoccupied. He then began to help with the food gathering, the butchering, and the fishing. He practiced hitting targets with his musket and throwing his knife. His keen eye and steady hand returned.

Evenings we canoed and watched the sunset. The rocking of the boat relaxed him. I would sit propped against his legs.

"Isn't Midge a delight?" I ventured one night.

"Hmm," Robert mumbled, disinterested.

"I think having our own child would enrich our lives, don't you?"

Robert stopped running his fingers through my hair. "I'm not sure, Madeleine. Have you thought about the care he would demand, pulling you from more important activities?"

"I think it's a matter of priorities. For me, nurturing a child is more important than discovering another river."

His hand slapped the side of the canoe. "So my explorations are not important?"

"No, Robert, that's not what I meant. I'm simply stating my own desires." The mood of the evening had been soiled. Oh, how he irked me!

Why was I attracted to him? He could test my patience with his tendency to see in blacks and whites and to quickly disregard my ideas. Yet I felt drawn to him, so completed by him. With him, I wondered what the next day would hold. He kept my life interesting.

A week later Robert fretted he should return to France to re-establish his royal grant. We were twisting hemp rope on the porch. Ellen, Wilhelm, and Francois were gone marking trails and scouting for trees for our supply of building timber. Midge slept under Full Moon's watchful eye. Claude was slaughtering and plucking hens for our supper. Robert studied his fingers while they pulled on the hemp, as if the hands held the answer to his dilemma. "I must go in person. A letter would not suffice."

He saw my sadness. "Mat-tee, it must be this way. We can wait a bit more, yes?"

Twist, pull, yank, twist. Repeat. I tried to focus on the rhythm of the ropemaking. Lye in the soaking solution stung my raw skin. But this was nothing compared to the emotional sting. How long had I waited for Robert? Eight years! Here he was going off again, first to France and then to the Mississippi Delta. God knows when I would see him again.

The silence was heavy. My mind churned. Did I truly love him? Did I want to wait another year? Have a child by him? Wake up next to him in my old age and care for him when he was elderly? Or had I had enough? Should I say good-bye?

I escaped to the "necessary," one of my best places for thinking.

Walking the long way back from the outbuilding, I sat on a boulder and reached into the lake, letting the cool water dribble down my arms, soothing my burning hands. I hiked my skirt up and dipped my bare feet in. My spine shuddered from the chill.

Except for my relationship with Robert, my life was settled at the age of thirty-seven. I was the first female to own property in this part of the world. Every day was productive with a goal to look forward to. The French colonials and the natives considered me a fair person who could talk the language and help heal their sick. Compared to twelve years ago when I lived with the Reverend Mother, God had blessed me with a solid sense of his presence.

So what to do about Robert? I lay back on the rock, eyes to the sky, and followed the floating clouds. "God, show me what to do, please. I don't think I can bear to wait, but I must respect Robert's desire to finish this one last leg of his journey."

As the white billows drifted by, I thought of the couples I knew. Each had distinctly different stories, their own share of joys and heartbreak. But each had similar cement in their relationship: They were utterly loyal to each other. Only with Robert had I felt that type of loyalty.

Robert was still working on the rope when I arrived back and didn't say a word as I resumed my task.

"Robert, I wonder. Might we marry before you leave? That way I would be the Lady LaSalle and represent your interests. Perhaps you would even leave me with child so I wouldn't be so lonely in your absence."

Without responding, Robert walked in the direction of the outhouse.

Upon returning, he said, "Madeleine, if you were Lady LaSalle, my creditors would go after you more than they do me. Your property would be jeopardized, and your name might be besmirched." He gathered up his finished rope. The hemp now looked like piles of large grass snakes lying coiled.

My fingers braided the hemp more quickly, trying to work out my frustration. If we didn't marry now, I had a feeling our union would never occur. The hemp snarled, and marinade burned my skin. I threw the twine into the bucket. Robert brought me a cool, damp rag. He took each of my sore, pruned hands and cleaned them. "Come, let's walk," he said.

We meandered around the meadow, watching Tonnere, not talking. Robert's closeness calmed me. I should only think about the present. Not the future, never the future anymore.

He led me to the dock, and we sat cooling our feet in the lake. A pike chased minnows, scattering them amidst the underwater rocks.

"Mat-tee." Robert placed my hands in his and stroked the palms. Lightly he began circling my inner hand with his finger. "There'll be another year."

I looked into his gray-blue eyes. "Robert, I want you to be my husband now, this summer, this year. I simply want you. Can't you understand that?"

"It is hard to believe a lady with your charm and abilities would want me. Especially when I cannot promise I'll stay by your side every day. You know my need to be on the move. Some days I think I am tired and growing older, that maybe this exploring should be left for the younger men. But then I think about helping you raise a child here at Parrot's Bay, and I feel restless and stifled."

"I know that, Robert. Over twelve years we've known each other, and you always have been the man to venture out. That's what I love about you. I can do the jobs that need to be done. You'll be missed when you're not with me, but I don't need you here." I kissed his palm, wrapped his fingers around my kiss, and closed his fist. I straightened up and said, "Let us marry. You can come and go as you please."

"What would you do if we had a child?"

"We don't have to have a child." Then I added, blushing, "I do know how to prevent that from happening."

He looked over at me sheepishly. "I should have guessed you might."

"I want to join with you, become one with you. Years ago you said that I wasn't ready. Now I'm ready. I don't want you to go across the ocean and then into the Gulf of Mexico without … without … " The heat rose in my face; my belly felt soft and tingly.

He shifted his weight, pressed my head toward him, and laced his fingers in my hair. He gave me a deep kiss. His tongue tantalized me.

Then, as if a fire just ignited between us and he might get burned, he pulled away as quick as lightening.

"Madeleine, we can't. Not until we marry. It is wrong."

"Then let's marry."

"No." He let out an exasperated sigh.

"Then let's become lovers."

"That's against God."

Realizing how deeply rooted his morality was, I backed off.

Our silence was painfully loud.

Through a large knothole in the dock's wooden structure, I could see the rocky bottom of the bay. Sunlight cut odd patterns in the clear water and sharpened the pebbles' colors to maroon, mustard, and ochre, giving them a shimmering appearance. The scene reminded me of the richly embroidered altar cloths adorning Catholic chapels.

"Robert, I have a compromise! You know the custom of mariage á la gamine where a couple seeks the blessing of the church and God, but they don't post the bans or have a legal document? Let us marry á la gamine. That way we can be lovers, and it won't be a sin in the eyes of God. In the eyes of your creditors, I'll still be Madeleine de Roybon D'Allone. We'll keep this a secret."

Was this the right solution for us? Robert and I would be united in God's eyes, but the people, who had hostile thoughts and intentions, would never know and could not hurt us.

Robert stared ahead, weighing this option. Then he slapped the dock and grinned. "A solution! You've got it!"

I leaned over, kissed him on the lips, and gave him an exuberant hug. Finally I was going to marry Robert!

Now, how should we implement our plans? The only chapel and priest within a day's travel was at Fort Frontenac, and LaBarre held that fort. LaSalle was blacklisted there. If he were seen there, he would likely be arrested.

We decided to go to the fort incognito as two newly arrived inhabitants, strangers to the fort's community. Times had changed, so we knew few people there. I would dress less provincially, using one of Ellen's dresses from Quebec and adding a flounce to the hem. Full Moon would dye my hair a russet color. Ellen clipped Robert's long curly hair (one of his trademark characteristics) short, and he brushed out his now long gray beard and bushy mustache. Then he donned the clothes of a farmer, not his customary voyageur garb, and shielded his eyes with a hat.

Claude transported us to a spot along the coast so we could walk into the fort. We had not shared our intention of marriage with our friends. They all surmised we were in costume to spy on the political environment.

The Eucharist would not be celebrated until the end of the service, so I squirmed and fidgeted through the confessional and homily. Finally as the priest prayed for the changing of the wafer into the body of Christ and the wine into the Savior's blood, Robert and I married ourselves. We placed silver rings on our middle fingers of our right hands in order to hide our new relationship.

While the priest said the benediction, we used his words as our marital blessing. There were no witnesses, no legal documents. But it was enough for Robert, who believed we were doing right in God's eyes. This secret, informal ceremony would protect me from any adversities that might come my way if I were legally married to him.

Robert and I could now join our bodies together without soiling our consciences. The physical craving I'd been fending off for years would soon be satisfied. And because of our union, I knew wherever he traveled, he'd always come home to me.

# PART SIX:

## The Pruning

# 29

# THE DEEP BLUE

On our first night as husband and wife, we stretched our bedrolls on the grassy knoll by the bay and lay there studying the stars, bodies tense and hot next to each other. As in most of his activities, Robert was direct and to the point on the topic of marital relations.

"Mat-tee, you know this may hurt you."

I shivered, not because of the pain I might be experiencing after nine years of abstinence, but by my husband's concreteness. Obviously he was not going to waste time relaxing me.

An unsatisfying and brief coupling happened on the second night as well. By the third night, I tried to talk with Robert about my needs. He looked at me startled as though, I—a woman—could possibly have an opinion about sex. I lay awake wondering how to break out of this pattern. I did not like the message I thought he was giving me: "You're my woman now, and I am going to treat you the way I think is best."

...

One week after our consummation, we went apple picking. The fruit hung on the trees—red, full, sweet-smelling, ripe for the harvesting. I asked Robert to bring one of the wooden ladders.

"What for?" he inquired.

"To climb to the apples high in the tree, silly. What did you think?" I noticed he carried an old blanket.

He walked on ahead and called over his shoulder, "If you bring the buckets, we'll be all set."

I fetched the ladder myself, balancing the two buckets on either end, and bracing the ladder on my shoulder. When I reached the orchard, Robert had already laid his blanket under the branches and was rocking the tree back and forth slowly. Apples fell plunking onto the ground, hitting other apples or even a branch on their way down.

"Stop, Robert."

"Why? This is the quickest way to collect our two buckets full." He continued to shake the tree.

"Quick your way may be, but our harvest is ruined. Look at those apples. Bruised and crushed to pulp in some places. Now please put your ideas aside for a minute and watch me." With alacrity, I balanced the ladder against the tree, placed a bucket on my left forearm, scrambled up the rungs, and, with finely tuned movements, separated the apples from their branches, leaving the buds of future apples intact. Within five minutes, my bucket was full. As I climbed down, I said to Robert, "Not only are the apples unhurt, but the parts of the tree needed to grow apples next year are intact."

Robert, seated on the blanket and surrounded by his fallen apples, had an interesting look: part hurt, part pleasure, and part confusion.

Sputtering at his thick headedness, I used my surge of frustration to express myself about his unsatisfactory lovemaking. "And for your information, you handle my body the way you handled that tree. Rock into it hard enough, and the deed is done. Do you want to know how to harvest *my* crop?"

I stood over him. He grinned from embarrassment. I offered him a coquettish smile and looked around. Seeing no one and aware that Claude and Wilhelm were out on the lake fishing, I moved apples out of our way, pushed him backward on the blanket, and pinned his shoulder down with my hand. I unbuttoned his shirt and caressed him. My touch made him tremulous. My knee pressed his thigh down, and I undid his britches. Robert groaned and attempted to sit up. Lowering myself onto him, I kissed him ardently.

"Relax, Robert. No one will be coming," I whispered.

Robert took the cue. Surrounded by the scent of apples and the rustle of leaves, we made love. When we were both satisfied, he collapsed onto the blanket, and I stretched out breathless along his side.

Robert said, "I never knew… I didn't realize… I should remember you can teach me a thing or two."

...

Iroquois besieged Fort Frontenac on October 26, 1683, two months after we became husband and wife. Most of the inhabitants had been slaughtered. One of a few dozen natives who escaped fled to Parrot's Bay to tell us. The Pro-English Iroquois, swimming in the predawn light, had crept up the bank and through a hole in the palisade. The twenty soldiers who tried to hold the fort were killed in their beds or at their posts.

Worse yet—the rumor circulated that LaSalle had incited the Iroquois, planned the strategy of using the river's bank, and sabotaged the palisade so it could be breached.

As the frightened savage talked, we plied him with refreshment and pummeled him with questions. Robert sat silently in the shadows so as not to be noticed. I could tell it was taking most of his willpower to hold back his temper.

Nine-year-old Francois listened; he bit his lips, and his eyes widened in bewilderment. As in all French-Native skirmishes, the half-breed boy was caught in between. And Midge, innocent Midge, propped up on pillows against the wall, played with her carved doll. At least her world was safe and happy.

...

For the next few days we fed the escapees and provided them with blankets or pelts for sleeping and kept busy as people came and went. Some had believed the rumor about LaSalle and were sputtering obscenities at him. Others, who had known Robert well in the past, were trying to explain the siege some other way.

The whole time Robert was absent.

At midnight, I was settled in bed but missing Robert by my side. In stealth, he approached our quarters and whispered. "Mat-tee, I must go tomorrow and get to Quebec before the last ship sails for France this winter. That gives me about three weeks."

He'd cleaned up, stopped at the food stores, and brought a plate of dinner with him. He forked food into his mouth as though he might not eat for a while, and he spouted off about LaBarre, his ineptitude and brashness. "I know it was he and his lieutenants who manipulated that siege. He wanted me to look bad and he look good. His Majesty must be informed."

As I watched him eating the cold ham and apples, I felt a deep sadness. Once more he would be gone from my life. Tears threatened to fall. *Oh, God,* I prayed silently, *Yet, again, give me strength. And certainly give Robert wisdom and courage.*

Outwardly I was composed and resigned, knowing this day of good-byes would come. "Aye, my love. Finish your supper, and then come to me. Let us have this one night together. I'll wake you before dawn and gather your supplies. Write me at each milestone. I'll be watching the heavens, knowing you are doing the same. And I'll be praying for you."

...

LaBarre regained Fort Frontenac for France November fourth. Scattered refugees trailed to our trading post, coming for basic supplies before returning to Cataraqui.

By the first part of December, our trading post was ready for winter; the necessary wood was gathered, crops were harvested, and a calf was slaughtered and smoked. We'd pickled fish from the lake. Then we decided to use our time building an icehouse, which would enable us to store fresh produce amidst blocks of ice. Midge would be able to have cool cow's milk next summer, and we could all enjoy cream and butter. Francois promised a delicacy he discovered in Quebec: flavored, chipped ice served in a cup.

As the old year made way for 1684, God's spirit in me was growing like a flourishing plant. Now I believed that when God said he would do something, he would do it for me out of his love.

...

In February Tonnere, harnessed to a sledge, waited at the lake's edge while Francois whispered encouragements and fed the horse apple pieces. Wilhelm and Claude had created a hole in the ice about two hundred feet from shore. As one sawed through the ice, making a two-foot-wide cubic hole, the other held wooden prongs into the frozen block, stabilizing it. Once cut, the cube was lifted up onto the ice-covered bay. Full Moon, heavy with child, wet a path, and I glided the block along that slippery chute on the frozen surface toward the shore.

Once we got to the sledge, together Francois and I lifted the ice block onto the carrier. Then Tonnere ambled to the icehouse, and Francois slid the block on to the sawdust-covered floor and stacked it.

The six of us kept at this harvesting all morning. The air was well below freezing, but the sun shone brightly warming our furs as we worked. I loved the fresh tingle in my nose on these crystal-white winter days. By early afternoon, the icehouse was half-filled with ice blocks, and by the next day there was no room left.

We built a cupboard in the main house to hold several blocks so our produce could be kept cool. No one imagined the price ice harvesting would cost us in the future.

...

Full Moon's difficult labor started before dawn a month later. Ellen and I chased the men out. The Ojibway woman started up a litany of complaints: It was our fault she couldn't get comfortable. I wasn't rubbing her belly gently enough, or I needed to massage her shoulders harder. The damp compress Ellen used was too hot—no, it was too cold.

As the labor intensified, Full Moon began cussing and shouting, first in Ojibway, then in French, knowing her words would irritate us.

By midday, my patience was spent. "Moon, silence yourself. You wanted this baby, remember. Quit complaining," I snapped at her.

She glared and let out a high-pitched stream of Ojibway, saying I couldn't possibly understand since I was a barren woman.

I left the room, fuming. Ellen followed me. "Mat-tee, Mat-tee, don't mind her."

"How can you stay so calm?" Ellen's demeanor mystified me. "In the childbirths I have attended, this is the only time the mother has been so, so... cranky. How can you stand it?"

"Remember the traits of Jesus that we talked about, his patience and his love?" she asked. "I have been relying on Jesus' spiritual power now. Otherwise Moon's attitude would bother me a great deal." Ellen went over to the ice cupboard and poured us both a mug of cool apple cider. "Why don't you fill yourself with that same power?"

"How do I do that?" I said as I sipped the thick, sweet juice.

"Ask Jesus to help you see her from his perspective. Your feelings may not alter immediately, but you will be given the power to change. See each moment as a spiritual challenge." She finished her mug and placed it on the counter. "I'll go back in. Why don't you take a break, and then take Moon some ice chips? I think she'd appreciate that."

When I reentered Full Moon's room a half hour later, I felt like a different woman. When I had confessed to Jesus my negative attitude and asked him to empower me with his positive one, remarkable peace came over me. Full Moon hadn't changed. In fact, she deliberately knocked the cup of ice chips out of my hand. But God loved her through me, and I experienced his Spirit transforming my responses. This was the day I was born anew by God's Spirit.

At sunset, Full Moon brought a healthy baby boy into the world. Claude named him Samuel Leonine.

...

On May 30 a letter arrived.

> Versailles
> April 10, 1684
> Dear Madeleine,
> We provincials have fallen out of the Court's favor. Even the former Governor Frontenac is being ridiculed as a bumpkin. While I wait for an audience with the king, my time is spent with the courtiers awaiting their turn to approach their monarch.
> The whole focus of the country is on the war with Spain. When I finally get to speak to the king, I will convince him that having these western lands is his best bet for dominating the Spanish colonies in America. Consolidating the forts from the Great Lakes to the Gulf of Mexico will guarantee France's supremacy over Spain. Waiting is so trying.
> Memories of you brighten my days. RLS.

...

"Now you mix the honey with the blueberries, crush them, and stir. That's how you make a syrup." In early June, Francois demonstrated how he made the flavored ice. "Then you take the pestle and smash the ice and pour the juice over the chips. And eat!" Proudly he handed me a mug of blue sweetened ice. My teeth ached as I sucked some from the cup. Swishing it around made my whole mouth numb, but I sucked up another bite and enjoyed the frozen sweetness.

"Our customers will walk miles to get this treat. Good job, Francois. How much is it worth in trade? The profits can be yours," I said, wondering what a cup of fruited ice could sell for.

Francois grinned, his teeth a deep blue from the iced dessert.

...

A letter came on June 15.

Versailles May 1, 1684
Dear Mat-tee,

The king has chosen me to execute his orders to place all North American lands under his rule. My enemy, Governor LaBarre, has been commanded to repair any wrongs he has done, such as returning the fort to me.

Three hundred and twenty people will travel to the Gulf of Mexico, including over a hundred soldiers, some workmen, masons, one surgeon, one Jesuit priest, some orphaned girls looking for husbands, and several families with a flock of children in their household.

Among those traveling with us will be my brother, Jean Cavelier, who has settled his differences with me. Nika and Tonty join us as well I am not as comfortable in the role of commander when my party goes beyond several dozen.

The king decided I am in charge of the land explorations, while Captain Beaujeu commands the fleet. But Beaujeu has already started taking issue with my decisions. This arrangement is riddled with problems.

This expedition is making me anxious. Colonizing the lands surrounding the Gulf of Mexico will be a formidable task. Beaujeu presses me for a specific destination west of Santo Domingo, and I have yet to place an X on his map, because the whole area is a diffuse, wet marshland with few landmarks.

Beaujeau says I am acting suspicious, bizarre and unbalanced. My intimate friends know my unsettled feelings, but the others give credence to Beaujeu's rumors about my mental condition.

When I am out of balance here, I bring forth a vision of your dark, clear eyes. Then I look deep within them and get my bearings. God grant me grace. RLS

...

Governor LaBarre tried to quash the Iroquois Five Nations during July 1684. He assembled two thousand French soldiers at Fort Frontenac for a show of strength, hoping to form allies of the Illinois, Miamis, Shawnees, and Ojibways. We at Parrot's Bay knew how intimidated these tribes were of the Iroquois Confederacy and how little use these natives would be in a battle. We also thought the governor's errand of peace was bogus; France wanted to go to war because such an act justified France's "protective presence." War stimulated the economy and brought monies from France to help sustain France's "supremacy" over the redskin.

As tension increased between the French government and the Iroquois warriors, more people came and left Parrot's Bay. Trading was lively, and our business thrived. Here in our sheltered bay, where we were self-sufficient, we lived in the illusion the world was at peace.

Francois had taken an interest in some Christian Hurons who taught the boy to shoot with a bow and arrow. He traded them his flavored ice for feathers and lessons. He was becoming a skilled archer.

The baby Sammy, looking like his mother, grew into a cuter urchin each day. I suspected that Sammy's father was not Claude, but an Ojibway. Because of the political turmoil, the Leonines hadn't gone to the fort for their baby's baptism. As time passed, the lack of this once important ritual didn't bother them.

Midge was walking. I loved to watch her hold onto Midnight's scruff, take tentative steps forward, lose her balance, and hit her bottom on the ground. Then she'd laugh. Midnight would sit patiently beside her so she could pull herself up on his fur. And the fun would start all over. I wished my life and my pleasures were that simple.

···

On September 2, 1684, a letter came from France.

> Dieppe, France
> July 17, 1684
> Mat-tee:
>
> We sail tomorrow, my dearest one. Captain Beaujeu and I have finally decided how much of what supplies we need and where to store them...
>
> Captain Beaujeu will be captaining the *Joly*. Captain Aigorn commands the *Amiable*. The king has given me a small frigate outright and a pilot, familiar with the North Atlantic, has been put in charge of her. A ketch follows behind us with livestock. I pray the irritation between Beaujeu and myself dissipates, as tension is not good for the men.
>
> Say prayers for us as we cross the Atlantic. RLS

···

Then on September 29, 1684, another letter arrived.

> LaRochelle, France
> August 8, 1684
> Dear Madeleine,
>
> A false start. The day we sailed, it rained heavily. By the second day, the sea was rolling. Then the mast of the *Joly* broke only forty leagues off La Rochelle. I believe Beaujeu might have set this "accident" up purposely to sabotage our venture and force a return to port. I must say the captain did work industriously to set the mast, but perhaps that was all a show. I feel unsettled by the personal relationships in which I am embroiled. The vagueness of our ultimate destination confuses me. I am troubled.
>
> *Adieu.* Your friend, Robert.

...

We traded a barrel of glass beads for a pregnant sow in March 1685, an unusual procurement for the eight of us at Parrot's Bay. The sow was due to have babies that following autumn, so we built a special pen in the barn. Tonnere and Midnight made various efforts to sniff and nuzzle her. Diversions like this kept our spirits up. Watching two-year-old Midge and one-year-old Sammy develop kept our daily routine lively. To further overcome the monotony, I daydreamed about my adventurer.

Captain Beaujeu mailed a letter, which I received June 15, 1685.

> Paris, France
> May 1, 1685
> Dear Mademoiselle D'Allone,
>
> Your friend the Sieur de LaSalle asked me to pen a brief report to you regarding his adventure in the Gulf of Mexico. I'm sure he will return to share the details. Suffice it to say, he and I have had our differences, but we did arrive safely in Santa Domingo in early March 1685.
>
> As captain of the *Joly*, I pressed forward with LaSalle to Matagorda Bay in the Gulf of Mexico. But there I considered it prudent to return to France. I had accomplished my goal: that of delivering LaSalle, his people, and his supplies safely to America.
>
> LaSalle and his party continued on the *Amiable* toward the Gulf of Mexico, followed by the Belle and the supply ketch.
>
> Your friend is a true visionary with all the problems that entails. His fervor and drive carry him forward. But his lack of both practicality and focus puts the venture on a shaky foundation. His irascibility is disturbing all around him. He and his followers need the hand of God.
>
> All hail to His Majesty Louis XIV!
> Your servant, Captain Beaujeu.

# 30
# ON THIN ICE

"The Edict of Nantes has been revoked!" I exclaimed on December 7, 1685, sitting down heavily in the nearest chair. A courier had arrived as we were finishing supper.

"*Mon Dieu*, now we're outlaws." Wilhelm fumed as he paced in front of the fire. "We must be watchful. Our beliefs are outside the law," he warned.

I knew what he meant. Under the Edict of Nantes, Louis XIV had been tolerant of Protestantism for years. Now, retraction of the Edict of Nantes made the Huguenots enemies of the Crown.

Wilhelm thought aloud. "Mat-tee, you're still registered with the Catholic priest at Fort Frontenac, are you not?" I nodded in agreement. Full Moon was nursing Sammy, one and a half years old. She ignored our conversation. Simple Claude listened, always willing to help but having no ideas.

Holding two-and-a-half-year-old Midge on her lap, Ellen was also nursing. Both mother and daughter were alert, Ellen to the issues, Midge to her mother's tension. This revocation of religious tolerance affected the Jenets more directly than either the Leonines or myself. Ellen's family had suffered severe persecution because of their reformed faith. The Migaults' dissension with Catholicism had caused great heartache.

Wilhelm proposed we at Parrot's Bay keep the Jenets' beliefs a secret. Thus he hoped no government representative, who showed up unannounced, possibly in the guise of coureur de bois or even a Catholic native would arrest his family.

Ellen disagreed with her husband's policy. "My dear, we can't keep our faith secret. Our loved ones have given up everything for what we believe to be true. I have no intention of keeping silent."

"We don't have to keep silent exactly," Wilhelm clarified. "But we can be circumspect. There is no need to walk into a trap just because you want to be a martyr." He stoked the fire, his movements tense. The burning apple wood mingled with the pine to create a sweet aroma. But we were not comforted.

"I don't want to be a martyr unless it is the Lord's desire. But I do want to show his truth to those who come by. All people should know their salvation comes through the grace of Christ. If I am persecuted for saying that, so be it." Ellen set her toddler on the floor, fastened her bodice, and went to fetch her Bible. Midge skipped over to her father and clambered up on Wilhelm's lap.

Ellen opened the large leather book. "Peter tells us that perseverance leads to character, that we should rejoice in our trials. This is the end of religious tolerance. Difficult times are upon us. We will be sharing in Christ's sufferings soon."

A shiver ran down my spine. My growing faith was still timid and shaky. Giving up control to God on a daily basis was unnatural and difficult. Usually I thought of myself first, before considering what God wanted. It took a disturbance in my soul, some loss of peace, to propel me toward God.

Ellen began to read the Bible aloud. But I needed to be alone, so I grabbed my cloak and stepped into the cold night. The moon was a bright crescent in the southern sky, encircled by stars and navy blackness. I breathed the chilled air and felt a frozen ache in my lungs.

I wasn't sure what to think. I wanted to be close to God, but I didn't know what to do about Catholic and Huguenot beliefs. I had been raised believing my salvation came from the church, its rituals, and sacraments. Reverend Mother Marie had reinforced these ideas.

Yet Ellen and Wilhelm had been teaching me to go to God directly, to seek his forgiveness without a human intercessor or reliance on church rituals. Often they told me I had been saved through grace and that I didn't need to "work" at being saved. "If you never take another sacrament again, God is still in your life, Mat-tee. He will always welcome you into heaven," they assured me.

"Oh, God," I said. "What do you have ahead for us? Will the Jenets be hunted down and arrested? On what path are you placing their feet? How should I practice my faith? I had imagined myself at Parrot's Bay for the rest of my life with Robert by my side. But it has been two years since I have seen him and a half-year since I heard about him. What are you doing with me? Please protect us here. Watch over Robert, wherever he is. Let him trust in you as he looks up at this moon and these stars. And help me to grow in my faith."

As I said these words into the night sky, I didn't doubt God would answer. I just wondered *how* he would answer.

...

On New Year's Day, 1686, I awoke from the dull heaviness of an immobilizing dream, my nightshift twisted around me. In the dream, our canoe had split in two, and I floated forward in the bow portion while Robert drifted backward in the stern. We were lost in a quilt work of stagnant pools, stringy puddles and meandering streams. Neither of us had any control.

Despite our increasing distance from one another in the dream, I could see my husband's confused expression. He kept turning his head looking for something. The humidity made it hard to breathe, and sweat poured down my bosom. Feelings of foreboding weighed me down.

Later, when Ellen and I were shelving preserves, I asked, "Ellen, do you give much credence to dreams?" Not waiting for her answer, I rushed to describe mine. I needed to talk about the dream, to regain my sense of reality.

Midge was babbling on the floor, so her mother handed the toddler a cut–up apple to quiet her. "Dreams have shed light on my thoughts.

They help me sort out loose ends. Sometimes God uses our dreams to communicate with us."

She climbed up a stool and asked me to pass the jars up. "God told Joseph and Mary about Jesus' birth by giving Joseph a dream." She reached for more jars and added, "But the devil probably uses our dreams too." Stepping down, she brushed her hands off on her apron. "What did you learn from your dream?"

I was silent. Fear? Confusion? Robert's or mine?

Without thinking, I said, "I wonder if the dream means Robert has lost his way?"

"Aye. Say that dream was a glimpse into reality, Mat-tee. What could you do about it? What choices do you have?" Ellen challenged me. I had no response. She went on, "God's providence is your only answer. Believe he is in control of what happens. Come, let's go read God's Word to see what it says."

We moved over to the rockers in front of the fire. I said, "How long will it take me to think like you, that I can go directly into the Bible and don't need to wait for the priest? My Catholic habits are still deeply rooted in me."

"That's not all bad. You can declare yourself a Catholic and not fear the judgment of the law against us non-Catholics." When Ellen saw my perplexed look, she added, "Mat-tee, I'm being sarcastic... somewhat. It would be wonderful if you thought more readily of God's Word and his Spirit. But worldly protection is yours because you're a Catholic. As long as you can say in good conscience you are a Catholic, then the bounty hunters out there to persecute the Protestants won't stand a chance with you."

Ellen thumbed through the Bible. My rocking was fast and erratic. "What would you say the dream taught you about yourself?" she asked.

"How anxious I am, about Robert and our future."

"Well, here's a verse for you: 'God has given you not a spirit of fear, but of power, love and a sound mind.' Think about that. Through the

Holy Spirit, you can replace your anxiety with a spirit of love, a strong heart, and common sense."

"How, Ellen? Even if God takes away my fear, I can't see how he could give me love and power. Robert is down there in the Gulf. I haven't seen him for over two years! Where's good in that?"

"I can't explain the process, Mat-tee. Transformations like this are nothing short of miraculous. But once the Holy Spirit gives you God's viewpoint on the situation, love and joy will follow. God changes our values. The earthly worries we have become trivial. He replaces what we yearn for on earth with desires that are more heaven-based."

Ellen reached for my hand. When she began to pray silently, I felt the strangest warmth wash over me, as though Ellen's peace was streaming out her fingertips into me. Then she prayed aloud.

"Thank you, Lord, for Mat-tee and the dream she had. You love her and want the best for her spiritually. Help her to see this from your divine perspective. Let her sorrow turn into joy, her fear into God-confidence. And Lord, give her a healthy and clear mind. She needs to know what you want her to do while she waits."

With that she raised me from the chair and gave me a firm, protective hug.

...

By his twelfth springtime, Francois, on Tonnere at a full run, could ride with no hands, and shoot an arrow or throw a tomahawk accurately at the same time. Aware of the tension between the white men and the natives, the boy said to me, "I'm caught in no-man's land, Mat-tee. The whites don't trust me because I'm a redskin, and the natives don't trust me because my white father is a Frenchman. That's why it's important for me to speak both French and Iroquois, to be skilled, and to be able to move well in both cultures."

His words were so much wiser than his years and triggered my idea that Parrot's Bay should have a ten-year-anniversary celebration. We would join together the white men and the red, the French and the natives, and the prosperous settlers and the travelers. We would roast a pig, serve a banquet, have competitions, and enjoy our bounty and our safety.

...

Georgette, Midge's pet, a cream-colored pig with a freckled hide as soft as a baby's behind, was as big as a barrel. Wilhelm would place his three-year-old daughter on the pig's back, put reins in her hands, and let his girl ride off. Georgette, in her devotion to Midge, was gentle with the toddler and waddled around the yard with Midge perched on her back, the little girl squealing with excitement.

In preparation for our feast in July of 1686, I was in the process of slaughtering Georgette's littermate, a castrated six-month-old. I sat on the hog's chest, raised my hunting knife and slit his jugular. Blood spurted.

At that very second, Midge, riding Georgette, entered the barnyard and saw me. Midge screamed in horror. Georgette took off at a run. Crying and pulling up on the reins, Midge squealed, and the pig squealed louder. I never knew pigs could trot so fast.

Ellen, hearing the commotion, ran from the house. Georgette, with Midge astride, barreled down the embankment. Midnight dove off the front porch and joined the fray. In seconds, Georgette reached the rocky beach and ran full throttle into the lake. Entering the water brought her up short. Due to the abrupt change of momentum, Midge was tossed over the pig's shoulders, flipped head over heels, and splashed into the water.

Midnight hit the water at a lope and grabbed Midge by her shirt.

Ellen flung herself into the lake and reached out for her daughter. Midge, startled by the plunge into the cold water but a good swimmer, came up sputtering and smiling.

I convulsed with laughter. Having quickly forgotten the horror of the butchering, the little girl found immense pleasure in her recent misadventure.

I corralled Georgette and headed to the barn to tie her up while I finished gutting the boar. When Wilhelm arrived, he helped me hoist the hog onto a hook to drain.

I described what happened to his daughter.

"She's got a great spirit, that little girl of mine: sensitive to the tough things in the world but resilient about the challenges that come her way. She'll go far in this new land," Wilhelm said with pride in his eyes.

...

Our celebration became the gathering point for soldiers, inhabitants, Christian and traditional savages, voyageurs, wives, and children. Twenty or more dogs joined Midnight and wandered around, begging tidbits and scruffings while guests used canine fur as napkins. With Tonnere and three other horses, Francois set up horse racing in the corral. Wilhelm created a swimming area with ropes and animal bladders and started water races. Then Claude and Full Moon had men, children, and women compete to see who could bring in the most and biggest fish within two hours.

The smells of a pig roasting, body odor, and unusual foods floated in the air. At noon, we laid out breads, jellies, pickled vegetables, cold roasted hens, and dried fruit. Blocks of ice kept barrels of spring water cool. The sky was cloudless, and it proved to be a hot, hot day.

Our trading post had grown from a one-room shelter to include two small houses, a full barn, a mill house, and a trading post with bakery ovens attached.

I circulated among the guests, speaking their language, and encouraging their accomplishments. I enjoyed the roles my life had given me: interpreter, trader, and sometimes even doctor or midwife. Nearly all the two hundred visitors were my acquaintances. We were mutually dependent for our quality of life.

That evening I danced with my visitors. We whites stomped with the natives to their drums, and then the reds cavorted to our fiddles and harmonicas. I thought about Robert. Much of his life's purpose was to affiliate the French with the natives, to secure this extensive land so that all could live in peace. And I felt thankful and proud.

A strange sound interrupted my reverie and made my ears ring. Looking around in the dusk, I spotted a Huron chief braying like a wolf under a full moon. Francois had just served him some flavored ice, and the chief must have taken a bite of the ice chips hastily, greedily. The coldness had set up an ache in what remained of his teeth. He howled. He spat the blue ice into his hand, studied it, let his mouth recover, and then grunted an enthusiastic "yup." Slowly, he licked the flavored ice, shoved it back into his mouth, and enjoyed the sensation.

Smiling, I patted him on the back and kept walking. Maybe the chief's encounter with the new dessert could teach us all something. If we bite into a new culture greedily, hastily, and without suspecting its impact on us, it could cause us pain. But if we enjoyed small tastes of it and relished it for how it provided something different and good, then we would spare ourselves pain. We might experience satisfaction regarding our cultural differences.

...

The party crowned our summer. Ten days later, Sammy broke out with a red rash, and his temperature soared. Full Moon came down with the same malady after two more days. Sammy turned delirious with fever. Moon's rash spread all over her body, making nursing miserable. Sammy lost his ability to suck and lay on his cot, listless.

Ellen and I suspended our work and gave our full attention to Full Moon and her son. Francois carried chipped ice in buckets so we could try to bring their fevers down. Wilhelm put up picture signs on our dock, at the mill, and along the horse corral: Sickness was here. Stay away. Claude would not leave his wife's side to fetch either priest of medicine man. When a rash appeared on Francois's skin, we knew his flush was not from hard work but he, too, had the same disease. Those of us with the blood of the white man were well, and those in our family who had Indian blood had fallen sick.

Was Full Moon right—that what ailed them was a white man's poison? Ellen stayed by their beds. I collected herbs for teas and poultices. Claude gave them icy baths and cleaned them up. Wilhelm kept our fires going for the hot water we needed and butchered a hen for broth. The trading post smelled like an infirmary.

Midge sat in the corner crying while her two playmates moaned on their beds. Midnight moved next to her, and the little girl rested her head on the dog's back, watching with a bewildered look.

By the middle of the night, the sick ones were resting quietly. Wilhelm read from the Bible. "The Lord said unto me, 'My grace is sufficient for thee: for my strength is made perfect in weakness.' Most gladly therefore will I rather glory in my infirmities, that the power of Christ may rest upon me." I fell asleep in the rocker wondering what it meant to glory in God's weaknesses.

No amount of herbs and poultices could break Sammy's fever. He succumbed to his fight after a five-day struggle. We placed his body, wrapped in his blanket, in the icehouse for a day so that Full Moon could gain enough strength to sit with us at Sammy's graveside. We buried the delightful two-year-old on July 21, 1686.

My heart ached for my friends.

When we placed Sammy in the ground, Wilhelm read these words:

> What shall we then say to these things? If God be for us, who can be against us? I am persuaded, that neither death, nor life, nor angels nor principalities nor powers, nor things present nor things to come, nor height, nor depth, nor any other creature, shall be able to separate us from the love of God, which is in Christ Jesus our Lord.

...

With death Parrot's Bay changed. Ellen overprotected Midge. Midge wiggled away from her mother, demanding independence. Wilhelm spent more time reading the Bible as though he needed answers. Francois struggled with the high fever only one day. When his energy returned, he found solace riding Tonnere. Claude worked harder, longer, and talked less than before, if such a thing were possible. Full Moon stayed in her cabin, not even venturing out to use the necessary; her sorrow was so deep and dark.

And I prayed more, asking God to show me his perspective. How could he, a loving God, allow the death of an innocent child? Where was God's goodness in all this?

I sat on the edge of the dock and watched. Storm clouds formed, backlit by the setting sun, billowing up into a thunderstorm. A mother loon and four chicks paddled out into the middle of the bay. Suddenly a chick was plucked from the line and disappeared, pulled under the water by a pike. From a treetop, a hoot owl swooped down to the nearby field, circled, hovered, and then flew back to his perch, carrying a furry critter in his talons.

The rhythm of nature. Life and death. The predator and the prey. Sunrise and sunset. A light of understanding flickered in my soul. The Creator had set up these rhythms, the order of the natural world, the laws of the physical universe. He thought the natural order was best for us, and he was not going to interfere with these laws unless a miracle was in order.

The mournful cry of the loon interrupted my thinking. Amidst the lake sounds, I thought I heard: "Faith is greater than understanding. Life is all about faith and the acceptance of my way."

I looked behind me on the dock expecting someone speaking to me. Wilhelm? Francois? No one was there.

"Mat-tee, just accept my way. The peace that passes all under-standing shall keep your heart and mind through my Son," the divine voice said.

I lay back on the warm wood of the boat dock and watched the evening clouds. Awe, fullness, peace—I felt these as the sun set.

And my faith grew.

...

The winter of 1687 was so cold we took extreme care when stoking the fires at night, and we stuffed rags in between the cabin logs' cracks to retain every bit of heat. Fresh snow fell nightly, covering over the dirty gray from the previous day. Parrot's Bay had frozen solid by January, so we anticipated harvesting our ice for a second year.

Robert had departed for France three years before. While I knew he had arrived in the Matagorda Bay area last year, there had been no word since. His absence created a gaping hole in my heart, which I filled as best I could through work, play, and my Parrot Bay family.

Every night I looked to the stars and wondered what constellations Robert was seeing. Every night I prayed God's blessing on him and my Parrot Bay's family. Every night I tried to yield my heart's cleft to the Creator and give thanks for this time of silence. Every night I sought the value in waiting.

...

In late March at dusk, Wilhelm padded out on to the ice to check our harvest spot. He wanted to be sure the cold snap wasn't refreezing the hole where we would cut ice blocks the next day. Ellen was telling Midge stories, and she could see Wilhelm's silhouette against the horizon as he walked out into the bay. I was in the barnyard scattering corn to the chickens.

Suddenly the ice cracked. Wife and daughter heard the noise. They saw Wilhelm disappear into the water. Ellen screamed. "Wilhelm's under the ice!"

Frantically Claude and I grabbed rope and planks and rushed to him, slipping on snow and sliding on icy rocks. I shimmied out on the planks. Claude held the end of a rope tied about my waist as a precaution. Wilhelm's fall had knocked his cap off, and it perched forlornly on the dark ice above the hole.

I lay cold on the plank, my head in the ice hole, looking for him. My mind pictured Wilhelm grasping for a handhold, then choking on the water as he slid into the freezing, dark bay. Had he kept his eyes open? Had he tried to climb out only to crack through again? Did his boots hold him down, water logged, ice cold? Or had he taken them off? Did he call out?

I cried out to God, sobbing.

Wilhelm was gone.

In the distance, I could hear Ellen's mournful howls.

I bellowed. To God, I screamed, "Enough is enough! Stop! Stop the pain!"

When I embraced my dear friend, I willed God's strength into her body. Ellen Jenet was a widow at twenty-seven years old.

...

Ellen and I moved around in a frozen stupor for days. Wilhelm's loss devastated her. I was in a dark, emotional pit where the cold blackness of the hole in the ice haunted me.

Francois sought comfort for hours in the woodland or with Tonnere. When Midge asked about her father for the first few days, her mother assured her that Papa had traveled to see Jesus. Midge then turned her concern on her mother, whose grief the little child could sense. Wilhelm would have comforted us with reading from the Bible, but Claude was illiterate, and Ellen was stupefied.

It was Midge who helped me.

"Mat-tee, read 'bout Jesus, 'bout how he loves us."

So I reached for the Bible, pulled Wilhelm's daughter up on my lap, and started reading.

> My sheep hear my voice, and I know them, and they follow me: and I give unto them eternal life; and they shall never perish ... I am the resurrection and the life; he that believes in me, though he were dead, yet shall he live ... Peace I leave with you and my peace I give unto you: not as the world gives, give I to you. Let not your heart be troubled, neither let it be afraid ... These things have I spoken

to you, that my joy might remain in you and that your joy might be full.

Reading the Bible began to heal me. I was starving for the Word of God. It was my bread. It quenched my thirst. It was my life.

Often I read aloud to Midge, Francois, and Ellen. If I had chosen to wait for a priest to comfort me, I would not have been able to survive that difficult time. I approached God in prayer hourly; such was the solace and strength he provided. Faith grew in proportion to my hearing God's Word.

...

As soon as the lake had thawed, a priest and a soldier arrived from Fort Frontenac. "We are here for Wilhelm Jenet, former captain in the governor's military," the soldier announced without preamble toward the end of April. I had met them by the dock's edge and silenced Midnight with a hand signal and the look. The dog slinked off. "Come up to the house, gentlemen. I'm sure some refreshment would be welcome," I said, scrambling to decide how to handle the situation.

As we approached the porch, I called ahead. "Ellen, they are here for Wilhelm." Giving her some time to think this through, I turned back to the men and warned them about the slippery embankment. "Watch it there."

The men untied their muddy boots and entered the lodge in their sock feet. They moved toward the fireplace but didn't take the offered seats.

"What is this about, sir? I am Captain Jenet's wife. Perhaps I can help you." Ellen spoke confidently, even though she had taken a seat in the rocker to hide her shaking knees. She was knitting with agitation.

The priest spoke. "It has come to our attention Captain Jenet has renounced the church. We would like to speak to him about that. Such behavior is no longer tolerated under His Majesty's law. The Edict of Nantes has been revoked. I am here to see if Jenet would like to make a confession and resume his standing as a Roman Catholic."

"And if he wouldn't, sir, make his confession? Then what?" Ellen looked the priest straight in the eye, knitting needles poised in her hands.

"Well, Madame, he would be put under arrest." The priest looked around. No evidence of a man in this dwelling was seen. Claude and Full Moon were living in their cabin, and Ellen had moved herself and the children in the main house with me since Wilhelm's death. No men's boots, no men's britches, no men's caps.

"Sir," Ellen said, addressing the priest, not calling him father or reverend as was proper. "Wilhelm is no longer here. He is unable to make that confession."

"Where may we find him?" the soldier asked.

"In heaven, sir," Ellen said, looking at the fireplace and the black and pine wreath mounted there since Wilhelm's death.

"In heaven, Madame?" the priest exclaimed. "We were told we would find him here."

Finding my voice, I stood in front of them. "Captain Jenet was drowned in the bay about one month ago. You will observe we are in mourning," I said, gesturing toward the black wreath, realizing they weren't picking up our subtle hints.

"What proof do we have that you are not hiding him, Madame Jenet?" the priest demanded of Ellen.

"None, sir."

Now timing can be everything. Midge ran in the front door just then, leading Georgette. The sight of the little girl leading a pig six times her size took them aback. The tension broke.

And it gave me an idea. As we had not recovered Wilhelm's body, proof of his death might be difficult.

"Honey," I called Midge over to me. Addressing the men, I said, "This young one is Captain Jenet's daughter, Migault. Midge, say hello to these men."

She grinned at them and said, "*Bonjour.*"

"Midge, would you please tell them where your daddy is. They are looking for him."

"Sirs, go look for my daddy in heaven. God has taken him to heaven. Right, *ma mere?*" With that, she skipped over to Ellen's lap, took the knitting out of her hands, and gave her mother a hug.

The soldier blushed. The priest cleared his throat. "The church gives blessings to this house because of the loss of your loved one." And he made the sign of the cross. They barely tied their boots so great was their haste to leave.

...

A peace conference in July 1687, between French leaders and the pro-British Iroquois chiefs, was held at Cataraqui. Governor Denonville, who had replaced LaBarre, invited Father Lamberville to moderate. For one peaceful day, the white men and the natives exchanged ideas.

But, on the second day, the governor's soldiers surrounded Fort Frontenac. They betrayed and captured the Iroquois. The French put their enemies in tethers and imprisoned them at the nearby Huron village. Fuming with anger, the Iroquois retaliated for the Cataraqui betrayal. One month later, Seneca and Onondaga tribes, part of the Five Nations, combined forces and committed themselves to overpowering the white man. Warriors unsheathed their knives, snuck up on the makeshift prison camp, and freed their leaders. Still enraged war parties spread out through Quebec. Hostilities between the French and the savages were as hot as the fires of Gehanna. An angry group of Onondaga warriors swept west, toward Parrot's Bay.

I learned this all later, when it was too late.

# 31

# SPILLED BLOOD

On that humid August morning in 1687, Francois led Tonnere as we hunted a mile from my trading post. Suddenly smoke rose on the horizon above Parrot's Bay. Seeing the plume of dirty sky, I wondered, *Is Claude burning brush? No. That can't be. It must be a thundercloud forming.* But Francois knew better. And in my heart, so did I. Hadn't we both seen the moccasin print in the silt? It was one—not of our trading partners—but of France's foe, the Iroquois's Onondaga people from across Lake Ontario. As a woman of New France, I would have no power to negotiate with them.

Francois leapt onto Tonnere's saddle despite his club foot, and rode off. I sprinted toward home, calling between gasps, "Don't let them see you." A deformed child was worse than garbage to a native.

Stopping short of our property, I crept behind a tree. In my yard, Ellen stood frozen, clutching Midge. One warrior guarded them. Claude lay dead, an arrow through his chest, his scalp bloody.

Smoke and soot filled the air, as a dozen Iroquois circled our burning house, gathering bounty. Our trade goods were strewn on the ground.

From my hiding place, I smelled sweat and war paint. Midge peered around her mother's enfolded arms. Another Iroquois dragged a stunned Full Moon out of the barn. They fastened her wrists and hobbled her ankles with rawhide. For once, the garrulous woman stood quiet; soot-stained tears smeared her face.

Then a flaming arrow flew toward the shingles of the barn roof and found purchase. Ellen raised her fists in the air and screamed. For that second, Midge was free from her mother's grasp. The warrior grabbed the child and tossed her to a comrade, who stuffed her mouth, trussed her, and laid her face down on the bottom of a canoe. Midge squirmed and grunted.

Ellen threw herself at the guard, scratching his face. His blood splattered her apron. The warrior slapped her and punched her gut. Her breath emptied out of her with a whoosh. Ellen's knees buckled, and she sank to the ground.

The warrior leapt on her like a starving wolf on a lamb. Pressing a large knife to her throat, he pinned her down. His free hand grabbed her thick skirts and undershirt, and he yanked them over her head. His face contorted with lustful exhilaration and hatred as he raped her.

She screamed again and again.

I tried to turn away but could not. Shame flooded me. Ellen was my best friend. We had seen the trading post prosper. Her gentle spirit had succored me through difficulties. I had grown into a better woman because of her faith.

And I knew how her violation felt. Had I not fled France because of my own humiliation? Had I not been devastated by my abuse while at Versailles?

What could I do? As the warrior ravaged Ellen, angry heat washed my body. I clenched my teeth, letting out a snarl.

Then I felt for the hunting knife strapped to my leg.

When the warrior was spent, Ellen's belly and thighs looked ashen against the brown earth. The Onondagan flipped his knife and sliced the skin on her forehead in a half moon. He raised the bloodied scalp of flowing blonde hair above his head and let out a feral whoop. Ellen moaned. Her eyes rolled back. Her chest writhed.

Horror started to invade my thoughts, but I slammed the gate on them. I focused on my options.

Ellen uttered feeble sobs. Her breathing rasped. She'd soon be dead from loss of blood. If I stole away to save myself, the savages would torture her until she died. Should I kill the warrior and bring down the wrath of the war party?

But Jesus had said not to kill. Yet this was our enemy, and the savage would kill me if I didn't kill him first.

Was it acceptable to kill my friend to spare her suffering? Wouldn't such a slaying still be murder in God's eyes? Shouldn't our Creator be the final arbiter of death? If I killed Ellen, would God understand?

As the warrior turned to count coup with his comrades, I made my decision. Staying low to the ground, I crawled to Ellen and whispered, "Godspeed. Christ is with you. Go be with Wilhelm. See our Jesus face-to-face."

Her eyes opened. Ellen smiled and gave an imperceptible nod of approval.

With the same gesture I used to slaughter our pigs, I slashed her throat. Ellen's blood spurted me in the eye. Bile rose. I swallowed it again and again. Her eyes quieted in death. She was peaceful now, entering a better world.

I lowered her lids. Then, to clear my vision, I wiped her blood away.

Every warrior's attention focused on Francois, who was being forced into the yard, leading Tonnere. Quick like a field mouse, I crawled back behind the tree.

The Iroquois laughed and pointed as the boy's clubfoot dragged behind him. Tonnere's ears flared backwards. The smell of blood unnerved him. Unfamiliar with horses, the natives kept their distance from the stallion while they bickered about what to do with Francois.

"He's a cripple. No good for anyone. Scalp him, I say!" one shouted. He wore four scalps on his belt, one of them Ellen's.

"But he's red skin. Look at him."

"Must be part white. A true native would have killed him at birth."

"You, take his scalp." The leader gestured to a young warrior, who drew his knife and stepped toward Francois.

I knew Francois was following their conversation. Realizing his life could be taken in a split second, the boy called out to the leader, "*Tasaten onywatenro*. Stay his hand. I can do well for your tribe. Let me show you."

Surprised, the leader asked. "You know our language? How can you, a cripple, do good for our tribe?"

"With this horse. We hunt well together. My leg makes no difference. Watch me." Francois held his head high, his back erect.

The leader surveyed the boy. "How do I know you won't ride away from us?"

"On my word as a red man. And I will ride naked to return as quickly as that squirrel can run to those woods." He pointed to the forest on the far side of the pasture.

The leader nodded.

Francois lifted up his bonds to be cut and then stripped off his clothes. Naked, he leaped on to Tonnere's saddle. He used his upper body strength to haul himself up by the mane, his good leg to spring high onto the horse's back, and his crippled leg to brace himself around the stallion's flank.

Boy and horse galloped across the field in a big loop. Francois, standing on Tonnere's back, pantomimed shooting a gun and then cocking an arrow and letting it fly. Some warriors muttered; all stared. I felt tears of pride well up. Would this earn the Iroquois' respect? Would they let Francois live?

Francois and Tonnere cantered back. But the horse did not stop at Francois's signal. Tonnere jogged to my hiding place, nickered for me, and tossed his head. The lead warrior strode over to the tree and held his knife to the horse's throat.

"Come out. Or I'll kill the animal."

I did not hesitate. The warrior looked at my blood-splattered face, glanced at Ellen's corpse, and grabbed me by my hair.

"Go ahead," I said in Iroquois as I looked him firmly in the eye. "Let me die and meet my God." Francois's performance had given me strength. I had little left to lose. I stroked Tonnere's muzzle. The stallion rolled his lips back as my fingers played with his nose.

Warriors chortled. Francois smiled.

The leader surveyed our trading area, our boat dock, and the canoes. He studied Francois, the horse, and me. How would they get Tonnere to their village? While a horse can swim across a narrow river, these marauders lived along the southern shore of Lake Ontario, one hundred miles of water away.

The leader assessed his captives and his treasures. He said, "Fill the boats with all the trade goods, the red skin woman, and child with white hair. Burn the place to the ground. We see you in our village when the moon is new."

Gesturing to me, he said, "You come with that horse and boy."

He tied the rope around my wrists and up around my neck. "You dress," he said to Francois.

Francois then asked permission to run into our lodge. When he returned, his satchel bulged with my diary and quills, our large Bible, my winter moccasins, Midge's doll, and his father's military cap.

Our trek to the Onondaga village in Oswego began.

We stopped to camp for the night several miles east of Fort Frontenac. Signaling Francois, I whispered, "Have you seen Midnight?" Francois, downcast, shook his head. I thought maybe that loyal dog had followed us.

When the Iroquois offered us roasted dog for our evening meal, a sickening feeling overcame me. I turned my back and, in the shadows, retched and sobbed. Grief pierced me. Francois, Midnight, and I had spent hours together romping, running, laughing, and growing. Midnight had saved my life. Curse them! Parrot's Bay was burned out. Midnight was dead, used as food for greedy Indians. Ellen, my dear Ellen, had suffered terribly. Then I, her friend, had killed her.

...

In order to cross the rivers our captors had to build a large raft to hold four people and one stallion. Tonnere, snorting and blowing, balked and bucked and would not board the floating logs. The horse needed a blindfold, Francois's words of endearment in his ear, and the boy's gentle hands on his flank. As tired as I was, I yearned to kick up a similar ruckus as the horse but dared not. No one would comfort me.

After a hot, sticky hike of ten days, we arrived at their Iroquois village in Oswego.

# 32

# SHADOW OF DEATH

Our captors pushed us ahead of them as we entered their village. I saw Onondaga Iroquois longhouses, standing fifteen feet tall and thirty feet long, spread out over many acres of green fields. Warriors led Francois and Tonnere away and put me in a small bark hut. Women clucked over my weakened condition. From what talk I could understand, they were trying to decide what to do with me.

Images of natives burning white people at the stake came to mind. Would I be brave if I had to face a death by fire? Or would my knowledge of their language and their ways save me, as it had Robert so often? When he returned north, would he be able to find me? Would I ever see him again?

A native girl had me sit and then tied me to the hut's center post. A pottery bowl of fresh water and another receptacle for waste were within reach. Corn bread and meat jerky lay on a block near my mat.

Time felt unreal, vague, and meaningless. For four days and four nights I was kept in this dimly lit dwelling. Twice a day a different native woman opened the flap letting fresh air in and gave me food and water She would stare at me. I would try to catch a glimpse of the outside, but the light was too bright. I marked the passing of a day with a finger line on the dirt floor.

Surprisingly, my time in solitude proved to be a balm. At first I sobbed, bewildered, exhausted, and grieving over Ellen's death. I believed she was with Wilhelm, living with Jesus in an unimaginably beautiful place. But would God forgive my taking her life into my own hands?

JULIE CATON

Because the hut was too dark to read the Bible, I recalled passages Annie, Wilhelm, and Ellen had read to me as I sat in the tenebrous stillness.

Eventually healing sleep settled over me.

...

During the four days I had heard or seen nothing of Francois, Full Moon, or Midge. When I fretted about Midge, I remembered the savages love children, usually adopting them as their own. And Midge, as her father had once said, was resilient and clever. Francois had already earned a safe place with the Iroquois if their treatment of him on our journey here was any proof. Full Moon was a native like her captors. As long as she kept her mouth shut, the Iroquois would tolerate her—probably.

I concentrated on listening and could distinguish the intervals of the day by the sounds the village made. After some practice, the camp hum melted into the background, and I could discern conversations among groups. I learned that the Iroquois warriors had been creating skirmishes throughout the countryside. Other Cataraqui captives were here, but I could not discover whom. The village was planning a victory dance, at which the captives would be presented to the tribe and their futures decided.

...

On the first day of September, two young women entered the tepee carrying bowls of steaming water and ointment.

"*Yias Madeleine. Taoten chias.* My name is Madeleine. What is yours?" I asked. The native girls were startled when I addressed them in their own language.

When the girls reproduced my name in their own language, they rendered my name "Watereen." The taller maiden with sleek, black hair said her name was Crow Feather, and the soft, curvaceous one was called Polished Rock. Crow Feather told me six white captives were in the village, including a little girl.

When these women sponged me off and rubbed bear grease on me (an appealing smell to them and pleasantly familiar to me), I felt renewed. They slipped a new deerskin tunic over my shoulders and braided my hair. I wore moccasins, leggings, and a skirt.

They led me to the central fires where tall greenwood stakes for burning captives had been raised. Would one be mine? A cold, sinking feeling ran through my body. I had to grip onto Crow Feather to keep from sliding to the ground. Each girl then held my arms. We took our place in the circle of gathered Iroquois.

Four nights and days in solitude had deepened my faith and assuaged my fear of death. I prayed, *Help me, Lord. Make me brave. If you want me to die now at this time in this place, so be it.*

Iroquois milled about. Midge, on the other side of the community circle, saw me and waved. A native woman spoke sharply to her, and her face changed to a confused, crestfallen look. I tried to smile reassuringly. Native drumming picked up speed as the chief, and his entourage entered the circle. The chief spoke about their victory in the north, the devastation they had caused the Quebec governor, and the bounty brought back.

Warriors came from outside the circle carrying canoes full of trade goods. Most of the goods were from the shelves at Parrot's Bay. My anger boiled, although I knew I must stay rational and calm.

Iron kettles, textiles, glass beads, bags of flour, and jars of preserves were laid at the chief's feet. I took a deep breath. I let go of my goods. After all, I had no control over them.

The rhythm of the drums changed. It now sounded like horses running.

From the outer circle, Tonnere loped toward the chief. Tonnere's harness was a bright-red rope, and Francois was wearing a red loincloth and red, knee-high moccasins flashing with white shells. The black stallion and the young man made a striking picture. Francois did tricks on the horse's back. The crowd expressed admiration with "oohs" and "aahs."

Halting the stallion just short of the chief, Francois swung down from Tonnere and bowed. Speaking in Iroquois, he offered himself and the stallion to the tribe. The crowd cheered.

Francois had learned the lessons well about cross-cultural understanding, diplomacy, and respecting the natives' way of life. With his humility and charm, he would be welcomed. For the first time since our captivity, I breathed a sigh of relief.

The stout warrior responsible for Ellen's suffering came forward, holding Full Moon and Midge by their arms. His face looked like a rotted pumpkin. The chief then asked a grieving mother who had lost her son in the skirmish at Cataraqui to adopt Midge. She came forward and gratefully took Midge away.

Full Moon was presented to an elderly native as her daughter. Full Moon did not look happy about this. I wondered how long the old woman would put up with Moon's complaining.

Next, the leader of the attack on Parrot's Bay beckoned to Polished Rock and Crow Feather to escort me to the chief. The warrior ordered me to introduce myself.

I lowered my gaze to the ground, remembering respect was shown in that manner. "Honored Chief, I am Madeleine de Roybon D'Allone, proprietress of the trading post, Parrot's Bay," I said in fluent Iroquois. "It honors me to be among your people."

A lie? Well, I did have respect for these people as much as for the French. I knew of atrocities being done on both sides. The royal dragoons had been as brutal to the Huguenots as Iroquois had been to French people.

"You speak our language? How?" He spoke with a lisp, due to missing teeth, but the old chief presented himself with dignity.

"The Creator *Hawendio* has given me a gift of languages. I learned yours from the Reverend Mother Marie of the Incarnation in Quebec." Confidence was returning to my shaking body. I said, "Perhaps I can assist you as an interpreter?" I glanced briefly at his face. Did I discern respect?

My captor thrust himself between his chief and me. The warrior's pumpkin face contorted with anger as he told the chief how I had stolen Ellen's death from him. He demanded my life as payment.

The chief looked at me with sorrow. Stringy, silver-gray hair fell over his face as he bowed his head and closed his eyes. Next to him my hostile captor stomped his feet and flexed his muscles. People remained quiet. The passing seconds, which held my life in the balance, unnerved me. I stopped breathing.

The chief raised his voice. "*Oskenrayehte.* This woman is warrior. Maybe she deserves death; maybe she doesn't. To know, she should run the gauntlet tomorrow. We will see her spirit."

My captor grunted. I exhaled my held breath.

Crow Feather and Polished Rock bowed their heads and guided me backward.

Male captives were then brought forward. Usually male prisoners, seen as a threat to the tribe, were sentenced to burn alive. One of the men, a coureur de bois judging from his clothes, begged to be permitted the gauntlet also. He understood some Iroquois and spoke haltingly. His captor cracked him on the head for speaking, and the captive sank to the ground, where he was instantly pinned by two young men.

The chief then said, "White man is brave man of the woods," and he ordered the man's captor to "take out the heart of your prize."

It all happened so fast; I was stunned. The Iroquois seized his knife, plunged it into the white man's diaphragm, and cut out his still-beating heart to the piercing screams of the victim. The warrior lifted the bloody organ above his head, gave out a war whoop, and took a bite out of the warm flesh. He then offered the coureur de bois's heart to the chief, who also took a bite from it.

I gasped and pushed bile down in my throat. Crow Feather and Polished Rock did not flinch. I hung onto their arms for support. The three surviving male prisoners were led to the stakes and tied. Iroquois set fire to the dry branches at their captives' feet.

Knowing these people venerated bravery, I forced myself to look at the flaming pyres. The smell of burning flesh assaulted my nostrils and my stomach revolted. Vomiting was the ultimate sign of weakness, so I swallowed hard.

As flames leapt upward, roasting their legs and licking their chests, I saw the horrified faces of the men contort in agony. I closed my eyes when I saw the flesh on one man's cheek blister and blacken just before he fainted.

My mind had frozen, except for the single message I kept repeating to myself: *Stand firm and strong. Then they may let you live.*

• • •

The sun set. The night sky was black.

At dawn, I would run the gauntlet.

I said, "I need to talk with my Creator, my *Hawendio*, Crow Feather," but she made no sign of leaving me. "If I were not a prisoner, I would go into the woods alone to seek my spiritual father. Do you understand? Please help me. Tomorrow I run the gauntlet. Tonight I need his power." I asked her for an oil lamp like Sleeping Willow had made me and for the Bible Francois had saved.

When she brought them, I requested solitude.

My time that night was an intense emotional battle. I raged about the loss of so many friends. I condemned myself for being so smug, so arrogant as to think we would be safe at Parrot's Bay. Maybe running the gauntlet was punishment for my pride. Fear choked me.

Robert had told me about the gauntlet, a native tradition and community test to discern the character of a captive. He had been a prisoner of the Iroquois several times. On one occasion he endured one. I remembered his tale:

"The tribal members line up in two rows about six feet apart. Every person carries his chosen weapon: a stick, hatchet, whip, handfuls of sand to throw in the captive's eyes. They strip the prisoner and shove him into the gauntlet, expecting him to run to the other end of the man-made tunnel. The natives want to observe the true character of their captive when he is under extreme duress. A rule of the competition: The captive can't be killed. If he emerges bravely from the ordeal, he is worthy of adoption. If he succumbs to the pain and torture, expresses weakness or fear, he is later killed—usually by burning at the stake."

"How did you manage it, Robert?" I'd asked.

"I ran fast, focusing on the end of the line. I concentrated on my breathing, held my head up high, and tried to ignore the blows and the cuts. I must have appeared brave because the tribe cheered me when I made it through."

"Don't you think it terribly cruel?"

"No more than placing poor souls in stocks or pillars, which we French do. In fact, it is over quicker and reveals more of the person's inner makings."

This conversation came back to me as I prepared myself for the next day's ordeal. Speed and physical strength were not going to win this experience for me. A sick, defeated feeling crept up. I was so tired.

I stretched myself out on the furs and whimpered.

I thought I heard Ellen's voice. *God has not given you a spirit of fear, Mat-tee, but a spirit of power, love, and a sound mind.*

*How does the Lord do that, Ellen?*

*Ask God for faith, Madeleine.*

So I started talking to God. "I'm so frightened, Lord. Help my lack of faith." I read Jesus' words and sang God's praise. Finally, a burden lifted off my shoulders. Involuntarily my arms rose up, hands open. A transformation was taking place.

Surrendering. Yielding.

I was giving up control to God.

He entered me.

And this time I felt peace. My anguish subsided, and I lay still. Serenity was all around.

On the mat, my body relaxed. Would I still be alive in the flesh by the end of the day? Or would I be with God?

In truth, the answer didn't make any difference. In either case, I was in God's hands.

# 33
# THE GAUNTLET

Iroquois pushed and shoved to get their place in parallel rows. I was led to the mouth of the gauntlet. An old man was swinging a spiked mallet, youthful warriors slapped hatchets against their palms and some urchins were juggling rotten fruit. I preferred not to think about these weapons but reflected on the two hundred human beings lined up to test my character. God loved each one.

The gauntlet is a living organism. It takes on a mood of its own, responding to the attitudes of the participants and of the captive. Would I be taunted and provoked, chided and harassed? Would I face this event in fearfulness or with courage and grace?

At the onset, I believed one thing: God was with me.

Crow Feather and Polished Rock pulled off my tunic. My nude body shivered. I heard jeering. The rough ground scratched my bare feet. Trying to immerse myself in the presence of the Spirit, I focused on the sky. Clouds puffed and billowed, white against bright blue. The sun warmed my breasts and back.

Then a warrior thrust me into the gauntlet.

What I remember was my walking tall and confident. I looked toward the horizon and not at the faces of the people. I breathed deeply, exhaling my fear and inhaling God's power. Somehow my feet hardened and found a sure path. I no longer felt vulnerable but wrapped in a protective shroud, that of God's love.

The sun's heat mingled with a breeze on my body. I could smell the people, their war paint, bear grease, and body odors. But I didn't see their faces, couldn't feel the pain they inflicted on me, or hear their taunts.

All I knew, all I experienced, was God's presence.

Then Crow Feather was placing a cape over my shoulders, and Polished Rock was offering me water.

I had emerged from the gauntlet and could still walk with confidence.

As I was led back to my tepee, I heard nothing for a few moments. Then a low rumbling of praise in Iroquois resounded through the tribe.

The girls did not tie me up, nor did they secure the flap. Instead they squatted, staring at me, silent.

In the background, the village hummed.

Finally Crow Feather spoke. "I have been with the tribe fifteen years and have seen five gauntlets. But you, Watereen, you... you were... you were—"

"What she is trying to say," Polished Rock interrupted, "is that never have we seen anybody like you. You have only a handful of marks on you, even though we saw knives slice you and whips lash you. You didn't cry out from pain. Your nakedness did not shame you. You carried yourself proud and sure."

"How can this be?" Crow Feather asked.

"Feather, let her rest," Polished Rock said. "We must cleanse those few wounds on her back. Mademoiselle Watereen, lie down. Feather, this lady warrior will talk to us later. Isn't that right, *Aweiachiayenrat*, White Heart?"

*Did she call me "White Heart?" What had happened?* With these thoughts in my head and the gentle hands of Polished Rock on my back, I fell asleep.

...

Several days later, I heard a scratching on my shelter's rawhide flap announcing a visitor. My back had healed. I had spent time with my two native companions reading from the Bible, and they had expressed admiration for this "Spirit" that had upheld me through the gauntlet.

The scratching continued. As it was midday and Crow Feather and Polished Rock had left me alone an hour earlier, I couldn't imagine whom it might be.

Julie Caton

"Come," I said.

A tiny, wizened native woman tucked her head in. In broken French, she asked if she might talk.

The day had an autumnal chill, so she had brought a bundle of firewood and asked in French if she could build up my fire to keep her bones warm. "At my age, any dampness sets me to aching." She added logs to the fire and seated herself cross-legged opposite me.

She was ancient with crosshatched lines covering her round face. Wispy, silver-white hair hung to her shoulders, and her neck and arms looked like golden-bronze, reptilian leather. Her widely placed eyes accented high cheekbones. These eyes captured mine; they were alert, curious and sympathetic.

"Welcome. I am Madeleine de Roybon D'Allone," I said in Iroquois.

"They call me Trees. And you are called 'White Heart,' are you not?"

"I have heard," I replied, "but I don't understand it."

"White Heart. That is what you were in the gauntlet."

To my perplexed look, she responded, "Your white body glowed ... Your back showed just a few marks. The rest of your body was untouched. You were looking up to sky the whole time. Your smooth, white arms reached high to the sun. After you were halfway down the line, the tribe stopped attacking and just watched. Your face reflected peace and love. We have called you 'White Heart' because that is what you looked like during the ordeal. A woman enshrouded in a pure, loving heart."

Trees repositioned a log, and it caught the flames. "I have only seen that expression once in my life. That is why I want to talk with you."

"Oh." That was all I could think to say, astonished by Trees's description of the gauntlet and me. We sat companionably watching the apple wood burn, not talking. Trees waited politely for me to initiate the conversation. Finally I inquired, "Trees, please speak what is on your mind."

"I am the adopted sister to the tribal chief. I was standing near you when you mentioned a name I haven't heard for forty-five winters: Reverend Mother Marie of the Incarnation. How did you know her?"

I told Trees my story of the Ursuline Convent, about working on the dictionaries, and Mother Marie's death in 1671. Trees's inquisitive look changed into one of sorrow. She didn't respond for a few moments. Then she explained, "I was her student shortly after she established the convent. My name was Teresa. My people were Huron. When my father and brothers were killed in the massacre in Huronia, my mother and I fled the area, walking cross-country to Quebec. The Reverend Mother welcomed us. She taught me French, and I taught her Iroquois. She shared with me the mysteries of the church and encouraged me to be baptized as a follower of Christ. I couldn't comprehend the love offered by Christ. But I yearned for it.

"Following my conversion, I stayed at the convent learning French ways. A Huron tribe from *Trois Riveres* offered to escort me to their village to teach their young girls."

Trees stretched her hands out over the fire, rubbed them, and continued talking. "But the Iroquois ambushed our party, killing our men. They took me captive and brought me here in 1643." Trees paused, reflecting.

"Today's chief is my adopted brother. To this day, I do not know why I was spared torture and death. Perhaps because the chief's wife had so much power and took a liking to me. Perhaps my prayers kept me from that danger. Perhaps the blood thirst of the tribe was not as intense as it has been in recent years."

I poured an herbal drink for Trees and said, "Mother Marie had told me about you."

Trees sipped the brew. "This tribe took me in and gave me freedom to worship Christ. They found me an Iroquois husband, and I had three beautiful children. Crow Feather is my daughter's daughter."

"And the other two?"

"God saw fit to take my sons last year—slaughtered in a battle with the French. Isn't that an odd turn of the sun?"

"I'm so sorry."

"My sons had been baptized secretly as young men. Because they were Iroquois, they could not practice Christian ways publicly. Our tribe allied themselves with the English who had rejected the Catholic Church and followed the reformed movement."

I nodded.

"I must keep my Catholic rituals to myself," Trees said. "Fortunately, I can openly profess Jesus Christ. I just can't practice the Mass or be seen in confession with a priest or hold a rosary in my hand. Doing so would bring shame on my family and threaten our alliance with the English settlers."

"How strange. Where I come from, the opposite is true. If I want to renounce the Catholic rituals, in the eyes of the French, I would be considered a lawbreaker, a Huguenot."

As we talked more, I discovered a true kindred spirit in Trees. We both had been uprooted, suffered losses, and found Jesus Christ. We both had to be careful about the outward expression of our faith.

Trees delighted in the idea that now she could hear the Word of God because I could read my Bible to her.

Her spiritual perspective on hardship encouraged me. "God is not punishing you, White Heart. He is pruning you, cutting away the dead wood, the branches in your life that don't bear any fruit. All these hardships will last only for a time. He loves you and wants you to be more like him."

Crow Feather scratched on the flap and brought us supper. Smiling at her grandmother, she presented three bowls of porridge topped with roasted apples. It was dark outside. Trees and I had talked the day away!

...

Crow Feather's older sister adopted the Jenet children. The Iroquois here respected Francois more highly than traders at Parrot's Bay had because of his skill with the horse and bow.

On the occasions when he sought me out, Francois would come with a question about his Catholic faith or a desire to reminisce about his parents. Despite his bereavement, he enjoyed his newly gained respect and the savages' natural way of living.

Midge played happily with the children and conversed well in their language, I often saw her cuddling the doll Francois had rescued from her burning home. When the little girl and I talked together, it was of the present. On rare occasions, Midge said, "I'll tell *Ma Mere* and *Mon Pere* that when I see them in heaven, Mat-tee," or "*Ma Mere* knows that happened, Mat-tee. She looks down on me from Jesus' house." Her childlike faith inspired me, and I encouraged her beliefs as best I could.

...

During the 1687 harvest season, God lavished the tribe with plentiful crops. The Iroquois held days of feasting. Trees came daily to hear me read the Bible. Many of the women, already touched by the faith of Trees and her family, had reached out to me. They asked if I would pray with them or read a word from the Lord. Often I was invited to their longhouses to share from their common pot.

Toward the end of November, while we sat in the privacy of my shelter, Trees broached a sensitive topic. The air smelled of pine boughs. "White Heart, would you consider letting me adopt you as my daughter? I am old, so I might be a burden to you if I were to become frail or weak, and would need you to care for me. Now my brother, the chief, has offered you to me to take the place of my missing sons. If you say 'yes,' you will be protected by my family."

Since the gauntlet and my acceptance into the village, I had assumed my role would be to take part in the forthcoming native—French-English diplomatic negotiations. Someday I expected to be returned to my country in exchange for the freedom of a captured Iroquois.

After a long silence, I said, "Trees, I love you. I would be honored to be a member of your family. But I'm not sure I am ready to trade all my French ways for a life completely and permanently with your people."

The old woman pressed. "You need protection, my daughter. If this tribe goes on the warpath next spring and we lose our fighting men, families will want revenge. By then, it will be too late for me to help you. You might be sacrificed at the stake."

"What about the possibility I might be ransomed? Your tribe needs money. Or perhaps your brother will exchange me for a captured warrior. Won't the French governor barter with Chief Flying Salmon for my return?"

"I don't know." Trees reached out to the Bible, opened the large leather cover, and ran her hand along the page. "What if he doesn't?"

The silence was heavy. I began thinking about my life under the French government. It had not been pleasant. Their hypocrisy galled me when I watched them deal with the natives. The regulations of living as a French woman were constraining and irrational. Because of the double standard in which women weren't permitted the same rights regarding property and ownership as the men, I had felt frustrated. Women had fewer political rights in 1687 Quebec than they had even ten years earlier.

The Iroquois gave their tribal women more status than the French did. Why would I *not* want to be adopted and become an Iroquois?

"Let me think and pray, Trees," I finally said. "I will give you my answer by the spring festival, *n'est-çe pas?*"

• • •

When ice started to melt on Lake Ontario in March 1688, one year had passed since Wilhelm had drowned. Ellen and I had awakened that morning facing a perfectly normal day, but by nightfall, our world had been turned upside down. An emotional sarcoma of loss and sadness had entered life, running its influence through so many aspects of our existence.

As I reflected on all the changes in the last year, the biggest one was my awareness of the power of the Holy Spirit.

Spring would be with us soon. And I had promised I would give Trees an answer about adoption in a few days. Where should my home be?

Several mornings later Trees noticed the circles under my eyes as soon as I stepped into the morning light. We walked to the river to do our ablutions.

"White Heart," Trees said, "I sense a sadness within you. You have been led elsewhere, *n'est-çe pas?*"

I hung my head, grateful for my friend's sensitivity. "I must embrace the Creator's gifts. In the last fifteen years, I have learned to think like both a French person and a savage, to talk with both tongues. These traits would not be used if I stayed in this village for the rest of my life." I looked deep into Trees's eyes. Immediately I saw her heartache at my decision. "Please forgive me, my dear mother. But I must trust in God's protection if my life is threatened by the wars."

Trees sighed and said, "Well, let's go back and have some tea and corn cakes. Let's read the Word. We don't know how long we will have together." The old woman put her hand in mine. It felt like warm sheepskin wrapped around bird-like bones.

That night I joined my Iroquois captors in their spring festival.

...

Forgetting to be polite, Crow Feather burst into my quarters on April 1, 1688. "White Heart, a priest is here for you. Come."

I straightened my hair and ran after her.

When we arrived at the chief's longhouse, their leader sat by the fire surrounded by the tribe's principle warriors and one old, tall Jesuit. The man wore a full habit and a large-brimmed, black hat. A salt and pepper beard framed an angular chin and hawk-like nose. A wooden crucifix hung around his waist. Chief Flying Salmon introduced me to Father Jerome Lamberville, famous for his bravery and his role in French-Native diplomacy. He had also been the unwitting pawn when the Quebec governor set a trap for the Iroquois chiefs in Cataraqui.

While Father Lamberville and I had never met, we knew each other by reputation. A flood of relief washed through me when I thought he might be here to make a ransom offer on my behalf.

As it turned out, that was not the purpose of the meeting.

Father Lamberville started the conversation in Iroquois. "Mademoiselle, the governor of Quebec has requested your presence at the diplomatic meetings taking place in Albany in May. Tribal warfare is heating up, and Denonville is considering alternative ways of quelling the tension. Your reputation precedes you as an astute negotiator and linguist. Even here in Oswego, you are being called the 'White Heart' and are considered a source of peace and healing. These natives trust few people of France as much as they trust you.

"While I am not in the position of bringing a ransom, I have received your chief's permission to relocate you as a captive to Albany for a season. Doing this will permit you to help settle intertribal disagreements before there is more bloodshed."

I tried to listen but was distracted by my emotional reaction to the priest himself, not to his message. Decades ago a Jesuit priest would have inspired a sense of familiarity and comfort in me. But in recent years, the sight of priests made me agitated and suspicious. Since my relationship with the Jenets had grown, I now viewed Catholicism through my Protestant friends' eyes. The church and its priests were more a hindrance to my relationship with God than a help.

I nodded politely and asked if I might consider the proposal overnight.

Chief Flying Salmon acknowledged that need and commanded Father Lamberville to return with me to my quarters to answer any further questions.

As we walked, we discussed the condition of Quebec. I was pleased to hear in unaltered, clear French the news: how Denonville was doing with the Indians (poorly), how Quebec had grown (large), how Fort Frontenac had been ruined since the Iroquois attacks of last year (abandoned!).

Maybe he had answers to my most pressing questions: Robert? And Parrot's Bay? My heart raced as we entered the hut. Trying to calm myself, I offered him some herbal tea and oatcakes. He sat cross-legged in front of my fire.

"Dare I ask you, Father, how Parrot's Bay fares?"

"Ah, your homestead. I'm sorry, Mademoiselle. I haven't seen it myself, but those who have said it was burned all to the ground. Wasn't it in flames when you were captured?"

I had been holding on to fantasies. Maybe someone had put the flames out and rebuilt it. Father Lamberville waited patiently for me to recover myself. I tried to breathe, but I had been holding this grief in for eight months.

"Father Lamberville, I can rebuild. If we can arrange a ransom, I can return to Parrot's Bay and start again."

"Ah, Mademoiselle." He sounded resigned. "When the fort was so devastated by the Iroquois, the nearby inhabitants slaughtered, and the land left to the wild animals, the government had little interest in seeing the trading post flourish. Within a few months, the governor confiscated Parrot's Bay and your land holdings. I was recently told that Denonville does not consider your original land grant to have been established properly. In his court's opinion, that land isn't yours. And it was never rightfully yours."

I jumped up. My face flushed with rage. A burning stick sprang out of the fire, showering red-hot embers onto the priest's robe. Father Lamberville calmly brushed them off. I paced the tepee, two steps one way, three steps another.

"Well, have you heard anything from Sieur de LaSalle? He was exploring the Gulf of Mexico."

The Jesuit's expression held a gnawing grief. "No, Mademoiselle. There has been no word."

I was desperate for space, air, and freedom. But I needed to hear more of what the priest said, as he had my future in his hands. I pulled back the flap and stood in the light, my back to Father Lamberville.

The air was cool, mingled with a touch of frost. *Breathe*, I told myself. *Breathe out. Breathe in.*

How could my land be stripped away from me? Why had Robert not returned? Injustice stung. At my core, I had believed I would make it back to Parrot's Bay and start my life over. Robert would join me.

Now I wasn't sure.

I thought, *O Lord. How much more?*

And the divine voice said to my heart, *My beloved, I won't give you more than you can handle.*

I gazed out over the village. People hovered by the central outdoor fires, skinning their game, making arrows, and stirring cooking pots. Children played with stones and sticks, laughing in their simple competitions. I saw Midge skipping in a pattern as other girls looked on, her white skin making no difference to anyone.

Regaining my composure, I came back to Father Lamberville and mumbled an apology. We conversed more, and the Jesuit said he was willing to request my ransom. "But I believe you will need to comply with the governor's request and go to Albany before we can accomplish that. Then I can advocate more effectively for you."

The whole time he was talking, I asked myself, *Do I want to do business for a governor and a monarchy that stripped me of my land, my livelihood, my very property?*

I studied the scorched holes at the bottom of the Jesuit robe.

Lamberville interrupted my thoughts. "Mademoiselle, I have another concern. Rumors circulated you had harbored Protestants, become a Huguenot yourself, and renounced the Mother Church. You do understand that—if that is true—there is little I can do for you. You would be considered an outlaw. The governor would not want you to return."

Now I had to decide that question that Wilhelm and Ellen and I had discussed for so many evenings. Was the Catholic Church my salvation? Or could I receive forgiveness for my sins and the blessing of the Holy Spirit outside the bounds of the church? Was I a Catholic, or was I a Huguenot?

Confusion overwhelmed my heart, and choices flooded my mind Gently, Father Lamberville asked if I wanted him to hear my confession.

"Father, give me time alone with God. Return when the sun sets. Please."

What should I do? Embrace the rituals of the Catholic Church and come to Jesus through the sacraments? Or come to him directly, shucking off the Catholic practices? I stared into the flames. Memories of Versailles' Court, of the Queen Mother, and of Reverend Marie of the Incarnation moved through my mind, and with them the beautiful rituals and meaningful liturgies of the Catholic Church.

Remembrances of the Huguenots on shipboard, then of Wilhelm and Ellen, of Annie and of their simple personal faith in Jesus flowed through my consciousness.

Spiritually, who was I? A Christ-one? I knew that beyond a shadow of a doubt. Jesus was my Lord and Savior.

But religiously, what was I? That was the issue facing me. That choice would influence the rest of my life.

I kneaded these thoughts around in my mind and heart. Slowly, a hunger for the familiar, mystical experience of partaking of the Holy Eucharist grew within me. While the Catholic Church had her faults, she had been there for me throughout my life. I had been baptized and married with the blessing of a Catholic priest. My husband was a firm believer, a religious man.

A peacefulness regarding these unique aspects of Catholicism settled on me. I could love Jesus personally, intimately, and still be a Catholic. I might have to forgive the church its hypocrisy and some of the priests their arrogance and inhumanity, but the Catholic Church was where I belonged, despite its faults.

As the sun sank below the horizon, Father Lamberville entered my small home, his head almost touching the smoke hole. I told him I wanted to confirm my loyalty to the church. Then I knelt before him, comfortable with the expected ritual of confession.

But I also knew that if this priest weren't available, I could speak directly to Jesus who was ever-present in my life.

The peace of God, which had been my saving grace throughout the last year, washed over me. I set aside my hatred and anger and submitted to God's desires for me. He loved me so much he had allowed his Son to be killed, nailed on a cross for my faults and for the evil in this world.

Now I would have to serve a governor who was acting unjust and un-Christian. But I would go to Albany and do my best as a woman who understood both the French ways and the natives' ways. With Christ's power, I would be fair and honest and would further these peace talks. I would wait for the ransom. I would persevere to see justice done regarding my property at Parrot's Bay.

And I would hope for Robert.

# Author's Note

This manuscript is a combination of eighty percent historical facts and twenty percent from the author's imagination. The chronology is true to history, including Madeleine's place at Versailles, her journey as a *fille du roi,* her role as creditor and fiancée to Robert LaSalle, her position as the first female property holder in Ontario at Parrot's Bay, her captivity, and her ransom.

LaSalle's travels, discoveries, assassination attempt, and political intrigues are based on historical fact as well. The Reverend Marie of the Incarnation was a living person, and her conversations with Madeleine are based on her correspondence left to the still-operating Ursuline Convent in Quebec City. Whenever I had an historical figure play a role, the facts surrounding that character were also true to life.

The fictionalized portions of the book involve Madeleine's struggle with her sexual abuse history and her feminine identity. Her crisis of faith and her spiritual journey are based on the author's experience as a psychologist and as a believer.

# RESOURCES

While the bibliography for this project's research is extensive, I am indebted particularly to the following sources:

On Robert de LaSalle, Anka Muhlstein's *LaSalle, Explorer of the North American Frontier*, Grasset and Fasquelle, 1992.

On Marie of the Incarnation, *Marie of the Incarnation: 1599–1672 Correspondence*, translated by Sister St. Dominic Kelly, 2004.

On New France, Olive P. Dickason's *The Myth of the Savage*, University of Alberta Press, 1984.

On French-Canadian culture, Peter N. Moogk's *La Novelle France*, Michigan State University Press, 2000.

On Huron Indians, Bruce Trigger's *The Children of Aataentsic: A History of the Huron People to 1660.* McGill-Queen University Press, 1976.

On Iroquois Indians, Anthony F.C. Wallace's *The Death and Rebirth of the Seneca*, Vintage Books, 1972.

On the Jesuit missionary endeavors, Lucien Campeau, S.J. *The Jesuit Mission Among the Hurons: 1634–1650*, Gontran Trottier, 1987.

# GROUP DISCUSSION

1. *White Heart* is about a *fille du roi* who travels to Canada to pick out a husband.

   Madeleine is confused about marriage and how to select a mate for life. What is your opinion about her decision to be a *fille du roi?* She has discussions about the meaning of love. What are the ingredients in the decision to marry someone? What is your opinion about "arranged or forced" marriages? What do you think love is?

2. One out of every three women in the U.S.A. has been sexually abused. Do you think Madeleine's experience of abuse and recovery was accurate? What factors helped her overcome her trauma symptoms? Comment on the differences and similarities of her sexual relationships with Tonato and Robert.

3. New France witnessed a great deal of political conflict. The debate was as follows: Should the towns and villages in New France consolidate for the purpose of strength in numbers and safety by proximity? Or should the colonists support exploration of the western lands and expansion of property for the betterment of French domination? Which would you have preferred and why?

4. The people of New France lived with the daily threat of Indian attacks. Many had experienced the terrorism of *les sauvage*. Do

you think our experience with terrorism today is similar or different? What suggestions do you have for a person dealing with daily threats of terror?

5. The Reverend Mother Marie of the Incarnation was a real-life missionary. She expressed her spiritual relationship in mystical terms. What is your opinion of Marie of the Incarnation? Would you like her for a mentor? Why or why not?

6. Madeleine found herself in the midst of various moral dilemmas. What were they? How did she manage them?

7. Robert and Madeleine discussed the difference between religion and one's spiritual life early in their relationship. Did you agree with their distinction? What theme did religion play in the characters' lives? Did any of the characters undergo spiritual growth? How important do you think a personal relationship with God is?

8. At least one time in their relationship, Robert lied to Madeleine. Was his lie justifiable? Should she forgive him? How does one forgive a wrong done in a relationship?

9. Madeleine had to adjust to several different cultures throughout her life. What were some of the cultural changes she had to make? How do you think she handled them? Have you had to adjust to cultural differences in your life? How did you manage the adjustment?

10. The value of waiting is a theme that runs throughout *White Heart*. Do you think waiting is something everyone has to do during his life? Is there a value in waiting? How did Madeleine's waiting periods influence her?

11. His fiancé describes Robert LaSalle as a man with two sides to his personality. Did you agree with this description? What was your opinion of Robert?

12. On several occasions, Madeleine had to live alone in complete solitude. How did Madeleine respond to solitude? What are your thoughts about living solitarily for a month or so? Even for forty-eight hours?